"A beautiful love story; sensitive, hard-hitting on the emotions."

—Catherine Anderson on *The River's Daughter*

"Brims with adventure, emotion, and detail."

—*Register-Guard* (Eugene, Oregon)
on *Spirit of the Eagle*

"Engrossing historical fiction. Highly recommended."

—*Kliatt* on *Spirit of the Eagle*

"Readers will be immediately drawn into this stirring novel. A powerful, exciting read."

—*Romantic Times* on *Daughter of the Mountain*

"Munn's knowledge of the period and locale is extensive, and she skillfully conjures the Seminoles' agonizing and brave stand-off with the government, as well as the terrifying risk taken by the slaves who joined them."

—*Publishers Weekly* on *Seminole Song*

"Vella Munn is one of today's best writers in providing her readers with an entertaining, fast-moving, and realistic novel. . . . [A] fascinating, well-researched, and exciting work of historical fiction."

—*Affaire de Coeur* on *Daughter of the Forest*

**By Vella Munn from Tom Doherty Associates**

# VELLA MUNN

# WIND
# WARRIOR

A TOM DOHERTY ASSOCIATES BOOK
NEW YORK

This is a work of fiction. All the characters and events portrayed in this book are either products of the author's imagination or are used fictitiously.

WIND WARRIOR

Copyright © 1998 by Vella Munn

A Forge Book
Published by Tom Doherty Associates, Inc.
175 Fifth Avenue
New York, NY 10010

Forge® is a registered trademark of Tom Doherty Associates, Inc.

ISBN: 0-812-53876-5
Library of Congress Catalog Card Number: 97-29880

First edition: April 1998
First mass market edition: March 1999

Printed in the United States of America

0  9  8  7  6  5  4  3  2  1

To the over-the-hill gang—long may we "labor."
My life is richer for Pat, who understands, Tallie
for her courage, and Mary Lou for her strength.
I love you gals.

They will be carried
To the nest of the eagle
And remain there in joy.
Joy fills the world.

*Chumash song*

WARRIO

The sight of two females compelled him to slip closer. If the leatherjackets had Indian women among them, he had no doubt of what they would be used for. This time he wouldn't stop until he'd spilled every drop of the men's blood; this time he wouldn't allow his anger and outrage to blind him to the need for caution.

No, he soon concluded, the women weren't prisoners. They rode handsome, strong horses adorned with ornate saddles and bridles. The heavier of the two was dressed in layers of black and gray, with a dark cloth covering over her head. If the new corporal was uncomfortable in the heat, surely her suffering must be even worse.

Was she being forced to wear that thing? Unlike Chumash women, who clothed themselves in short fringed buckskin skirts, this one's long, heavy skirt must touch the ground when she walked.

Continuing his study of her, he took in her bowed back, her hands gripping the reins and folded like those of the padres at prayer. She looked only at the ground, as if afraid of her surroundings or so caught within her thoughts that she was unaware of anything else. If her horse hadn't continued to plod along, she would be as motionless as the dead. Despite the little he could see of her, he knew she wasn't young.

The other woman, too, had on a long skirt, but in a great many ways she was different. This one's loose white blouse left most of her arms bare and exposed her throat and neck. What he could see of her flesh was dark and smooth. She had nothing on her head except for a black mass of hair pulled off her neck and caught in a knot so thick it made him wonder if her hair reached below her waist. Even from here, he could tell she was young, no longer a child but not yet weighed down by life as his wife was.

This one seemed possessed of an endless curiosity about her surroundings because she turned her head first in one direction and then the other, taking in the world with the intensity of a young fox. Sometimes she stared down at the ground near her horse's feet; other times she rose in the saddle and studied the horizon. He was too far away to know what was in her eyes, and yet he sensed she was trying to commit the land to memory.

She would have to do more than that if she intended to live here. She would need deep-running strength to hunt and till the land, to draw water out of springs, to survive the hot summer and heavy rains of spring.

Without knowing why it should matter to him, he wondered what would happen to her if he took her into the mountains and forced her to stay there through winter storms. Would she cower where he placed her or die of exposure trying to escape? Would she understand what the wolves and coyotes said when they threw their voices into the air, or would she hate and fear sounds that were as familiar to him as his heart's beating?

What had brought the women here? Would they be followed by more?

Fighting the unwanted thought and accompanying emotion, he took careful note of the five. The leatherjacket he'd wounded had been carried away, accompanied by his corporal. Now three newcomers were retracing the earlier steps, maybe replacing those who had left. Three when before there had been two?

And Spanish women?

The enemy had passed from directly in front of him and would soon be out of sight. He would wait until there was no risk of being spotted and then follow them so he'd know whether they were heading for La Purisima or continuing north. Much as he wanted to get back to his people, his return would have to wait until he discovered whether the fat corporal had been replaced by someone even more committed to ridding the land of what Fathers Joseph and Patricio called wild Indians.

Wild Indians! No matter how many times Black Wolf had heard the padres and leatherjackets call his people that, he didn't understand. Wild was a grizzly, an elk, a deer, a cougar, a wolf. Just because the Chumash—some Chumash—refused to bend their backs to the work ordered by the missionaries and reject Sun and Moon, the spirits that dwell in whirlwinds, Humqaq, didn't mean they were animals.

Motionless, Black Wolf watched as, step by dusty step, the plodding group pulled away from him. The prickling at his back caused by the sun briefly distracted him, but he could escape from the heat in a few minutes. For now—

The younger woman swiveled in her saddle and looked behind her. Back straight, she took in her surroundings until she was staring at where he was instead of down at the ground like the others. He knew she couldn't possibly see him because, like Wolf, he had learned how to remain hidden.

It didn't matter. It was time for her to comprehend that she didn't belong here. Feeling strong and fierce, he stood and revealed himself. He held aloft his spear, then aimed it at her. Although she started, her gaze remained locked on him. She neither cried out nor motioned to the others.

Not understanding, he returned her study.

# 2

Barely believing what she'd seen, Lucita Concha Arguello Rodriguez kept her reaction to herself. Still, she shivered despite the day's heat.

For a moment, she stared at her hands holding her mount's reins, but curiosity and apprehension became too much for her, and she again glanced at the horizon, then rose in the saddle and lifted a hand to shade her eyes.

Her father, Cpl. Sebastian Rodriguez, insisted that the savages around La Purisima Concepcion were little more than animals. According to him, the viceroy of New Spain, whom the Spanish Crown had entrusted with responsibility for developing the missions, should have placed the fledgling colonies under military, not Catholic, domain. That way, the savages would be made to respect and fear armed soldiers even if they were too feeble of mind to grasp the concept of a righteous God.

As a result of her father's harangues, she had half-expected to see the Indians down on four legs, but this one—a warrior, she remembered her father calling the man—had stood erect and proud, unclothed when she'd never seen a grown man undressed. Although she'd been too far away to look into his eyes, she'd sensed a certain intelligence about him. More than that, he'd pointed his weapon at her in acknowledgment.

Not simply acknowledgment. He'd warned, threatened. She should tell her father. He would know—

"Lucita! What are you doing?"

Teeth clenched, she faced her mother, who was riding on her left. Senora Margarita Inez Delores Rodriguez had drawn her short but sturdy body even straighter, and Lucita found herself wondering if her mother's bones were possessed of unnatural strength. No matter how tired Margarita might be, she never allowed herself to sag. If it hadn't been for the bright splotches of heat on her cheeks and the moisture glistening on her temples, Lucita would believe her mother felt nothing of the day's nearly insufferable heat.

"Doing?" Lucita stalled. "Trying to stay awake."

"You are calling attention to yourself with your constant moving about." Mouth pursed, Margarita stared at Lucita's exposed throat. "God warns against immodesty; you know that."

Oh, yes, she knew all about God's constraints and warnings, thanks to the lessons that had begun before she was old enough to understand what was being said to her. If she told her mother what she thought she'd seen on that dry and desolate hill, their conversation would turn into a lecture about the ungodly Indians destined to spend eternity in hell unless they sought salvation, and today Lucita couldn't take another lecture. Besides, it was too late for her father to do anything about the savage. As long as she was surrounded by soldiers, she was safe, wasn't she?

"We will be living in this land, Mother," she ventured. "Surely it isn't wrong for me to learn all I can about it."

"I did not say you should not exhibit curiosity about your surroundings, but your father's men . . . they have been too long without. . . . They look at you and—"

Before she could decide whether to ask her mother to continue, a rabbit sprang from the brush in front of her. Pulling on the reins to keep her horse from shying, she pointed at the little creature. "It's so different from home. I did not realize . . ."

Her voice trailed off as she thought of Mexico City with its university, majestic cathedrals, and massive government buildings. If she'd had any choice, maybe she would still be there, but she didn't, even if her parents didn't understand her reasons for begging to be allowed to accompany them here.

"The world beyond your soul does not matter, Lucita. Only your relationship with God does."

"I know, Mother," she said as she always did. "Still, surely God would not take offense because I am curious about a land so few will ever see?"

"Was the Son of God distracted from his tasks by where his feet walked? No. He knew and embraced his mission just as I do, as you should."

"You are right, Mother. Please forgive me."

"It is not my forgiveness you must seek."

"I know," she muttered and bowed her head in a gesture of acceptance. A few moments later she heard her mother's soft whispering and knew she'd once again lost herself in prayer. Unless disturbed, Margarita wouldn't be aware of where her physical body was until she'd finished, which might take the better part of an hour.

Despite herself, Lucita didn't attempt the familiar journey to her own soul. Instead, she looked out from under her lashes at the dry, soft hills surrounding them. Although the land was quite different from her home in the Valley of Anáhuac, sheltered by the snowcapped peaks of Popocatepetl and Iztaccihuatl, she loved the clean smell of the air here and felt alive in a way she never had before.

Unfortunately, the everlasting creaking of leather and wagons, the endless thud of hooves, even the occasional snorts and sighs of the plodding animals made it almost impossible for her to concentrate on anything else. Still, there must be other sounds, sounds that would tell her more about this uncivilized place that would become her home.

*Even rabbits made sounds, didn't they?* she pondered. Their little bodies looked all but weightless, but it seemed impossible that they could move through the brush and dry grasses without disturbing the plants in some way. She'd heard the soldiers her father had brought with him grumble about how they might have to supplement the meat provided by the mission's cows with deer. Did deer call out the way cows did? Was it possible that some understanding, some form of communication, passed between deer and rabbits, between deer and bears and wolves even?

The warrior, if that's what he'd been, knew about deer sounds and how rabbits moved, whether wolves felt remorse at taking life.

Certain her mother would disapprove because she was once again drawing attention to herself but unable to stop, Lucita ran her free hand over the back of her neck in an attempt to wipe away the sweat that had pooled there. *"Not sweat,"* she heard her mother say. *"A lady is beyond such things."*

Well, lady or not, her body reacted to the heat in the same way the soldiers' bodies did.

A hot breeze fanned a few strands of hair about her cheeks and throat, making her thankful that she'd put on a loose blouse with lace sleeves. Perhaps it was immodest—the way the soldiers looked at her made her uncomfortable—but how could her mother stand the layers of heavy black cloth? It was summer. Surely even God understood that a person needed bare forearms and throat in order to survive the heat.

The warrior . . .

Her thoughts hung up on the word, forcing her to wonder what it meant to be a wild man who cared not at all whether he wore anything, who was free to do what he wanted, who lived with deer and rabbits instead of surrounded by walls as she'd been all her life. Who would have gone through his entire life with no knowledge of God if it hadn't been for the padres.

"Mother?" She kept her voice low so the others couldn't hear.

"Yes." Although Margarita looked at her, her eyes didn't quite focus, and Lucita knew the older woman was still lost within her prayers.

"Are there ever times—I mean, you are so close to God. You have embraced him and he has embraced you, but was it always that way?"

A frown disturbed Margarita's usually immobile features. "Why do you ask?"

*Because I'm not sure it will ever be like that for me.* "I was wondering. . . . I mean, you were so determined to come here that—"

"It is my calling, Lucita, as it must become yours. God wants me to save the savages' souls."

"You never questioned that calling?"

"No. Never."

"But this land—you didn't know what it was going to be like. Surely you had questions about how you would tend to your personal needs, where you would live, whether we would have a roof over our heads."

"I trust in God. As long as I live for him, he provides. And I pray daily that you will one day accept him as I do."

"I do accept. How can you—"

"I know what lives inside my daughter's heart. You have not immersed yourself, without reservation, in a religious way of life. You have—" She glanced over at her husband. "Your father's blood runs through your veins."

"I don't know his thoughts; he has never shared them with me."

"It does not matter. The military is his life; you have seen that passion, and it has made its impact on you."

Was that it? Feeling suddenly heavy and old, Lucita simply nodded before letting her mother go back to her meditations.

Although they seldom spoke, the two unkempt soldiers her father commanded remained close to each other; not that she blamed them. Despite her mother's attempt to keep her isolated from the soldiers at Santa Barbara during their stay there, she'd felt compelled to learn everything she could about what their future might be like, and the only way she could do that was by talking to those who already lived in Alta California.

Although most of them had been reluctant to speak to her, a corporal's daughter, she'd persisted until she'd learned something about the area's past. One event stood out in her mind. It had happened more than thirty years ago, but the soldiers still talked about the night when over eight hundred armed savages attacked the mission at San Diego, burning it to the ground and murdering Fr. Luis Jayme.

The attack at La Purisima that had led to her father being assigned there had taken no lives and hadn't been part of a massive attack. In fact, she'd caught a glimpse of the soldier who'd been wounded and overheard Cpl. Roberto Galvez arguing with her father that the viceroy had no right ordering him replaced since the savages around La Purisima were cowards.

Not that her father had cared about Corporal Galvez's pride or would ever make the mistake of dismissing the enemy.

Leaning forward, she fixed her gaze on her father's straight back. Every line in his body, even the way he rode his horse, spoke of a man who was a soldier at his core. He'd killed before; she had no doubt that he was capable of and willing to kill again.

The small of his back throbbed, but Cpl. Sebastian Rodriguez refused to acknowledge it, just as he ignored the sweat pouring down the sides of his head and the miserable excuses for soldiers who had been assigned to him.

In more than twenty years spent in service to his country, he had never felt so ill-equipped for an assignment, and if he'd thought it would do any good, he would have sailed to Spain to present himself before the viceroy or even the king. Unfortunately, Corporal Rodriguez knew what the answer would be. The Spanish Crown had already spent a fortune setting up the California missions, and the military was hard-pressed to maintain the troops it now had, let alone commissioning additional men.

It wasn't true; there were more soldiers than necessary whiling away their days at the presidios while he was expected to restore order at La Purisima all but single-handedly, and if he failed—

His wife and daughter had been speaking to each other, but they'd now fallen silent. If he'd had any choice in the matter, the two would be in Mexico where they belonged, but that, like the number of men under his control and his being ordered here, was out of his hands. Margarita and Lucita might believe their entreaties had had an effect on him, but they were wrong. Instead, he and his family were pawns in the hands of powerful priests who believed it was time for the missions to become civilized. Men of God who'd never been out of their homeland and knew nothing about conditions here had decided that sending Spanish women to at least one of the missions was the way to accomplish that. He'd been sent to La Purisima not because of his military record but because he was married to a deeply religious woman, a woman who, the viceroy had ordered, would accompany him. The fact that Sebastian had a grown daughter only solidified the priests' argument.

Teeth clenched, Sebastian rode out the waves of shame that overtook him whenever he thought about that. He was a soldier, a proven fighter! He'd led the men under him against untold enemies of the Crown. His record should speak for itself! He hadn't outlived his usefulness, lost his ability to plan and strategize, to fight, just because age had crept up on him!

His jaw ached and he forced himself to release the tension there, but that did little to calm him. Instead he, once again, vowed to prove himself to his superiors. He *would* crush the so-called rebellion here, and when he was done he *would* demand the respect due him.

Anything else was incomprehensible, and terrifying.

Black Wolf's legs easily kept pace with the slow-moving group, and although his side bothered him, he remained strong. If he hadn't had to concentrate on remaining hidden, he might have grown impatient waiting for them. As it was, he split his attention between the newcomers and the land that was as familiar as his son's features.

In their foolishness, those who had built La Purisima had chosen a valley surrounded by low tree-covered hills. As a result, a Chumash could easily remain hidden while slipping close enough to see what was happening at the mission. He did that now.

Summer had burned his world. Winter would lash at it, and those of the People who lived in the hills with him would be hard-put to find enough game to fill their bellies, but from the beginning of time the Chumash had performed the ceremony honoring Kakunupmawa, the sun, and *Kakunupmawa* had once again grown in strength and warmth and spring had returned. It would happen again and again for all time as long as there were still Chumash not trapped within the mission.

Grunting, Black Wolf wrapped his fingers around the charm stone he carried on a thong around his neck. Talks with Frogs had given it to him so he would be invisible to arrows and protected from illness. The shaman hadn't known whether the charm stone would keep him safe from Spanish swords and muskets, but it had never occurred to him not to accept the sacred talisman.

Kakunupmawa had lost much of its energy and light by the time the newcomers finished the gentle drop into the rich, fertile valley his people called Algsacupi. The setting sun glinted off the buildings' tile roofs and seemed to penetrate the heavy adobe walls, but although the leatherjackets and women continued toward the church, he had no desire to risk venturing closer. Besides, he knew what the church's interior looked like, just as he knew about the cemetery with its too-many small crosses, the death-smelling infirmary, what it was like to live confined in the small, cramped dormitory.

Amused, he watched the leatherjackets dismount and stagger about. The leader with the plumed helmet was the last to swing out of his saddle and seemed to be taking great pains not to reveal any discomfort. He stood beside his motionless horse for several minutes as if concerned about the animal's welfare, but Black Wolf guessed he didn't trust his legs to do more. Finally, however, he stepped toward the two waiting padres.

At that, the hot, bitter taste of hatred coated Black Wolf's mouth and darkened his vision. Fists clenched, he remained crouched behind a boulder and studied the interaction among the men. The padres wore their usual flowing gray garments, but they had pushed back their head coverings, revealing their heads.

He would have to be standing only a few feet away from tall, skinny Father Joseph to hear him because the man's wispy, childlike voice never carried. In truth, if it were only the two of them, he might have approached Father Joseph and asked whether his once broken knee still pained him, maybe even offered to help him back to his feet after praying on the hard adobe floor.

Father Patricio was different.

Sharp pain on his upper thigh distracted Black Wolf. Careful not to reveal himself, he slid off the boulder, only then slapping at the wasp that had stung him. Looking around, he saw that where the boulder met the ground was being used as a wasp nest, something he would have noticed if he hadn't been so intent on the scene below. After running his nail over his thigh to dislodge the stinger, he looked around for a safer vantage point. A fiery sensation remained, but he'd been stung before and knew the discomfort would soon subside. Besides, that pain was nothing compared to what he'd suffered at Father Patricio's hands.

Black Wolf was surprised to see the leatherjacket leader lift his hands toward the black-clothed woman and help her to the ground and wondered if she was too frail to do such a simple task on her own. He had never seen a Spanish woman. Maybe they were all like newborn fawns.

When the bareheaded woman with the great mass of midnight hair jumped lightly to the ground, he decided he'd been wrong. It still puzzled him that the other woman had required help, because she now dropped to her knees in front of the men of God and bowed so low to the ground that her head touched earth, but the ways of women weren't his concern. What mattered was whether his people were in danger from this new military presence, whether the new leatherjackets had come to exact their brand of punishment on him—if they ever caught him.

The kneeling woman looked up at the other woman and then tugged on her skirt hem. After several seconds, the stander knelt, but instead of lowering her head, she looked up at first Father Patricio and then Father Joseph. By turn, the padres placed their hands on the women's heads, giving their blessing.

It seemed to Black Wolf that Father Patricio remained with the bareheaded woman longer than with the other.

The younger of the two was the first to regain her feet. Once she had, she put her hands on the other woman's shoulders. Then the younger woman slipped her fingers around the other's elbows and helped her stand.

When the wind shifted, the stench of boiling fat assaulted Black Wolf's nostrils. Although he couldn't see the large, dark vats where fat from slaughtered cattle was boiled, he all too easily remembered standing for hours over the containers while endlessly stirring the slime that, when melted, was stored in large skin bags until needed to make the candles that lit the small, dark rooms.

The slaves the padres called neophytes surrendered their youth and strength to tallow rendering. As long as the padres remained at La Purisima, as long as they were protected by armed leatherjackets, more and more Chumash children would be forced to fill their lungs with the wretched stench.

A spasm snaking from palm to forearm served as notice that he'd gripped his spear too tightly. He should know how to keep his emotions under control. After all, denying what he felt had kept him alive during the years when the child now known as Black Wolf had been a prisoner here.

But it was so hard.

The all too quickly approaching night made Lucita think of a storm-tossed wind. She'd been so young when her mother took her to the ocean so they could watch her father leave for the first of what became an endless parade of leave-takings. She couldn't remember where the viceroy had sent him that time or how long he'd been gone or whether her mother had shown any emotion at either his leaving or his return, but she would never forget the feel of the wind as it slapped her cheeks and tangled her hair. She knew why she was being reminded of that now; except for these few buildings and wooden corrals, there was nothing but wilderness.

"We are delighted to have you here," Father Joseph said, his soft voice only partly separating her from her memories and reactions. "For years I prayed the Lord would see fit to send women to help spread his word in ways that are beyond the ability of men. And now, finally, my prayer is answered. Surely the Lord's ways are both mysterious and wonderful."

"God is all-wise, all-knowing," her mother said. "It is not for us to question his timing."

"No, Senora Margarita, it is not. I trust he looked over you during your journey."

As her mother told Father Joseph about the small, cramped packer ship they'd spent seemingly endless days and nights on while traveling up from Compostela to San Diego, Lucita tried to concentrate, but her mother, like the others, had become disembodied voices. Lucita was grateful for the opportunity to stand, and yet the long hours on horseback had been wearing and she looked forward to sleeping. Sleeping? It seemed unlikely that she could quiet the whirlwind of impressions that filled her mind enough for that to happen.

If only they'd reached the mission earlier in the day. As it was, she would probably have to wait until after evening prayers and supper to gather any impression of her new home. She was aware of several long whitish buildings, the church with its companario and three bells, a fountain and overflowing rock-lined pond, a number of trees of various types, and beyond them some nearly hidden smaller buildings. She'd expected fortification such as adobe walls enclosing the mission, but there was nothing in the way of protection.

Something smelled horrible, the stench familiar and yet stronger than anything she'd ever encountered. The sounds of cattle, pigs, sheep, goats, and other animals pulled her attention toward the wooden pens. She'd spotted a water-filled ditch on the way in and wondered where it led to and whether it watered the large garden. Most of all, she wanted to see where the Indians lived and if they looked like the wild one she'd seen earlier.

"Daughter, did you not hear the father?" Margarita asked sharply. "Honestly, it is so hard to get one's children to pay their elders proper respect."

"Your daughter is not a child," Father Patricio said. He'd tilted his head to one side and was smiling faintly. "She is a woman."

"A woman who should be married," her father insisted.

"Sebastian." Her mother's voice, as usual, was carefully balanced between peacekeeping and pacifying. "The padres are not concerned with what goes on within our household."

Father Joseph shifted his weight, winced, and cupped his hand over his right knee. "Indeed the Church acknowledges that some matters are the responsibility of parents. However, that responsibility is easily accepted and dealt with if the Church's teachings are faithfully followed."

Her stomach knotted, but Lucita refused to let her reaction show. She and her father had never been close, never reached out or shared. Things had got worse since she'd threatened to run away if she was forced to marry the man her father had chosen for her. There were times when she believed it would be easier if she simply acquiesced, but if she did, she would spend her life with a stern-faced man determined to carve out a hacienda in the Texas territory. More than that, she'd seen Ermano De Leon ride a horse to death, seen the emaciated condition of his cattle.

"I am most interested in learning how you have been able to bring the Church into this wild land," she said, deliberately turning the subject in another direction.

"I am glad you are, my child," Father Patricio said. The pot-bellied man with oversize hands smiled at her again, showing crooked teeth, one of them black. "However, that can wait until you have eaten and rested. We have instructed the cooks to prepare a meal worthy of our new commander and his family. The neophytes will tend to your horses. There is no reason for us to stand out here, no reason at all."

Lucita's mother cleared her throat. "Is it dangerous? I am sorry. I do not mean to sound ungrateful or to take our thoughts from the task of doing the Lord's work, but it has been on my mind so much. Do we have anything to fear from the wild Indians?"

# 3

The newcomer, obviously an Indian, wore nothing beyond a diaperlike garment that looked in danger of sliding off his hips.

Although she wanted to hear the answer to her mother's question about their safety, Lucita couldn't take her eyes or thoughts
off the man who'd just approached them. He stood a respectful
distance away, strangely long arms hanging at his sides, his head
bowed. She wanted to believe they had nothing to fear from him,
but she'd never seen someone so uncivilized-looking.

His black, tangled hair fell to the top of his prominent shoulder blades. He was some five or six inches taller than she was, not
particularly well muscled, his deep and beautiful eyes set a little
too close together. A broad and flared nose dominated his features,
and she gained no impression of his mouth beyond the fact that
she could see his tongue.

"Come here," Father Patricio ordered. "No, no. Do not do
that!" Springing forward, he struck the Indian on his cheek. "Have
you no modesty?"

The man had slid a hand inside his dirty garment and had
been scratching himself there. As the blow rocked him, he winced
and shuffled backward, then stared fixedly at the ground.

"I apologize, dear ladies," Father Patricio said, flashing what made Lucita think of a dog's teeth, sharp and cruel. "We try so hard to civilize these creatures, but I doubt our work will ever be done, especially with the adults."

"But to hit them—"

"Lucita! Silence," her father warned. "The padre does as he must. The enemy understands violence; it's what keeps them in line."

"Unfortunately, you are right," Father Patricio muttered, but something in his eyes made her believe he didn't regret what he'd done. "They persist in going about like animals, and I fear their acceptance of the Lord will never be complete."

"Surely not, Father," Margarita gasped. "Without God, their souls will spend eternity in hell. They must understand that; they must!"

Father Patricio sighed. "We try, my dear lady. But as you can see, it is not an easy task." He glared at the Indian. "You cannot fathom the joy we felt when we received word that you were coming. To have a true servant of the Lord working with us . . ."

Overcome by what Lucita assumed to be joy, the surprisingly fit-looking (in spite of his rounded stomach) padre folded his hands under his chin and gazed skyward. Although she felt pressure to express herself in the same way, Lucita couldn't take her gaze off the Indian with the reddening handprint on his cheek. A young man, his flesh seemed too large for his body. His ribs and shoulder blades stood out, and his belly, or what should have been one, had sunk deep between the sheltering bones.

The greatest lesson, she now realized, was in his eyes, which spoke of uncounted emotions felt but unsaid. They seemed on fire, confused, afraid, and angry all at the same time, the look a frightening twin of what she'd seen in the eyes of babies with no mother's breast to suckle.

"My mother asked if we had anything to fear from the savages. Do we?" she asked although her father undoubtedly wanted her to remain silent.

"Not most of them." Father Patricio waved a dismissive hand

at the Indian, then said something she only half-understood because although most of his words were Spanish, a few were foreign to her. "They are gentle, if dull-witted, children," he said when he was done. "I will not try to tell you different. However, fortunately, the neophytes are deer, not bears."

"Not all of them," Father Joseph said.

"What do you mean?" she asked although an Indian had wounded a soldier, an act that had set in motion the reasons for her father having been sent here.

"What he means"—Father Patricio spoke without looking at his companion—"is that there are a few beyond saving. The devil's children. They—"

"Father Patricio, I must protest!" Father Joseph interrupted. "They are lost. Not—"

Father Patricio held up the hand that had so recently been used to punish. "You are too kind to them when they do not deserve such words. Perhaps our guests are not interested—"

"I am," her father interrupted. "Unfortunately, my predecessor was of no mind to discuss conditions here which I mean to rectify as quickly as possible."

"Of course, of course." Father Patricio nodded repeatedly. "I, we will be happy to answer any and all questions. For now . . . the *lost* ones, as Father Joseph so charitably calls them, are not under our care. Either they still live like animals in the mountains, or they have run away. Those who run . . ." His eyes closed and he seemed lost within himself. "They are the worst."

"But we *must* reach out to them," Margarita protested. "It is God's law that all hear and believe in his word."

"Perhaps, senora, you will succeed where we have failed," Father Joseph said after an uncomfortable silence. "Father Patricio and I have differing approaches to discipline, but in truth, neither of us has been entirely successful. Certainly we want to hear your thoughts on how those creatures might be saved from the devil's clutches."

Shade by shade Margarita's cheeks grew redder. "I did not mean—please—it was not my intention to find fault. To have brought this many heathens into the light is proof of your dedication. I simply—"

Father Joseph reached out as if to touch Margarita's forearm but stopped before the contact could be made. "I understand, dear lady. I, too, came here ignorant of the conditions I would find, not the least of which is their persistence in clinging to their heathen superstitions. My soul burned with the need to spread the Lord's word. It still burns and I daily thank him for what we have been able to accomplish, but there are those incapable of accepting the truth."

"We no longer believe we have failed." Father Patricio glanced at the horizon as if seeking something out there, then turned his gaze not to Margarita, but on her daughter. "We now understand that the minds of some of these creatures are incapable of comprehending what gives us our greatest joy."

Lucita wanted to ask if those "creatures," as the padres called them, were ever treated with dignity instead of violence, but she remained silent. Her mother tolerated no argument, no questioning, and Lucita had been a dutiful child. Her father, harsh and rough and unapproachable, intimidated her; it had always been easier not to speak to him. But she'd learned she had the desperate courage necessary to fight to come here instead of marrying a man who had laughed during a horse's final moments of life. That courage, born of what she'd learned about survival while caring for some of the city's orphans last year, continued to boil within her. Someday it might break free, and if it did—

Father Patricio was still studying her. Uncomfortable, she first tried to ignore him and then returned his gaze. The corner of his mouth lifted almost imperceptibly, giving her yet another glimpse of his teeth.

"Come, come, you must be starving," Father Joseph said. "We would be remiss in our heartfelt appreciation if we didn't properly feed you. We wish living conditions could be more in keeping with what you left behind, but this is not civilized New Spain, or has the name Mexico become official? We are so out of touch here."

"Both are used equally," her mother explained. "I do not concern myself with politics, so you must ask my husband for . . ." She glanced at Sebastian, who seemed bored with the conversation. "I must ask again. Are our lives in danger?"

Father Joseph seemed to settle within himself, his body looking even less substantial than it had a moment ago. "I would love to give your heart rest, dear lady, but your husband's presence, along with that of the other soldiers, is proof that we dare not become complacent. The military force granted to the missions is far less than we would wish for, and La Purisima is unique among the missions in that it was not built with security as its primary goal. As you can see, there are no walls for fortification. I must caution you and your daughter to always think of your safety."

Father Joseph's speech filled Lucita with the unease she'd begun to master, and she couldn't help looking beyond the cluster of adobe buildings, corrals, and gardens to the shadowed foothills. The world out there was an unknown, mysterious, frightening.

And the warrior she'd seen was part of that world.

Night seemed to take forever to coat the land during the long, hot days of summer, but Black Wolf waited with the patience of one whose life has always been ruled by the seasons. After slipping a little closer, he contented himself by watching the increased activity and noting the newcomers' weapons. He'd been afraid there might be extra muskets in the wagon but saw no sign of them as the leatherjackets went about unloading it.

Before long, the two women entered the padres' quarters, followed a few minutes later by the leatherjacket's leader. The man's way of walking put Black Wolf in mind of a bull standing watch over its herd. He was dangerous, bold and confident. Because of the activity from the *pozolera*, or kitchen, Black Wolf knew food was being brought to them. It wouldn't be the bland *atole* made from grain cooked into porridge that, for days on end was all the mission Indians had to eat.

Anger at this inequality surged through him, but he'd spent

much of his childhood with his emotions clamped inside him and knew how to reach beyond them.

With the newcomers no longer in sight—the other leather-jackets had now finished caring for their mounts and had entered the large sleeping room where they would live with those already there—his time for learning through his eyes came to an end.

Taking advantage of the lengthening shadows, he slipped closer, stopping only when he caught the sweet aroma of ripening pears from the trees the first padres had planted. There wasn't much he missed about the mission, but he would never forget the wonderful taste of pears and grapes and other fruits. He smiled as he thought of how many grapes had found their way into his belly instead of the bulky leather sack he'd been given to collect what the padres used to make wine—wine that served as a vital part of what wound up in trading vessels and made the mission prosperous.

Movement in the grasses beneath the chinaberry tree that supplied the padres with the seeds they used for their rosaries caught Black Wolf's attention. A number of chickens must have found something to their liking there, if the small cloud of dust was any indication. His gaze was next drawn to the sheep pen, and his thoughts went back to the bruises he'd suffered while trying to shear the cantankerous creatures. Those bruises were nothing compared to those from the beatings administered by Father Patricio.

Stopping the thought, he traced the wolf outline on the back of his hand, felt strength flow through him, gave thanks to his spirit for freedom.

Someone was walking toward the sheep, a man who moved as if his legs had no interest in or strength for the task. After unlatching the wooden and leather gate, he stepped inside, shaking his head as the animals backed away from him. Still, shuffling, the man—an Indian—stalked the bulky creatures. Perhaps he was so intent on his task that nothing else mattered or he hadn't brought his mind to what he obviously didn't want to do. The reason wasn't important, reality was that he'd left the gate open a crack, and as the sheep continued to evade him, first one and then a few and finally the entire herd left confinement.

Bleating, the sheep ran as if only half-comprehending that their world had suddenly expanded. Most of them remained bunched together, colliding with each other and whirling in aimless directions. A few, however, wasted no time in running as fast as their thin legs could take them.

Instead of trying to overtake them, their tender had stopped to close the gate and was now yelling for help. What adults Black Wolf could see were laughing and looked not at all inclined to offer assistance, but several children obviously saw this as an adventure, since they immediately rushed at the milling sheep and began tackling those they could reach, which only added to the din.

To Black Wolf, the answer to this problem was a simple matter of placing a large amount of grain inside the corral. In a few minutes the sheep would settle down and willingly return to what they considered their home, but was it possible that such a conclusion was beyond the neophytes' comprehension? For many, the years of mission life had robbed them of their ability to live as their ancestors had; had it also stolen from them the gift of thought?

Not all of the children were milling about. One, a boy on the brink of manhood, had taken off after the animals running toward the foothills, toward Black Wolf. He remained where he was until the boy was far enough away from the mission that low-growing oak trees hid him from those below.

Then, his movements slow, Black Wolf stood. "I am unarmed," he said in Chumash.

Pulling to a stop, the boy stared at him. Black Wolf repeated himself, then asked if the boy understood.

"Yes. What are you doing here?"

"Watching. You have nothing to fear from me."

"You . . . you are not a neophyte, are you?"

"Once, but no longer."

His head cocked to one side, the boy folded his arms over his naked chest and raised his chin in a defiant gesture. "You saw the new leatherjackets, didn't you? That is why you are here."

"Yes." Shrieks and laughter along with the sounds the sheep made cut into the night air. "I cannot leave until I understand what is happening," he said.

After a glance at the now disappearing sheep he'd nearly overtaken, the boy shrugged. "I know of Chumash like you, men, women, and children who hide from the leatherjackets and padres and refuse to accept the Lord."

Black Wolf could have told the boy that their ancestors had always worshiped Sun Spirit and, in turn, Sun Spirit had blessed the land with water and food, but he didn't dare waste time explaining what the child should have begun learning while still an infant.

"You and I speak the same language," Black Wolf said. "The language of our grandfathers and their grandfathers. That makes us brothers."

"But you are wild. An animal."

Whatever the padres' teachings, they hadn't robbed this youngster of his honesty; he should be grateful for that. "An animal does not have the power of speech; I do."

Confusion aged the boy's features. He pulled his lower lip into his mouth and briefly chewed on it. "The padres say that the Chumash who forsake their teachings and refuse to live under the Lord's blanket will spend eternity in hell."

Hell meant nothing to Black Wolf. His grandfather and grandfather's grandfather knew that C'oyinashup, the Lower World, was the home of misshapen dark beings who might cause evil mischief and harm to humans, but there was no fire there, no burning. When he'd taken *tolache*, the dreaming drink, and found his way to his guardian spirit, Wolf, he'd brought back with him a soul-deep belief in his ancestors' world; hell existed only in the minds of those who called themselves Catholic missionaries.

"We will not speak tonight of the white man's belief," he told the boy. "You have sheep to capture, and I dare not stay. Tell me, quickly, of those who came today. The new leader, is he like the fat corporal before him, lazy and given to drinking much wine? Or does he speak of revenge for what I did to the leatherjacket?"

"You stabbed—"

"He was forcing himself on a Chumash woman. I stopped him."

The boy blinked, and his mouth sagged. "He . . . the leatherjackets say that he will never again be able to bury himself in a woman."

"Ah. So I succeeded."

What might be taken as a chuckle passed the boy's lips. "The leatherjackets wanted to kill you."

"The one I gelded nearly did." Black Wolf touched his side. "What do you know of revenge talk?"

"Nothing. Nothing. I have not been close to them. I do not want—"

"Perhaps the padres spoke of the newcomers before they arrived?"

"It is my job to scrape hides. The padres seldom come where I am."

Frustrated, Black Wolf mentioned the women. "I do not understand why they are here," he admitted. "Are they to service the leatherjackets?"

"I do not think so. The woman in black? I heard it said that she is married to the new corporal. Surely he will not share her with men who are lesser than him."

"And the younger one?"

"In the women's faces I saw a great deal that was the same. I think maybe they are mother and daughter."

No Chumash mother would turn her daughter over to the enemy. The Spanish women had come willingly; at least, he believed they had. Besides, he had heard that Spanish maidens were much prized. If she mated with many soldiers, wouldn't she lose all worth?

"You know nothing of the women's reason for being here?"

"No. The older one knelt at Father Joseph's feet and kissed his shoes. Perhaps she is here to serve God."

Perhaps, but simply accepting that would leave him ignorant when his life and the lives of his people were at stake. No matter what the risk to himself, he had to learn more.

"I would like to believe I can trust you," he told the boy. "If you learn anything that might tell me whether those I live with will remain safe, will you tell me?"

"The padres do not share secrets with me. Father Patricio is so quick to anger, so—"

"Then leave."

"What? Where would I go? How would I live?"

Stinging words aimed at telling the boy he could never call himself a man if he was afraid to escape this half-existence were on the tip of Black Wolf's tongue, but he remembered the days and nights when fear had held him in chains. Fortunately, his grandfather Lame Deer had understood and done what he couldn't do for himself.

"With me, if that is what you want."

"With—what is it like in the mountains?" The question came quickly. "Is it true that great bears attack and babies starve because there is not enough food for them? I could not—that is not living."

"Khus? Bears? Starvation? Who told you that?"

"The padres."

"They lie!" Before the boy could say anything, Black Wolf went on. "Bears feed on nuts and insects, small forest creatures, and fish. Not once has one threatened my people. To see a grizzly means one will share that grizzly's strength and courage, and blessed be the Chumash who takes Khus as his spirit."

"No children die?"

"Tell me this and then I will answer you. There are many Chumash buried within the cemetery, are there not?"

"Y-es."

"Chumash who die before their time in this world should be over?"

"Y-es."

"What takes them?"

For the length of time it took for Black Wolf to twice pull air into his lungs no one spoke. Then, sounding older than he had before, the boy said, "The padres call what happens by many names: consumption, chicken pox, measles, smallpox, and the sex poison that destroys bone and muscle."

"Before the newcomers came there were no such diseases among the Chumash."

"That is what I heard, but maybe it will not long matter. Maybe soon there will be no more of us."

"Do not say that!" Night had settled itself over them, filling Black Wolf with the need to hold his son in his arms while Fox Running fell asleep. Instead, he grabbed the boy's wrist and pulled him toward him. "Great Eagle, Coyote of the Sky, Sun, Moon, Morning Star—they are the gods which made the Chumash out of fine white rock. Our gods will never turn from us."

"Great Eagle, Morning Star? The padres never let us speak of them. They say . . . they say these are the words of a disbeliever who will spend eternity in hell."

"The padres' God turns a blind eye while the cemetery fills. I cannot accept that. For me there is nothing except Chupu."

"Chupu?"

"You do not know the name of your ancestors' god?"

When the boy said nothing, only strained to free himself, Black Wolf turned his gaze toward Wotoko, which the padres called west. The ocean waited there, as ageless as Chupu. Maybe this captive would never see the ocean. Maybe he would never join in the festival to honor Kakunupmawa, the sun.

For that he hated the padres and anyone who believed as they did.

# 4

Reactions rigidly clamped into submission, Lucita forced herself to step inside the darkened room lit by two slender candles. After a substantial and surprisingly well-seasoned dinner of mutton, corn, pears, and baked bread, her mother had accompanied the padres to chapel while Sebastian had gone, she supposed, to oversee the soldiers' settling in. However, although her mother wanted her to join her in evening prayers, she needed this time alone even more.

So this adobe box with its high ceiling, cool walls, and stark interior was where she would spend the foreseeable future. The inescapable fact caused her to press her hand over her mouth to stifle a whimper.

Heavy wooden shutters had been set in the too-small windows, and although the heavy coverings were open tonight, that gave her little sense of space. She hadn't expected the living quarters to be so cramped and lifeless, so stark. Life back home had been a simple existence, not because her father hadn't selected a large, well-built home as befitted his position, but because her mother kept it sparsely furnished, insisting that one's devotion to God's commandments could and must be exhibited in all aspects of life.

The large sums Margarita turned over to the Church had occasionally aroused her husband's ire, but a man dedicated to building a military career knew better than to appear opposed to the Church in any way. As a result, Lucita grew up feeling she had more in common with the poor country farmers than her prosperous neighbors.

Just the same, this inhospitable room was almost beyond her comprehension. Taking courage in hand, she picked up one of the candles from the wooden table. Blackish smoke billowed out from the flame and had already made its unpleasant impact on the air.

In addition to the table, the room contained two hard, narrow beds, each covered, it appeared, by a single hide blanket. How could she possibly sleep under the skin of something that had recently been alive?

Casting off the morose question, she slowly walked around the room, taking in the rough-finished chairs that accompanied the table, a small, empty bookshelf against one wall, a crude painting of the crucifixion hanging over the bed farthest from the door. Chests had been placed at the foot of each bed, and because there was nothing else, she assumed that the one by her bed was where she would place her personal belongings. At least, everything she owned would easily fit in the small container.

She'd taken note of the different plants, trees, and grasses on the way here, and although they showed the impact of having been without water for too much time, they spoke of life and carried intriguing fragrances. Surely no one would mind if she borrowed one of the wine goblets and used it to hold a simple bouquet.

Cheered by the thought of being able to do something to improve the conditions of the room, she again set about inventorying her surroundings, but it didn't take long enough. In less than a minute she knew everything there was to know about this too-tight place. The floor was dirt-tracked tile. The adobe walls, maybe two feet thick and cold to the touch despite the warm, stale air, were more gray than white. Other than the beds and chairs, there was nowhere to sit. She could only pray the winters weren't too harsh and she'd be able to spend most of her waking hours out-of-doors.

Taking one of the candles with her, she stepped outside. The moon, full and golden and rich, dominated the night sky. The heaven was alive with stars, and she felt closer to God at this moment than she ever did inside a church.

Although Father Joseph had explained that the rest of the nineteen missions had been built in a square with an inner courtyard, La Purisima was different. The fortlike design had been abandoned because of the likelihood of an earthquake, and it stretched out in a single unprotected line consisting of three main buildings, the livestock pens, gardens, and what appeared to be an extensive water system.

She felt vulnerable and alone, and yet her determination to understand this place she couldn't quite believe existed propelled her forward. When she'd arrived, the settlement had been filled with people, the vast majority of them Indians, but she could no longer see or hear them. Maybe they went to their villages at night; maybe they were housed nearby. The heathens hadn't known about Catholicism before the padres arrived. Did they, even those who'd been baptized, still perform pagan rituals?

There was so much she didn't understand, so many questions clamoring inside her, so many doubts and fears and—yes—excitement.

Her attention on what lay at her feet, she half-shuffled, half-walked. She had it in mind to go to the chapel, not to pray, although she would once she stepped inside, but to see if her mother was done with her devotions and ready to join her in the cavelike place that had become their home. However, she'd taken no more than a dozen steps when she was distracted by the sound of running water. By holding her candle at arm's length, she located an adobe brick–lined ditch. Filled with clear water, the ditch obviously came from higher ground beyond the church.

She shouldn't try to follow it to its source. Despite the padres' reassurance that wild animals seldom ventured close and had never attacked a human here and that she couldn't imagine savages like the one she'd seen on her way here being foolish enough to test the military strength, the world beyond the mission represented mystery and the unknown.

Still, she hadn't yet convinced her feet to stop walking. Maybe it was the need to stretch her legs after hours on horseback. Maybe it was the need to replace the unknown with knowledge.

And maybe . . .

Father Joseph seemed favorably disposed toward answering her questions about how the mission functioned, but for now she had to rely on the imagination her mother insisted kept her from blindly accepting God's word.

Would she spend the rest of her life here?

Her mind closed itself off from the question, refused to acknowledge it had even been asked, and she reassured herself that she wouldn't go so far that she could no longer see the buildings. Thanks to the moon and stars as well as her candle, it wasn't as if she were stumbling about like a blind woman. All she wanted was to get a little exercise, observe, and learn, not think beyond the work and planning it had taken to create this outpost of civilization and religion in the middle of nothing.

Because her senses were tuned to anything she might see, hear, or smell, it wasn't long before she came to the conclusion that the murmur of sound she now heard came from somewhere in the trees a distance from the padres' quarters. The soldiers were sitting outside their quarters, so it couldn't be them. If the neophytes spent their nights among the trees, they were entitled to their privacy.

Still, it couldn't hurt if she took a quick look at where they lived, could it?

Silent, she started down a narrow but well-worn path. She imagined the neophytes trudging to and from here as the endless days piled up and drew comparisons between their lot and her own, only it wasn't the same. Her father had a much-respected reputation as a military leader, and her mother was known throughout the city for her pious works, but those were her parents' accomplishments.

When she first sensed the presence, she was momentarily grateful for the distraction from her thoughts, but that quickly changed. A man stood a few feet away and half-hidden by a low-growing brush, one arm hanging at his side. The other held what in the poor light looked like a long wooden branch. She made out his unclothed chest, something hanging around his neck, long hair trailing over his shoulders, muscled legs.

Incapable of speech, she took a backward step. To her horror, he matched her pace.

"Go away!" she gasped. "Oh please, go!"

He did nothing to indicate she'd broken the charged silence. He might be deaf or too lacking in intelligence to comprehend her words. "I'll call the padres. My father . . . my father will make you leave."

Only dimly aware of what she was doing, she retreated a few more feet. As before, the Indian kept pace. Her heart pounded and each breath she took sounded desperate and strangled. By contrast, the man made not the slightest sound.

"You . . . you . . . they will punish you! How dare—"

"Silence!"

Her mouth hung open. Her throat burned from the need to finish what she'd begun, but this Indian, this savage, had ordered her not to speak, and she was obeying.

"Why are they here?" he asked in a voice as deep as the night.

"What? I . . . You have no right. . . ." His Spanish, although accented, was perfectly understandable. In contrast, the Indians who'd waited on them while they ate had communicated with grunts and gestures.

"Why are they here?" he repeated.

"I-I . . ."

"Answer me!"

"Go away!" she squeaked. "If you don't, I'll scream."

"No. You will not."

"What? I—"

"One sound and I will kill you."

Maybe what he was holding onto moved in her direction; maybe she'd only imagined it. Not that it mattered, because she believed him with every fiber in her. Shaking, she forced herself not to run.

"I ask you this." The words came from deep inside him. "Will the leatherjackets attack my people?"

"Le-atherjackets?"

"You call them soldiers. Do they plan war with my people?"

Despite the question, he didn't sound afraid. In truth, she couldn't imagine him fearing anything. Her father had always seemed so powerful and unreachable, but much of that, she knew, was because of the uniform he wore, the weapons he carried, his huge horse. This all but naked man needed none of those things because his strength and courage came from a place she couldn't fathom and knew better than to try to deny.

"Your . . . people?"

Pointing, he indicated the distant hills. "The Chumash who are free."

"Chumash? Free?"

"Not slaves or captives like those the padres call neophytes but men, women, and children who live the way Chupu designed."

The word *Chupu* should have meant nothing to her, but there was something deep and respect-filled in his tone that made her wonder if it was his word for God. Despite her fear, her brain came back to life. "You . . . you were out there today, weren't you?" she gasped. "On the way here, I looked up and saw . . . saw you."

He nodded.

*God help me.* "And you followed me here?" Fear tasted both hot and cold in her throat.

"I had to."

She couldn't say how far apart they were standing. At least, he wasn't close enough that he could grab her without effort. That should have given her some measure of comfort, but it didn't because this whatever he was with his strong, unhampered legs could overtake her as easily as a hunting dog retrieved a wounded bird. She'd heard her father and his fellow officers talk about war; she believed she knew what it meant to fear death at the hands of the enemy.

And this man was her enemy.

"If . . . if you harm me, my father and his men will hunt you down."

"No, they will not, because my medicine is too strong." He gripped whatever it was he wore around his neck, then touched the back of his right forearm. "I prayed to my spirit, and Wolf answered. I am safe, tonight. Listen to me. Listen and believe. If I had wanted you dead, your blood would now be staining the ground."

Shock briefly rendered her speechless. "What . . . what do you want?"

"Your father is chief of the leatherjackets?"

"Chief? You mean their commander? Yes." Saying that made her feel a little more in control because surely this simple creature had been taught to fear well–trained and armed troops.

"Why is he here?"

"Why? To . . . it is his job."

"His job is to command five men?"

"Y-es." *Only five.*

"And why are they here?"

Pain sliced into her temple, and she couldn't stop herself from pressing the palm of her hand against it. She'd spent much of last year caring for the parentless children the Church supported. The experience had taken her beyond the sheltered life of her childhood, but she'd never expected to be standing here talking to an armed savage. He'd been built for a physical life. His black hair had been fashioned by the wind, and his dense voice put her in mind of hard earth. It was all too easy to imagine him being absorbed by the night, but if he was, she would never know whether he was human or part of the land.

"I don't understand your question." Was that her voice? It sounded so small and hesitant, frightened.

He took a step forward, loomed over her, blocked out the moon. "Your father and his men, are they going to hunt my people down? Kill them?"

Her father had killed. No matter how many times her mother had begged him not to speak of such things around his daughter, Sebastian bragged about the blood he'd shed and the lives he'd taken.

"Let me go, please."

"I cannot."

*Cannot?* "I won't tell anyone. Please, I . . . I have never hurt anyone, never wanted to. All I want is . . ."

It had been on the tip of her tongue to tell him that all she wanted out of life was not to have to marry a man who disgusted and frightened her, but he couldn't possibly understand what she was talking about.

"Soon I will walk away from you," he said, and for some insane reason she believed him. "But first I must have the truth."

Tonight the wind was a playful child. She felt it caress her cheeks, tangle itself in her hair, sing through the grasses. The air smelled new and clean, and when she should be thinking of nothing except how to go on living it calmed her.

"My father seldom speaks to me," she admitted.

"Why not?"

"He wanted a son. When I was born, he turned his back on me." Why had she told this man that?

"He does not call you his daughter?"

"Yes, of course. When he must," she amended. "But . . . it doesn't matter." Suddenly on the verge of crying, she fought the need to run, an impulse that would surely result in that shaft penetrating her heart. "You . . . you think my father and the other soldiers are here because they want to kill you?"

He laughed. "I would be a fool to think otherwise. I attacked one of them, made him no longer a man."

"You?" *Oh, God!*

"Yes. I will not lie about that. The soldiers must have their revenge, but I care not just for myself. There are women and children. Old men and babies."

*Babies!* "He wouldn't . . ."

There wasn't enough air in her lungs. Desperate for more, she took a deep breath, and it now seemed as if the air smelled not just of grass and earth but of the Indian—the savage—as well.

"Do not lie to me."

"I'm not! I . . . I do not know what my father's orders are."

"But you can learn."

"You want me to ask—" To her shock, she gave a short and

bitter laugh. "He won't tell me his plans. That's the last thing he would ever do."

The savage had slid a few inches away from her in the last few minutes. Now he put an end to the distance by striding forward, gripping her wrist, and pulling her off balance. Why didn't she scream?

"I say this to you," he said. He stood so close that she felt his breath on her cheek. "Return to your father; find safety in his presence. If you tell him of me, it makes no difference because he will never find me. But you . . . you will know that I am here. Watching. Waiting for the time to speak to you again. And when I do, you must tell me the truth, or your life will end."

He could do that; she had no doubt of it. Her muscles felt weak and she had to bite down on the inside of her mouth to keep from crying out, and yet she didn't hate him for making her feel this way.

He was courage, desperate courage.

And she admired him as she'd never admired another human being.

The woman had made little noise as she hurried away from him. She'd long disappeared from sight and he should be seeking a place of greater safety, but he couldn't put his thoughts to that.

Despite the danger, Black Wolf knew he'd been right to confront her. It hadn't taken much to make her afraid of him, and her strength had been nothing compared to his. When he grabbed her, he'd wondered if her heart might stop beating, but he no longer did. She might be small and quiet and move as if she didn't want to call attention to herself, but hidden courage ran through her, courage he couldn't help but admire.

He didn't know whether she would seek the truth from her father and could only pray she now wanted that truth for herself.

His stomach cramped, letting him know he would spend the night hungry, but he'd experienced hunger many times in his life, and as long as he didn't weaken from lack of food, it didn't matter.

Aware of the need for the deepest shadows, he slipped close

to the nearest building, his thoughts too complex to put his mind to seeking shelter in the hills. The young woman believed her father didn't love her. She hadn't said those words, but they existed in the way she held her body, the tone in her voice. He was proud to have a son, but he would love a daughter just as fiercely; his heart could not beat any other way.

The Spanish were so different from him and his people; he would never understand them.

Suddenly angry at himself, Black Wolf spun on his heels and took the first long stride that would take him away from the mission. What the young woman felt and thought wasn't his concern. All he needed from her was knowledge about her father and the rest of the leatherjackets. She hadn't been able to tell him tonight, but soon she might have the answer, and he would force it from her.

# 5

Lucita gripped the dry leather cord that served as the handle to where she now lived. By the murmur coming from within she knew her mother was praying; the sound made her want to laugh, to cry. She was safe! Safe.

What was it the savage had said, that he'd prayed to his spirit asking for safety tonight and that a wolf had answered? Only he hadn't been talking about a pack of animals; she was convinced of that. Obviously he believed he had a spiritual relationship with whatever it was he called Wolf.

How insane! How barbaric! God and Christ, the saints and apostles, angels, dwelled in the heavens, not some fierce creature that made her shiver just thinking about what the animal was capable of. But she *had* spoken to the Indian, felt his intensity and the depth of his belief.

"What are you doing?"

Alarmed, she whirled around, tearing a nail on the rough cord. "Father!" she gasped in recognition. "I . . . I did not hear you."

"Obviously. Have you taken leave of your senses?" A spray of spittle landed on her chin. "Fool! You should be inside, not wandering about after dark. If I knew you were going to act so irresponsibly, I would have never allowed you to accompany me."

*Tell him! Tell him!* "I . . . I was on horseback for so long. I needed to stretch my legs."

"I forbid it."

"I did not mean to defy you." Mindful that others might hear, she kept her voice low. "It is just that this place fascinates me. I wanted to explore—"

"Explore! You have no idea what it is like to be in hostile land, how to act." Although he'd been on the move since before daybreak, he still wore his uniform and carried his sword. He stood, feet wide apart as if supporting a weary body, right hand on the hilt of his weapon. "You do not belong here."

"Where would you have me? Married to a man determined to take me to Texas?"

Before her father could reply, the door opened and her mother stood there. "Stop it! Please, stop it!"

Lucita's father, little more than a hulking shadow, spun toward his wife. "Do not attempt to order me, woman. I will say what I wish to my daughter."

"Everyone can hear." The words rushed out, soft yet determined. "I was in the middle of my prayers. Do you have no consideration for—"

"You are always praying." His voice, so much lower than his wife's high one, was filled with disgust. "Go back inside. Tell God everything; whimper about your unsatisfactory marriage to a brute of a man. It means nothing to me. Leave me alone with my daughter."

"She is my daughter, too."

Ignoring the comment, Sebastian grabbed Lucita's arm and propelled her inside. The room smelled of hot tallow, and the shadows had been forced into the corners.

"What were you doing?" he demanded.

*Tell him! Tell him!* Warning herself of the folly of trying to free herself from his firm grip, Lucita concentrated on her answer. "I told you," she said, her voice low. "Walking."

"I asked my men. None of them saw you for nearly an hour."

Had it been that long? She should be telling him about the savage, should have gone looking for her father the moment she returned. But she hadn't.

"I will not abide your silence, Lucita. Where were you?"

"Trying to get my bearings." The lie came so easily that it shocked her. "I didn't mean to frighten you. If I'd thought—"

"Do you think I'm capable of fear?"

She had so little understanding of this man who must have once held her in his arms that she couldn't possibly answer his question. "What do you want me to say?"

"Nothing." He released her. "Tonight you will listen."

Her mother had closed the door behind them and was leaning against it, her eyes darting between daughter and husband. Margarita chose her battles with her husband carefully. Obviously, she had decided not to risk his wrath tonight.

Taking her cue from her mother, Lucita nodded but said nothing. Spittle formed at the corner of Sebastian's mouth as it so often did when he spoke, not because his emotions had brought him to the brink of self-control, but because a knife wound had severed some of the muscles there. That limp side, so at odds with the rest of him, held her attention.

"There is much at stake for me here, much I am determined to accomplish," he said after wiping his mouth with a practiced gesture. "I have decided to sleep with my men so they will understand that we must function as a unit. I realize it is of little consequence to you and your mother and you would rather I didn't burden you with the details of my position, but none of us have a choice in this."

Her father wasn't a man who felt sorry for himself. Neither, however, did he hold back if he felt his knowledge was superior, which he obviously did tonight, like so many times before.

"Nothing would do but your mother accompany me. I tried to educate her as to the hardships and dangers, but that didn't matter to her, only her damnable promises to God."

"Sebastian!"

He acknowledged his wife by spearing her with a sharp look.

"I know all about the vows you made to convert the heathens; how could it be otherwise, thanks to your constant reminders? I have never stood between you and what you believe is your mission, but neither am I going to remain silent while you and your daughter risk our lives."

The savage had spoken of his people, calling them Chumash. Maybe he had a wife and children, parents and brothers and sisters. When he returned to wherever they lived, was there ever animosity between him and the others? Maybe savages were incapable of complex emotions, but—

"Lucita? Are you listening?"

"Yes, Father."

"Yes, you are." Sebastian sat on one of the two beds, but his body remained as ramrod straight as it had been all day. "Must I remind you that a soldier was wounded here in a way which demonstrates the greatest depravity? His attacker *must* be hunted down and punished, or other savages will believe they can get away with such an atrocity. Control of the savages is essential to the success of the mission system, and to the glory of Spain. I accept the challenge; it's what my whole life has been about. The viceroy did not send me here so I could look after the safety of two women."

"I never asked—," Lucita began.

"Certainly not! The last thing I would allow is for my daughter or wife to commandeer one of the sparse troops for their personal use."

"Do you really believe there will be trouble?" She forced the question.

He snorted, the unresponsive part of his mouth at odds with the rest of his expression. "There already has been. I will not allow it to escalate."

"No, of course not."

*"You will know that I am here. . . . Waiting for the time to speak to you again. And when I do, you must tell me the truth, or your life will end."*

"But . . . how are you going to find the Indian responsible?"

"That is none of your concern."

"Father, please. The thought of you putting yourself in danger . . ." The words died as she asked herself what his death would mean to her. "Mother and I will be working with the Indians. It is possible we will overhear something that could be of use to you. If we could help—"

"Help? You? You don't know enough to remain inside after dark."

She should tell him it wouldn't happen again, but she couldn't. "I . . . I keep thinking about how vast everything is here. How can you possibly find one man?"

"Not a man. A stupid, vicious animal. He needs food and water. When he goes after those things, we will be waiting for him. And if he has convinced others that rebellion is possible, they will meet his fate."

*"I prayed to my spirit, and Wolf answered. I am safe, tonight."* "That is it? You will patrol the creeks?"

"How little you know! Just stay out of my troops' way." Standing, he stalked toward her. "I want you here. Here! Do you understand?"

"Sebastian," Margarita interrupted. "Your daughter and I are at La Purisima to minister to the souls of the Indians. We *have* to have contact with them. The Lord—"

Sebastian shook his graying head. "I order you not to make my task any harder than it is. Think about every movement you make; weigh the wisdom of it carefully. That is what I am asking of you."

He might have used the word *ask,* but there was no question to what he'd just said.

"Father?"

His response was to glare at her.

"I'm not questioning you," she said. "I just need to understand something."

He shifted his weight, his jaw clamping taut, which made her wonder if the scars he'd received over the years pained him tonight. She wanted to care for him, but he had never shown any weakness and she'd learned a great deal about keeping her feelings to herself from him.

"I've heard you say that the best way to defeat an enemy is to attack when they aren't expecting," she said. "Do you consider all wild Indians your enemy or just that one?"

"Lucita!" her mother exclaimed. "Our concern is with the neophytes' souls, not what happens to heathens incapable of hearing the Lord's word."

"I know, Mother." She'd already asked so many questions about her father's plans that she may have aroused his suspicion. Still, she didn't know enough, not because the savage might demand information of her, but because—maybe because she hoped to prevent any more blood from being shed.

Choosing her words carefully, she went on. "The neophytes once lived with those beyond our reach. If Father and the others attack the savages, how will the neophytes react?"

Her mother, so sure of herself when it came to religious matters, opened her mouth but said nothing.

Slapping his hands together, her father declared, "If only you had been born a boy! What a soldier you would have made. I will never allow a weapon in the hands of the neophytes, never take my eyes off them. Give a wolf back its fangs and it will regain the courage to attack."

Maybe, but the wild Indian had weapons and freedom and yet he hadn't harmed her. Why that was came to her quickly—a reminder she would be a fool to forget. The Indian had no desire to slit her throat as long as he thought he could learn something from her.

"The savages here have never attacked, have they?" she asked. "Not like what happened in San Diego?"

She expected him to dismiss her question as womanly nonsense, but he didn't. "That is because the military presence keeps them in line. My predecessor became complacent and it nearly cost one of his men his life. It will *not* happen again. Order *will* be restored."

*By making an example of one savage?*

With a grunt that sounded too much like a groan, her father reached the door and then turned back toward her. "If you were a man, we could talk the night away, but I do not have the time to waste discussing military strategy with you. I want to know where you are at all times. I will tell you where you can go and when."

"I'm not a child. I know—"

"Lucita," her mother interrupted. "Do not argue with your father. She will do as you say, Sebastian. I promise."

"I will hold you to that," he said and closed the door between them.

Without bothering to knock, Sebastian stepped inside the padres' quarters. The men of God had been sitting at a table with their heads bent over something Father Joseph was writing. They looked up at the corporal, and then, without saying anything, Father Patricio reached for the jug near his elbow.

"The soil here produces some of the finest grapes in the country," he explained as he handed the jug to Sebastian. "And our wine is unsurpassed."

The padre was right. Smooth and yet with the fire Sebastian's belly craved, three swallows passed in rapid succession. "Excellent," he proclaimed.

"We allow ourselves a nightly drink. It fortifies the blood and helps us sleep. Besides, what little we take for ourselves is not missed," Father Joseph explained as Father Patricio pulled up the only spare chair in the room so Sebastian could sit down.

"Then you are able to supply the Crown with a wine export which meets expectations?" Sebastian asked although he already knew the answer. His hip ached and his left calf threatened to cramp, but he refused to acknowledge either discomfort.

"More than meet," Father Joseph said proudly. "No other mission's wine commands a higher price, or is more favorably accepted. In fact, Pablo Portola, the merchant who has been servicing us for several years, has become a wealthy man."

"You are to be commended," Sebastian said and took another swallow, then placed the jug on the table. Although he would like nothing better than the oblivion of drink, it wouldn't happen tonight because duty came first, not the least of which was recording the name Pablo Portola to memory.

"Tell me, how often does this merchant visit and what, beyond wine, do you export?"

As the chattering, hand-fluttering padres launched into an explanation of their efforts to meet the Crown's expectation that the missions be profitable, Sebastian concentrated not so much on what they were saying as on learning all he could about the two. In truth, he cared not at all about the various crops and other goods that Senor Portola bought and eventually took to Spain. Of the two, Father Joseph struck him as less worldly. Everything they accomplished, according to him, was done for the glory to God. Father Patricio, in contrast, had a stronger grasp of what existed beyond the mission and the reality of secular life. He was more likely to speak first, and if he contradicted anything Father Joseph said, the whisper-voiced padre acquiesced. Sebastian recorded his interpretation to memory.

"I appreciate your attempts to educate me," he said finally. "And doubtless I will want to know more. However, one thing remains foremost in my mind."

"Of course," Father Patricio broke in. "And let us say, we are delighted to have you here. Delighted. Your predecessor—what can we say? Of course he was humiliated to have the viceroy order him replaced, but the blow to his reputation was not foremost in his mind."

"Patricio, please," Father Joseph warned. "The corporal is not interested in—"

"But I am. If I am to succeed where Corporal Galvez failed, I must know what his failings were."

"Yes, yes." Father Patricio smiled the rat-faced smile Sebastian already loathed. "I was going to say—there is no lack of female companionship here. They are willing, available. Corporal Galvez had a healthy appetite for such things."

"Which he won't be able to satisfy if he is ordered to sea." Not caring that the gesture showed the marked differences between the sides of his mouth, Sebastian grinned. "I have always maintained that a soldier who is able to satisfy his sexual needs makes a better fighter."

Father Joseph looked uncomfortable with that, but Father Patricio nodded agreement. If, as Sebastian had surmised, Father Patricio carried more weight here than his companion did, there would be no problem with his troops making use of the females — not that that would have made a difference.

"You have both been here a number of years, have you not?" he asked. Then, without giving them time to answer, he continued. "I trust that your knowledge of the terrain and conditions is extensive. Beyond that, I believe I can rely on your knowledge when it comes to educating myself about the savages."

"Of course, of course," Father Patricio said. "Anything you want—"

"For now, only one thing." He'd been leaning back in the chair in an effort to rest as much of his body as possible. Now he rocked forward. "I had a long conversation with the wounded soldier. He professes to remember little of the incident and insists he was doing nothing to have incurred anyone's wrath. However . . ." Sebastian paused deliberately. "The nature of his injury leads me to believe otherwise."

Father Joseph dropped his gaze but not so Father Patricio. "When he was found, his pants were down around his knees."

"So perhaps Senor Turi was expending himself inside someone's wife and that neophyte took exception to his actions?"

"No. No."

"How can you be certain?"

"Because no neophyte would do what that creature did." Father Patricio held up a fisted hand. "They know better."

"Hm. But someone wielded that knife."

Not breaking eye contact, Father Patricio reached for the wine jug, wiped the neck and lifted it, but didn't drink.

"It is my understanding that Turi suffered so from blood loss and pain that he lapsed into unconsciousness and thus was unable to supply any information beyond the obvious."

"True, true," Father Joseph said. "I argued to have him remain here until he was fully recovered, but when the corporal received word that he was being relieved of leadership here he insisted on leaving immediately and taking Senor Turi with him."

Sebastian already knew that. However, he believed that more could be learned by listening and observing than by flaunting one's knowledge. However, the time had come for him to reveal what he'd uncovered. He explained that his conversation with Turi had been profitable, not only because Turi had begun to remember more about the incident, but also because he was more willing to share those memories with Sebastian than with his commander.

"Something was described to me." Sebastian spoke slowly and deliberately. "I hope this particular detail will expose the savage's identity."

Father Patricio licked his lips; Father Joseph looked decidedly uneasy.

"Turi remembers a mark, a scar on the back of the hand holding the knife. He has no doubt that it was a wolf's head."

Both padres sucked in their breath, and something passed between them that Sebastian didn't, yet, understand but vowed to.

"Black Wolf," Father Patricio hissed.

The harsh noise sliced through Lucita's dream of standing in the dark while even darker eyes stared back at her. Springing up from the uncomfortable bed, she struggled to remember where she was and how she'd got there.

When the inharmonious clanging was repeated, she looked over at her mother, who appeared just as confused, then hurried to her feet and stared out the window. She couldn't see the church but surmised that someone was ringing the three campaigner bells. Dawn had just begun to slide past the night, and now that her heartbeat was returning to normal, all she wanted was to crawl back into bed.

"Prayers," her mother announced. "Hurry and dress yourself."

· By forcing herself not to think beyond the act of slipping out of her nightgown and into the dress she'd worn yesterday—a necessity, because she hadn't yet unpacked the rest of her limited wardrobe—Lucita managed to be ready by the time her mother was. Yawning, she stepped outside.

A ragged current of human movement flowed past; she estimated that nearly two hundred Indians were heading toward the church. Not sure whether she was expected to join them, she let her mother lead the way.

Margarita, head bowed under her mantilla and hands clasped over her chest, paid no attention to the still-ringing bells that topped the solid church. The double front doors were open to let the Indians in, but Margarita touched Lucita's shoulder indicating she should follow her to the side entrance. Once inside, she found herself in the sacristy, where Father Joseph sat on a wooden bench, a trio of heavy candles in a recessed shelf behind him illuminating one side of his face.

"Welcome, ladies." Father Joseph's delicate smile took years off his age. "I wondered if you would be too weary for morning prayers after your long journey."

"A child of God is never too tired for devotions," Margarita replied. "Giving praise washes away earthly concerns."

Nodding, Father Joseph rose and walked over to the arched cloth-covered opening leading to the worship hall. He drew the curtain back a few inches, and Lucita could see the silent Indians, men and boys on one side, women, girls, and babies on the other. There were no benches, and everyone knelt on worn tile. Despite the many bodies, the silence was eerie, a sense of tension palatable. Only when the church was full did Father Joseph step into the room. At her mother's prompting, she fell in line behind the padre and took her place to the left of the reredos, where she, too, knelt.

The sermon, spoken in both Spanish and Chumash, wandered from denouncement of one earthly sin to another and went on for more than an hour. After giving heartfelt thanks for a safe journey through a land alive with so much beauty, Lucita's mind wandered. Her knees first ached and then became numb, and she worried her mother wouldn't be able to stand afterward. From time to time a child or infant began to cry, but he or she was immediately silenced by fingers clamped over a tiny nose and mouth, which effectively prevented the crier from drawing breath. Upset by such harsh treatment, she vowed to ask Father Joseph about it afterward. In the meantime, she took in impressions. Like the neophyte who'd approached the padres yesterday, many of the men wore only skimpy diaperlike garments. In contrast, the women had on blouses and skirts that rendered them modest by any standards. No one wore shoes. Hair length appeared to be according to personal preference, since many women had cut theirs short while a number of men let theirs flow over their shoulders. Although she'd occasionally glimpsed the Indians of Mexico, she was surprised by how dark the neophytes' skin was. Even her tanned arms didn't come close.

What first and then relentlessly made its impression on her was that no one in that stale-smelling, cramped space returned her gaze. She tried to tell herself that they were lost in the sermon, but as far as she could determine, nothing Father Joseph said elicited any reaction from them. Maybe it didn't matter to them. And maybe they didn't dare exhibit emotion any more than they dared let their babies cry.

At long last Father Joseph appeared to run out of breath, because he abruptly extended his arms in a gesture that gave everyone permission to rise. The blandness, the nothingness, was gone, replaced by—she'd seen fear in the eyes of the orphans she'd tried to comfort and knew that emotion all too well. It was here now, alive and overwhelming.

"My children, I am certain you realized there was no confession this morning," Father Joseph said, speaking in Spanish for the first time. "No penance for sins. In celebration of the arrival of God's new agents, you are excused."

A mutter ran through the crowd, but it quickly died away and the dark eyes remained downcast. Despite that, Lucita caught glimpses of lingering apprehension and a sense of foreboding rose in her.

The Indians were still filing out when the bells again began to ring. Following the stragglers, she watched as they split off into several groups. Many started toward the kitchen while others headed away from the mission proper. There was still no sound beyond that of bare feet on earth, an occasional cough.

"Lucita!"

Her mother's voice spun her around. Margarita stood braced against the church's exterior wall, her features grim. Laced in with displeasure was a hint of pain.

"We are here to minister to the Indians' souls, not try to become them," Margarita warned as Lucita offered her arm for support.

"But . . ." No, she couldn't say what was on her mind. "Aren't you fascinated by what their lives are like? Where are they heading? What are they going to do with the rest of their day?"

The answer to that came to her in bits and pieces that made up a whole she didn't want. The Indians had split up after morning mass so the unmarried ones could eat their dipper of *atole* in the communal kitchen while those who were married ate the same gray porridge made from ground grain in their own huts, which were perhaps an eighth of a mile from the church. Once that was over, the bells called them to the lavanderia and cistern area, where an elderly Indian referred to as the majordomo separated the neophytes into several groups. One made up of men yoked the oxen and drove them toward the fields, and for the rest of the day dust kicked up by digging tools drifted over everything. Still other men were put to work making bricks from clay, straw, sand, and water, and she learned that each worker was required to make forty bricks a day. The same materials were used to mold roof tiles that were then placed in kilns to bake. Those responsible for keeping the kilns hot streamed sweat.

The women's work struck Lucita as equally mind-numbing. Thanks to the water supply created by an extensive system of aqueducts, clay pipes, reservoirs, and dams, a dozen women were kept busy cleaning the mission's clothing. Others wove either wool into coarse serge or hemp into cloth, their roughened fingers never at rest. Like the men, they had daily quotas to fill. Children as young as six or seven worked; the younger ones were placed under the care of several elderly women.

To Lucita's way of thinking, those responsible for rendering tallow into soap and candles had the most disgusting job. How could they force themselves to bend over huge metal pots filled with the fat of slaughtered animals while low fires slowly melted the fat so it could be drawn off and stored in skin bags before being melted again in the large rotating candle dipper?

She wanted to observe those working the olive crusher and the large whipsaw used to turn trees into boards and processing the hides used as trading goods, but there was only so much she could accomplish in one day, particularly because the bells announcing religious service rang three more times before dark. By then she felt both physically and emotionally drained and wondered how the Indians kept up the pace.

"How do they do it?" she asked Father Patricio when she spotted the younger padre outside the building he shared with Father Joseph. "Is their work ever done?"

Father Patricio lifted a goblet filled with deep red wine to his lips and swallowed. "The Lord's work is never done, my child. Surely you know that."

"Yes, of course. But—"

"I saw you watching the woman with the newborn twins," he interrupted. "Granted, her lot is harder than most, but her years of service to the Lord are limited. She must give herself to him now so she can assure herself of a place in heaven."

"But she looks so weak." Lucita nearly pointed out that providing adequate milk for her children was sapping the woman's strength, but she'd never talked to a man about such things.

"There are many weak and sickly neophytes among us, Lucita. If you have not yet been inside the infirmaries"—he pointed toward a barely visible building on the other side of the aqueduct—"perhaps you do not know the extent of the problem. They fall ill with alarming regularity; many die."

Instead of admitting that she hadn't yet committed herself to what would be her work here, she asked for an estimate of what he meant by many.

"We do not count the losses," he informed her. "It is the Lord's way of testing those who once were heathens and might return to that state if those of us who are enlightened do not fill their minds and days."

She'd once believed that busy hands were preferable to idleness, but that was before she'd looked into the eyes of orphans who had never known what it was to be loved. Yes, the Church put a roof over those children's heads and made sure their bellies didn't go empty. The priests addressed the orphans' religious needs and responsibilities, taught service and penance. What they didn't provide were caring arms and a warm chest. She'd tried to fill the crying need, but her arms could only encompass so many.

That was what those sweet twins needed, not a mother with bleeding hands and aching back, but one with enough energy to rock them to sleep.

"But what if that mother dies?" Lucita asked. "What is to become of her children?"

"They will be given to another with the ability to nourish them."

A woman who already had her own child, or children, to care for. It wasn't right! What was the harm in decreasing quotas or requiring one less religious service a day or giving them something more substantial to eat?

Not trusting her ability to speak, she tried to focus on the sky. The dust from the fields had finally settled, giving her a clear view of the heavens for the first time in hours. During the seemingly endless journey from Mexico to Alta California she'd often filled her sleepless nights with stargazing. It wasn't dark enough yet so she could make out that many stars, but the promise was there.

Father Patricio, his wine goblet now empty, had gone inside. She stood alone, watching as the world around her changed from the one dominated by the sun to something softer, quieter, lonely and yet rich with the opportunity for thought.

The neophytes were either inside the dormitories—a separate one for girls over twelve years of age to protect them from "insult," she'd been told—or in the straw huts she'd glimpsed. Her father, whom she hadn't seen all day, was undoubtedly with the other soldiers, while her mother had gone into the small chapel in the monastery building. She, alone, remained outside.

Maybe.

# 6

"There ain't nuttin' to it. All you gotta do is get your hands on one of the gals. After that it's do as you wanna, 'cause there ain't no one gonna stop you."

The soldier who'd been speaking fell silent with his mouth hanging open when Sebastian entered their sleeping quarters, but it didn't matter because he'd already heard enough.

"Go on," he challenged. "What were you saying?"

The speaker glanced nervously at the two who'd accompanied Sebastian to the mission. "Nuttin'. Just educating them on how things is around here."

"Are you? Well, now it's my turn."

As he expected, the five men straightened and gave him their undivided attention, at least as much as they could considering the late hour. Their uniforms were a joke, as was their physical condition, but they were all he had.

"I have additional information about the savage I've vowed to capture," he said. "It doesn't matter to me whether I take him alive or send his head to the viceroy as proof."

They all nodded agreement, but no one asked how he planned

to put an end to Black Wolf—proof to him that they weren't much more intelligent than the Indians.

"Thanks to the padres," Sebastian continued, "I know who he is, and that he grew up at the mission."

"He's a neophyte?"

"He was years ago, but he escaped. The padres tried to convince Corporal Galvez that Black Wolf is capable of entering and leaving the mission at will because he knows it so well, but my predecessor did nothing to either stop or apprehend him. That's how he managed to attack Turi."

"You mean he could be out there right now?"

"No, of course not," he insisted, although he had no way of knowing. "I'm certain he's aware of my arrival and that will keep him away, at least for a while. However, Father Patricio informed me that he's a curious and cautious creature. He's going to want to know what my presence means, and when he tries, we will be ready for him."

"How?"

Although he'd already pondered that while preparing his strategy, Sebastian gave the question additional thought before speaking. "Black Wolf has avoided detection because he knows how to blend in with the neophytes, but some of them, I am convinced, have been helping him."

That caused the men to grumble among themselves. Sebastian hoped to take advantage of their outrage as a way of making them feel personally responsible for the mission's security.

"I intend to ferret out those who have knowledge of the savage. They will be 'encouraged' to reveal everything they know."

"How you gonna do that?"

By answer, Sebastian touched the hilt of his sword.

Uneasy and yet determined, Lucita stepped inside the infirmary. Exploration of the mission and discussion of her duties and responsibilities with the padres had filled the first two days, but it was time to make good on her vow to utilize the nursing skills she'd learned at the orphanage. The padres had been pleased to learn she had experience working with the ill and injured, al-

though she'd sensed they were waiting for her to prove herself—
not that she was surprised. They'd been relieved to hear that she'd
been exposed to a number of illnesses but had never gotten sick.
She prayed that her good health would continue.

The only light in the cramped, stench-ridden structure came
from two small, high windows. There were six beds, four of them
filled today. Someone coughed, a deep, racking sound, and she
winced at the thought of the pain that must go with the cough.
Whoever was in the bed closest to the door propped him or herself up on an elbow and stared at her. The rest remained motionless.

Forcing herself, she approached the closest bed and discovered that the patient was a boy perhaps nine or ten years old. He'd
lain back down but watched her every movement. Naked, he had
a bloodstained bandage around his ankle, and from the knee
down his leg looked painfully swollen, the smell made her stomach recoil. When she began removing the wrapping, he offered
no resistance, but his fingers and jaw clenched. She wanted to re-
assure him that she wasn't going to hurt him, but she didn't know
how to say it in Chumash. Where was his mother?

What she saw shocked her so that the question died. The flesh
around the wound was so red and swollen that it was difficult to
tell exactly what was wrong with it. Forcing herself, she touched
his toes, and discovered that they were hot. Looking into his eyes,
she saw what she had feared: fever.

"What happened?" she asked in Spanish. When he gave no
indication he understood, she nearly repeated herself, but what
was the point?

Returning her attention to the injury, she took careful note of
the ragged flesh and exposed bone. Had he been tilling the soil
and injured himself with the tool he'd been using? As she looked
around, her gaze settled on the small table that held a bowl and
a mound of rags. Thinking the bowl must have water that she
could use to wash away the dried blood, she started to pick it up,
but the liquid was filthy. Recoiling, she searched for decent water
and bandages that hadn't already been used but couldn't find
either.

Appalled, she started toward the door thinking to find Father Joseph, whom she felt comfortable talking to, but she hadn't looked at the other patients yet. With her hands fisted, she approached the bed closest to the boy. The man in it appeared to be sleeping. From the way his facial features had sunken in, at first she thought he was elderly; then she remembered that she hadn't seen any truly old people.

Did none of the neophytes live long enough to reach old age?

His breathing was raspy and quick; his thin chest rose and fell, rose and fell. Dark veins stood out on the backs of his slack hands, and although it was her Christian duty to offer him some comfort, she couldn't yet force herself to grasp those useless hands.

The warrior she'd seen the other night knew what this place looked and smelled and felt like; he had to! No wonder he was determined to keep his people away from this hell.

*Hell.* Thinking of what should be a place of healing in such terms should have shocked her, but she was aware that it didn't because it was the truth.

More determined now, she placed her hand on the man's shoulder, discovering that he had no excess flesh, nothing, it seemed, between skin and bone. His mouth hung open and yet with each breath his lips quivered as he pulled in air through his mouth.

He was dying.

Alone.

None of those in the other beds were in immediate danger of dying, although both of the women were weak and feverish. Perhaps she should return to the man, but if he died today, certainly he wouldn't want her to be the one to watch that happen. If he had family—she hated to think of him without any—they should be here with him.

Just as the boy's mother should be with her child.

Awareness of the room's spent air suddenly hit Lucita, making her wonder how she'd managed to remain in here so long without feeling as if she might choke. Hurrying to the door, she flung it open and stepped outside, breathing deeply.

She couldn't lift the dying man or the two women, but the boy—

The youth was watching her again, his body angled toward her, eyes too bright. One hand clamped his knee, and she remembered that he hadn't looked at his wounded foot when she removed the bandage. Returning to him, she slid her hands under him and lifted. Groaning, he first tried to lean away from her, and then, when she refused to release him, he wrapped his arms around her neck. He felt so small, a sick child looking for comfort, that she had to fight tears.

Although she hadn't said anything to him, he seemed to know what she had in mind, because his thin body strained toward the outside before she'd taken a single step.

Someone had cut down a large tree not far from the door, and she carried the boy over to the stump and eased him onto it. Then she hurried back inside for the scrap of a blanket that had been at the foot of his bed and used it as a pad between his injured foot and the stump.

When she was finished, he smiled at her, the gesture tentative and fevered. Clamping down on a sob, she ruffled his hair and was leaning over to place a kiss on his forehead when a sound distracted her. Looking up, she spotted her mother.

"Lucita! What if he carries some disease?" Margarita gasped.

"He's injured, Mother. The air in the infirmary is horrible. That anyone gets well breathing that is a miracle."

Hands clasped over her breasts, Margarita took a moment to study her daughter. As always, her first reaction was that she'd given life to one of God's truly beautiful creatures. A child who hears too much praise grows up spoiled; Margarita knew that. Still, surely there was no harm in clutching her sense of pride about her only offspring to herself.

And what warmed her heart even on the most chilling of days was that Lucita's heart was just as beautiful. Wasn't what she'd just done proof of that?

"There are not many miracles in that place, Lucita," she made herself say. Although it was morning and she'd slept soundly because her husband hadn't demanded his husbandly rights, she suddenly felt old and exhausted at the thought of her daughter's willingness to enter that world. "I spoke to Father Joseph about that. He says many enter, but few leave the infirmary."

"No." Lucita sighed. "I don't imagine they do. Have you been inside it yet?"

"Briefly last night. Lucita, why didn't you wait for one of the padres to accompany you? To even considering tending to the needs of those unwashed alone—"

"Mother," Lucita interrupted as her parent knew she would. "You know what I told Father, that I was determined to see if I could minister to the neophytes' health needs here. That's what convinced him to let me come."

Margarita was far from convinced of that, but until she'd had the opportunity to speak openly and privately to the corporal, she remained in the dark about the man's true intentions regarding their daughter.

"Their spiritual needs must come first," she said, the words tumbling easily from their lips.

"That's your task, Mother." Lucita smiled, then fell silent as she rearranged the blanket she'd placed under the boy's foot. "I would never pretend to have your skills in that regard."

"It could happen. If you would turn your mind completely to religious pursuits . . ." Although she'd intended to say a great deal more, Margarita let her words fade off. The daughter she loved nearly as much as she loved her God was too worldly for the life she would have chosen for her.

"You are right," she said instead. "The land here is very different from what we left behind. I thought I had prepared myself for the primitive conditions we would find, but I never thought I would feel so . . . so alone."

Disbelief coated Lucita's features, but it was too late for Margarita to take away the words.

"You, too?" Lucita whispered. Straightening, she pointed toward the horizon. "It is as if there is no end to the nothingness."

"Are you sorry you came?"

"What choice did I have?"

Lucita smiled, but because Margarita had studied her daughter's every expression and gesture from the day of her birth, she knew it was forced.

A silence that felt both companionable and unfinished stretched between them until Lucita announced that she needed to bring a supply of clean water into the infirmary. Margarita started to insist Lucita order neophytes to do the work, but the creatures appeared so lacking in intelligence that she didn't see how they could understand the simplest of orders. Somehow, soon, she and Lucita would have to learn how to communicate with those they were determined to minister to.

When she could no longer see her daughter, Margarita walked over to the infirmary entrance, but instead of going inside, she stopped and looked around. The sense of loneliness remained, but only because she'd briefly put earthly concerns before her relationship with God. Lucita was right. Her task at the mission was to show the neophytes the path to salvation. She would begin by . . .

Maybe because she'd heard it so much of her life, she was able to isolate the sounds of horses and men from the constant din. This morning on the way to chapel, her husband had told her that his first priority was to make sure the men newly under him were proficient in fighting techniques. Plans for punishment and revenge would begin as soon as possible. She'd made the mistake of asking him if he thought that was necessary, and he'd retorted that only a fool couldn't understand that the only way to make sure the king's troops and religious institutions were safe from attack was by remaining ever at the ready and destroying any and all rebels.

Hand clamped over her mouth, Margarita reached deep inside her for a calming prayer, but it was slow to come. Instead, her mind insisted on going back to that long ago day when her father had refused to hear her desperate plea that she be allowed to become a nun.

She was his property, he'd insisted, and thus he was within his rights to plan her future in a way that was most advantageous to him. Six months later she'd found herself married to Sebastian, a man she would never understand and had nothing in common with. A man who, although she struggled to hide her reaction, sometimes frightened her.

Black Wolf stood in the middle of more sun-faded wooden crosses than there were numbers in his head. On this warm summer night three days after he'd confronted the corporal's daughter, it seemed as if the stakes marking where his people had been buried rivaled the stars in the sky.

Making a fist, he slammed it against the nearest stake, shattering the wood. Although sharp pain warned him not to repeat the impulsive gesture, he didn't regret what he'd done. This place called a cemetery wasn't the way of his ancestors. He ached to dig up the bones of those who no longer walked on this earth and carry them to Siliyik, the sacred enclosure in the hills where they would be honored with singing, dancing, and a large nighttime fire. After the mourning ceremony, the graves would be marked by the rib bones of whales and red, black, and white planks that reached for the sky, as it had been done since the beginning of time, and maybe the souls of the dead ones would find their way to the land of Similaqsa.

A barely perceptible whisper of movement pulled him out of himself. Alert and cautious, he waited. The young woman had run from him, and yet he didn't believe she'd told anyone about him, because if she had, they would have looked for him. Instead, the leatherjackets had marched and patrolled the open spaces beyond the mission and then marched again, always, it seemed, under the corporal's eye. Whoever came his way tonight walked in ignorance of his presence.

The sound repeated itself, telling him that a lone person was responsible. The imprisoned Chumash avoided this place as much as possible, and if Wolf didn't walk beside him he would be elsewhere himself. The newcomer might be a leatherjacket, but Black Wolf didn't think so because their swords and muskets made their own hated racket.

Confusion furrowed his brow when light from the stars told

him it was the young Spanish woman. Her steps slow as if her mind was somewhere other than on her feet, she entered the cemetery. Then she stopped and, like him, touched one of the crosses. Unlike him, her contact was made with fingers and not fist. He'd seen glimpses of her since their meeting, but she'd always been too close to the buildings for him to risk approaching her. He should be glad to see her so he could demand she tell him more than the little she had the other night, but this place was for his people, not the newcomers.

"Go back where you belong," he hissed. "Do not disturb the bones of my people."

She started and gave a little cry but didn't run. Instead, to his surprise, she came toward him, trying not to step on the ground directly below the crosses, an impossible task.

"I'm alone," she whispered.

"I know."

"Yes, you must. I had no idea . . ." Her whisper trailed off. "I still can't believe there are so many graves."

"My people are dying." The words ground up from deep inside him, and he couldn't begin to think how to stop them.

"Yes," she whispered. "They are."

He'd expected—wanted—her to tell him he was wrong, that this too-quiet place couldn't possibly mean his people were leaving the land of their ancestors, but she didn't.

"It is night," he said instead of reminding her of his earlier warning. "Why are you here?"

"Why?" She breathed the word, allowed it to flow into the night. "Because . . . it has been such a disturbing day. So many things . . . I have so much to think about." She raked her hand through her hair. "A neophyte died a little while ago while I held his hand. I knew he was going to; I prayed for his soul, but . . . Are—if you try to touch me, I'll scream."

"If you do, perhaps your father's men will kill me. Is that what you want?"

She stood far enough away that he couldn't touch her, and yet he didn't sense she feared contact from him. Her reaction, along with unanswerable and fascinating questions about what was going on inside her, made him want to demand she keep nothing from him.

"Who was he?" he asked.

"He?"

"The man who died?"

"I don't know. I never learned his name, and the others in the infirmary—I can't talk to them, so I don't know anything."

"He will be buried here, but maybe that spot will not be marked with a cross."

"I won't let that happen."

"It matters to you?"

"Yes, it does! I watched him die because I couldn't help him; *he* matters to me."

"You knew I was waiting for you," Black Wolf said because he didn't want to deal with what she'd just told him. Her only value, he reminded himself, lay in what he might be able to force out of her. "You should have remained by your father's side."

"Maybe I should have, but . . . You wanted answers from me." Her whisper seemed as light as a bird's wing, comforting almost. "Answers about what his plans are."

"You know that thing?"

"No. Yes. I—what is your name?"

The padres had called him James, but he'd left that behind when he fled. "Black Wolf. What do they call you?" He asked.

"Lucita Concha Arguello Rodriguez."

"Lu-cita?"

"It means 'bringer of light.' My mother wanted me to become a nun and spread the Lord's word."

"Is that what you are, a nun?"

Her sharp laugh put him in mind of a knife slicing through hide. "No. No."

"You do not want that?"

"Want?" There wasn't enough light; he couldn't look into her eyes and draw out her thoughts. "There's no higher calling. My mother, it's what she wanted for herself, but—why am I telling you this?" She sounded angry, but whether at him or herself he couldn't tell. "You can't possibly understand. You've never . . ."

"What have I never?"

She took a loud and ragged breath. "I . . . I was going to say you have never been forced to do something that wasn't right for you, but I don't know you."

He wanted to agree with her, because they came from different worlds and no bridge would ever be built between those worlds, but they were both standing here, talking instead of attacking or retreating, sharing the truth of what the soil beneath their feet contained. Soon he would ask himself why that was, ask why he didn't hate her and why, he believed, she felt the same way toward him.

"Black Wolf," she said. "Why are you called that?"

"Wolf is my *'atisbwin*. When I sought a spirit helper, Wolf came to me in my dreams."

" 'Atis-bwin? What is that?"

"It does not matter. You will never understand!"

Her body tensed and he readied himself to spring at her in case she tried to flee. "What do you mean, a wolf came to you in your dreams?"

"If I say the words, you will call me a heathen."

"No, I won't!"

"The padres do."

Rocking back as if he'd struck her, she said, "I'm not a man of God. I'm not a nun. I'm a woman trying to understand what it is to be a Chumash."

"You do not order me to renounce my pagan gods?" he challenged.

Arms wrapped around her middle, she spoke through clenched teeth. "I have never known anyone who wasn't a Catholic, never known there was any other way to be, until now. Black Wolf. Your name says so much about what you are, while mine is a constant reminder of what another person wanted me to be. Please, tell me about your spirit helper, your dreams."

"No. They are mine, not yours. Lucita, you left your people tonight not just because you needed to think. I believe you were wondering if I would find you again. What is the truth you carry within you?"

She sucked in a noisy breath. "I . . . I want to tell you to be careful."

"I am in danger?"

"Yes. He—my father—he wants to make an example of whoever wounded that soldier."

"An example?"

"He . . . Black Wolf, if he captures you, he'll kill you."

"He does not know who I am, where to look for me."

"But he's determined. He won't rest until . . . I know him."

He'd opened his mouth to ask her to tell him more when the sound of approaching footsteps captured his attention. Launching himself at her, he grabbed her and pulled her tight against him, his free hand clamped over her mouth. Every line of her body tensed, but she didn't try to fight him, and after a moment he slackened his grip.

The footsteps came closer, slow and steady. Because his knife hung at his hip, he would have to shove Lucita aside in order to attack, but the stranger didn't know he was here, which gave him the advantage. And he would kill if that's what it took to assure he would go on living.

"Lucita!" a woman cried out. "Lucita, where are you?"

"My mother," Lucita whispered against his hand. "Don't—please don't."

"Lucita?" Margarita repeated. "Is that you?"

Before Lucita could decide whether Black Wolf would allow her to speak or slit her throat to ensure her silence, the warrior pushed her away from him, and she knew he'd left because her nerve endings told her.

"I'm here, Mother," she managed.

Because she was cloaked in her everlasting black, Margarita was in the middle of the cemetery before Lucita could fully separate her from the night.

"Thank the Lord!" Margarita clutched her against her soft,

ample bosom. "When I realized you weren't in our quarters, I became frantic. Lucita, if your father knew you were out here—"

"Mother, look around you. Do you know what this is?"

Still holding onto her, Margarita took in her surroundings. "The cemetery," she said in a small voice.

"There are so many . . . So many graves."

"This land is harsh. The wild animals—"

"Wild animals aren't responsible."

Black Wolf had stood in the middle of this evidence of death, his tone and the way he held himself telling her how deeply it affected him. Was it possible that he'd said what he had because he sensed she had the same reaction?

"Then what?" Margarita pressed.

"I don't want to think about it, but after working in the infirmary I don't have any choice. Mother, La Purisima hasn't been here that many years. There shouldn't have been this many deaths."

Margarita released her and pulled her mantilla close around her throat. "I pray their souls had been saved before they met their maker."

Saved by her God? What about the Chumash god?

Three small crosses had been placed close to a larger one, but none were marked, and Lucita had no way of knowing whether they were related. She hoped not, because if they were, perhaps a mother or father and three children had all died at the same time.

Maybe Black Wolf knew.

"Lucita, we have to go inside, now!"

Eyes misting, Lucita caressed the closest of the small crosses. The finish was rough and a sliver poked into her fingertip. She pulled it out with her teeth, then again placed her hand on the simple marking.

Had this forgotten child ever known the freedom Black Wolf fought for so fiercely?

# 7

The mission far behind him, Black Wolf lifted his eyes to the sky and gave thanks to Moon for protecting him tonight. The girl hadn't told him anything he didn't already know. The leatherjackets wanted him dead; if they managed to find his village, they would attack it, either killing or capturing any who stood in their way. His task was clear: he must keep the enemy from his people by giving them tracks leading elsewhere to follow.

But first . . .

Watching Lucita and her mother together had done things to him he hadn't wanted and yet had no desire to fight. Instead of melting into the night the way caution dictated, he'd remained just out of sight while the two women embraced, their indistinct words carrying only emotion. And in the silence that enveloped him after they left he remembered how his son felt in his arms, the sound of the child's laughter. Need as powerful as a wildfire flowed through him.

Choosing his footing carefully, he trotted toward the foothills, legs and lungs and heart as strong as his spirit, his recently injured ribs unimportant. It would take him most of the night to reach the shelter he'd built for Fox Running and the boy's mother.

By then, even Black Wolf's body would cry out for rest, but that was all right because, tired, he might forget that Lucita hadn't run from him, had sought him out.

The last of the stars had disappeared when Black Wolf stepped into the trees that sheltered his people's low mountain village. As he did, he caught the aroma of cooking meat and his belly loudly reminded him of how long he'd gone without food. Over one shoulder he carried the carcass of the doe his sinew-backed bow had brought down during the night. He would partake of someone else's food this morning, but soon his people would eat what he had provided.

There were only two tule-and-willow-thatched huts in this new place they called home, unlike years past, when as many as thirty families had lived in separate but closely placed homes. At least, the two structures were large enough that everyone had adequate sleeping room, but it never ceased to bother him that they were forced to live as fugitives.

Cooking fires were going in both huts, as witnessed by the twin trails of smoke coming out of the roof holes. Walks at Night, the village *wot,* or chief, lived in the larger of the two, but sharing what he knew with the man he would one day replace would have to wait. Both excited and strangely nervous, Black Wolf pushed aside the tule mat that served as the smaller hut's door and entered. The moment he did, the mutter of early-morning voices faded and he felt all attention fix on him. Standing motionless, he gave everyone time to recognize him.

"He returns!" an elderly man called out.

"Black Wolf? You were gone so long, we thought—"

"What did you see? My sister—is she well?"

"Are there more cattle? Is it safe to go after them?"

Unable to sort out the various questions, he lowered the deer carcass to the ground and held up his hand indicating he would answer everyone in time. But for now—"Fox Running? Where is he?"

A shy giggle came from the direction of his family's sleeping quarters. He turned toward the sound, his mouth spreading into an unrestrained grin as a naked long-legged boy pushed himself to his feet. The child took a few steps, then stopped, staring.

"There you are, little hunter," Black Wolf said. "What have you been doing? Do you still have the gift I left with you? Surely you have not grown so old in less than a moon that you no longer play with Seal?"

At the name of the steatite effigy he'd given Fox Running in the spring, the boy cried out, "Father!"

"My son."

Dropping to his knees, Black Wolf held out his arms. As the warm and wiggling body launched itself at him, his throat closed and his head filled with a prayer of thankfulness.

His son was life and energy, high-pitched laughter and surprisingly strong arms now wrapped so tight around his throat that he had to struggle to breathe.

"Is that you?" He ached to grip his son with all the strength in him but didn't dare. Instead he listened to the pounding of the smaller heart pressed against his chest. "You are so big. How many fish have you eaten? How many acorns?"

Pulling back slightly, Fox Running held up both hands, his fingers widespread. "Bunches and bunches."

"You eat more than I do. Maybe you will grow up to be a giant."

Obviously delighted with that possibility, Fox Running punched his father's chest. Pretending to be overwhelmed, Black Wolf rocked back and then sprawled onto the ground. His son landed on top of him, pinning him to the ground. Fox Running's squeal echoed throughout the hut.

"I surrender! You are no longer a baby; soon you will be a man."

"I am so big. Big like a bear."

"Yes, yes, you are," Black Wolf laughed and clutched the boy to him. Fox Running smelled of the straw and reeds used to make his bed. A hint of wood smoke clung to his tangled hair. What set his heart to hammering went beyond the joy of being with the person who meant the most in life to him. The boy was healthy.

Black Wolf would thank his wife for that.

Still holding Fox Running, Black Wolf looked around but couldn't see Rabbit Dancing. The thought that something might have happened to her chilled him, but before he could ask, the others crowded in with insistent questions about what he'd seen and heard at the mission. He answered as best he could but kept his explanations short. Soon enough they would know about the new leatherjackets, but not until he'd discussed that with his *wot* and the shaman.

Finally someone thrust a coiled reed basket filled with roasted fish at him. He ate quickly and steadily, amused because his son was making a game out of snatching tidbits out from under his nose.

"You have not eaten for a long time," the woman who'd fed him observed.

"There was much to do, and I did not often think about my belly. I wish I had brought back more." He indicated the deer carcass.

"There is still a mountain of food at the mission?"

"Much is grown and the herds continue to increase, but a great deal is sent elsewhere while the captive ones go hungry."

"It is not right!"

"No, it is not." Fox Running was now making a pile out of the tiny fish bones, intent on his task. "Where is his mother?" Black Wolf asked. "She is well?"

The woman nodded and pointed toward a hanging woven tule blanket that closed off a section of hut that hadn't been designated for his family. Wondering what was so important that Rabbit Dancing hadn't come out to greet him, he left his son and pushed aside the blanket.

Little light invaded the small area, and it took several seconds for his eyes to adjust to the gloom. He saw his wife first as a crouched form, then realized she was looking up at him.

"My husband," she whispered. Although she smiled at him, she didn't reach for him.

"I greet you, my wife. And, again, I thank you for my son."

"He eats like a man." Her voice was low, gentle and understanding. "He is no longer our baby."

"No, he is not."

Waiting for her to explain what she was doing, he gave silent thanks to the gods responsible for giving their son life. Rabbit Dancing had not danced during the last Hutash, the harvest ceremony, not because she didn't want to but because in the past year her legs had become slow to respond to her command. He had said nothing to Lame Deer when his grandfather told him he was to marry Rabbit Dancing because it wasn't for a boy to question his grandfather's wisdom, but Rabbit Dancing already had two grown children. A widow, she had lived with her eldest son.

"She is a skilled healer," Lame Deer had said. "The shaman listens when she speaks. Her hands have magic in them; I fear you will need that magic."

Lame Deer had gone to the *'antap* seeking affirmation that Rabbit Dancing's time of childbearing wasn't yet over, and when he received it he'd encouraged his son to sleep with her often. Black Wolf had done as he'd been ordered, and his own prayers had been answered: he had a son. However, Rabbit Dancing had nearly bled to death while giving birth, and since then he seldom reached for her because their coupling pained her; no more children had begun to grow inside her.

"I asked," he told her. If she didn't want to embrace him, he would respect her wishes. "They assured me that you are well."

"I am. But he is not."

Only then did Black Wolf realize his wife was kneeling beside a blanketed figure. Squatting, he took in a feverish face, closed eyes, a slowly and painfully rising chest. The man, an Indian, looked more dead than alive. His right hand was tightly wrapped; the bandage was bloodstained.

"What happened?"

"If I say, it will only anger you."

"You are afraid of my anger?"

"I know you, my husband. You believe your shoulders are broad enough to carry the burdens of all who walk your way. I . . . I sometimes wish you cared about nothing except hunting and gossip."

"Sometimes I wish there was nothing more to put my mind

to," he admitted. "Must I wait until he wakes before I know the truth?"

"No." She sighed. Then: "They cut off his hand."

*They* could only mean the leatherjackets. "Tell me," he ordered through clenched teeth.

Rabbit Dancing's explanation didn't take long. The injured man had been a slave at San Luis Obispo de Tolosa, to the north. For reasons he hadn't explained, he'd tried to run away. Recaptured, he'd been forced to kneel before the padre there as the mutilation took place.

"Despite his wound, he again ran," she continued, her voice thick with emotion. "I do not think he knew where he was going. Two of our braves found him, more dead than alive, near Tinliw and brought him back here."

"The shaman has been with him?"

She nodded. "Talks with Frogs has done much magic, surrounding him with curing stones and packing sage and willow bark around what is left of his hand."

"He will live?"

Her silence said too much. Black Wolf wanted to touch the injured man, say something that might help, but he had not yet been to the sweat house and was unclean from being around the leatherjackets.

"Where is Talks with Frogs?" he asked. "He should be here with you."

"I do not mind, my husband. Many have need of a shaman's powers these days, and there is little for me to do until it is time to collect sage and piñon nuts. Fox Running wants to be with the older children, and I let him because he is lonely when you are gone."

His throat constricted. "I do not want it like that."

"I know. I know. Black Wolf, there is another thing, something . . ."

"What?"

"This one." She indicated the unconscious man. "There is more wrong with him than the loss of what he must have to hunt and fight."

Because he'd never doubted his wife's wisdom about health and sickness, he merely waited.

"I fear his fever comes from the white men's illness."

Black Wolf took an involuntary step back. Then he grabbed his wife and tried to pull her with him, but she resisted and he broke off the contact. "You risk too much! What if you become sick?"

"It is too late, my husband," she whispered. "I spent much time with him before the fever came; if it is going to attack me, the danger began before I knew to protect myself."

"No!"

"Enough! I will not let you add my weight to the burdens you carry. And I beg you, do not remain with him. Do not touch him."

When she said that, he realized that she'd kept her body between his and the patient. "You cannot sacrifice yourself," he insisted. "I—"

"Listen to me, Black Wolf. I do what I believe is necessary. When the fever hit him, I thought about moving him away from the others, but I could not do that without help and I would not take the risk of asking someone to carry him, be touched by the air he breathes."

Placing her hand on her patient's cheek, she assured herself that his face was turned away from them. "I have not allowed Fox Running in here," she whispered. "I . . . I have not touched him in two days."

The thought of their son lying wasted and unresponsive shook Black Wolf deeply, and fear for his wife's health only increased the blow's impact. "There is nothing you can do for him? No herbs?"

"I have tried silktassel bush leaf, myrth, but nothing has strength against what the strangers brought here."

*My people are dying.* He'd told Lucita that and here was proof. How would she react if he forced her to see this?

"Leave him! You can do nothing for him."

"I wish it was that easy," she whispered. "But what if I carry the disease? Do you want me to walk among our people?"

A furious and yet helpless curse pressed past Black Wolf's lips, and Rabbit Dancing blinked back tears.

"Go," she whispered. "Please. I will not have you like him. I will not!"

"But you—"

"Go!"

She'd never been able to order her warrior husband, had never so much as tried. The fact that he'd turned his back on her and was walking out of the room served as proof that he knew she was right. Sinking into herself, Rabbit Dancing clamped her hands over her shoulders and began rocking back and forth, but pride kept her from crying.

Maybe Black Wolf would never know how much she loved him. He was so much younger than her, all energy and health when those things had begun to fade from her. They had their son in common, that and their love of being Chumash, but her husband's world existed far beyond her.

"I will not allow this to be the end of me!" she whispered harshly. "We have not had enough time together, my husband! There must be more. There must!"

When Black Wolf returned to the central area, he was bombarded by questions about how friends and relatives were doing. He gave some answers freely, such as the effort he'd gone through to ensure that the enemy couldn't track him here; others, because he knew the pain they would inflict, took longer.

Fox Running had gone outside, and finally Black Wolf used that as his excuse to leave. By now, summer's heat had settled over the camp, adding to his need for sleep, but that could wait.

As he hoped, he spotted Talks with Frogs sitting outside the *temescal* used for sweat baths.

"I heard you had returned. I waited here because what we say is not for many ears," the shaman said. "Our *wot* has gone hunting, but I do not wish to wait for his return." The short, paunchy man patted the ground beside him, and Black Wolf sat down.

"I must go back," Black Wolf said, his gaze locked on a cluster of seedlings growing in the shade of a large pine. He wondered how many of them would survive.

The shaman pressed his hand over his eyes, his thick knuckles turning white from the effort. "I see danger."

*Danger.* "It does not matter. I have no choice."

"What do you want of me?"

"Must I ask?"

Sighing, Talks with Frogs shook his graying head. "I do not want to do this, Black Wolf. My eyes tell me things that . . ."

Talks with Frogs was not a man given to silence. "I would not have a spirit helper if you had not shared your wisdom with me and my grandfather," Black Wolf pressed. "I cannot do this thing without you."

Instead of acknowledging him, Talks with Frogs got to his feet and entered the *temescal* through the roof entrance. Black Wolf followed him, climbing slowly down the interior ladder. Even before he reached the dirt floor, his sense of peace grew. The hot, nearly smokeless fire was already going, which made him believe Talks with Frogs had known they'd be doing this.

Black Wolf waited until until his shaman had seated himself and then did the same. He immediately began to sweat, and his lungs felt as if they might close down. He shouldn't have allowed so much time to pass without renewing himself here. The thought made him ask himself if he'd ever do this again.

Ever see his son again.

No! Not as long as Wolf walked beside him!

When Talks with Frogs began chanting, sounds without meaning washed over Black Wolf. Surrendering to the sensation, he mentally took himself back to the mission, not because he wanted to, but because it was important that his people know as much as he did. He "stared" at the padres, "heard" the commanding bells, "smelled" the stench of melting tallow, "slammed" his fist against a careless cross.

"You do not want to be at that place," Talks with Frogs said, his voice a deep singsong. "Your heart beats fast and you cannot swallow."

*Yes.*

"You ask yourself if there could have been another way. If you had not plunged your spear into a leatherjacket, they would not now be hunting you."

*I know.*

"But that was yesterday's step and you did what a warrior must do. You can only walk in today."

*Yes.*

"You are right to go back; your people's future depends on what you learn."

*Because of what I did.*

"Seek the shadows, Black Wolf, your spirit always with you. Do what you must. Slip close to the leatherjackets and listen to what they say. Step into where they live and count their weapons. Ah! I hear your heart pounding, feel your determination. You want to seize the enemy's muskets, lances, and swords and bring them here so that strength will be in the hands of your people."

*Yes.*

"Be wise, Black Wolf. Put wisdom before all else. If you do not, your son will grow up without a father."

*No!*

"You sense danger. It comes on *cenhes,* the wind, but it is not a *nunasis.* There is no danger from a hate-filled supernatural being."

"I do not fear *nunasis.* I never have."

"Because your *skaluks* is so strong. No one's, not even mine, is stronger. But perhaps even Wolf lacks the power to protect you now."

"No!"

"I pray you are right. Listen to me. You remember when the leatherjackets rode down on your parents' village and murdered your father and threw a rope around your neck and dragged you off to live as a slave."

*I will kill—*

"Listen to me! Never forget the feel of that rope, but do not let your need for revenge rule you. Hatred is unwise, dangerous. Ah! Fear wants to wrap itself around you, but you turn your back on it, try to deny it. I say this to you—do not surrender to fear as a child does no matter what you must face. Instead, take the knowledge born from that time and those emotions and make them part of everything you are and do."

"I already have," he whispered.

Talks with Frogs rocked back and forth, his arms uplifted, eyes closed. "Yes. Yes. You carry much wisdom inside your heart and mind. That and more courage than most of our warriors."

The shaman lowered his arms and grabbed Black Wolf's ankle. "Wisdom lives in your heart, in your head. The courage of Wolf gives your muscles strength. These things are gifts from your *skaluks*. I pray . . . I pray the gifts will be enough."

His hold became tighter, but despite the sharp pain, Black Wolf didn't try to pull free.

"We are one now, one," Talks with Frogs said. "I walk in yesterday with you, know—ah!"

"What?"

The shaman's mouth worked and his lids fell and rose. Still, several seconds passed before he spoke. "This last time at the mission was different from those that came before. You saw and heard and experienced things you never have. I see inside you and know this."

*Tell him everything; hold nothing back.* "There is a new corporal," he said. "He walks like a bull and is always armed. He has vowed to kill me."

"No." The word came out a hiss. "That is not it. Not all of it."

Leaning forward, Talks with Frogs gulped in a deep breath. Black Wolf imagined his essence being sucked deep into the shaman and, along with it, perhaps more knowledge about his thoughts and emotions than he had.

"You do not yet understand the meaning behind this new experience," the shaman continued, "but it is changing you."

"Is this good? Wise?"

"I cannot answer. Only you can." Still holding onto Black Wolf's ankle, Talks with Frogs wiped sweat off the side of his neck with a trembling hand. "Dark clouds press around you. I hear your heart beating, hear the sounds of the leatherjackets' horses and weapons. You do not run, because that has never been your way, but I say to you that standing to fight may be the end of you."

Black Wolf had never questioned his shaman's wisdom. Hadn't Talks with Frogs been the first to know Rabbit Dancing was carrying his son, that it would not rain all through the hot days of this summer?

"I am not afraid of death." *Better mine than my son's.*

"A wise man does not fear what comes for all of us. What I say to you is that great danger waits for you. Your people need you; your son needs you. Do not ever forget those things."

"What must I do?"

The shaman released his grip on Black Wolf's ankle and took hold of his wrist. Eyes closed, he again chanted. The meaning behind the sounds, known only to Talks with Frogs, went on and on. Finally: "Danger, danger for all of us. A leatherjacket with blood on his hands and murder in his eyes."

"Sebastian Rodriguez."

"How do you know his name?"

"His daughter told me."

"His daughter?"

"I forced the truth from her."

"Black Wolf, no!"

Startled by the shock in the shaman's voice, Black Wolf nearly touched him, but he dared not pull a spirit man out of his walk with those spirits.

"You killed her?" Talks with Frogs asked. "Her father's need for revenge—"

"No. I did nothing to harm her," he said and then told Talks with Frogs everything he could remember about the time he'd spent with Lucita.

"She did not run from you, did not cry out? That cannot be."

"That is what my warrior's heart told me, and yet it happened."

"I do not understand this woman."

"Neither do I," Black Wolf admitted. "After our first meeting, I again sought her out. She looked into my eyes and said she had not spoken of me to her father, and I believe her."

"But what she told you may no longer be."

Talks with Frogs placed Black Wolf's hand against his chest and held it there while he prayed.

"The spirits have spoken," the shaman whispered while the fire snapped and hissed. "The danger which surrounds you touches all Chumash. We must know whether we are safe here— or whether we must flee, again."

Sweat ran off Black Wolf, and he felt weak. Despite that, he nodded. "If I want to call myself a man, my eyes and ears must be where the enemy is. It can be no other way."

"Ah! Take your charm stone with you. Take your strongest spear, your truest arrows. Never close your eyes. Walk always like a deer being stalked by a cougar."

"I will."

"I pray for you, Black Wolf. As long as we both draw breath, I pray for you."


"Wife. I want you."

A furtive glance told Margarita that Lucita had overheard her father's command, a fact that forced her to retreat into herself. Surrounded by silence, she stood and made her heavy-footed way to the door. When she opened it and peeked out, she saw that Sebastian was already heading toward the private space next to the soldiers' quarters that he'd claimed as his own. Certain the padres were watching and knew why she was following her husband, she kept her eyes downcast.

*I submit, my Lord. Always I will submit. It is the cross I bear.*

"Don't look so shocked," Sebastian admonished when they were alone in the room she'd been able to avoid so far. "It isn't a sin for a man and wife to be together before the sun sets."

"But . . . I thought you were busy." The room smelled of dry leather and his unwashed body.

"I have been; I have. But I don't have to tell you about my needs, do I?"

"No." Without waiting for him to order her to do so, she began removing her shoes. Most times his urges took such powerful hold of him that he didn't object to her retaining as much clothing as possible. All that mattered to him was that he have access to the most private part of her.

"Tell me." Hands on his hips, he watched her. "Do you regret coming to La Purisima?"

What she regretted but would never tell him was that her determination to minister to the neophyte's souls meant that for the first time in his career she had accompanied her husband on a mission. Always before she'd waved him off with relief lightening her load; she hadn't asked herself how he satisfied his needs while they were apart.

"The need for salvation is immense," she said in a rotelike tone. "My heart is glad God has chosen me to be one of the instruments for that task."

"Hm. And I daresay your relief at not having to force Lucita to marry Senor De Leon is just as great."

She kept her head bowed, but her senses hummed as she attempted to judge his mood. "If you had insisted, I would not have stood in your way. You know that."

"Hm. Tell me—no, no, go on. Now the stockings. Tell me, what do you believe my plans are for her future?"

Still not meeting her husband's eyes, Margarita slid her hands under her skirt. "To secure an advantageous marriage for her."

"Correct! I don't want either of you to forget that."

"Senor De Leon is wealthy. Why didn't you—"

"Why?" He seemed to be pondering that, and she regretted not having the courage to ask him before. "Because my mind was taken up with the details of this new assignment. Besides . . ." The working side of his mouth curled inward. "California is a land embraced by wealthy and ambitious men."

"Have . . . have you told her that?"

"There is no need. The decision as to her future is mine. It will do you no good to stall, Margarita. I want what is mine, and I want it now."

Her body feeling hot and cold at the same time, she did as he'd ordered, exposing her legs. Once done with her stockings, she immediately smoothed her skirt down around her limbs.

"What are you hiding from?" he challenged. "Do you think I haven't seen everything you have to offer, such as it is?"

He wasn't going to berate her today, was he? *I turn myself over to you, Lord. If it is your desire that I do this I will, but—*

Sebastian's broad hands clamped around her waist, and he pulled her close. Then he demanded she undress him. She did so, not thinking, working automatically.

"Have you no curiosity, Wife?" he asked as he bunched her skirts around her hips. "It doesn't matter why I want you now instead of tonight?"

"I . . . why?"

"Because I have something more important to do then. I will be meeting with all adult male neophytes."

"What—"

"It is time for them to learn who is in charge." As if to prove his point, he pressed a thumbnail into her thigh. "And for them to understand I will not rest until I have Black Wolf in chains. Or dead."

# 8

---

Walks at Night took two bites of venison and then passed the tightly woven basket to the man on his left. As the other adults did the same, Black Wolf felt his belly tighten. Tonight's meal was taking place in the *wot*'s hut as proof that having Black Wolf back among them represented a special occasion. Although he wanted to eat with his son and wife, he understood how important his presence was. What bothered him wasn't the endless questions about what he'd seen and heard and done but how little his people had to eat.

"When will you leave?" his friend Much Rain asked.

"I am not sure," he answered. "First I will spend time with my son."

"And with your wife?" Much Rain gave him a teasing glance. "You have been gone from her bed for a long time."

"That will not happen," he admitted softly so the others wouldn't hear.

"Poor Black Wolf. He is so ugly, so unmanly, that even his own wife cannot abide to sleep with him." Much Rain's features sobered. "I am sorry. I should not have joked about this. It is wise that she keep herself apart from you until she knows that the danger has passed."

Although it was more complicated than that and surely Much Rain understood, Black Wolf agreed and then asked his friend when he'd last gone fishing.

"Three days ago, but my spear remained dry. There is little water in the creeks now; you know that. I want to go to the sea, but it is so far and the journey dangerous. My heart weeps because we have been forced to leave what should be our valley home."

Much Rain was one of the tribe's better fishermen, and his frustration at his inability to provide for his people was etched in his too-dark eyes.

"I have listened to you speak of the richness at the mission, their crops and livestock," Much Rain went on. "They make us live like grub seekers while they sell everything they do not need to sustain life. It is not right! I cannot sit here doing nothing."

"Neither can I."

Reluctantly Black Wolf turned toward his *wot,* who had just entered the conversation. Although he knew what was coming, he remained silent.

"This time you will not travel to the mission alone," Walks at Night said. "I have spoken to the Paha, the Ksen, and with the shaman. It is wrong that we are hungry. It will be no more."

"My *wot,* I escape discovery because there is only one of me. A single deer slips easily through the forest, but a herd is easy to find."

"That is true, but we have no choice. If we remain like hibernating mice, we will starve. Tell me, Black Wolf, if I were dead and you had become leader, would you say any different from what I just have?"

Feeling both trapped and resigned, Black Wolf shook his head. Nothing, not even his life, was more important than giving his son and the other children the food they needed to turn them into strong adults.

After much discussion, it was decided that Much Rain and his young, healthy wife, Willow, along with three other men would accompany Black Wolf. Willow had just announced that she was carrying their first child and was determined the child be born full of courage, and what better way to instill courage in the unborn than by enabling him or her to accompany his or her parents on a perilous journey?

Black Wolf spent the evening with his son. Although Fox Running's ability to concentrate on any one thing for more than a few minutes was limited, his father didn't mind. The boy's high-pitched chatter filled the air as they played and talked, but at length his laughter turned into a whine and then tears.

"Are you tired, little man?" Black Wolf asked.

"No. Tell me a story about whales."

"I already did, twice."

"Tell me another one. This time, this time there has to be a grizzly and a sea monster and five elk and an eagle and—I want an eagle for my spirit helper. Lots of eagles. Have a whole bunch of them in the story."

"Wait a minute. I can't put all that into one tale."

"Yes, you can."

Touched by his son's confidence in him, Black Wolf pressed the boy against him. "All right," he said when the emotion that had clogged his throat receded. "But I want you to lie down with me while I tell it. Once we are rested, we can get up again."

Fox Running grumbled that he didn't need to rest but didn't object when Black Wolf stretched out on his mat and held the boy against his side. Black Wolf kept his voice to a whisper, his hand gently rubbing the small, warm back. As Fox Running's breathing slowed, Black Wolf pressed his lips against the boy's forehead.

"Listen to me, child of my heart," he whispered. "I love you as I have never loved before. Because you exist, I know why my father gave up his life for me. Thoughts of you bring sunlight to my days and strength to my body. You are why I live, why I will not run from the enemy, why I risk my life when I would rather be with you."

Fox Running snuggled closer but gave no other indication he'd heard.

"Wolf gives me the courage to do what I must, but if you did not exist, I would not care whether I had a *skaluks*."

The boy sighed, the sound ending in a soft squeak that brought a smile to Black Wolf's lips.

"Leaving you is so hard, my child..So very hard. I would give anything to . . ." Throat constricted, Black Wolf matched his breathing to that of his son; he would always remember the way the boy's body, limp and trusting, fit against his.

Finally, because sleep was still far from him, Black Wolf got up and made his way to where his wife was. She started as he entered the makeshift shelter, her reaction letting him know that she'd been dozing beside her inert patient.

"He still lives?" Black Wolf asked.

"Yes," she whispered back. "But not for long. His lungs do not have the strength to fight what rages inside him."

Coming a couple of steps closer, he listened. She was right. Every breath took so much effort that he hurt for the unconscious man. "His fever is no less?"

"No. I hate this! Hate what is happening to our people!"

Rabbit Dancing was like a slow-moving river. Although she walked as if she had nothing to do and no concerns, beneath the surface she churned. Perhaps it was her depth that he admired the most about her.

"So do I, my wife. Most of all, I hate having to be away from our son."

She hadn't yet looked up at him; that didn't change as she went on. "You do what you must," she said, whispering again. "You alone of our people understand the newcomers' language. When our son is older, you will teach him what he needs to know so he can carry on your wisdom, but for now . . ."

Now Rabbit Dancing had to comfort Fox Running when he cried for his father, a fact that tore Black Wolf apart. "I pray it will not always be so," he admitted.

"So do I, my husband, but what we want and what must be done cannot always be held in the same hand."

Nodding, he ran his hand over her long graying hair.

She looked up at him, her mouth soft. "It is good to have you here, but I fear that this sickness will touch you."

"It already has."

"What?" she gasped.

"At the mission. I stood outside the infirmary, walked in the cemetery. And yet I remain well because Talks with Frogs has blessed this." He indicated his charm stone.

"I pray you are right. Black Wolf, what happens between a man and his shaman should be for them alone, but I cannot let it be like that now. Please, what did Talks with Frogs say to you?"

Taking a breath, he forced himself to continue. "He called his spirits around him and looked into the future. He saw danger there."

"For you?"

"Yes."

Other than briefly lacing her fingers together, Rabbit Dancing gave no indication of her reaction. Scooting closer to her patient, she laid the back of her hand against his forehead. Black Wolf wanted to believe the man's illness would die with him but had seen it spread so quickly among the Chumash that it seemed capable of outrunning the swiftest deer.

"Our son sleeps," he said softly. "I would like to be like him, full of energy and curiosity about his world."

"I wish you could be, too, my husband. The enemy robbed you of so much of your childhood."

That was the past; he refused to dwell there when only the future mattered. "If anything happens to me," he said, "if I dïe, take Fox Running far from here. Keep him safe."

"Black Wolf, this is where the bones of our ancestors are buried. Our legends come from this land. Everything we are springs from this ground."

Why couldn't his wife be like the women forced to live at the mission? Along with their freedom they seemed to have lost their ability to feel, to think, to look into the future, to embrace the past.

"I know," was all he could say.

Rabbit Dancing tucked the deer hide blanket around her patient's body and got to her feet. She first pushed her hair back from where it had slid across her cheek and neck and then reached for but didn't touch Black Wolf.

Her sigh came from deep within her. "I will do as you ask, my husband, not because I want to hear your words, but because they live within me as well. If I must raise our son without you, I promise it will be in a safe place."

He needed to ask her where she planned to take Fox Running, but the question would have to wait, because she wasn't done speaking.

"What you ask of me," she whispered, "I ask of you."

"You speak of your death? That will not—" he began, then stopped himself because they'd always been honest with each other. "I promise. Whatever I must do to keep him safe, I will."

Rabbit Dancing's eyes glistened. He didn't want to think of her dying, not just because Fox Running needed his mother, but because she was a good woman, gentle and wise, peaceful when he might be wild.

"There are some who say it is foolish to bring more children into the village when we cannot promise them safety and enough food," she said. "But I say that without babies, there will be no more Chumash."

Rabbit Dancing seldom had her woman's bleeding anymore. He hated placing his seed inside her only to see her pain when her body didn't begin to swell with life. Still, they might never again be man and wife.

"Earlier you did not want me in this place," he told her. "You have changed your mind?"

Her mouth worked and a thin line of tears slid down her cheeks. "I want . . . I want you."

He held out his hand, but she didn't take it. Instead: "Go! Please go, husband of my heart."

Fighting not the need to release himself inside her but his desire to comfort her, he remained where he was.

"You believe your faith protects you from illness," she whispered. "I want to share that belief, but I prayed over this one." She indicated her patient. "So has the shaman and still he is dying. Go. When you return we will . . ."

Once again she was alone. Hoping to protect herself against that pain, Rabbit Dancing busied herself by first finger-combing her hair and then braiding it, but finally the silence caught her in its grip. Dropping to her knees, she wiped sweat from her patient's temple.

"He *will* return," she whispered. "And when he does, his seed will be strong and my desire for him even stronger. It will be different then, my body no longer old.

"Yes," she continued. "The spirits protect him, guide his feet. Surely they want his courage to run through the veins of all his children. Our children."

Split between fear for Rabbit Dancing, exhaustion, and apprehension about tomorrow, Black Wolf fell into a light sleep all too easily invaded by discomforting dreams. His son kicked him lightly once, waking him. He tried to bury himself in nothing again but couldn't find his way back to oblivion.

Wolf would lead him where he needed to go and guide his feet. Wolf, his *skaluks*, knew what was in his heart. *Walk with me into the future. Show me what will become of my people. Tell me what I must do to protect them. This I ask of you, beg of you.*

Shadows swirled closer. Made up of grays and black, they settled over him, softly trapping him. He couldn't tell whether they were warm or cold, wondered briefly if they now encompassed the entire world of the Chumash, and then it no longer mattered. Someone—maybe him—floated into the great dark shape. It seemed a wonderful place to be.

For a long time there was nothing, and then the grays and blacks returned and Black Wolf—at least what of him he could command—embraced the shaded world and pulled it in around him.

He wasn't alone. Forcing his heavy legs to walk, he approached the figure. Only he'd been wrong, as there were two figures.

*Black Wolf, my son,* one of them said without words.

*Black Wolf, son of my son.*

Although the two men were surrounded by mist, making it impossible for Black Wolf to make out their faces, he knew their voices. The spirits of his father and grandfather had come from the resting place of all Chumash spirits and were waiting for him; either that or his dream-self had found its way to them.

*Where are we?* he asked.

*We do not know. Maybe C'oyinashup. Maybe 'Alapay.*

The difference between the lower and upper world was great, and he should care which it was, but he didn't. His grandfather showed himself first. Although Black Wolf's memories of Lame Deer were of a man imprinted by time, the years had blown away, leaving a warrior in his prime. His eyes glowed with a red light, and his mouth hung slightly open like that of a panting animal.

*You are well?* Black Wolf asked, but his grandfather didn't answer.

Carrying a broken spear, Black Wolf's father stepped close to a fire that hadn't been there before. As Black Wolf watched, his father threw the spear into the fire, but before it could be consumed, it began to rain and the fire went out.

*What does that mean?* he demanded. *What does that mean?* His grandfather was still panting. His chest heaved as if he couldn't catch his breath.

*Answer me! What are you doing?*

The two men had started to kneel beside the embers, but he must have startled them, as they suddenly looked up. Their eyes changed color and when he looked deep into them he saw a world of spring-green grass.

*Are you looking into the future? Is that what you see?*

They were gone; perhaps they'd floated up to join the smoke, but he couldn't be sure. The gray and black shadows were returning, and he felt an almost overwhelming desire to lose himself in the dark colors, but he couldn't because his spirit still belonged to his earthly body.

The only sounds were his son's soft grunts and groans. Fox Running had pulled himself into a tight ball, his head resting on his father's outstretched arm. Black Wolf absently brushed the boy's coarse hair back from his face and then slid his arm out from under the surprisingly heavy head.

To dream of one's dead ancestors meant a warning of danger.

Suddenly cold, Black Wolf sat up. No light reached the sleeping area, which meant the sun was a long way from chasing away the night. He had been unable to give his father a Chumash burial. Despite his sorrow over a task not completed, he had been careful not to think about his father in the evenings. To have both men in the same dream—

Preparing himself for what might be the inevitable, he vowed to take along a tule blanket in the morning so his people would have something to carry his body back in. Much Rain and the others who accompanied him would see his burden and know but not question, because no Chumash ever asked another about his thoughts of death. Even Rabbit Dancing would remain silent; only her eyes would speak.

Not thinking, Black Wolf clutched his son to him. The boy stirred and let out a small squeak but remained a limp and trusting bundle in his arms.

"I love you," he whispered. "And if it takes my death to keep you safe, I gladly sacrifice myself."

A week had passed since she'd seen Black Wolf, and in that time Lucita had come to half-believe he'd been a figment of her imagination. Her days were taken up with what she had to do in the infirmary, and what little time was left over was spent either in prayer or watching the neophytes, particularly the children.

Another neophyte, a middle-aged woman, had died, but Lucita concentrated on the fact that the boy with the wounded leg seemed to be getting better. The last time she'd taken him outside, another boy a few years older than the one she called Midnight because his eyes reminded her of that had joined them. From the way the two acted around each other she decided they were related, brothers perhaps. She still had no idea where their mother was or if the woman was alive but would continue to watch and observe and encourage the older one to visit.

But not this afternoon, she reminded herself as she left the infirmary and started toward the kitchen for a late lunch. Once she'd eaten—

"You heathen! How dare you defy me!"

Stifling a scream, Lucita lifted her skirts off the ground and ran to the back of the small monastery building. She'd recognized her father's furious voice but had no idea who he was yelling at or why.

A horse's excited whinny sliced through the air, making it impossible for her to hear anything else. As her gaze settled on the activity around the prancing animal, she saw that her father held his sword at the throat of a nearly naked Indian. The Indian jerked away but abruptly stopped. He couldn't escape because his arms were lashed behind him and a rope had been tied around his neck. Cpl. Sebastian Rodriguez held the end of the rope, and as she watched, horrified, her father yanked, pulling his captive within a hair's width of the deadly point.

"Father, no!"

She didn't remember starting to run and had no idea what she was going to do once she reached them, but she couldn't let her father kill a helpless prisoner; she couldn't!

Ignoring her, Sebastian held the rope as if he were a vaquero controlling a wild horse. "Savage!" he bellowed. "How dare you defy me!"

Features hard, he increased the tension on the rope. Desperate to escape the sword point, the Indian threw himself to one side, but as he did, her father yanked down, pulling the Indian off balance.

"No!" she screamed. Reaching her father, she tried to grab his wrist, but he first drew his hand away and then shoved her, hard knuckles grinding into her throat. Gasping, she staggered back.

"Do *not* interfere, Lucita!"

A thin ribbon of red welled on the Indian's throat. For a terrified instant she feared the captive was Black Wolf, but this poor creature lacked Black Wolf's height and musculature. "What has he done? My God, what are you doing?"

"Done? I issued an order. Instead of obeying, he tried to run away. Now I will teach him a lesson the others will never forget!"

Kicking out, her father delivered a blow between the Indian's legs. The captive doubled over, and as he did, her father brought his fist down on the back of the man's neck. The neophyte sprawled onto the ground and struggled to turn onto his side, but her father placed his boot on the exposed neck.

Her throat throbbed from where she'd been pushed, but it couldn't possibly be as painful as what the prisoner was experiencing. To her horror, her father pulled a short length of rope off his belt. Woven into the rope were a number of small rocks.

"Don't! My God, I beg of you, don't!"

"Silence!"

His order struck her with as much force as the unexpected blow had. Still, because the Indian's life might depend on her, she refused to retreat from the fury in her father's eyes.

"You might kill him."

"Good! Then all of these miserable beasts will know my power."

Black Wolf had run, had escaped, and now lived far from the mission's influence. If he was ever recaptured, his punishment would equal or be worse than what faced the bound man.

"You have already hurt him." She explored. "Surely he understands—"

"Silence."

Her father was back under control, as witnessed by the restraint in his order, only that could be even more dangerous than his earlier fury. Reining in her own emotions, she locked her hands by her sides and forced herself to wait. Catching movement out of the corner of her eye, she realized their argument had drawn attention. Both padres were striding toward them; her mother hurried to catch up with them. Two of the soldiers stood maybe twenty feet away, prompting Lucita to wonder why she hadn't noticed them before. By contrast, the neophytes had retreated and were clustered together, their voices low and yet harsh.

His movement slow and deliberate, her father lifted his arm

and brought the whip down on the exposed back. The Indian shuddered and gasped, his breath going on and on. Again the whip struck him, this time leaving several red welts. The second gasp ended in a sob.

"Stop it!" Her legs numb, she staggered forward and tried to intercept the whip. Despite her attempt, it again connected with vulnerable flesh, and this time the Indian screamed. The sound hadn't ended before the other neophytes took up the cry, reminding her of frightened puppies.

"Leave me!" her father ordered. He'd raised his hand, the whip aimed at her. "Leave me or suffer the consequences."

*Run. Hide. You can't help*— But what if this were Black Wolf?

"He's bleeding, Father. My God, you'll kill him."

Unbelieving, she saw the rock-weighted rope coming toward her, the movement both swift and yet so slow she should have had time to escape, and yet suddenly her arm felt on fire. He'd struck her! In front of the priests and her mother and the other soldiers, her father had taken a whip to her!

"Sebastian, I beg of you!"

Not understanding how her mother had managed to wrap her arms around her without her knowing she was going to do it, Lucita could only gape and struggle to make sense of the nightmare. Instead of reducing her to tears, her injury instantly hardened her. She felt herself tremble but knew her reaction came from something far different from fear.

"Lock her up!" Sebastian ordered, his eyes locked on hers, hatred arcing between them. "She is not to step outside until I give my word."

"You can't—," Lucita began, but her mother silenced her by clamping her hand over her mouth.

"She means no disrespect, Sebastian." Margarita's voice had taken on the defeated tone Lucita hated and would have destroyed if only she'd known how. "She is overwrought. She—"

"Get her out of my sight!"

Sobbing, Margarita wrapped her arms even tighter around Lucita's waist and began dragging her away. Everything in Lucita screamed at her to stay and do what she could to try to save the captive's life, to let her father know he'd destroyed something between them, but would risking being struck again accomplish anything?

Her mother could barely speak for her sobs. "Please, please, he did not mean—"

"Yes, he did."

Her voice had been stripped of emotion, and in the few minutes it took for her mother to half-guide, half-drag her to the storehouse her father had pointed at, Lucita accepted that whatever love or respect or admiration she might once have had for her father had died today.

"I hate him," she hissed as the door closed behind her and the shadows took over.

"No. You cannot. He gave you life, kept a roof over your head."

But she could.

# 9

The heavy wooden door slammed behind her. Unable to face it, Lucita forced herself to concentrate on her surroundings, but there was no window in the grain-filled room. Darkness pressed around her, trapped her in her thoughts, and made it impossible to ignore her throbbing arm.

If she were free, she wouldn't rest until her father had been forced to acknowledge her outrage, her wrath, her hatred of him. In her mind, she saw herself pounding his chest, clawing his flesh, screaming like some demented creature. The image gave her a small measure of pleasure until she remembered how easily and totally he'd dismissed her.

Her father cared nothing about her emotions, her heart, even the condition of her flesh. It mattered not at all to him that she'd been appalled and horrified by his treatment of the runaway, but then why should it?

Her father didn't understand her any more than she understood him. They were strangers, two people united by blood and precious little else; she'd been a fool to think it might be otherwise.

Moving about by feel, she found a bulging burlap sack that

smelled of grain and sat on it. Suddenly weak and half-sick, she leaned forward and rested her head in her hands, breathing deeply until her mind cleared. *His* lash had torn a furrow in her upper arm, and although it would soon stop bleeding and eventually heal, she'd carry the scar to her grave.

She'd been in windowless rooms before; it wasn't as if such an existence were foreign to her. And yet . . .

Unable to lie to herself, she faced her fear's source. Never before had she been locked up and denied the simple act of walking about free. Darkness wasn't terrifying when a way to freedom remained, but when escape depended on the whim and will of someone else, someone who might even now be denying her existence—

"Mother." She whispered the word. "You don't want this for me; I know you don't. Why do you allow him . . ."

Her mother wasn't here, and it did no good to ask questions of the stifling air. Besides, Margarita would never oppose her husband. Lucita had been saved from having to marry Ermano not because her mother had successfully pleaded her case to her father, but because Sebastian believed he could secure a more advantageous—for him—marriage for his only child. In the meantime, he was determined to keep her near him, to protect his property.

Desperate for something to put her mind to other than her situation, she mentally placed herself outside. Instead of settling her attention on the mission, she went beyond, not just to the mistletoe-laden oaks, rabbit burrows, and aggressive blue jays, but to Black Wolf. Wherever he was, the warrior could look up at the sky, embrace the breeze, inhale the scent of the wilderness. Maybe he was with his wife and child, holding—

"Aarg!"

Jumping to her feet, she staggered about, stopping only when she hit her shin against something that refused to give. Ignoring the new discomfort, she held her breath until what she'd heard made horrible sense. A man was screaming, each agony-filled cry punctuated by the sharp sound of a whip against flesh.

The shrieks went on and on, sometimes little more than an exhausted whimper, too often high and sharp and inhuman. Sobbing and shaking, she clamped her hands over her ears and struggled to deny the pain in her arm, but the sound penetrated her mind and soul and her wound pulsed.

Her father was capable of beating a man to death, relished his control over life and death. If he so desired, nothing would stop him until no beating heart remained in the helpless, hapless neophyte. Sick to the point of nausea, she dropped to her knees and began praying, but her words made little sense and she couldn't complete a single sentence.

The unnatural night encompassed her, trapping her as surely as that poor creature had been trapped. Waves of something that might be fear and might be anger but probably was a tangled combination of the two sliced into her and stopped the useless prayers.

God, her God, wasn't going to stop the beating any more than he would lead her out of this prison. Salvation, for her, lay in waiting for someone else to unlock the door. As for the neophyte—

"Let him die quickly. Please, let it be over for him!"

Horrified by what she'd just said, she nevertheless repeated her plea, but all too soon her mouth clamped shut. Barely breathing now, hating what she was doing and yet having no choice, she listened. Her tears, which had died along with her prayers, began again. Either the Indian had fallen unconscious or her father had exhausted himself.

There was another possibility, that her stupid, hated, and yet necessary words had been answered and a life had ended. Wondering if she could ever make herself pray again or ever want to, she waited and waited, but the world beyond her remained silent.

Careful this time, she began a slow and deliberate search of her surroundings, because the alternative was to do nothing and her body, her soul even, demanded action. When her fingers found nothing new, she rested her head against a wall, the cool adobe penetrating her cheek and cooling a little of the heat left behind by her tears. She wanted to do the same with her arm, but just touching it made pain shudder through her. She was now thankful she couldn't see and that her mother had brought her here, because that way she hadn't had to watch.

"Lucita?"

Startled, she straightened. The voice was male, but with so much adobe between her and whoever had spoken, she wasn't sure of the speaker's identity.

"Lucita."

Father Patricio. "What?" she asked, surprised by how hard it was to form the word.

"It is over."

*Over.* "Is he dead?"

"Yes. Not that it matters."

*Not that it matters?* Rage boiled up from deep inside her, but she forced herself to remain silent.

"Do not waste your energy mourning the neophyte, Lucita. He was destined to sacrifice himself so the others better understand the consequences of trying to defy the corporal."

"Destined?" She could barely believe what she'd heard. "My father killed him. That is not a sacrifice."

"You question God's law? Do you not remember Job's words? 'As it hath pleased the Lord, so is it done. Blessed be the name of the Lord.'"

"God didn't make that whip. My father did. He decided to strike and strike and go on striking—"

"Your father has a mission here; you know that. What do you want, for Senor Turi's attacker to go unpunished?"

Was the padre talking about the wounded soldier? "He didn't; the neophyte wasn't—"

"Listen to me. We believe that creature had knowledge of where Black Wolf is. It was his duty to reveal that location, but he didn't. He knew the consequences."

"Black Wolf?"

His head cocked to one side, Father Patricio concentrated on the tone of Lucita's voice. She'd said the savage's name so quickly that he couldn't help wondering if she'd heard or even spoken it before. The possibility confused him and he debated whether he should tell her father, but that would wait. In the meantime, it was just him and the striking young woman with the unbelievably alive eyes.

"We have discovered the identity of Tori's attacker," he said. "Your father is committed to seeing him punished."

"By . . . by murdering a man?"

"Not a man," he corrected. "Never forget that they are heathens, Lucita, even those who have been baptized and profess to have abandoned their primitive gods. I know Black Wolf; both Father Joseph and I do. He grew up here." Believing he'd said enough, he fell silent.

"What—this Black Wolf?" Her voice sounded muffled. "If my father captures him, what will he do to him?"

"That is not for me to say," he expanded as an image of Black Wolf just beginning his growth into manhood filled his mind. If he could go back to that time, have Black Wolf again—"The corporal spoke of exacting on the savage what was done to his victim, for beginnings."

"No!"

"Lucita!" Pressing his hand against the wall, he imagined being able to touch her. "How dare you question the will of God! Do you not believe the words of the Scriptures? 'An eye for an eye.'"

"My father is behind this—God had nothing to do with it."

"Lucita! The Lord's hand is in all things. Surely you do not question that. Are you listening to me?" he demanded when she didn't respond.

"Did my father send you?"

"No. I came here on my own."

Forcing himself to concentrate on something beside Lucita, he looked around, but the neophytes had retreated to their quarters, the corporal had left to meet with his soldiers, and Father Joseph hadn't yet appeared to pray over the neophyte's body.

Assured that they wouldn't be disturbed, Father Patricio spoke again. "My child, I sense confusion inside you, and it pains me. I fear you have been touched by the devil. Surely it is he who placed those thoughts in your head, he who turned you from the path of belief and uniformity with God's will. It is my duty to lead you back into the fold."

"Please, leave me alone."

"I cannot do that." *Such a ripe creature, untouched and pure, deeply troubled.* "Lucita, get down on your knees. Pray. Pray for forgiveness and light."

"I—"

"Down! Clasp your hands in surrender and humility. Bow your head so the Lord knows you are repentant. Only then can you begin to hope for salvation."

"Father, I—"

"Lucita! There is only one way you will be released from this darkness, and that is by turning your soul back over to God."

"How?"

Nothing she could have said would have pleased him more. "By accepting my outstretched hand, my child," he replied. "By allowing me to guide you. You are not the first. There have been many, many who needed me to show them the way."

Lucita couldn't say how long Father Patricio had stood outside her prison. He'd gone on and on about humility and God's will and the necessity of begging for forgiveness while she'd tried to shut out his words, tried not to think or be. Now he was gone, but although she was grateful for the silence, she continued to struggle to remain above the fear that lapped at her.

The room was both too small and too large. She felt lost in it, small and insignificant. At the same time, she half-believed she'd become a giant in danger of being squeezed to death in the confining space.

Whenever the walls pressed in too tightly, she fastened her thoughts on Black Wolf and imagined him running free through the woods. He would stop to slake his thirst at a clear-running stream. There would be fish and frogs and plants that thrive surrounded by water, one after another of them catching his attention.

Because he understood that world that seemed so strange to her, Black Wolf knew which animals fed on what plant life and where to find deer, elk, even wolves and cougars. He could look at a cloud and know whether it carried rain and how hard the wind would blow and if—

A scraping sound jerked her out of her thoughts. Scrambling to her feet, she faced in the direction the sound was coming from and waited.

As daylight flooded her cavernlike world, she made out a large shadowy figure. The man stood motionless, arms folded over his broad chest, breathing loudly.

"Come here, now!"

Obeying her father, she stepped closer, stopping shy of the opening only because her eyes hadn't yet adjusted to the loss of darkness.

"Did you hear me? Come here!"

Lifting her hand to shield her eyes, she took another few steps. Once again she stopped while she was still out of her father's reach.

"Father Patricio informed me that he spoke to you," Sebastian said, his words clipped and cold. "He told you to look to your soul?"

"Yes."

"And have you?"

The question she needed to answer was not whether she had begun the effort of rescuing her soul from everlasting ruin, but whether she wanted to give her father the answer he demanded.

"I have prayed," she said.

"Praise the Lord."

Recognizing her mother's voice, Lucita peered past her father. Margarita had pulled her mantilla tightly over her head and was holding onto the knot under her chin with white-knuckled fingers. Margarita stared, not at her daughter, but down at the ground.

Grunting, Sebastian turned back toward Lucita. Now that she

could see clearly, she took note of how pale and tight the flesh around his scarred lip looked and was puzzled by it.

"I will *not* suffer your disobedience ever again, do you understand," he said. It wasn't a question.

Teeth clenched, her cheeks and arm on fire, she returned his stare.

"Did you hear me!" His harsh voice echoed throughout the room she could barely wait to leave. "You will never stand in my way again, *never.*"

"Yes," she whispered. "I hear you."

Striding forward, Sebastian grabbed her wrists and yanked her toward him. "You hear, but will you obey?"

*Give him what he wants.* But despite the yammering inside her, she remained silent, because what happened here and now might have a great deal to do with whether her father ever took a whip or other instrument of torture and death to a neophyte, whether he ever saw her as his equal, someone who held him accountable.

"For God's sake, Lucita. Answer him."

"I can't," she told her mother, because she wasn't ready to speak to her father yet. Her fingers were becoming numb, not because he was careless in his handling of her but because he was determined to exhibit his mastery over her; she knew that. "He's trying to force me to say he was right and I was wrong," she said. "But I won't."

"Damn you!"

Yanked off balance, she somehow managed to keep her eyes locked on her father's. She'd never noticed how incredibly hard they were; either that, or she hadn't allowed herself to see what lurked beneath the surface.

"Lucita!" Her mother sounded on the verge of hysteria. "That savage, he had to be sacrificed. Don't you see?"

"No, I don't see," she shot back.

Deliberately, cruelly, her father squeezed until she feared her wrists would snap under his grip. Pain slashed through her, and she had to bite back a scream, but in an insane way, she felt proud of her ability to deny him his pleasure.

"What would you rather I do?" Sebastian goaded. "Perhaps I

should tell the viceroy that I did not do my duty because it displeased my daughter?"

"I know—"

"You know nothing!"

Dizzy, she struggled to remain on her feet. Because she was still determined not to let him know how much he was hurting her, she tried to look beyond him and her mother, but it was impossible to focus on anything except this room and what was taking place within it. Besides, otherwise she might be forced to stare at the dead man's body.

"She is worthless!" her father suddenly hissed. With a final twist of his fingers, he shoved her away from him and whirled on his wife. "I am done with her."

"My husband, no! Please."

"You heard me, woman. This daughter who is not a daughter shames me. I should have insisted she marry Senor De Leon. Perhaps he would have taught her obedience."

"She is overwrought, Sebastian," Margarita pleaded. "This wild land, the primitive accommodations and food, the need for God's hand here—"

"More like God's fist. Hear me, both of you. I will be rid of my daughter as soon as it can be arranged. There is a man, a wealthy merchant. When Senor Portola arrives, I intend to speak to him about a marriage contract. Neither of you will oppose me in this. Do you understand!"

"Yes, my husband."

"You do, but does she? Listen to me, Lucita. Today you shamed me before my men and the padres and stood in the way of my duty. That will never happen again. Never! Nothing—" He glared at her. "Nothing would please me more than to have you spend the rest of your life on board some miserable ship. Anywhere as long as I'm rid of you."

Father Joseph would disapprove and it meant less wine for export, but Father Patricio handed Sebastian a full jug and then waited while the flush-faced corporal drank. They were standing a few feet from the body of the dead neophyte, and although the flies were already buzzing around it, he didn't say anything about their leaving.

"Perhaps he didn't know anything after all," he ventured, indicating the body. "Surely your lashes would have freed his tongue if he did."

"It doesn't matter," Sebastian spit.

"But you—"

"It doesn't matter," he repeated, his voice even more strident than it had been the first time. "The others saw. They won't forget the consequences of disobeying me."

*Neither will your daughter,* Father Patricio thought. "True," he said. "What do you intend to do now?"

He couldn't be sure, but it seemed that the corporal hesitated just a moment before answering. According to him, he'd had no time to do anything beyond ascertaining conditions at the mission, but as soon as he'd convinced himself that his men, both those who'd already been stationed here and the newcomers, were fit for extensive forays into the wilderness, he intended to expand his search for both Black Wolf and the rest of the savages.

Corporal Rodriguez seemed to be trying too hard to prove himself equal to the task at hand although he'd certainly handled the situation with the neophyte in a most aggressive way. Corporal Galvez had been easy to figure out since nothing mattered to him except getting through the days with as little effort as possible, that and making the most of his leisure. This new military man was a different creature, a fact Father Patricio had no intention of forgetting.

"I spoke to your daughter a few minutes ago," he said once the corporal had run down. "Tried to get her to see the error of her action."

"What? She is my responsibility, *mine.*"

A responsibility the corporal was failing at. "As a man of God, it is my duty to serve the souls of all my parishioners," he pointed out.

"I forbid it!"

Anger blazed through him, but he refused to let it show. He'd offered the wine in part because he'd wanted to tell the corporal that he suspected Lucita had had prior knowledge of Black Wolf but no longer had any intention of doing that.

In fact, there was precious little he wanted to share with the man.

# 10

Willow worked her way into the crook of Much Rain's arm and trailed her fingers over his ribs, but although his body responded, the warrior kept his attention on Black Wolf. A total of six Chumash had left the mountains before dawn, and while their early conversation had been about what food and perhaps even weapons they might find at the mission and bring back with them, as they neared the valley much of the talk had died away.

Much Rain had filled his time with thoughts of whether his first child would be a boy or a girl. Although he'd told Willow he wanted a girl so she could be taught to prepare tasty meals and massage his feet after a day of hunting, he'd long studied Black Wolf's sure-legged and quick-witted son. Nothing would make Much Rain prouder than to help guide his own son to manhood. What, he wondered, gave his friend the most pleasure about being a father?

Throughout the miles of walking, Black Wolf had led the way, and although Much Rain had occasionally joined him, his friend hadn't been much interested in conversation. They'd stopped near a small lake where neophytes were sometimes sent to fish and two of the warriors were now testing their skill in that regard, but although Much Rain would have liked to join them, the need to talk to Black Wolf was stronger.

"Remember last winter when you and I were following that elk," Much Rain said as he sat down near his friend. Out of the corner of his eye he could see Willow studying him with that small secret smile meant for just the two of them. "We kept praying it would snow so it would slow him and we could easily follow his tracks, but it didn't happen. Instead, my moccasin developed a hole and you lost an arrow trying to bring down a crow. I think it is not so wise that we tell our children of our failings."

"Perhaps," Black Wolf said, sounding distracted.

"What is it?" Much Rain insisted. "If you are concerned about our safety, do not keep it to yourself."

"It is not that."

"Then what?"

Finally he had Black Wolf's attention. "You and the others sleep all your nights in Chumash land and your bodies and thoughts have remained Chumash, but it is different with me."

"It cannot be helped. Someone must watch the leatherjackets, and who better than you, who understands their language?"

"I know." Black Wolf picked a blade of grass and began chewing on it.

"Still this bothers you?"

"Yes." He rubbed the back of his neck. "I feel unclean."

It was on the tip of Much Rain's tongue to tell Black Wolf to walk into the lake, but then he understood that his friend was talking about another kind of dirt.

"You purified yourself and the shaman blessed you," Much Rain pointed out.

"And after that I had dreams about the dead."

"No!"

Black Wolf said nothing, but it didn't matter because his eyes revealed the truth. "Does anyone know this?" Much Rain asked.

"Only you. My friend, my soul is heavy, and I fear it will stand between me and what we have come here to accomplish."

Much Rain's own soul now weighed more than it had a moment ago, but as silence stretched between them, he searched inside himself for answers. Finally he straightened, discovering that Black Wolf was looking at him.

"The others and I will wait here," he said firmly. "And when you return from Humqaq, we will take from the bounty of those who have taken from us. Our prayers for you will ride on your shoulders as you do what you must, and the gods will purify your heart and mind."

"Wait here? But the danger—"

"Do not concern yourself with us, old man." Forcing a smile, he patted Black Wolf's muscled arm. "Do you think we are so foolish as to loudly proclaim our presence?"

"Of course not, but . . ."

"But what?"

"Nothing." Black Wolf sighed.

"You think I do not know what you are thinking?" he asked. When Black Wolf's grandfather had brought him to the village, Much Rain had resented Black Wolf, not just because he was taller and stronger but because he was wise and questioning in a way he'd never seen in someone not of advanced age, but now he knew that wisdom increased a man's burden.

"You warn and caution because you fear your unclean state has placed us in danger; do not deny that," he insisted.

Black Wolf blinked but continued to hold his gaze. Again he sighed. "If it were you, you would carry the same fears."

"What Chumash would not? Listen to me, my friend. Go to Humqaq; purify yourself. We will be here when you return. There is none who would question what you are doing."

As a result of the three hours she'd been forced to spend in prayer for her soul, Lucita's knees protested her every movement. However, that had taken her thoughts off her injured arm and wrists, at least a little. Father Joseph had stood over her for at the better part of an hour, his gentle features pained. Neither of them had said anything, Lucita because shame and hate and confusion warred inside her and until she'd come to grips with what had happened between her and her father, she needed to keep her emotions to herself.

Father Joseph had been replaced by Father Patricio, who'd clamped his hand over her head and beseeched God over and over again to look kindly upon her, to forgive and enlighten. With his help and instruction, the priest maintained, she could again become one of God's children.

She'd tried to turn her soul over to his caretaking as she'd done so many times throughout her life, but the image of the dead Indian had remained, haunting her thoughts and closing her mind off from anything else.

Now, aching in both body and spirit, she slipped outside the small chapel next to the padres' quarters and drank in hot, clean air. Her mother, who'd been ordered to leave her side, might be waiting for her in their room, but she couldn't face her yet. A sense of apprehension touched Lucita's nerve endings, and looking around, she noticed that one of the soldiers was watching her. Of course. Her father must have insisted they not let her out of their sight.

Feeling half-wild and hungry for something she couldn't express, she started toward the too-silent graveyard but stopped because she knew she would find no solace or answers there today. The mission with its thick walls, ponderous arched columns, heavy tile roofs, and persistent, morose bells only added to her sense of being trapped. No matter what she might say, no matter how honestly she might express herself, no one would ever understand why she felt on the brink of exploding. No one except, maybe, Black Wolf.

She spent the evening working in the infirmary. When Father Joseph briefly joined her, they spoke, not about what had happened earlier, but about his hope that Senor Portola would be able to make good on his promise to consult with a doctor about treatment for blindness caused by eye injuries, since that had happened to three neophytes. Because she'd prepared a tea poultice under a physician's instruction for an orphan's infected eye, she told Father Joseph about that. Although the soft-spoken man was encouraged that there might be something he could try, he lamented that it would be months before Senor Portola could bring any tea leaves here.

"He is a good man," Father Joseph said. "Rich, as is expected for someone who has devoted himself to his business the way he has, but he knows how isolated we are and strives to bring us news of the outside world."

"My father told me about him," was all she could think to say.

When he was ready to leave. Father Joseph entreated her to come with him. However, although she would never feel comfortable in a building filled with unresponsive people, some beyond her help, she busied herself with changing Midnight's bandage. To her delight, all of the swelling was gone.

"Do you understand?" she asked, pointing at the still-red flesh. "Maybe the infection has been defeated."

The boy split his attention between her and his injury, and although he said nothing, his eyes carried their own message.

To her surprise, it was dark when she stepped outside. If a soldier was waiting for her to emerge, she couldn't see him, and because she hadn't thought to bring a candle with her, perhaps she'd escaped undetected. Her mother and Father Joseph knew where she'd been. So, she expected, did her father, if he cared.

Thoughts of her father flooded her mind, but this time she wasn't swamped by memories of the awful thing he'd done. Instead, she focused on the reason behind his action. He was determined to punish Black Wolf, and if it meant killing a neophyte to make the others fear his power, so be it. To him, all that mattered was that the Indians become so terrified that they reveal anything they might know about the warrior.

What if it had been Black Wolf today?

Unable to take herself beyond the horrible question, she made her way through the dark to the horse corral. Because she couldn't tell one shape from another, she whistled softly and then made a chirping sound until one of the creatures started toward her.

More chirping and clicking brought the big-headed, short-legged mare she'd ridden on her way here close enough that she was able to reach out and touch the animal. She couldn't keep her thoughts off how far the animal might carry her and, in truth, didn't try. Turning slowly, she took in the night.

Saddles and bridles were kept in a nearby lean-to, but how could she lift a saddle onto the animal's back when her wrists still throbbed? What was she thinking? She'd been forbidden to do anything without her father's permission and she'd never disobeyed him, never so much as thought about turning her back on her Church's teachings and dictates.

But she'd never seen death before either, death at her father's hands.

Never felt terror for a Chumash warrior.

As the mare nuzzled the side of her neck, her thoughts and emotions went to the hills beyond and to freedom. Silence and peace.

Her father had wounded her deliberately and cruelly, with no regard for her as a human being, his daughter. And yet he expected her to beg both God and him for forgiveness?

*I cannot!*

*Not yet.*

An icy cold gripping her, she stepped into the lean-to and began feeling around. Refusing to acknowledge the pain in her shoulder and wrists, she lifted the lightest saddle she could find and brought it and a bridle into the corral. If she was discovered — no, she couldn't think about that.

When the mare was ready, she climbed onto the saddle and again scanned her surroundings. Sudden light spilling out from the soldiers' quarters captured her attention, and she feared the figure illuminated by the just-lit candle was her father but then realized it was one of the men under his command. He stood with his legs far apart and his hands bracing his body against the wall. Because his pants were down around his ankles, at first she thought he was relieving himself and started to turn away. Then she realized he had someone pinned between him and the wall. Straining, she studied the other figure until she realized it was either a slightly built woman or a child.

Revulsion and horror slammed into her. The padres had informed her that unmarried Indian girls lived in their separate quarters so they would be protected from insult, but what she was seeing was insult; it had to be!

A cry of alarm pressed against her lips, but she didn't allow it freedom. Her father had done as he wanted to her; the same was now happening between the soldier and girl, and nothing Lucita said or did would change that.

The everlasting stench of tallow reached her on the wind, made up her mind for her.

Because of the way the buildings had been arranged, she could leave without having to get any closer to the quarterly. She took that route, afraid, not believing what she was doing, yet knowing she had no choice if she wanted to avoid madness.

Or maybe what she was doing was proof of her madness.

Sick to the point of nausea, Margarita paced from one end of the tiny room to the other, It seemed as if the night had already lasted for half of her life and no amount of prayer would make it morning.

Her daughter was gone! When she'd first woken, Margarita had told herself that Lucita was either in the chapel seeking peace for her heart or busying her hands and body by working in the infirmary, but she'd checked both of those places and then the garden, the various animal corrals, even tiptoed around the girls' quarters.

"Where are you?" she moaned aloud. "My God, my God, where are you?"

She'd come back inside because she was afraid Sebastian would see her wandering about, but now she was discovering that the fear of discovery was less than the need to go on looking. After once again dropping to her knees and uttering another prayer for her daughter's safety and guidance for herself, she pushed open the heavy door and stepped outside. The air out here was cleaner and cooler and might help clear her head. Was there anywhere she hadn't checked? Maybe the chapel again.

As she turned in that direction, she caught movement out of the corner of her eye and froze. A cold sense of dread clamped around her as her husband walked toward her.

"Where is she?" he asked.

Her mouth flopped open, but nothing came out.

"What kind of a fool do you think I am!"

"I never—"

"Enough!" he bellowed. "I swear, if I had known that marriage to you would be like this, I would have never bowed before God with you."

"Sebastian!"

"Sebastian what?" he challenged but didn't give her time to respond. "You forget something, Wife. You married a soldier. And a soldier learns to listen and look and observe or he dies. You've been searching for her for well over an hour, but you haven't found her, have you?"

The last, she knew, wasn't a question but a challenge. Sebastian had never struck her; he didn't need to because she'd always cowered before his size and strength and temper. If that temper was ever unleashed on Lucita—

"What are you going to do?" she managed.

"Disown her."

"What? No! Please, she—"

"Don't try to make excuses for her, Wife." He made it sound like a curse. "And don't try to tell me she doesn't know what she's doing. She's run off."

Hearing him say that brought yet another wave of nausea. "Find her, please," she begged. "She might—there are wild animals out there."

"And savages," he pointed out unnecessarily. "No, I'm not going to disown her." He spoke so calmly and quietly that for a half-second she let down her guard. "She is much too valuable to me for that."

Because he saw her as goods to be sold to the highest bidder.

"When she returns—and she will return once she gets a taste of the wilderness—I will teach her obedience."

"Sebastian!"

"Sebastian, Sebastian. Is that all you can say? Your daughter has shamed and disobeyed me for the last time, Margarita. She is a wild horse who needs to be broken to ride. As soon as I have accomplished that, I intend to turn her over to a man who will keep her on a short rein. A man who will pay me handsomely for the pleasure."

*I hate you. I hate you.* "Then you aren't going to look for her?"

"Why should I?" he asked and laughed that heart-chilling laugh of his. "Trust me on this, Wife. She will be back as soon as her belly knots in hunger."

**Point Concepcion**

Drinking in the taste and sound and feel and energy of the ocean, Lucita finally allowed her mare to stop. What little remained of night still embraced her, the moon not strong or full enough to bathe her surroundings in silver light. There might be wild animals out there, bears and cougars, wolves. Still, she hugged this darkness for the simple reason that she had chosen it instead of having it thrust on her.

Dismounting, she gave the mare its head so it could graze but held onto the reins because without the horse, she would be utterly alone.

*Alone.*

*For the first time in her life, truly and completely alone.*

"You aren't afraid, are you?" she asked, her voice thin and small and high. The horse chewed, vigorous crunching easily heard above the sounds of unseen waves.

"No, of course you aren't because you accept whatever happens; you do not question. Night or day makes no difference."

The mare sucked in a noisy breath as if testing the grass's quality before taking another bite.

"How simple it is for you. You eat and sleep and suffer people on your back, but you do not think, do you? You do not question or doubt. You don't even care why I made you walk all those hours. Why? Why did I?"

Unnerved by the near-hysterical tone in her voice, she pressed a throbbing hand over her throat and told herself that the mare would surely warn her if a dangerous animal approached.

"Black Wolf." His name whispered from her. "I was so afraid

for him. I thought—I must have thought I could find him out here and warn him. . . ."

For a moment she wondered if she'd said everything she needed to, but then: "The other day Father Joseph told me we weren't that far from the sea and that there was a decent trail leading to it. That's why we're here, not just because we found the trail but because I love the ocean. It makes me feel peaceful, and I need that now. Do you understand? I need peace more than I do human company."

When the mare gave no indication it had heard or cared, Lucita ceased her useless talk. The sea rushing back and forth along the coast had always filled her with a sense of restless energy, but tonight she was too tired to be caught up in it. Leading the mare, she made her way to a cliff that overlooked the bay and sat cross-legged on damp grass and sand.

"Listen," she told the mare. "It's a lullaby. The sea is singing to the world, and the moon and stars are here because they want to hear the song. We are blessed, you and I, because we are part of it."

*Blessed?* At the word, her thoughts tangled and tumbled. She wanted to tell herself, to believe, that peace and understanding would soon fill her and the awful turmoil inside would be over, but she couldn't.

"I don't know him! He calls himself my father, but he's a stranger to me." She ran her fingers over her upper arm, feeling torn fabric and a long welt but no longer pain. "Maybe . . . maybe he's a stranger to himself."

Once again she fell silent, overwhelmed by the possibility that Cpl. Sebastian Rodriguez might be or had ever been anything but sure of his place in the world. The simple truth, at least the one she'd always believed, was that he allowed nothing, or no one, to stand in the way of his determination to fulfill his mission in life. She—his daughter—had dared to resist his authority, and he'd proven himself capable of and determined to squash her. More than that, he would do whatever he decided was necessary to destroy Black Wolf.

Point Concepcion? She wondered who had named it that,

whether ships ever docked here, whether the Indians who lived with Black Wolf fished in the surf. Then, because she couldn't stop the questions, she wondered if Black Wolf himself had ever stood on this spot and what he thought about when he heard the churning sea and lonely-sounding birds.

Lucita dozed off as it was getting light. Every time she tried to stir herself enough to seek a more comfortable place to stretch out, exhaustion reached out to claim her, and she didn't care enough to fight. She couldn't lie on her side because that position increased the aching in her shoulders, but it didn't matter because there were other positions she could assume and the dreams that washed over her took her somewhere safe. They weren't really dreams, more like snatches of thought and emotion, endless questions about the rest of her life.

Finally daylight pressed against her eyelids and brought her to a sitting position. After a moment of confusion, she faced reality. Although she'd tied the mare's reins to a bush, either her knot had been clumsy or the mare determined to free itself. Either way, Lucita was alone.

Hunger gnawed at her and she berated herself for not having brought something to eat, but she'd been so desperate to put everything the mission represented behind her that she hadn't.

Only now—now she would have to return because otherwise she'd starve.

How helpless she was, how useless! The savages, as the padres called them, could sustain themselves forever in the wilderness. They knew how to take from the land, build shelters, raise families, survive, flourish even, while she . . .

"I am sorry," she whispered as an image of her mother returned. "I do not want to worry you. Please believe me, I wasn't running from you. I should have told you what I was doing. Next time . . ."

Shaken by the thought, she tried to tell herself there would be no next time. If she managed to get back to the mission with its food and water and walls and roof, she'd remain where the soldiers' weapons could protect her and she wouldn't starve. However, she only had to look at her purple and swollen wrists to know she might not be able to keep that promise.

Looking around, she spotted the trail and walked over to it. Not yet acknowledging what she was doing, she began back-tracking. Aware of the need for both caution and vigilance, she kept her eyes on what she could see of the horizon and fought the sense of loneliness that was no longer her friend. Once she spotted a distant deer and her features relaxed because the deer represented the freedom she'd so desperately sought yesterday. Twice quail scattered as she came close to where they'd been feeding, their reaction to her presence reminding her of the always nervous neophytes. Going back; she was going back. No matter how much she hurried, it would take most of the day to return to the mission on foot. Her father either had already sent his men out to look for her or was searching for her himself. When, not if, she saw him again, she would have to face his wrath, try to explain herself when she didn't understand.

She could remain here, hide from him for the rest of her life—her short, hard life.

*Lord, please look after me. Guide my feet and decisions, listen . . .*

What was the merchant's name? Senor Portola. He was expected any day, wasn't he? Could she marry a man she didn't know yet? Would he want her?

If she remained alive, did she have any other choice?

A high whistling sound sent shock waves through her, instantly pulling her away from her disjointed thoughts. Balanced on her toes, she tried to make sense of what she'd heard but couldn't remember enough of what it had sounded like.

There, on a slight rise to her left, form and movement. More than a little afraid, she faced whatever it was and waited, because there was no alternative. As a result of the sun's position, it was impossible for her to make out more than a large four-legged shadow.

Four-legged? Her horse?

Stepping closer, she realized she was right, but what else she saw quickly stripped her of her sense of relief. A nearly naked Indian had hold of the mare's reins and was staring at her as if he could command her with nothing more than the look in his eyes.

Black Wolf's eyes—even though she hadn't seen him in daylight before, she had no doubt that it was him. If he'd followed her here, taken her horse, and decided to confront her, she should be afraid, shouldn't she? But her emotions around the man—she would never call him a savage—weren't that simple. He represented a wild courage she'd never known existed, and instead of feeling overwhelmed or inadequate, she hungered for what he took for granted.

Step by step, she closed the distance between them, and although she was still trying to make sense of the fact that he was here, it seemed right. She remained aware of her empty belly, her aching body, questions about the rest of her life, but dismissed those things because at this moment Black Wolf was everything.

"It is you," he said when he was close enough that she could see his chest slowly rise and fall. "I was not sure."

"You—how long have you been here?" she asked.

"Not long. I traveled through the night."

"Why?"

"Because Humqaq is here."

"Humqaq?"

"It is a sacred place."

"Sacred?"

"To my people. To yours it means nothing."

*It wouldn't be like that if you'd tell me.* "I . . . I did not mean to disturb—I'm on my way back . . ." She couldn't make herself say the word *home*, not with him looking part and parcel of his surroundings, now that she could finally see him in the daylight. He seemed larger somehow, his eyes so dark that they took her back into the night. She could see what was on the thong around his neck and wondered at the meaning behind what to her seemed nothing more than a small polished stone.

"Why are you here?" he asked.

"I—it doesn't matter." She couldn't meet his eyes.

"To you it does." His voice was soft yet probing. "Your body speaks of the battles inside you."

"Battles?" she murmured. "How did you . . ."

When her words faded, Black Wolf slid his hand down the mare's rein and then pulled up, forcing the animal to stop eating. "She should not feed with a bit in her mouth," he said.

*Thank you for not pushing me.* "I know. I should have taken it off her, but I was afraid she would get away if I had nothing to hold onto."

"She did anyway."

Black Wolf couldn't possibly concern himself with the way she cared for her mount, and, for now at least, neither did she.

"Thank you for bringing her to me," she said as he handed her the reins. The mare shoved a warm nose against her shoulder; the contact jarred her still-swollen right wrist, and she held it against her middle in a self-protective gesture.

Black Wolf pointed. "What is that?"

"I, ah, I hurt myself."

Without asking permission, he took hold of her forearm and brought her hand close to him. Next his eyes went to the slashed sleeve and he frowned. "Not you. Someone who sought to injure you. Who?"

"Please, don't ask. I . . ." There was a mark of some kind on the back of his forearm, not a scar and yet not something he'd been born with, but she couldn't concentrate on it.

He touched her wrist with fingers so gentle she easily imagined them caressing a newborn. Still, she shivered, torn between her need for tenderness and the desire to break free. Her mother had always warned her not to let a man touch her in an intimate way, but was this what she meant?

"Who did this?" he repeated.

"My . . . father." She frantically searched for a way to take back the answer, but it was too late.

Mouth tight, he leveled his dark-eyed gaze at her until she felt compelled to return it. Although he remained silent, she sensed his question and knew she would give him the truth.

"I tried to stop him from beating a neophyte to death," she said.

"He killed—"

"Yes!" she blurted. "Black Wolf?" With no idea of what she was going to say, she placed her hand on his forearm.

"Tell me," he pressed.

"My father . . ." No, she couldn't be a coward, especially when Black Wolf's life might depend on his knowing everything. "He believed the neophyte knew more about you than he was telling."

"Me?"

"Yes. Oh, God, I don't know how, but somehow he found out you're the one responsible for wounding that soldier. He's vowed to make you pay."

# 11

His thoughts firmly on the untold ways his people's lives had changed since horses had been brought here, Black Wolf slipped off the mare's bridle. Before releasing it to feed, he whispered into its ear, smiling despite himself at the way the mare kept twitching it.

"What were you doing?" Lucita asked.

"Letting her know of me and you so she will not forget and wander off."

He could tell she didn't know whether to believe him but didn't try to explain because if they remained here, she would see the truth of his words.

In all honesty, he wanted to turn his back on this young woman with her bright eyes and sober mouth and, most of all, what she'd just told him, but if he did, a river would always remain between them, and they'd already come so far.

"Sit," he said. "We must talk and when we are done, you will return to the mission."

"I know," she whispered. "I shouldn't be—I was getting ready to leave when I saw you."

"I do not understand. No one knows where you are?"

"No."

"Why?"

"I wasn't thinking; I saw things I couldn't handle; it was as if I was going to shatter and all I could think about was getting away. But . . ." Face now buried in her hands, she went on. "No matter what happens, I have to go back."

Although that was her world, he wished she could remain near Humqaq forever, learn of its sacredness. "You are certain it is me your father searches for?" he asked.

"Yes. He knows your name."

Not a neophyte but a man had died yesterday because of him. It was possible the man hadn't known anything and simply hadn't been able to convince the corporal of that, but that didn't lessen Black Wolf's sense of responsibility and regret.

"What are you thinking?" she asked, and he wondered how long he'd been silent.

"Thinking?" Drawing in a deep breath, he made the decision to open a part of himself to her. "When I was learning to become a man, my grandfather warned me not to allow myself to be ruled by emotion and instinct, but it happened when I saw a leather-jacket attacking one of my people. Now I must live the rest of my life with the consequences of what I did."

"So must I, Black Wolf. So must I."

She was talking about what had caused her to flee the mission, but although he needed to know everything she could tell him, he wasn't ready to hear yesterday's details yet.

"You have not asked how I learned your language," he said instead.

"I . . . I wondered, but . . . you are right; I didn't."

"It was forced upon me."

"Forced?"

"I was too young to fight, a child, when the padres who came before the ones who are here now captured me."

She clenched her teeth at the word *captured* but didn't drop her gaze from his, and he again admired her courage.

"Leatherjackets attacked my village." The memory took him into himself, forced him to relive the nightmare. "The padres will say they came so the Chumash could be baptized, but that is not the truth of it. Some of our warriors were killed, my father among them."

"Black Wolf, no!"

Her exclamation left him feeling wounded when he believed he'd made his peace with his father's death. Speaking around the emotion took effort, and yet he wanted her to look into his past because that might help her understand who he and the rest of his people were today.

"A rope was thrown over me, and I was forced to go with the leatherjackets. When we reached the mission, the padres felt my arms and legs, made me stand naked in front of them while they studied me."

Her mouth slid open, but she said nothing, and he wondered how much she understood of what he was trying to explain. Father Joseph had told him that the Spanish protected their daughters and wives from the world beyond their homes and kept them innocent and pure and ignorant, but a woman who had watched a man being beaten to death had stepped outside those walls.

"When they were done, they said I was to serve them, not work in the fields or tannery or tend the animals."

"It . . . it must have been easier."

No, she didn't know. "The padres insisted I learn their language," he said. "I wanted to hold onto my ancestors' tongue, but they refused to let me speak it in their presence."

"But the neophytes speak Chumash."

"It was different for me."

She leaned forward, her knees drawn up against her body, eyes intent.

Restless, he gripped his charm stone and pulled the thong taut against his neck. "Lucita, when I learned your language, I came to understand a great deal. The padres called us children and prayed we would see their light and be saved, that when we died our souls would go, not to hell, but heaven. But when services were over, my people returned to the fields and tannery and were made to work until they could no longer. The only escape was death."

The day had promised bright sunlight, but a low, light fog had formed and was now spreading itself over the landscape. He felt himself being absorbed by grayness.

"I prayed for a death yesterday," she whispered. "And for that man's soul to find peace."

"Peace in the afterlife of the Catholic or the Chumash?"

She opened her mouth but didn't say anything. Driven by a force he couldn't fathom, he continued. "We were Chumash since the beginning of time, Lucita. That man's father and father's father and all who came before them were warriors, but now we are told that was wrong and we must become this thing called neophytes. I am not here with you so we can throw words at each other. What I pray to the Chumash gods for is that you see the true world of my people, not what others tell you."

"How?"

Holding the charm stone so she could see both it and his wolf tattoo, he continued. "The padres want the world to believe they are saving our souls, but that is not the truth."

"Then what is?"

"The padres are here at the command of the inspector general, who obeys the king's orders. There would not be missions if your king had not been worried because those you call Russians were on land the Spanish had claimed for their own. He ordered the Church to establish outposts so the Russians would see Spain's strength and leave. Lucita, your God did not send the padres here. Your king did. Whatever they must do in order to tame what they consider Spanish land, they will. And if it takes the lives of all of my people, so be it."

Instead of arguing, she kept her eyes locked on his, and in the silence that followed he wondered if there was anything he wouldn't tell her.

"You—the padres told *you* about Spanish royalty, about the Russian presence?"

"Ha! I was not that important to them, but I listened and I learned. Many things."

"What things?"

Why had he said what he had? Feeling trapped, he sought a

way to end what they were talking about, but maybe she was the only Spaniard to truly listen to a Chumash. If so, it was vital she see what was happening through Chumash eyes—at least, as much as he could bring himself to reveal.

"There are memories which will not leave me," he admitted. "Instead of fighting them as I once did, I now keep them bound within me. What I can say is that when Father Patricio took over for the old padre, I became his houseboy, served him."

She didn't move so much as a muscle, which he took to mean she wasn't looking beneath his words for the truth they rode on. "Lucita, Father Patricio tried to steal my soul."

"Your soul?"

"He ripped it from my heart, squeezed, and made it bleed." He *had* to stop speaking. Otherwise . . .

She frowned. "Why would he do that?"

What an innocent she was. "Because nothing mattered except his need for me." He forced out the words. "He calls himself a man of God, but I spit upon that image."

"Black Wolf! No!"

"No? Listen to me, Lucita. Your father killed a helpless man yesterday, but he is not the only one capable of doing unspeakable things."

Her eyes were hollowing out. Every line of her body had become tense and alert like a doe sensing danger. "That's why you fled the mission?" she whispered. "Because of Father Patricio?"

"In part. I was a child when I was taken from my village and had forgotten a great deal, but when my grandfather brought me back home, soon it was as if I had never left. I am no longer a child; who and what I now am can never be taken from me."

"What is your life like now? Please tell me."

The padres refused to let his people speak of the Earth Goddess, Hatash; *molmoloq iku,* who were the First People; and Kakunupmawa, the sun, and worshiping them resulted in a beating, but Lucita had no weapons, no force beyond her words. Still, that wasn't the only reason he dug deep inside himself for the answer.

His voice as impassive as he could make it, he told her about what Chumash life had been like before the first foreign explorer arrived and this land was theirs. She hung onto every word of how his ancestors had hunted and gathered, how they used reeds, deergrass, and three-leaf sumac to make their baskets, how they had built their round, thatched homes from willow, whale rib bones, and bulrush or cattails, the whistles, flutes, and bull-roarers that provided his people with music. Most of all she wanted to hear about Chumash gods and beliefs.

"What does it matter?" he asked. "The time may come when there are none left to believe."

"How can you say that? There are hundreds of Chumash living in the missions."

"Those Chumash's hearts and souls have been taken from them."

"Don't say that!"

"When you look into their eyes, do you see pride and joy? Do they walk in freedom?"

She shuddered. "No. No, they don't."

For an instant he thought she was going to touch him, but although the distance between them decreased, the contact wasn't made. "Maybe you're stronger because of what you were forced to do," she whispered. "What is it like to be a Chumash woman? Does her father own her? Can he tell her who she must marry and how she must speak, when she can speak?"

"That is not the way of the Chumash. Marriage strengthens the tribe. My wife was chosen for me because she is wise and thoughtful where I am quick to act. Her hands are those of a healer; my grandfather wanted to surround me with healing magic."

"Maybe that's why you're still alive."

"Maybe. And maybe it is because I embrace Humqaq."

A crow flew overhead, its harsh cry momentarily making hearing anything else impossible. When it had left, Lucita repositioned herself so that she was now sitting on her left hip. "This is Humqaq? It . . . it doesn't feel different from anywhere else."

She had pushed him too far today. Already he'd told her more than was safe, but her voice was like that of a songbird, gentle and filled with whispers of freedom. And she had fought to save the life of one of his people.

"Humqaq is not at this spot," he said.

"But close?"

"Yes."

"Will I ever see it?"

"It is not for you," he told her. "Only those who have prepared themselves and know the truth about our ancestors and spirits and gods belong there."

"I don't, do I?" she whispered. "Humqaq, wherever it is, is your place."

"Yes, and when I know you are safe, I will go to it."

She said nothing for several minutes. Then: "Do you ever doubt yourself, Black Wolf?"

"Doubt?"

"I do." She got to her feet, brushed grass and leaves off her skirt, and looked around. "Sometimes I think I doubt everything about myself."

"That is not right."

"I know." Although she laughed a little, she sounded desperate. "I want . . . I want my mother's faith. To have the depth of faith you do. I think I even want my father's conviction. He . . . he beat a man until he died because he believed he had a right and a need to do that. It was a horrible thing, horrible! And yet . . ."

She kept looking around, her eyes darting from one thing to another. He felt overwhelmed by the need to help her in her search, but he didn't know what she was looking for.

"My mother has never doubted her belief in God, never questioned it. It isn't that simple for me anymore." She ran her fingers deep within the mass of her hair as if she were trying to hide within it.

"Your mother does not know what is in your heart?" he asked.

"How can she if I don't? Sometimes . . . sometimes I feel as if there's a storm inside me and all I want to do is scream."

It wouldn't take much for her to start screaming this morning, but if she did, would it shatter her? Not sure what, if anything, she needed from him, he spread his fingers over his knees and waited.

Suddenly her restless movements ceased, and she looked up at the sky, drawing his attention there. He spotted a hawk, its flight slow and easy, as if it had been born for nothing except riding the breezes.

"I wish I was a bird," she whispered. "To never have to come to earth again. A bird doesn't think; at least, I don't believe it does. It doesn't cry when something dies, does it? It doesn't question whether there needs to be death and . . ."

She clutched her bruised wrist, winced but didn't let go, and he wasn't sure whether the pain registered with her. If it didn't, it was because the agony inside her head was far greater.

Leaning down, she picked up the bridle and started toward the mare almost as if she'd forgotten he was here. The horse shied when she approached it, but she muttered something he couldn't hear and it stood still, its hide shivering slightly. After putting on the bridle, she swung into the saddle.

Only then did she look at him.

"Fight for your freedom, Black Wolf," she said in a voice that was both weak and strong. "Don't ever let anyone take it from you."


"She isn't here, Corporal. Perhaps your daughter overslept and that is why she isn't at mass."

If Father Patricio had been a neophyte, Sebastian would have run his sword through him. As it was, the corporal saw no reason to feed his curiosity.

"Don't concern yourself with her, Padre. She is my responsibility, not yours."

"But—"

"Mine," he insisted. Not caring who might see, he leaned down and put his face inches from the padre's. "If you had done the job you were sent here to accomplish, there would have been no need for me. If you say anything to anyone about what goes on within my family, that is what I will tell the viceroy."

As Sebastian expected, Father Patricio blanched. Then he

looked around, his eyes widening as he realized that what was intended to be a private conversation at the side of the church was far from that.

"You wouldn't know who you are looking for if it hadn't been for me," the padre said after a long silence. "I have knowledge of Black Wolf, not you."

"You think I wouldn't have gained that knowledge without you?" He snorted. "Look, it is not my intention to cause problems between us; that will serve neither of us. However, I do insist you keep your thoughts regarding my family to yourself. We will not have to have this discussion again, will we?"

His head bobbing up and down on his thick neck, Father Patricio slid away. "I meant nothing of a negative nature," he said. "I care about all my lambs; Lucita is one of them."

"Perhaps." Deciding to let it go at that, Sebastian spun on his heels and stalked toward where his men were waiting for breakfast to be served. In retrospect, he was glad he and the padre had this conversation since it had solidified their relationship and taught the potbellied man who was in charge.

What had he told Lucita the other day? That they would have had a great deal in common if she'd been a son? What that would be like was beyond his comprehension, just as he would never understand why she'd run away. It didn't matter; she'd be back soon if the savages didn't get her. And if they did—

Irritated with himself, he shook off the thought. The time he'd spent at the presidio had given him the opportunity to talk to other members of the military about the Chumash. He'd learned that although they were a lazy lot with no resistance to disease and very rarely given to an uprising, they weren't stupid. And, he now believed, Black Wolf was the least stupid of them all. Black Wolf knew the folly, the insanity, of harming a Spanish woman, especially the daughter of a military man. If the warrior happened to come across her, he would slip away unnoticed.

Maybe not, Sebastian amended. Maybe he'd insist she return to the mission so soldiers wouldn't come looking for her, even bring her back himself.

The corporal's men looked up as he approached, but nothing about their demeanor gave him any indication of whether they knew about his altercation with the padre.

"These are your orders," he said. "I want two of you"—he pointed—"to head south in search of the merchant. He is due, and I want to be assured that he does not meet with any problems. The rest are to remain here and outside. I do not want the neophytes to forget for a moment our presence."

Long minutes passed before Black Wolf started toward the great sea that had always provided for his people but might one day be taken from them. Because answers from the spirits came only to those who had opened their minds and let them become like morning mist, he fought to keep from thinking about the girl/woman who'd ridden away from him.

The climb to the cliffs overlooking the sea called for strength and balance, and he took pleasure in what his legs were capable of. It felt good to scramble over boulders, balance himself on narrow ledges, work his way around the brush that clung to the thin earth here. Sweat ran down his back and his chest stung from scratches caused by the brush, but those things, like the act of climbing itself, kept his mind too full for thoughts of anything beyond himself, at least for a while.

The hawk he and Lucita had spotted earlier seemed to be studying him, circling and diving and climbing and then doing it all over again, never leaving. When he could, he stared back and challenged the creature to do the same. The hawk continued its travels through the sky, showing its superiority, and he prayed his son would one day see himself in the winged creature.

Finally, when his muscles burned and he had to fight to take enough air into his lungs, he reached the top of the cliff. Far below, waves pounded against the shore, roaring in both determination and pleasure.

It was right. He understood determination and felt pleasure at having reached the sacred place his grandfather had brought him to the fall he became a man. Only his grandfather's and father's spirits could join him these days, but he sensed he wasn't alone and was happy.

At least as happy as a man who carried the burden of his people and the awful consequences of his rash act could be.

After resting a few moments, he slowly made his way to the sacred opening and stretched out on his belly, peering down. The Miswaskin River became one with the sea here, but although it boiled with life, his people never fished at this spot because to do so would anger the spirits.

The Miswaskin, instead of drawing together for the final rush to the great water, had split itself in two. Much of the river spilled joyously into the sea, but some of it had found this other route.

As awed now as he'd been the first time he saw it, he marveled at the way the water threw itself out into space at the top of the cliff and then plunged to a deep and quiet pool sheltered by the rocks he'd just climbed. The only way to reach the shadowed pool was by climbing down a rope placed there by long-dead Chumash and often repaired and strengthened.

He took hold of the rope, his fingers digging into the knots that slowed and guided his descent. As he worked his way downward, he thought of the rope Lucita's father had used on the captive, but what he touched today brought, not death, but access to sacred water and, he hoped, peace for his heart and mind.

Despite the strain to his shoulders, he didn't try to hurry, because Humqaq was a place for thought and contemplation, for questions asked and answered by one's spirits and ancestors, but only for those who showed proper respect, who understood.

*Feel my presence, sacred one. Touch my heart and listen to what is in my head. I seek peace and have come here because this is what Humqaq promises. My flesh is not soiled; it holds no remnants of the enemy. I am clean. My thoughts are clean. I seek only . . .*

Margarita, driven to distraction by worry for her daughter, had been on her way to the infirmary with the faint hope that she'd find her there when the door swung open and Lucita stepped out.

"Praise the Lord," Margarita gasped. "It is you, really you."

"Yes, Mother," Lucita said, her tone distant.

For a moment they stood looking at each other, and then Margarita held out her arms and Lucita hurried to her and finished the embrace. Telling herself she wasn't going to cry, she wasn't, Margarita held onto the healthy and alive young body until she trusted herself to speak.

"Where . . . where have you been? You were gone all night. All night and *he* refused to look for you."

"Did he? Where is he?"

How distant she sounded. "With Father Patricio. I don't know what they have to say to each other, but . . ."

"I'm sorry, Mother," Lucita whispered. "Please believe me, I would have given anything not to worry you, but I couldn't help . . . And then when I got back, I wanted to see how my patients—Midnight is better. I was so afraid my being gone had harmed him, but . . . he's going to live. Thank God, he's going to live."

Margarita wanted to tell Lucita that only madness could account for what she'd done yesterday and the way she was talking right now, but maybe it wasn't that after all. Maybe the need to hold onto sanity had been responsible.

"You're back," she said with a sob. "That's all that matters."

"No, it doesn't. I . . ." Lucita's voice fell off and Margarita wondered if her daughter was going to cry, but then she began to speak again.

"I went to the sea," she said. "Almost, anyway. And I saw . . . I know why my father didn't look for me."

She'd been about to say something about what she'd seen out there, but either thoughts of her father had intruded or she'd deliberately changed the subject.

"He insisted you'd return when you were hungry," Margarita said. "I begged him to find you because of the wild Indians and animals, but he wouldn't listen."

"Did you expect it to be any different?"

There was something new and unfathomable in her daughter's voice. Pushing back, she looked into Lucita's tired but still-beautiful eyes. "No," she said. "I did not."

Lucita sighed. "But he was right. I had to return. I had no choice."

"Are you going to tell him?"

"No. Not yet."


Much Rain snored in Willow's ear, waking her from her nap. Sitting up, she looked down at her husband. They'd made love a little while ago, and from experience she knew he wouldn't wake until bodily needs made their presence known.

They'd been waiting for Black Wolf since yesterday, and although the men were content to sit doing nothing until he returned, her hands and legs didn't know how to be idle. After relieving herself in the bushes, she took in her surroundings, irritated to see that not a single Chumash warrior was awake.

Men! They did so little work! When Much Rain shifted position and reached out his hand to where she'd been, her thoughts softened. He might have no understanding of what it took to constantly prepare food, care for children, and help ready the village for winter, but no one was a better fisherman and together they had explored the delights of what it meant to be a married man and woman.

Just the same, she had no one to talk to and nothing to do. When she was a child, there'd been her sister to spend her days with, but about the time Black Wolf returned Oak Leaf had gone to the mission to sell a pair of moccasins she'd made, never to return. It was said that Oak Leaf had allowed herself to be baptized and now was highly prized as a seamstress. Although Willow never told anyone this, she was curious about Oak Leaf's life and whether she ever thought of her childhood with her sister.

Willow and the warriors were far enough away from the mission that they could talk and she and Much Rain could make love without fear of being overheard. If she moved swiftly, she could approach the mission, see if she could easily spot her sister, and return before her husband woke up. Apprehension clutched at her as she contemplated the risks of what she wanted to do. Black Wolf had insisted they wait until he returned and it was night to go after the foodstuffs because it was all but impossible for six adults to remain unobserved, but one—

In the end, Willow's memories made her decision for her. After placing a light kiss on Much Rain's forehead, she slipped away. Because she'd gathered birds' eggs under the adult birds' sharp eyes, she knew how to move slowly and carefully, but it was hard to concentrate on that when she thought of what she would say to her sister if she saw her.

Once Willow was close enough that she could hear the neophytes in the garden, she lay on her stomach for a long time while trying to gather her courage around her, but although she now realized that a number of women were working among the rows of corn, she couldn't see them.

Pressing her hand against her stomach, she vowed that her and Much Rain's child would be born with courage in his heart because not just his father, but his mother as well, had taken risks.

"Oak Leaf, your little sister is no longer a child," she whispered. "She is a married woman about to become a mother. I want you to know that and to learn if you have children of your own and are happy."

*Oak Leaf couldn't possibly be happy, could she?* Willow wondered as she crawled closer and closer to the sweet-smelling corn. If it was true that Oak Leaf spent her days sewing for the padres, she wouldn't be outside, but maybe one of the laboring women knew her and could relay a message.

Saddened by the thought that she might not see Oak Leaf after all, Willow rose to a crouching position. For the first time she was able to see legs and arms and even bent heads. The neophyte women's clothing was in a state of disrepair, but a number of them wore hide blouses and skirts like her, a fact that held her motionless as she worked her idea around in her mind. It wasn't unheard of for a Chumash warrior to adorn himself like one of the neophytes in order to move about them. Why not her?

Her heart felt as if it had become lodged in her throat, but she hadn't seen her sister in five winters and might never again be this close to her. Standing, she looked all around, assuring herself that there were no leatherjackets about. Then, her bare feet treading lightly on the summer-hot ground, she walked toward the neophytes.

From where he sat on the top of the turkey coop Mundo Uriarte watched the young woman. The soldier couldn't say when he'd first spotted her; maybe it was the way she conducted herself that had initially caught his attention. Unlike Corporal Sebastian, Mundo was no newcomer to this post and knew who belonged and who didn't. The squaw didn't. Smiling, he jumped down and began making his way toward the cornfield. The female neophytes were his for the taking; hadn't he just had his way with one last night? However, mounting one of them provided no challenge and damn little satisfaction. It had to be different with the savages; he'd long wanted to test his theory, and what better opportunity than this? It mattered not at all what she was doing here or whether she'd come alone or with others, because he wasn't stupid like Turi. Turi—he couldn't even remember the man's first name—had dragged his squaw into the bushes, which had been all the opportunity the animal called Black Wolf had needed to exact his brand of revenge.

But Mundo knew to take the woman in the middle of the rows of corn because no savage, not even Black Wolf, would risk being discovered and the neophytes wouldn't lift a finger to stop him from having his fun.

As for the squaw—

Reaching the first cornstalk, Mundo pulled his knife free just in case. Then, his organ already pulsing in anticipation, he lengthened his stride.

# 12

The land was alive with the sounds of crickets and other insects, but despite that, Black Wolf heard the faint howl of his spirit that accompanied the waves of power and courage now washing through him and gave his heartfelt thanks. Strengthened anew, he ran like a deer, like a coyote, alive, more animal than human.

Measuring time by the beats of his heart, he eventually reached the harsh rock outcropping above the hated scar on what had once been his ancestors' hunting grounds and announced himself by pulling an owl's call from deep inside him. His greeting was immediately answered, not by the long single note that would have told him that all was well but by a series of quick yelps like those of a frightened dog. Alarmed, he closed his hand around his knife.

The small hollow behind the rocks held no light, but because his senses were as keen as his namesake's, he quickly determined that all were there. He wanted to believe he had overreacted, but then he smelled the blood.

"What is it?" Although low, his voice sang with concern, and he cursed himself for having been gone so long.

"Willow." came the too-simple answer.

Much Rain spoke from the ground; Black Wolf dropped to his

knees and reached out until he found a strong male arm. "What happened?"

"Leatherjackets." Much Rain sounded nothing like his usual lighthearted self. In the time Black Wolf had been gone, his friend had aged and pain had become part of him.

"Willow? She is dead?"

"N-o."

This wavering voice couldn't possibly belong to Willow—he didn't want it to be her—but he had known her too long and shared too many conversations with her to convince himself otherwise. Releasing Much Rain, he scooted closer. His searching fingers found another arm, this one smaller, softer, and stripped of the muscle that had made Willow a valuable member of the tribe.

He wanted to hear her speak again because everything he needed to know might be in her words, but maybe every breath and heartbeat she possessed was needed to remain alive. Taking her limp hand, he placed it against his chest and willed his own health to enter her.

"What happened?" he asked.

For too long no one spoke, but then Much Rain began. His clipped and hard warrior's voice reminded Black Wolf of a fox warning the enemy away from his mate.

"Two leatherjackets have left, but we do not know how long they will be gone. My wife . . ." Much Rain's voice trailed off and he placed his hand first over his wife's breasts and then settling on her torn belly. "Thinking she might find her sister, she went into the cornfields. Brave, so brave, she would not remain behind."

"I . . . I am not—"

"Hush, my wife. Hold onto your strength."

But there might not be enough. The smell of blood and Willow's inability to speak told Black Wolf that.

The telling came slowly, one reluctant word after another, but finally he understood that Willow had been discovered by a leatherjacket. She'd tried to make the enemy believe she was a neophyte, but either her clothing had given her away or the leatherjacket had cared only that he'd found a woman alone.

"He had his way with her." Much Rain spoke through clenched

teeth, helplessness and rage barely held in check. "Again and again. He violated—"

"My husband . . ."

"It is all right," Much Rain whispered as he took his wife in his arms. "And then he stabbed her here."

Her belly—drenched in blood.

"Chupu!"

Although he regretted his outburst, Black Wolf would never regret calling on the Chumash god. He knew the extent of her injury and that the life inside her couldn't possibly have survived. Hurting, he again took Willow's now clammy hand and pressed it against his chest. He prayed to Chupu, to Wolf, to the *'alchuklash,* shaman's who understood the heavens and the effect the heavens had on the life of his people.

"My . . . baby," Willow whispered.

*Gone,* Black Wolf mouthed. Despite the horrible truth, he tried to share his being with the young woman, to will her to live and one day be capable of carrying another child, but part of him remained with his warrior's heart, where the need for revenge beat, made strong by what Lucita had told him about her father's brand of justice. He sensed the same emotion in Much Rain and the others and knew that if they weren't careful, hatred might consume all of them.

Much Rain was whispering to his wife, his voice deep and hard and yet soft, as if caressing her. Black Wolf prayed that Willow's violation hadn't taken too long and she hadn't been undone by fear and loneliness, but maybe the gods had been elsewhere then and hadn't heard her pleas.

Maybe they had been at Humqaq with him.

*No, please! Surely I was not so selfish as to take all power for myself, not when she needed . . .*

Faint movement pulled him from unwanted thoughts and self-hatred, but when he focused on what was happening, he wished he had remained in prayer. Much Rain had leaned forward and was pressing his lips against his wife's. Willow's fingers were limp in his; all muscle and bone seemed to have been stripped from them.

Much Rain groaned, the sound that of a man who had had his heart ripped from him, who had ceased to be human and now embraced what it was to be animal. He straightened, then leaned forward again, bending his back so he could kiss that place where his child had been growing.

Black Wolf's eyes burned; heat surged through him like a lightning-caused forest fire, and yet he didn't feel like crying. Desperate, he massaged Willow's fingers, but there was no response. When she left them for another place he couldn't say; maybe she had died one nerve at a time, fighting for both herself and her unborn infant.

"Willow! Come back!"

Shaken out of himself, Black Wolf grabbed his friend's arm and prevented him from jumping to his feet. "Stay with her," he insisted. "Her spirit needs you."

Much Rain struggled, but his body lacked the strength it needed to break free. Finally, sobbing, the young brave clutched his wife to him and began rocking back and forth like a father comforting a child. Black Wolf stroked his friend's hot shoulder, placed his fingers against the back of his neck, and probed until he found the hard knot there. Using the same motions his wife did when she ministered to his sore muscles, he kneaded and massaged, and at length Much Rain's body no longer felt as if it might shatter.

"She did not die alone." Black Wolf was forced to whisper because his throat had been gripped by a powerful hand. "You were with her."

"I should have been with her earlier! Should not have let her go alone!"

"No. No."

"I tried . . . She was crawling to me when I found her. I carried her, prayed for her, but Chupu did not answer."

*Maybe because he was with me.* Guilt slammed into Black Wolf until even whispering was beyond him. Still, he rocked with Much Rain as the warrior had just done for his dying wife, ran his fingers over Willow's face, and gently closed her eyes.

"I will kill—"

"Much Rain, no!" one of the others who'd been standing by called out. "You made a promise to her."

A violent shudder tore through Much Rain, and Black Wolf wondered if they shared the same spasm, born from the same place and at the same time.

"I made a vow to a living woman, but she is dead," Much Rain hissed. "And . . . so is our child."

In his mind, Black Wolf saw a knife plunging into a softly rounded belly, heard the leatherjacket laugh, felt Willow's scream. If Chupu had been with her, two lives might not have ended today.

"Much Rain, listen to me." His throat closed down and he had to swallow before he could speak again. "If you allow revenge to rule you, you, too, might die."

"It does not matter. My heart is dead."

"It will begin to beat again," he whispered. "The time will come when you once more hear the redwings and meadowlarks sing."

"No."

"Yes. Listen to me. Listen and believe. I was once dead because the padres had done that thing to me. My heart was no longer Chumash, but that changed because those I loved and who loved me surrounded me. The same will happen for you."

He readied himself for another argument, but Much Rain said nothing, only breathed deep and quick like a man who had tried to outrun a deer. Black Wolf couldn't say why he'd been so determined to take his friend away from himself and the grief that waited for him but didn't regret what he'd done.

The enemy didn't like to touch the dead. As soon as life left someone, the body was treated as if it had never existed, thrown into the ground and quickly covered. It might be different one padre to another or if a leatherjacket lost someone he loved, but Black Wolf would never understand why the enemy turned their back on a dead Chumash when there was nothing to fear from death and the journey to the other world should not be done alone.

Much Rain knew that even if he knew nothing else, he might hold his wife and unborn child until after the sun set and in the holding begin to heal himself. Respecting his friend's journey,

Black Wolf left him, joining the others as they sat together in a tight, softly chanting group. He blended his voice to theirs in prayer but couldn't give himself entirely to the ceremony that was as old as his people. Before leaving them, he'd prayed to Wolf and Chupu that these people, his people, would be successful in their search for food.

But then he'd gone to Humqaq to purify himself, had thought only of himself.

Somehow he would atone for that.

When their prayers were over, Black Wolf gathered the four warriors around him. Seeing the look in his friend's eyes tore at him and fed his growing fury.

"The leatherjacket who killed this woman will have boasted of his deed, and their corporal will have instructed his men to look for more savages," he warned. "When the others return, it will become even more dangerous for us. Her body must be taken to where it belongs. Only *her* body, not more Chumash."

No one mentioned the child — not that they had to. Sounding exhausted, Much Rain again voiced his desire to do to his wife's killer what had been done to her.

"Not today, my friend." Black Wolf held up the blanket he'd brought for his own body in case he died. "I could not bury my father as is our way, and that regret has never left me. You will never find peace if you do not follow the way of our ancestors. Return to the village of our childhood and carry her inside the sacred stone slabs. Dance the swordfish dance, sing to her, tend the night fire, dig her grave, and place her in it with the baby basket she made for your child."

A strangled cry was Much Rain's only response.

A wolf was without equal. Created to hunt and kill, its keen senses made it possible for it to survive through the harshest winter, to run for hours in order to bring down large prey. Black Wolf breathed in those things that were precious about his spirit until he wondered if his arms and legs would ever tire. True, his head pounded and he felt confused, but that was all right because today he was a predator and nothing else.

The drying cornstalks shook and rattled in the wind, but still he moved quietly, stealthily, confidently. Willow had no more need for Chupu, and he had pulled the god into him, turning his belief into a weapon.

Several neophytes looked up, startled, as he approached them. One, a little girl, disappeared into the midst of the plants, but a heavyset woman regarded him with small, watery eyes.

"Where is he?" Black Wolf asked. Maybe he should have explained himself more fully, but a predator doesn't speak.

"The leatherjacket?" the woman asked, and yet he had the feeling she already knew whom he was talking about. "Is she dead?"

So news of the rape and stabbing had reached all ears. Not surprised, he nodded.

The woman drew her dirt-stained hand over her dry mouth. "I heard her cry out, heard him order her to be silent."

"You did not try to stop him?"

"How?" She lifted her hands in a helpless gesture. "They have weapons while we . . ." Jaw sagging, she stared at the knife Black Wolf held. "What are you going to do?"

He didn't move.

"You cannot! They are too strong!" Looking startled, she clamped her hand over her mouth and spoke around her fingers. "You are not one of us, are you?"

He shook his head.

"I remember . . . my mother taught me how to weave baskets before I was brought here." She sighed. "I tried to teach my daughters the same skill, but there are not enough rushes or tule at the mission, and the padres force my girls to live in the *monjerio* and I seldom see them."

"The murdered woman whose name I must not say again made fine baskets," he told her. "She had just finished the one she planned to place her baby in."

The woman's features sagged. "Her child—"

"Died with her."

Hand still clamped over her mouth, the woman paced back and forth like an old horse looking for a way out of its corral. The three men who'd been working with her had stopped what they were doing and stared but made no move to join the conversation. All Black Wolf cared was that they didn't betray him.

"His belly is as big as that of a woman about to give birth. No female neophyte is safe around him." The woman stared at the ground. "He has little hair and shoulders so broad that maybe his mother was a mule."

"Where is he?"

"There." She pointed toward where the horses were kept. "I want you to take this knowledge with you. What he did to the woman, he has done the same to my eldest daughter."

"No." Despite his protest, Black Wolf wasn't surprised.

Her eyes filled and spilled over, but she didn't seem aware that she was crying. "At least he did not take a knife to my child, but she is defiled. Life here is so different," she whispered. "Not what I knew as a small child. My mother taught me how to make fine baskets, to gather berries and acorns, to roast bulbs. I . . . I tell my daughters not to fight the leatherjackets, so that they may live."

The smell of horse sweat and manure clogged Black Wolf's nostrils and the never-ending snorts, thuds, and chewing sounds made his ears ring, but he still had his eyes and he hadn't forgotten what the neophyte woman had said to him, her helpless anger.

The corral had been constructed out of tightly packed sticks held together with rope, but by moving like a wolf, staying in the shadows and peering through the slitlike openings, he managed to catch glimpses of what was going on inside. It was possible that the murdering leatherjacket had left the area, but until Black Wolf knew that for certain, he would be patient.

If this had been his father's time, he would have gone to battle naked except for the knife lashed to his waist so his body wouldn't be encumbered, but if he did, he risked catching the attention of the padres or leatherjackets when he must take on the look of a neophyte.

A horse snorted and shied, drawing his attention to what had startled the animal. It didn't take long. A big-bellied man wearing a uniform unequal to the task of adequately covering him stood at the opposite side of the corral. He carried a slender whip in one hand; a coil of rope hung from the other. Slinking like a coyote after a rabbit, the leatherjacket attempted to separate the tallest horse from the others. Black Wolf could have told him that a handful of grain would bring the animal to him, but if the man wanted to exhaust himself this way, so be it.

A studied look in all directions convinced Black Wolf that no one was paying attention to what the man was doing. Filled with what was instinct for his spirit, he closed the distance between him and the rope-tied gate and let himself in, leaving the gate open so he would have a way of escaping. He glided rather than walked, presenting himself as being of no more importance than blades of glass. A couple of the horses glanced his way but found him unimportant, for which he thanked Wolf.

A growl began low in his throat, making him wonder if he'd ceased to be a man entirely and become a cougar. A cougar or a wolf, it didn't matter. What did was that he reach his prey.

The leatherjacket was losing patience, as witnessed by his set jaw and the hard way he gripped the whip. The pain giver twitched, lifted, was slowly lowered, and Black Wolf understood that no matter how much the man might hate this horse, he did not dare vent himself on it until he'd trapped it.

An almost painful spasm brought Black Wolf back to himself, and he realized he'd been clenching his teeth, but how could his reaction be any different? In his mind's eye, he went back to when this creature—he would not call him a man—had stalked Much Rain's wife, trapped her, violated her, stabbed her. Suddenly protecting the horse became as important as avenging her death.

Once again a growl waited on his lips, and he smiled. He knew how to hunt and kill. Before he'd accepted the leatherjackets as his enemy, he had hunted only to provide for his people, killed only because they needed to eat, but the knowledge was in him, and this time he would not end his journey by giving thanks to the souls of the creatures who had given up their lives so others might live because the leatherjacket had no soul.

Intent as he was on his goal, he still kept a part of himself separate from the act and thus knew when his world changed. Poised on the balls of his feet, he turned so he could see behind him. For the briefest of moments he thought Lucita had found him, but before he was forced to deal with that, the approaching woman's features came into focus.

The elderly neophyte nodded, once, her work-broken body suddenly younger, and she made a small gesture as if reaching for her eyes, then stopped. Black Wolf continued to look back at her, his message as silent as hers as he thanked her for telling him where to look. Then, light as a fawn, she was gone.

He swung back around, isolated the leatherjacket from the four-legged creatures, started toward him again. Black Wolf's body felt so hot that he wondered if he might burst into flames—not that it mattered, because he had come here to do one thing and would not stop until—

The horse to his left reached out a white muzzle and sniffed deeply, then snorted. The sound was still echoing when Black Wolf slipped around the horse and put it between him and his prey. Although he hadn't touched the horse, they stood so close that he could feel its energy build and knew it might shy away at any instant. The animal snorted again and took a hesitant step backward.

Out of the corner of his eye Black Wolf saw the leatherjacket pause in his relentless pursuit of the other horse and begin to turn. The distance between them was too great; Black Wolf couldn't overpower him in time to prevent an outcry. But maybe, maybe—

Howling like a wolf, his Wolf, he rammed his shoulder against the white-muzzled horse. The instant he did, the animal squealed and plunged ahead. He heard a human bellow, but the sharpest tones died under thudding hooves. Strength flowed into him as he gathered himself and sprang.

Lashing pain cut through him, but he didn't waste time by trying to make sense of it. The leatherjacket had squared around to face him, the whip-holding hand uplifted. He'd dropped his rope and was fumbling for whatever weapon he carried at his waist.

"No!" Black Wolf bellowed. Propelled by his words, he slammed into the leatherjacket, the effort throwing the man backward and onto the ground.

A cloud of dust half-blinded Black Wolf, but he didn't need to see. Once again pain bit into him, along the side of his neck this time, and he knew the whip had found him. Acting on instinct, he reached for the man's wrist, but the massive belly was in the way.

A howl, or maybe a growl, burst from Black Wolf. At the same time, he felt two beefy arms lock around his head. Desperate for freedom, he tried to throw himself to one side, but the enemy had shifted his attack so that he now held Black Wolf's hair with one hand while the other—

A jarring, numbing sensation rocketed through Black Wolf. For an instant he thought his head had been ripped from his neck, but that couldn't be it because he was still alive. Once more something slammed into him, and despite the haze threatening to encompass him, he realized the leatherjacket had slammed his fist into his jaw.

A Chumash did not fight this way. A Chumash—

He barely felt the third blow, but it must have been a powerful one, because his limbs now seemed to be those of a newborn infant and he couldn't tell whether he still gripped his knife.

A newborn, a baby at its mother's breast.

Willow. Dead.

Her baby murdered without having ever felt its mother's arms.

Rage became a storm inside him. His muscles still wouldn't answer his call, belonged to no one.

And yet—

Black Wolf felt his fingers tighten and something dig into his palm and knew he hadn't dropped his knife after all; if nothing else, the powerful need to survive remained with him. The leatherjacket called out for help, and although the horses made a great deal of noise, Black Wolf had no doubt that the man's companions would hear.

He was Black Wolf, protected and guided by Wolf. He had

survived imprisonment, become free, become a Chumash, and now—

"No!" Energized by the sound of his voice and something hot and powerful, he threw himself backward with such force that he broke free. His scalp felt as if it had been torn from his skull, and tears he had no control over completed the job the dust had begun.

*Run!*

But he couldn't. Not until—

His growl became a howl, long and deep and primitive. It was still echoing when he lifted his knife over his enemy's thrashing body and drove it home.

# 13

"Lucita! I need you, now!"

Heart pounding, Lucita scrambled to her feet and cast about trying to get her bearings. She knew she was in the chapel but had been either so lost in pleas for peace and understanding or so overwhelmed by what had happened over the last few days that she'd lost her hold on reality. It was on the tip of her tongue to ask her father how he'd known she was here, but she didn't. Careful to remain a safe distance from him, she tried to assess his mood.

"It has happened again! Damnation! And this time—didn't you hear me, girl? I need you."

"What happened again?" she asked, stalling.

"One of my men has been attacked."

Suddenly cold, she took an involuntary step, then stopped because her father barred her way. As she feared, he used that opportunity to grab her. Fortunately, his grip on her upper arm wasn't tight enough that her circulation was cut off, and she half-believed he didn't have punishment in mind.

Although she was capable of moving on her own, he hauled her outside and pulled her toward the soldiers' quarters, giving her scant opportunity to take in her surroundings. Because the padres insisted on keeping the door to their private chapel closed at all times—to prevent the neophytes from taking anything, they said—she had no idea what had been going on outside.

"In here." After yanking open the door leading to the soldiers' quarters, Sebastian shoved her inside.

Someone was groaning, the sound sharp and wild and loud enough that it was almost a scream. Although she'd never been inside this building, it held no interest for her as she hurried to the small cot holding a large man. The soldier had been at the mission when she and her family arrived, and her father hadn't bothered to introduce her to him—not that his name mattered right now.

"Stabbed him," her father boomed. "The godless devil left his knife in him."

Thinking the injured man must have got into a fight with another soldier, she knelt beside him and leaned close. Despite the blood, the quavering cries, and the way the heavy body jerked about as if trying to destroy the cot, she now knew her first conclusion had been wrong. The knife hilt barely visible within the rolls of belly fat had been made of bone, not metal.

Looking around, she noted that two other soldiers were in the room, leaning against a wall instead of near their companion. Her father might have ordered her here, but she would never ask for his assistance.

"I need water," she told the soldiers. "As hot as you can make it."

"You are going to scald him?" the shorter of the two asked.

She shook her head but didn't bother explaining that she couldn't decide how or if to remove the knife until she could see the area better,—an impossible task until some of the blood had been washed away. After a momentary argument, the shorter soldier hurried off, soon followed by his companion. Her father yelled at the second man to return, but he either didn't hear or pretended not to.

The wounded man still thrashed back and forth, but in the

few minutes she'd been here his movements had slackened, making her wonder if he'd come to the end of his strength. She placed the back of her hand against his forehead, not surprised to find it both cold and sweat-soaked.

"How long ago was he hurt?" she asked.

"I don't know," her father said. "Not long. The horses—the noise they were making made us wonder if a wild animal had gotten in with them. It took us a while to calm them. That's when we found Mundo."

"Mundo," she whispered as her patient ceased to be a soldier and became someone with a deeper, more intimate identity. "Mundo, can you hear me?"

The man's eyes, which had been darting around the room like those of a captive bird seeking freedom, settled on her. Despite everything she needed to do, she took a moment to grip his hand and thought of how much healing she'd been able to accomplish simply by rocking a feverish child. Mundo gripped back with so much strength that she was afraid he'd break her fingers. In contrast, his legs now spasmed ineffectively, and by the sudden stench she knew he'd lost control of his bodily functions.

"Don't talk," she told him, although she wasn't sure he was capable of speech. The doctors who visited the orphanage had explained that a body's natural response to grave injury was to go into shock and that shock could kill.

It necessitated digging into him with the nails of her free hand, but finally she forced him to release her, then rubbed his flesh where she'd left her mark. He continued to stare at her, but the bright gleam she'd seen there a few minutes ago was being replaced by a telling dullness.

He still wore his uniform, but someone had ripped the fabric away from the wound. Gently she ran her hands over the exposed injury. She wished she had no idea how deep the blade had buried itself in him, but she'd seen a Chumash knife; the length was enough to penetrate his gut even with the layers of fat.

What was it the nuns had told her—that God worked through their fingers and if a patient's belief was strong enough, fingers alone could perform a miracle? But she didn't have a nun's faith. Still, she would do everything she could.

"Get it out of him!" her father ordered. He'd no sooner spoken when the injured man screeched, then fell silent.

She wanted nothing more than to obey her father's command. The instrument of injury and possibly death was an obscenity, but pulling it out—even if she could get a decent grip on it—might injure him further. That was what she told her father.

"He cannot live with it in him," Sebastian countered. "Either you do it or I will."

Yes, he would, his actions perhaps no different from when he'd lashed that neophyte to death. "I never said I wouldn't, but I must examine him first," she said. "And I can't do that until I have the means to clean him."

"Ha! Those worthless beasts won't return until they've gotten themselves drunk. I called for you because you have skills in such things and the padres—don't try to tell me you don't have the stomach for this."

He'd probably summoned her instead of Father Joseph as punishment for her earlier actions. "You want it out now?"

"Of course. That knife is an abomination. Damnation, Lucita—"

"Father, I can't perform a miracle. His chances . . ." Unwilling to say more in Mundo's presence, she simply looked at her father.

He met her somber gaze with one of his own. "I've seen all manner of wounds," he said in a low tone. "I know what we are facing."

A few days ago her father had said that if she'd been a boy they would have had a great deal in common, and at this moment, maybe for the first time in her life, they were thinking the same thoughts.

"He's going to fight me," she whispered. "I need you to hold him."

For a moment she thought she saw hesitation in her father's features, but the look was gone so quickly she couldn't be sure. When Sebastian positioned himself on the opposite side of the cot and leaned over the man, pinning his arms to his side, she found herself on the verge of tears; there wasn't time to ask if it was possible for her and her father to work together.

When she touched the torn flesh, the seemingly unconscious soldier tried to buck away from her. A weaker man couldn't have held him in place, but her father stayed with Mundo, cursing, ordering, occasionally seeming to bellow with him.

The knife had gone straight in and wasn't close to the heart, but she had no way of knowing how many organs had been penetrated—certainly the muscles controlling his bowels, muscles he could not live without. The man was dying; maybe the only thing she could do for him was free him from what was causing his death. Steeling herself for what she must do, she nevertheless was vaguely aware that someone else had entered the room but didn't look up.

"What are you doing?" Margarita demanded. "Lucita! How can you touch—he is bleeding, unclean!"

"He's hurt."

"Sebastian! I will not have my daughter—"

"Silence! This man needs her skills."

No amount of skill would save this life, and she and her father knew that. Taking advantage of her patient's momentary interest in the argument, Lucita quickly wrapped the hem of her blouse around her fingers and gripped what of the knife was exposed. Something inside her screamed, demanded that she leave, insisted that this scene, this dying, be carried out without her. Instead, eyes shut and teeth clenched, she pulled.

The howling scream silenced her parents and put her father to work trying to control the now wildly thrashing Mundo. Not allowing herself to think beyond the moment, she cast aside the knife and leaned forward, stopping the flood of blood with the heel of her hand.

"Who did it?" Sebastian demanded. "Damnation, tell me!"

"Stop!" Lucita ordered her patient. "You must lie still. Otherwise you'll bleed to death."

"Lucita?" Her mother's voice became a whimper. "Your blouse—what have you done?"

"What I must," she answered distractedly, then grabbed the

soldier's ruined shirt and used that to cover the wound. Mundo's shaking had become so pronounced that her father was hard-pressed to keep him on the cot, and she nearly convinced herself that none of the trembling came from her.

"My child, my child," Margarita whimpered. "Dear Lord, please take her from this. Protect her and shield her from this horror."

"Shut up!" Sebastian bellowed. "The Lord has nothing to do with what happened. A savage, a damnable savage—look at that knife! It's one of those animals."

"Please, Sebastian. Do not say such things in our daughter's presence. She is a maiden, innocent."

*Innocent? What was that?* Her parents' argument continued around her, punctuated by her patient's hoarse sobs. His cries and the wound claimed her and answered her question about innocence. Whatever that state might be, it no longer had anything to do with her.

Finally, unable to tolerate her parents' arguing, she sent her mother to ask the padres for silktassel bush leaves and European myrth, which she then used to clean and pack the site. Loss of blood had finally rendered Mundo so weak that her father no longer needed to restrain him.

"Let me know if there is any change," Sebastian said as he got to his feet. "If you can get through to him, make sure he tells you who attacked him."

"Where are you going?"

"That is none of your concern."

His boots slapped the ground with every step, giving sound and weight to Sebastian's emotions. He looked around for the soldiers, but neither of them was nearby, the worthless curs!

Thinking to take himself to where he would find some peace and quiet for thinking, he headed for the horse corral, but before he could reach it, he spotted Father Patricio coming toward him.

"What has been going on?" Father Patricio demanded. "All that commotion—"

"If you were so curious, why weren't you there?"

"Because I was occupied with the mission's finances. Senor Portola will not be able to linger, and I want to be ready for him. What happened?"

Sebastian told him.

"Mundo has no idea who attacked him? You are certain?"

"I told you, he hasn't spoken since we found him."

"But you have your suspicions, don't you?"

For a man of God, Father Patricio had a remarkable grasp on reality. "I daresay we are thinking the same thing."

"What are you going to do about it? How many soldiers will that creature attack before he's stopped?"

The question was precisely why Sebastian had wanted to avoid the padre. Damnation, didn't Father Patricio understand how difficult it was to bring down one man when that man moved ghostlike wherever he willed? But if the corporal said that, Father Patricio might say and would surely think him unequal to the task, and he couldn't tolerate, couldn't abide, that.

"No more," he said. "What happened today will never happen again."

Skepticism danced in Father Patricio's eyes. "How can you say that?"

"Because . . ." Just when he thought he might falter, his mind clicked down on a plan. "I will no longer wait for Black Wolf to come to me."

Margarita remained with Lucita after her father left, but it was clear this was the last place she wanted to be. As Mundo lapsed into unconsciousness, Lucita asked her mother to pray for him. Muttering that she had to be in a place of God before God could clearly hear her, Margarita slipped away.

"You aren't alone," Lucita whispered when it was just she and her patient. "I won't let you do this alone."

Taking Mundo's trembling hand, she held it for what seemed like hours. Occasionally he stirred, and when he did she again and again told him she was with him and wouldn't leave, that her mother and the padres were praying for him. Sunlight briefly made its presence known through the too-small window, but before long, the shadows took over.

Mundo, who had looked so fierce and unapproachable before, had sunken into himself, become smaller somehow. Sweat poured from his body, and no matter what she did, his wound continued to seep. She was aware of the stench of his ruined body, her bloody blouse, the discarded knife nearby, the sticky stains on her fingers. Most of all she was aware of her inability to pray.

An Indian had done this.

Awareness of a change in the room pulled her out of herself, and she realized Mundo had opened his eyes and was staring at her, only she wasn't sure he could actually see her.

"Get him away from me!" Mundo bellowed with unexpected strength.

"Easy, easy," she whispered. "You are safe."

"No! No! Damnation!"

"Shoo. Quiet," she crooned, hoping her soft and feminine voice would make an impact. "You are all right."

"Savage!"

"I know." *I know.*

"His arm—knife . . . his arm, no!"

"What about his arm?" she asked because it seemed to her that Mundo was more afraid of that than the weapon he was seeing in his mind.

"What is that! Something . . . something . . . No! Not a . . . wolf."

*Black Wolf!*

No more than a half hour after Mundo had spoken his last words, Lucita released his limp hand and got to her feet. She walked to the door on nerveless feet and stepped outside, retreating momentarily from the sunlight, but before long her eyes adjusted and she took in her surroundings.

Her father and the two soldiers along with three saddled horses were near the entrance to the church, and in the middle of the small, tight group stood Father Patricio.

All eyes turned her way as she approached, but she didn't try to acknowledge anyone except her father. Neither could she rouse herself enough to ask what they were planning to do.

"It's over?" he asked.

"Yes."

"Did he say anything?"

"No," she managed. "Nothing."

Lucita had been untruthful. Father Patricio had no doubt of that, but still he didn't believe the time was right to tell Sebastian of his suspicions. Instead, he waited until the girl had left before returning to the conversation they'd been having.

"I do not understand," he said to Sebastian. "Obviously Black Wolf can come and go at will, and yet you intend to leave the mission undefended?"

Sebastian looked irritated and Father Patricio was worried the corporal might ride away without saying anything. "Black Wolf has no quarrel with you, Padre. Has he ever threatened you or Father Joseph?"

"No."

"Then you will not be in any danger while we are gone."

"But where—"

"Do I need to draw you a picture?" Sebastian snapped. "He is getting bolder and bolder and undoubtedly now believes he can do whatever he wants without fear of reprisal. The next time he attacks, he won't be alone."

Despite himself, Father Patricio stared at the distant haze.

"Yes!" Sebastian sounded excited. "Things have escalated to the point where they demand immediate attention. The wild Indians live somewhere in the hills. There is only one way to assure that attack won't come, and that's by stomping on the snakes' den."

"I thought you said your men weren't ready for that."

"I have no choice. As soon as I've collected the others, I will accomplish what I was sent here to do."

"Lucita, where are you going?"

Too exhausted to speak, Lucita slowly turned.

Catching up to her, Margarita tentatively fingered her dirty sleeve. "Throw it away, please. The washwoman will never be able to get all the blood out, and even if they could, I couldn't abide seeing you in it again. I'll order one of the seamstresses to make you another. Certainly the padres can spare enough cloth for that."

She'd watched a man die today, and her mother was talking about her attire. "It doesn't matter."

"Not matter? How can you stand to wear it?"

"Mother, there is nothing repulsive about blood."

"That is not what I said. We cherish the blood of God's Son, but that soldier only rarely stepped inside the church or took communion."

"That was Mundo's decision, just as mine was to try to save his life." The sun felt hot. Added to what she'd absorbed of her patient's fever, she felt as if she might burst into flames. If only she could reach the trees, the ocean.

No, not the ocean.

"I do not understand you, Lucita," Margarita went on. "Look at your hands."

She did as she was told. To her, the dark stains served as a mockery of her efforts to keep Mundo alive.

"I'm not sure I understand myself," she whispered. For a heartbeat, she wanted to rest her heavy head on her mother's shoulder. Then she remembered how small and vulnerable Margarita had looked earlier and the impulse died.

"It is this untamed land," Margarita whispered after a too-long silence. "You should be back in Mexico City, safe and surrounded by others who embrace and are capable of understanding what the Church is about. Everything is . . . so different here." Reaching out, Margarita touched Lucita's cheek but only briefly. "It is changing you."

# 14

Lucita's father rode at the head of the small band of leather-jackets moving south from the mission. In addition to the corporal Black Wolf saw only two grim-faced men; he didn't have to ask what had had happened to the final man. Lids lowered against the hot afternoon sun, he watched until the group disappeared from view. Only then did he stand and brush dirt and leaves from him.

Never before had he seen the mission left undefended, which meant they believed their destination and their task there were more important than keeping the mission protected. Their mounts carried sleeping blankets, and he guessed the bulging leather bags contained foodstuff.

He was responsible for this. He!

If he could walk backward through time, not allow himself to be driven by instinct, keep his hand off his knife, he would— maybe—but it was too late for that.

*Speed my people's feet as they make their way home; keep that home safe from the enemy. Wrap Much Rain's heart in eagle down and give him the courage to face tomorrow.*

His prayers for the others over, he turned his thoughts to

what he must accomplish. Even with the leatherjackets gone, he was hesitant to enter the mission grounds. However, he had no choice.

Holding his body so still that he ceased to think of himself as separate from the rocks, he listened. The sound of many voices carried to him, and even if he hadn't seen the neophytes at work, he would have known how many were about this afternoon.

*Guide my feet, my spirit. Understand my need for knowledge and bring that knowledge to me. My people's safety depends on what I do and learn today.*

After sending a silent message of love to his son, he clambered onto a nearby boulder and lifted his face toward the heavens. He thought he saw the outline of a frog in a cloud formation, but Frog was the shaman's spirit, while he trusted in Wolf.

His throat filled, his mouth opened, and he let forth with the cry that had led him into manhood. The howl rose, spread, thinned, and yet remained deep, and he imagined it drifting upward until it, and he, became one with the clouds.

At length nothing remained of the sound he'd made, but still he waited for his spirit's answer. The cloud ceased to be a frog and became a five-legged horse and then a leafless tree.

Confused, he repeated his howl, but once again his message was met with silence. The tree was no more, nothing else showed itself to him for a long, long time, and then—

The sound began as a thin whisper, which slowly, steadily, grew deeper. No throat, either human or wolf, could sustain itself that long, but then Wolf was a spirit and his laws were his own.

*I wait for your wisdom. Please, reveal to me what I must do.*

The howl ended abruptly, and Black Wolf felt as if he himself had stretched out in the silence and ceased to exist. Once again he let his thoughts go to his son, then to the stranger-woman who maybe understood him in ways no one else had and to his need to step far back in time to where only the seasons existed and his grandfather's grandfather waited.

Wolf, calling to him. The cry deep and strong.

*I must think like a predator, that is what you warn, is it not?*

A single, sharp answer.

Feeling as strong as Wolf's voice, he jumped down and began slinking toward the mission. He wondered if the older woman he'd spoken to earlier had kept her knowledge of him to herself. Maybe her hatred of the leatherjackets remained as strong as before and she believed he'd done right by attacking Willow's killer, or maybe she had spent so many years here that fear of the padres and leatherjackets had loosened her tongue. However her thoughts went, he didn't dare risk his life by trying to talk to her. Still, there was another who might tell him the truth.

When he'd slipped as close as he dared in the daylight, he sat and leaned against a fallen tree trunk and waited for dark, as patient as his namesake. He had just been brought to the mission when this tree gave up its life. Because he had not yet had the Chumash beaten out of him, he had cried out as the tree fell and begun to pray that its spirit would find a new home, but then the padre had laid a whip across his back and he'd learned to be silent.

The lesson of silence, if nothing else, had remained with him, he thought as he spotted two neophytes struggling under the weight of something. They were followed by Lucita and her mother. The neophytes stopped just outside the cemetery and began digging into the unyielding earth. Sunset had come and gone by the time the neophytes finished their task. Only then did the padres arrive, their heads bowed as if the world around them were of no consequence. With the leatherjackets gone, shouldn't they be concerned with their safety?

Despite the need to absorb everything, he couldn't take his eyes off Lucita. Although she'd remained close to her mother the whole time it had taken for the grave to be dug, she seemed separate from what was happening, as if her thoughts, her soul even, resided somewhere else. Even now while the padres prayed and her mother sprinkled handfuls of dirt on the body, Lucita remained motionless.

She should not be part of this!

Perhaps she heard him; perhaps the thought had come to her on its own. Either way, Lucita abruptly left the small gathering, and other than her mother, who was staring after her, no one seemed to notice. When the padres were done, they, too, walked away, leaving only the neophytes to cover the body and Lucita's mother to pray. They'd just buried the leatherjacket he'd attacked; after seeing the size and width of the body, he had no doubt of that.

It was dark when the church bells rang, telling both Black Wolf and those who lived within the mission that the time for night prayer had once again arrived. As the sound of bare feet slapping on earth reached him, he cautiously started forward, reminding himself that the padres might have left those few they trusted to remain outside as guards.

It wasn't right! His heart understood that he should hide from the leatherjackets, but to fear his own kind, those who had once been as one with him and who might again know what it was to be Chumash!

The door to the leatherjackets' quarters was locked, making it necessary for him to slip around to the side where the window was, but he had no choice, hoisting himself onto the sill and making himself as small as possible before looking back. It didn't matter why the leatherjackets lived so close to the padres or why they all slept near the putrid tallow-rendering place. What did matter was that there was no hiding from the memories.

He knew the smell, the feel, the size, maybe even the taste of what Father Patricio called home. How many times had he prayed he'd never have to enter the cell-like enclosure again, and how many times had his prayers gone unanswered?

Despite his struggles, he ceased to be a man and became a child again. Although years had passed, he still felt Father Patricio's hands on him and heard the man's whispered orders, felt himself tremble.

Barely aware of what he was doing, he lowered himself back onto the ground and stared up at the small opening he would have to climb through if he hoped to capture what weapons the leatherjackets might have left behind. He didn't need to enter Father Patricio's living place, didn't have to trap himself inside that prison!

Wolf had given him courage countless times. Wolf would once again fill his body with strength, and he would remain a warrior, no longer a helpless child. This he believed.

His back pressed against the leatherjackets' wall because he couldn't force himself to be any closer to Father Patricio's essence, he howled, careful to keep the sound no louder than a whisper. What might have been nothing but could be danger caused him to whirl back around. The darkness was complete, and his eyes soon ached from the strain of trying to see. His ears told him that no one was there, and yet—

Eyes, red and hot.

Sucking in air, he leaned forward. A rush of warmth surged through him as he accepted that Wolf had come to him in the night and was staring back at him.

*You hear my heart beating, my spirit. You know my greatest fear. You understand that certain things will never leave me and that I will always need you.*

The amber eyes momentarily disappeared and then reappeared, and Black Wolf knew his spirit had blinked. He now made out the faintest of outlines and in his mind saw the great head with its open, grinning mouth and killing teeth.

He had nothing to fear. Wolf was with him.

One step became two, but before he could take another he stopped, because he was only a man and a man does not carelessly touch his spirit.

"Thank you," he whispered.

Another light glow appeared, but this one had nothing to do with the spirit world. Angry because someone had opened a door and was stepping outside, candle in hand, he balled his fingers into fists and stalked toward the intruder. Wolf was gone, taking his burning eyes with him.

Sheltered by the night, Black Wolf belatedly remembered where he was and why he'd come here. Wolf would not protect him from his stupidity.

"Black Wolf?" a soft and familiar voice said. "Please, I know you are there."

Lucita belonged to another world, one he'd lost touch with in the past few minutes, and returning to it took every bit of concentration at his command.

She held her candle in front of her as she came closer. The glow wreathed her features in shadow and light, making him think of how the world looked when lightning spit forth from the sky.

"I heard that howl," she whispered. "Please, where are you?"

What would she think if he told her that much of the sound had come from his spirit? Wondering if she would call him a liar, he waited for her to draw closer. The first time they'd met, he'd forcefully silenced her, but he no longer feared she would reveal his presence. Perhaps that was all he knew about her.

Her flickering image took on substance, and at length the candlelight revealed him as well.

"I knew it," she said, her low voice emotionless. "Why are you here? The danger . . ."

"My people need the leatherjackets' weapons. We are unarmed."

"Unarmed!" She threw the word at him. "Do not tell me that! Don't ever try to tell me that."

"What I do should not matter to you," he said.

"It does, damn it! Don't you understand that!"

He'd never guessed she could be like this, hating him as completely as he hated Father Patricio. "Go back inside, Lucita," he told her. "Either that or call someone to kill me."

He heard her quick intake of breath and caught a glimpse of the rage in her eyes. "Don't speak to me of killing, Black Wolf," she said. "Not after what you did."

She took a long, heavy step toward him, then stopped, the arm holding the candle uplifted as if she wanted to strike him with it. "Where is your knife, Black Wolf?"

Instead of answering, he reached out and yanked the candle from her, then held it up so he could study her better. Instead of trying to defend herself, she let her arm drop to her side, and exhaustion etched her features.

"I took it out of him today." She spoke slowly, every word a drumbeat. "Reached into a man and pulled out the knife you'd placed there even though I knew it wouldn't make any difference."

"Why did you, then?"

She blinked several times and he guessed she hadn't expected the question. He didn't want to think about what she'd just said, didn't want to imagine her trying to stem the flow of blood he'd been responsible for.

"Because I couldn't stand to have that awful reminder of what you're capable of."

*I am sorry. I did not want that for you.*

"You were with him when he was buried," he said instead.

"How—you saw, didn't you? If . . . if you did, then you know my father and the others aren't here. That's why you are, isn't it? Because you know the mission is undefended."

"Where did they go?"

"I don't know. He confides in Father Patricio, not me."

"I do not believe you," Black Wolf said, although maybe he did.

"I don't care! Nothing matters to me right now, nothing!"

Her outburst propelled him into action. Without thinking, he dropped the candle and seized her, clamping his hand over her mouth. She felt so small and slight in his arms, in contrast to the beefy leatherjacket, and yet she'd had the strength and courage to try to save the man's life.

"I am sorry," he whispered into her ear.

When she didn't try to break free, he slowly, cautiously, released his hold enough that she could speak around his hand.

"Sorry?" she mouthed.

"You should not be part of what happened."

"What would you rather I did? Hide while he died in agony? Damn you, Black Wolf."

"What would you have me do?" he threw back at her. "Let a death go unavenged?"

"Yes!"

Before he could silence her again, she shook her head and continued. "What death are you talking about? No, don't tell me. I can't take any more dying, Black Wolf. I may want you in hell, but I will not have a hand in that."

Was that what it was to be civilized? If so, then the padres were right to call him and his people savages, and yet he believed her to be a gentle woman.

"Black Wolf?"

The strength had seeped out of her voice, leaving her sounding like a small child, and yet his arms knew they were not holding a child.

"What?"

"That was you howling, wasn't it?"

She didn't want to know the truth behind the man's death, and he should not tell her, but there was lightning and thunder between them, and even if he knew how, he would not try to stop the storm that was playing itself out in words that maybe did not matter.

"I called, yes," he told her. "And I was answered."

He felt her muscles tense and allowed her the freedom to turn toward him. The candle had gone out when he'd dropped it, leaving them in darkness.

"I . . . I have prayed to God my entire life," she said. "When I was a child, I prayed my parents would love each other and that they would have other children and . . . When I went to work in an orphanage and fell in love with sick children and babies, I prayed for them."

"Did your God hear then?"

"I . . . maybe. Sometimes." She breathed low and quick, like someone out of breath who does not want others to know. "What happened out here a few minutes ago . . . I don't want to admit what I heard. If I could make myself believe only one throat made those sounds, I would, but . . ."

So this was why she hadn't tried to run away. "You heard my spirit, Lucita."

In response, she shook her head, the motion quick and violent, but she didn't call him a liar and he wondered if her belief might one day become as deep as his.

"Will you try to stop me tonight?" he asked.

"From what?"

He indicated the leatherjackets' quarters. "My people's weapons are as nothing. If we are to remain free, we must have strength."

A shudder ran the length of her, and for reasons he didn't dare face he longed to wrap his body around hers and make her safe, but even if she allowed him to, that was impossible.

"I hate this," she said fiercely. "Watching my father and the other soldiers ride out talking of revenge, all I could think about was that they must be looking for women and children, your son. You. No." The word came out as part of a deep sigh. "I won't stop you. Oh, God, what am I saying?"

She sagged against him, and without weighing the wisdom of his action, he breathed in her scent. For a time that wasn't nearly long enough, the heat of their separate bodies became one and he thought of nothing else, knew nothing else, but the sharing didn't last long enough because she pushed away, and he let her go.

"What are you going to do?" she asked. "Kill someone else?"

"If I must."

"No. No. No." The word became a chant. "Why did you do it? What did he do to you?"

"To me, nothing."

"Then why—"

"He destroyed a Chumash woman, Lucita. Forced himself on her, tore into her and beat her. You think me a savage because I stabbed him, but he did the same to my friend's wife."

"Oh, God!"

Anger flowed into him from a place he couldn't fathom, and he didn't try to hold back what else needed to be said. "She was with child. His knife destroyed two lives and left her husband wishing for his own death."

"No."

"She died as I watched, Lucita. Just as her killer died as you watched."

At that she sagged, making him wonder if she was going to lose consciousness, but although it seemed to take all her strength to remain on her feet, he sensed her battle and knew she was going to win. She said nothing, but then there was nothing left to say.

When she pulled free, he thought she might run away. In truth, he wanted her gone, because as long as they stood like this he couldn't think. Instead, she took his hand and rotated it until his palm faced down. Her fingertips were like butterfly wings as she explored the back of his forearm.

"Before he died, Mundo said that the Indian who stabbed him had the outline of a wolf's head here."

"And that was when you knew it was me?"

"Maybe . . . maybe I did before that."

"And still you came to me tonight?"

"Yes." Releasing him, she drew in a breath. "I . . . we both experienced death today. Each of us did what little we could to make someone's dying easier."

"Yes."

She took a small step, and he knew she was getting ready to leave. The sense of both freedom and loss pummeled him, caused his own retreat. Neither of them had spoken of what tomorrow might bring; neither had asked whether they might see each other again.

And yet, somehow, he knew they were not finished.


He had just slipped out of the window after an unsuccessful search for weapons—two rusted swords were all he'd found— when the door to where the padres lived opened. Letting night envelop him, he studied the approaching figure until he was convinced it was Father Patricio. The padre had removed his head covering, and his hands hung at his sides, drawing Black Wolf's attention to their large size. The priest's steps were slow and shuffling, making Black Wolf wonder why the man hadn't brought a candle with him. True, the moon was out, but with the leather-jackets gone, wouldn't the padre want to know all he could about his surroundings . . . unless he didn't want anyone to see him?

Father Patricio was heading toward the *monjerio,* his walk purposeful and firm as if he could hardly wait to reach where the unmarried girls spent the night. Clamping his reaction into submission, Black Wolf pulled in his surroundings and assured himself that only he and the padre shared this place; then, although there was a great deal to risk, he stepped forward.

"Has your God given you eyes that see in the dark, Padre?" he asked.

"Wha—who?" Father Patricio's head jerked up and he lifted his hands as if to protect himself.

"It is me." He spoke firmly, confidently, not caring how much hatred rode with the words. "Black Wolf."

The padre's feet seemed to be dancing without his being aware of their movement. When he abruptly lifted his cape over his head, Black Wolf wondered if the man really thought doing that would protect him.

"I have not come to kill you, Padre," he said. "You have nothing to fear from me, tonight."

"Heathen!"

"Yes," he said, his voice full of pride. "In your eyes, I am that. Padre, those who guard you are not here tonight. Are you such a fool that you did not think of that before exposing yourself?"

"You know why they are gone. After what you did—"

"What I did. Or perhaps you do not care that the leatherjacket murdered one of my people."

Retreating a few feet, Father Patricio looked around him, his head bobbing like a branch caught in the river. Black Wolf wanted him to try to either run or call out for help because then, like his namesake, he could attack, but he had made the padre a promise that he would be safe tonight. More than that, if he turned from his word, Lucita would know.

"I do not lie. It is not the way of a Chumash warrior. And I have no secrets. Tell me, what takes you to the *monjerio* on a dangerous night?"

"Get out of here! You have no right—"

"It is you who has no right!"

"Damnable heathen!"

Gathering his muscles, Black Wolf launched himself at the padre and clamped his hands around the man's throat. Father Patricio's strangled scream put him in mind of a buzzard driven from feeding; it would bring others to see what was wrong, but he only needed a few seconds.

"Leave them alone!" His teeth were clenched as he spoke. "You call yourself a man of God, but it is a lie. I hate you for what you do. And a Chumash who hates lives with the need for revenge." He increased his hold. "I have a question and you will tell me the truth."

A gurgling served as the padre's response.

"Where has the corporal gone?"

# 15

It was nearly dawn by the time Sebastian and his men met up with the soldiers he'd sent ahead to find the merchant. After introductions were completed, Sebastian explained that he had immediate need for his men to quell a potential Indian uprising, but instead of taking off, he accepted Senor Portola's offer of a simple meal. In truth, Sebastian was all too happy to oblige since he didn't know when he might have another opportunity to take his measure of the man.

"So it's true, is it?" Pablo said as he cut a slab of black bread for Sebastian. "There have been problems at La Purisima."

*More than the rumormongers have yet gotten hold of.* "Some, but not for much longer."

"You have a plan to end it?"

"Indeed." As he'd expected, Pablo was well armed and accompanied by a couple of men who were responsible for the half-dozen pack mules. Beyond that, the merchant's musket and sword were of the finest quality, his clothing expensive, his personal horse a powerful-looking creature. Pablo himself was a handsome man with an alert bearing.

"Do you mind telling me what you intend to do?" Senor Portola asked. "I promise I won't tell the savages."

Sebastian made a show of laughing at the joke. "I'm certain you won't, since that would hardly be to your advantage. There wouldn't be a problem if they hadn't been allowed to carry out their miserable lives unchallenged. They have grown bold; one of their warriors has become a killer."

"No!"

"I am afraid so," he said and described the latest assault, dividing blame between Mundo for shirking his duties and Black Wolf for his savagery.

"What an appalling incident. What are—"

Not giving the merchant time to finish his sentence, Sebastian launched into an explanation of his commitment to finding where the wild Indians lived and then attacking their village. If it took wiping out the entire population, so be it, but he would prefer to return to the mission with a large number of new neophytes in tow. He said nothing about the hard reality that nothing about his present post had gone the way he'd anticipated, about his growing anger and the sleepless nights.

"I'm certain the padres will be delighted," Pablo said, his expression grave. "A mission can always use more hands to do the work."

"True—not that that is my primary concern."

"No, I daresay yours is of a military nature."

"That and safeguarding my family."

"Your family?"

Smiling to himself at how easily he'd worked the conversation around, Sebastian explained that he'd brought his wife and young unmarried daughter here as a courtesy to the Church. He briefly described his wife's religious duties, then began talking about Lucita.

As he went on about her healing skills, her quick intellect, and the fact that she'd recently broken off a financially advantageous engagement, he was certain Pablo's interest was growing.

"What can I say?" He trusted his sigh would be taken as that of an indulgent father. "Lucita can have her pick of men, so if she insists one suitor doesn't live up to her expectations I can hardly argue that she'll never have another opportunity. It isn't as if I'm in a position of needing to improve my financial standing."

"Hm. It seems strange, then, that she wants to isolate herself here."

"It does, doesn't it. However, she wanted to experience at least a little of the world before settling down. All I want is her happiness." The last stuck in his craw, and he hoped Pablo wouldn't press him further. If only he could make sure Lucita knew what was expected of her when Pablo arrived and that the merchant would be suitably impressed.

Should he say more about Lucita, or would the merchant believe he was deliberately singing her praises? Taking advantage of the fact that he'd just been poured another cup of wine, he studied his surroundings. They'd met up with Pablo while he was passing through a small, narrow gully with low hills all around. In all his years, Sebastian had never allowed his troops to let down their guard while in such a vulnerable position. If the Chumash attacked, he and the others would be hard-pressed to defend themselves. However, as he reminded himself, so far he'd seen no evidence of organization among the Indians.

"The padres are most proud of their wine," he said. "You must deal with hundreds of wines; surely you are in a position to judge quality. Are they right to be boasting?"

"Indeed," Pablo said with a smile. "In fact, sampling the current stock is what I enjoy most about visiting La Purisima. So, what does your wife think of conditions there?"

As the men continued their conversation, the wind carried their voices to the east where Black Wolf lay on his belly on one of the rises overlooking the group of men and animals. He couldn't hear what they were saying and didn't care, because what mattered was that the leatherjacket represented danger to his people. More than once Black Wolf's thoughts strayed to his hand in things and what he might have done differently, but whenever he did, he remembered watching a young, dying Chumash woman and hearing the helpless cries of her husband. The Spanish surely called him a savage for what he'd done afterward, but he'd been an animal then, a wolf, an attacker driven by the need for revenge.

Shaking his head, he concentrated. The leatherjackets had left their horses grouped together some distance from the merchant's animals, and although their reins had been looped around convenient trees, no one was watching them. He couldn't possibly disarm the men, but if they were on foot—

Corporal Sebastian, although in earnest conversation with the merchant, occasionally scanned his surroundings, which was all Black Wolf needed to see to convince him that he wouldn't be able to get any closer without being seen. Still, he wanted to take advantage of the fact that the leatherjackets were away from their mounts.

*Wolf Spirit, bring your thoughts to me today. Make your strength and cunning mine. A wolf attacks; a wolf does not fear death. Is that what you want of me?*

Sensing a presence behind him, he turned, but he saw nothing except for the deep shade cast by trees.

*I need your wisdom today, need to become you. If it is within my power to bring the horses to the ground I will do so, but not if it would result in my death. What—*

He'd been wrong. The darkness under the nearest tree wasn't a shadow after all; at least, he didn't think so. Instead, he believed he was looking at a grizzly. Or maybe it was a changing shaman as had revealed itself to him after he'd fought with the first leatherjacket.

A grizzly.

A slow smile touched his lips, and he lifted his head to the heavens to thank Chupu and Great Eagle, but mostly his prayers were to Wolf, who, he believed, had sent him the truth.

Scrambling to his knees but keeping his head low so he wouldn't be seen, he reached deep into his throat for the necessary sounds. Then, cupping his hands over his mouth, he chuffed and growled. A couple of the horses arched their necks and looked about, but the others gave no indication they'd heard. He crawled closer, the journey slow and laborious, but he continued making the sounds of a grizzly and the horses became more and more agitated, no longer eating, some of them straining against the reins, blowing out excited breaths. So did the mules, but because they'd been securely tied he doubted they could break free.

Only once he was close enough so he could see that the men had been eating dried meat did they take notice of the horses' actions. The corporal barked an order, and two of the leatherjackets jumped to their feet and started toward the horses. At that moment, Black Wolf, too, stood. Although the effort tore at his throat, he bellowed. No one looked his way. Instead all eyes were on the horses as first one and then the others snapped their reins and began galloping away. Laughing silently, he watched as the leatherjackets sprinted after them.

Two days after her father left, Father Joseph took Lucita's arm and guided her toward the merchant Pablo Portola. Considering his long trip here, she expected the newcomer's stench to make her stomach rebel, but it didn't. Remarkably clean in contrast to the two scruffy men in charge of the pack mules, he put her in mind of a caballero, with his fitted *calzonera* that flared out at the bottom, allowing him freedom of movement. His broad-brimmed sombrero shielded his face and saved it from being sunburned. Because of the shade the sombrero provided, it was difficult to judge his age, but he carried himself as if he was fit and healthy. He'd unbuttoned his vest to reveal a ruffled white shirt.

"Lucita." Father Joseph gave her a gentle nudge while her mother hovered nearby. "Do you have nothing to say to the senor?"

"Of course I do." She extended her hand, hopefully hiding her embarrassment at momentarily being at a loss for words. "Welcome. It has been so long since we have heard any news of the world. I hope you will be able to stay long enough to tell us a great deal."

Senor Portola closed her fingers within his own and lightly kissed the back of her hand. "I wish it could be longer, senorita. However, I have a ship waiting to sail and must leave for the presidio tomorrow. Given recent events, I wish it could be different. I do not like seeing La Purisima unprotected."

Obviously Senor Pablo was a man of wealth, as witnessed by

his dress and horse, the only one with enough energy to still hold up its head. She wanted to believe he had a kindly demeanor after what she'd experienced lately, but maybe she was only trying to convince herself of that.

"I had the opportunity to speak briefly with your father," he said. It seemed he was about to say more, but he didn't, leaving her to wonder what he and her father had discussed.

Although the merchant had released her hand, he continued to gaze down at her; then he gave her a quick grin. "I confess Corporal Sebastian told me enough about you that I was most eager to reach La Purisima, which I did as soon as possible, considering. . . . There are not many single young women in this country, and to discover you are as beautiful as he stated—well, I am pleased. Most pleased."

"He said I was beautiful?"

"Yes indeed. Unfortunately, there was an . . . incident before we had spent more than an hour together. Otherwise, I doubt there'd be a single thing I don't know about you."

Although she was certain he'd left something important unsaid, she didn't know enough about the man to press him for details. Besides, the only way she could keep from going crazy wondering what her father was doing was by refusing to think about either him or Black Wolf.

"You must be exhausted from your long travels," she said. "Hopefully there will be food to your liking."

"Yes, yes," her mother agreed. "We want to do all we can to make you comfortable. Your business sounds fascinating. I'd love to hear about your travels."

To Lucita's surprise, being with Pablo, as he asked her to call him, turned out to be easier than she'd expected. As they ate, he explained that he'd grown up in the shipping business at his father's side and, after taking over, had devoted all his energy to expansion, but because the padres needed to be brought up-to-date about Church matters, neither she nor her mother pressed for more personal information.

Both Lucita and Father Joseph were delighted to hear that the merchant had brought along a measure of tea leaves, and when Father Joseph told him about her work in the infirmary, he asked her to show it to him.

"Are you sure you want to do this?" she asked as they stood outside the infirmary door.

"I know what I'll find in there, Lucita," he told her. "What interests me is your reaction."

Off balance because of his intense scrutiny, she nevertheless wasted little time in checking on her patients' status. She waited until she was done with the others before going to Midnight's bed. As had happened twice before, the older boy was with him.

"Oh, wonderful!" she exclaimed. "Look at his leg."

Pablo leaned close. "I see what was a nasty wound well on its way to healing."

"I was so worried infection would kill him, but he's going to live." Remembering what Father Joseph had said about Midnight, she impulsively hugged the boy and then sighed.

"What is it?"

"He'll have to return to work. I argued to give him a little more time for the wound to close over, but . . ."

"But the mission must continue to function."

"Yes." She didn't care if she sounded angry. "Nothing is more important."

"To the padres, true, but it's different with you, isn't it?"

He might be challenging her, but she couldn't pretend not to have an opinion. She explained that Midnight's work was both dangerous and dirty and she was afraid he wouldn't be given the opportunity to adequately cover his injury, thus undermining the strides they'd made.

"Do you want me to speak in his behalf?" Pablo asked.

"What? No, no, this isn't your concern."

Surprised by his offer, she turned her attention to the older child. "I think they must be brothers," she explained. "One day he watched me clean Midnight's wound, and the next day I found him doing it himself. It does my heart good to see so much love between them."

"Remarkable, remarkable," Pablo said. Then he held out his

arm, indicating he wanted her to loop hers through his. Both hesitant and warmed by the gesture, she did so.

"You are a gem," he said with a grin as they stepped outside. "A rare gem."

"What do you mean?"

"You have opinions and aren't afraid to show your emotions."

Confused, she frowned up at him.

"It's just that I don't think I've ever met a woman who expresses herself as openly as you do."

"You disapprove?"

"Not at all." He patted her hand. "Please let me explain. Over the years I have discovered that most ladies are willing to listen and agree to anything a man — a well-situated man particularly — says, which flatters a man's ego but tells that man little about the lady."

"My social skills are rather primitive," she admitted, even though she'd never imagined she'd say that to someone she'd just met. "I've lived a sheltered life."

"So have I. Oh, not in the way you have, but I must admit I have not been in the company of women as much as I would have liked. It is an unfortunate consequence of the way I earn my living."

"Do you enjoy what you do?" she asked, not just to be polite but because she honestly wanted to know.

"I have never experienced any other way of life, so I'm not sure how studied my answer is, but yes. Sailing is in my blood. I love the seas, the challenge, even the danger."

"Danger?"

"Mostly from the weather. Nature is an unkind master. The risks are never-ending and may someday take my life or the lives of the men under my employ. But nature simply is. It does not hate, does not scheme, has no ulterior motives."

She'd never heard a man say something like that, making her wonder if he sometimes questioned life's deeper meanings. Now she asked him that.

"Often." He chuckled. "Much more often than my parents,

particularly my father, wished I had. Do not misunderstand me—my father was a dedicated businessman, and I learned a great deal from him, but I could never be satisfied thinking only of ships and cargo. I want to know why the winds blow the way they do, whether it is possible to anticipate a storm, why people act the way they do. There were times when my father and I believed we had nothing in common."

"Do you still?"

"He is dead, Lucita. Lost in a storm." Although his words were matter-of-fact, his tone gave away his regret.

"You miss him, don't you?" she asked.

"Every day. I'm sorry. I didn't mean to bring you out here so I could talk about that."

"It's all right."

"Yes," he said softly. "I imagine it is. Senorita, let me be frank. I am accustomed to people deferring to me; position comes with wealth. But I don't want it to be like that between you and me."

"You don't?"

Stopping, he waited until she was facing him. "I want to be frank with you because you were frank with me in there. Business concerns have taken my youth. I do not regret that I passed my twenties and thirties alone, but I just turned forty."

She hadn't thought he was that old.

"I don't want to be alone anymore."

"You don't," she almost said but realized in time how stupid it would sound. "Being here"—she indicated the valley and what lay beyond it—"can make a person lonely."

"Especially a young, vibrant woman. Surely you want more than this, Lucita."

*Surely.*

"If you want, I will court you. In truth, I would like nothing better, but this is not the setting for a lengthy courtship worthy of a woman of your sensibilities, grace, and attractiveness. I intend to be honest with you and hope you will be the same in return."

*Courtship?* "I . . . would like that."

"Good. Your father says you are headstrong and that any man who takes you for a wife will need to manage you with a firm hand."

"And you decided to accept the challenge because you are used to wielding that firm hand?" He wanted honesty; she would give it to him.

To her surprise, he chuckled. "In business, yes. But in my personal life, never. My mother came from farming stock, the only girl in a family with six children, and although she knew nothing about making a living from the sea when she and my father were married, she never shirked work. My parents sacrificed and eventually succeeded together. Even my sister had her own role within the company until she married a spice merchant and convinced him to take his business into both England and France. As a result, his wealth has more than doubled."

"Why are you telling me this?" she asked, although maybe she already understood.

"Because I believe you are a great deal like my mother and sister, a woman with a mind and a will. A woman who needs more from life than what she has found thus far."

Pablo walked Lucita back to her quarters in silence, not because he had nothing to say to her, but because his thoughts were too complex to allow for conversation. Realizing they only had a couple of minutes left together and knowing how busy he'd be in the morning, he stopped and waited until she was facing him.

"How do you feel about living here?" he asked.

"Feel? I told you, there's a great deal for me to do. I've never felt more needed."

"What about concerns for your personal safety? I'm certain you've guessed that your father and I talked about the problems he's been having with the savages. Don't you feel at risk here?"

"No," she said so quickly that it left him puzzled. "No, I don't."

"Why not?"

"Because . . ." She drew away a little and looked around at the dark. "I . . . I am doing necessary work. The wild Indians know that if they harm me, those who are ill or injured will have to rely on Father Joseph, and he has so many other duties."

"Then you believe savages are capable of complex thought?"

"You don't?"

He liked being challenged by her. "A reasonable question, Lucita. However, instead of answering, I believe I must tell you what happened while your father and I were together."

She cocked her head to one side but gave no indication of being surprised by his words, and he guessed he hadn't been as adept at keeping things to himself as he'd hoped. He told her everything about the stampede, that he'd offered the loan of his big gelding and mules to assist in rounding up the horses and of the hours it had taken to retrieve three of the beasts.

"I didn't want to leave before your father had recovered the rest of his mounts," he finished, "but he understood the time constraints I'm under and insisted he could make do with what he had."

"And after he has all his horses back? What is he going to do then?"

"I'm not certain. It depends on how long it takes before none of his men are on foot, but the last we spoke, he remained determined to find the savages' village."

"I see."

"How can you be so calm?" he pressed. "I don't see how you can feel safe here. If there is a rogue grizzly, one that has gone mad—grizzlies have no fear of man, and it takes nothing to provoke them to attack. If the horses hadn't broken free, it might have slaughtered—"

"Did you see it?" she interrupted.

"No," he admitted. "And that puzzles me. I've observed a number of bears during my years in this country, and I've never seen one act the way this one did. It was almost as if it was deliberately trying to frighten the horses. It succeeded."

"Yes," she said. "It did."

# 16

Pablo left before noon the next day, his pack animals all but lost under their burdens. He'd saved his final and most lengthy good-bye for Lucita, promising he'd return as soon as possible and asking her to constantly be on the lookout. She did the same to him, surprising herself by how deeply she meant it. No man—at least not one of her race—had ever made her feel so special or confided so much to her.

Her father and the others were gone for a week, during which Lucita lived in fear that they would find Black Wolf's village. By contrast, every prayer session run by the padres began and ended with a plea to God to guide the soldiers in a successful mission.

Sickened by the images conjured up inside her—particularly if the soldiers attacked women and children as well as warriors— she tried to fill her own prayers with a plea for understanding of what was happening both in her world and inside her heart, but no matter how hard she tried, she couldn't completely silence the neophytes' chanting.

Although she tried to keep busy both mentally and physically, the days dragged. If it hadn't been for the pleasure she'd gained from seeing Midnight able to work again, she wasn't sure how she would have coped. She was still concerned that his wound shouldn't be exposed to filth, but he was obviously happy to be able to walk, and there was no missing the pleasure he gained from being in his brother's company.

One afternoon she was sitting with a small group of children too young to work when loud, sudden shouts brought her to her feet. Her first thought was that the soldiers had returned with proof of their success, and she vowed that no matter what the consequences, she wouldn't force herself to be part of whatever celebration took place.

The youngest girl began crying as the shouting continued. Muttering calming words, Lucita lifted the child in her arms and gave her a reassuring hug. When she had quieted, Lucita transferred the slight weight to her hip and slowly followed the others toward the main trail leading to the mission.

A quick appraisal assured her that none of the soldiers had suffered any injury. Another, hesitant appraisal gave her the answer she needed. There were no prisoners.

But if there'd been no survivors—

"It's all right," she crooned to the child whose grip on her throat belied her slight build. She looked around for the girl's mother, belatedly remembering that the woman had been sent to the olive mill for the day.

"What are you afraid of?" she gently asked, although the girl spoke little Spanish. "I won't let anything happen to you. No matter what it takes, I'll keep you safe."

Maybe language didn't matter, Lucita thought as the girl snuggled against her. Maybe love didn't need words. At the thought, her eyes burned and she took in her world through a blur she understood as completely as she understood what she felt for this child.

The soldiers and their mounts looked exhausted. She felt sorry for the horses, but even when her father's face contorted as he dismounted, she couldn't conjure up a breath of sympathy for him.

Sebastian waved his hand in a gesture of dismissal, then glared at the small troop as the men turned their horses over to the neophytes and started toward the kitchen. Both padres joined him, and although she was certain her presence wasn't wanted, she stepped closer. Because of the noise, she couldn't hear what her father was saying, but his grim expression said a great deal.

When he looked at her, for several heartbeats she didn't think he'd seen her; either that or he considered her unimportant. Then: "Put that creature down."

She retreated a little but continued to hold onto the child who now stared openmouthed at Lucita's father.

"Did you hear me?" he demanded. "I will not have you lugging that filthy creature around."

How could caring for a child be wrong? However, she was wise enough to know her father was in no mood for an argument, especially from her. She wasn't ready to deprive herself of those trusting arms around her neck, but Corporal Sebastian had gone off to murder those he considered savages, and this bright-eyed child might be in danger.

"You saw nothing?" Father Joseph asked as the little girl ran off.

"Nothing," Sebastian admitted, his features stony. "I have no doubt that Senor Portola told you about the horses being frightened off."

"He said there was a grizzly," Lucita replied warily.

"So it appears. It took two days before we captured the last of those miserable nags, and by then they were in no mood for a lengthy trip."

"You forced them?"

"Only to the extent that was wise and prudent, Lucita. I sorely wanted to lay a whip to them, but to what purpose?" He stopped while he rubbed the scar at his mouth. "I am accustomed to fighting an enemy willing to do battle, but the savages are animals hiding in caves."

Black Wolf had said nothing about the Chumash living in caves—not that she would tell her father that. In the time he'd been gone, Sebastian's usually clean-shaven cheeks had taken on a dusky hue that gave him a sinister quality. Dirt had caked around his neck; more dirt covered his uniform.

Father Patricio, who had been standing slightly behind Father Joseph, cleared his throat. Not all of the savages had been in hiding, he said. Black Wolf himself had been here just after the soldiers left, his presence a mockery to the king's army.

"Black Wolf!" Sebastian reached for his sword. "That animal— that murdering animal! I swear, I'll—"

A shout drew Lucita's attention from her father's reaction. One of the soldiers had emerged from their quarters and was yelling that it had been broken into.

She started to follow her father and the padres, who were trying to keep up with him, but her mother, who had said not so much as a word to acknowledge her husband's return, stopped her.

"This is men's concern, Lucita," she said as Sebastian stepped inside. "It has nothing to do with us."

Hours later, Lucita looked up from her task of making sure the children ate at least a bite of peach as protection against rickets to see her mother gesturing for her.

"It is your father." Margarita's mouth looked strained. "He wants to talk to you. Please, whatever he says, agree with him."

*Not all chains are visible, are they?* Lucita silently asked her mother as she walked with her to the padres' chapel. When they entered it, Lucita saw that the candles were lit. The soft glow spreading over the crudely drawn religious pictures took her back to her childhood, when simply being in a room like this gave her a sense of peace.

Her father was sitting on one of the wooden bench while the two padres, also seated, faced him. One of the soldiers stood slightly behind Sebastian, looking as if he wasn't part of whatever was going on.

She received no more than a quick glance from her father, but it was enough; he considered her no more important than the waiting soldier.

"I want all of you to know that I have made my decision," Sebastian said. He was still dirty and unshaven, but bread crumbs and a stain covered the front of his uniform—proof that he'd eaten. "The savages defy us. My God, they murdered one of my men and tried to kill another."

Father Joseph crossed himself at her father's profane use of the Lord's name, but Father Patricio gave no indication of his reaction.

After wiping spit from the ruined side of his mouth, Sebastian continued. "The Crown in its ignorance believes a skeleton troop can maintain control and quell any uprising, but I am not so deluded. It is impossible for so few to prevent a bloodbath."

"Sebastian!" Lucita's mother gasped. "Do you really believe—"

"What are you doing here?"

"You said—"

"I said I wanted *her.*" He jerked a finger at Lucita. "I have no need for you."

Her chin quivering, hands moving nervously, Margarita backed out of the chapel. Lucita felt torn between the need to run after her mother and comfort her and the even stronger need to insist her father not treat his wife like a beast of burden. But she had begged Lucita not to incur Sebastian's wrath, and no matter how much effort it took, she would remain silent. Besides, it was vital she hear her father.

"I have no choice in this," Sebastian said, his words clipped as if they were the last thing he wanted to say. "I must request more troops."

"Amen," Father Joseph responded.

Ignoring the padre, her father went on. Because he dared not leave the mission unprotected, he had decided to go alone to the presidio, where he would commission for additional manpower. He expected to be gone the better part of a week. In the meantime, the soldiers were to separate the adult male neophytes from the others and do whatever it took to assure they not forget who was in charge.

"If you must make an example of one or more of them, fine. No one will be allowed about at night, and I want at least two soldiers on duty at all times. Any neophyte shirking or leaving their work will be shot—no exceptions."

A sense of horror at the image conjured up left Lucita weak and shaking. If only she knew how to make the neophytes understand her, maybe she could warn them.

When the soldier asked for verification of his rights and responsibilities, Lucita noticed that both padres were paying close attention. That made sense, since they were responsible for the neophytes' souls and assuring the mission's work continue to be done and were perhaps concerned that the corporal's orders would put that work in jeopardy. But why had she been ordered here?

With an abrupt wave of his hand, her father dismissed the others. To her surprise, the padres said nothing about the fact that they were being ordered to leave a place of worship. She started to follow them, but Sebastian told her to remain.

"You will go with me," he said after the door closed behind the slow-walking Father Joseph. "It is foolish to keep you isolated from eligible men."

"To the presidio? What can I—"

"Silence! I swear, you are more trouble than the savages." Glowering, he indicated that he wanted her to sit across from him. She did as he ordered but didn't try to break the silence.

"You spoke with Senor Portola?" he asked.

"Yes."

"And?"

"He wasn't here long, Father." Uncomfortable saying anything of a personal nature, she wanted to keep it to a minimum. "We had only a short time to talk."

"What about?"

"Many things." A glare was all it took for her to understand that he wouldn't be satisfied with that. "He has traveled so many places and had so many experiences. They fascinated me."

"You did not irritate him, did you?"

She almost snapped that she had enough social graces to know when to stop pressing an issue but thought better of it. "No, I did not. I showed him what I've been doing in the infirmary because he seemed most interested."

"Did he? What do you think of him as a man?"

The question didn't surprise her; somehow she'd known they would come to this point.

"I was most favorably impressed," she admitted. "He is worldly and yet there is a gentleness to him I found most appealing."

Sebastian nodded and then frowned. "And yet he didn't spend more than a few hours in your company."

"This time. But he will return."

"Of course he will. He has business here."

She paused, then gave him what he wanted. "Not just business, Father. He wants to see me again."

The proprietary look she hated and feared took hold of his features. "Does he," Sebastian muttered. "Does he indeed. And when will that be? The next time the padres have sufficient trade goods?"

"No. He . . . he'll be back as soon as he can arrange it."

"Then he was taken with you?"

"Yes."

"Yes. Is that all you can say? Why is he in such a hurry to return?"

"Because . . ." When he leaned forward, invading her space, she finished. "He spoke of courtship."

"Indeed! Hm." Getting to his feet, he began pacing. "He reached the presidio several days ago. Perhaps his business there is already finished and he is on his way back. And if he has been delayed and you show up with me, he may take it as a sign that we are too eager for a union. No, no, I do not want you with me after all."

Unable to silence a sigh of relief, she started to stand, but he stepped toward her and she sank back down.

"You will conduct yourself in a manner which meets with my approval," he said. "And if Senor Portola arrives before my return, you will be as gracious and accommodating as possible. Do you understand?"

She nodded.

"I hope you do." His mouth thinned. "Because if I find fault, any fault, with your behavior, you will regret the day you were born. And so will your mother."

* * *

Long after her father left, Lucita finally emerged from the chapel and closed the door behind her, but instead of looking for something to satisfy her hunger, she pressed her cheek against the door and let the night sounds surround her.

She had prayed and then prayed again, asking God to help guide her through what lay ahead and assist her in making decisions that could dictate the course of her life forever, but if God had listened, if he cared, he hadn't made himself known to her.

Her father would make her life miserable if she remained at La Purisima in an unmarried state, that misery spilling over to her mother. The world Lucita had once known in Mexico City had become a distant memory—not that it mattered, because she couldn't go back there by herself. Pablo was little more than a stranger; despite her favorable impression of him, how could she imagine them as husband and wife, being part of his world?

*I feel so lost.* Her prayer, if that's what it was, brought her to the brink of tears. *As if I don't belong anywhere. Is that what you want for me, Lord? Will I best serve you by becoming some man's wife? But what about the neophytes? If I leave, what will happen to them?*

*What will happen to my mother?*

An owl hooted, pulling her away from the thoughts that had been overwhelming her. A sudden chill caused her to rub her arms, but although a faint breeze was blowing, it had nothing to do with how she felt.

Spotting her mother, she stopped and nearly turned away, then walked over to her. Margarita's face was etched with unease, but she didn't say anything.

"It's all right," Lucita said reassuringly. "He wanted to know about my impression of Senor Portola."

"And?"

"I'm certain he sees Pablo as a suitable husband."

"I'm certain he does." Fists clenched, Margarita stared into her beautiful daughter's eyes. Lucita hadn't said everything about what she and her father had discussed; her mother was certain of that. She could only pray that in time her daughter would unburden herself. In the meantime, Margarita would be there for her, encouraging and lending what support she could.

"What about you?" she asked. "Do you see Pablo as a suitable husband?"

"I don't know. I've just met him."

"A wise answer." Taking Lucita's capable hand, she squeezed it. For a moment she nearly convinced herself not to say more, but she'd spent so many years silent and no longer could remain so.

"I am not one to give advice about matters of the heart, Lucita," she said. "What I hope you will heed, what I pray will carry you through this decision, is my counsel to listen to your heart."

"My heart doesn't know what it wants."

"I think it does, Lucita, if you open yourself up to it."

"How?"

"Only you can decide that."

Fog drifted up from the surf to cover the cliff with a damp, lacy layer. From where she sat on the tired mare, Lucita tried to determine where the sand left off and the ocean began, but the water was in constant movement, swallowing and then releasing the beach.

A thousand times during the ride here, she'd come within a heartbeat of convincing herself to return to the mission, but whenever she started to turn her horse's head, reality slammed into her.

If her father couldn't arrange a marriage with Pablo, he'd find someone else. Whatever her fate, she would never again see this wild and intriguing country. Never again speak to the savage, the killer, who maybe was the only human being who understood her.

Her mother had been the one with the wisdom to tell her to seek solitude, and although Margarita had been shocked when, an hour after her father left, she'd announced that she needed to be away from the mission for a while, her mother hadn't tried to stop her. Margarita had brought up the danger from savages and wild animals, but Lucita had pointed out that she'd been alone in the wilderness before and had been safe.

"The land calls to me, Mother," she'd said. "I feel at peace out there, more content than I've been in years. God—surely God won't desert me."

"You aren't afraid?"

"Of the wilderness, no. Never."

Her mother hadn't looked convinced, but all she'd said was that she'd pray for her.

After securing the mare's front legs with loose-fitting ropes so there wouldn't be a repeat of what had happened the first time, Lucita sank to the ground and pressed her hands over her hot, tired eyes.

She must be insane! What other explanation was there for what she'd done?

Most women had no quarrel with marriage. She'd seen the excitement in her friends' eyes when they announced their betrothal and later, after they were married, they giggled about their "wifely duties," some of them hinting that what happened in bed was the best part of being wed.

But her mother had never spoken of "wifely duties," only pursed her lips and clenched her fists before walking slowly toward her husband.

Since coming to La Purisima, Lucita had seen a soldier forcing himself on a woman and at least three couplings between neophytes. Although her mother had been horrified and begged the padres to insist the neophytes do "such things" in private, gentle Father Joseph had muttered that the Indians were carrying out God's command to be fruitful and were incapable of comprehending that their mating might offend anyone.

*Fruitful. Wifely duties.* All Lucita knew was that the act was carried out by the neophytes with great enthusiasm and sounds that sent shivers down her spine.

Opening her eyes, she waited for the world to come back into focus. Black Wolf had called it Humqaq. That was his church, where he went to pray to his gods or spirits or whatever they were.

It couldn't be! There was only one God, the deity she'd worshiped her entire life. How could Black Wolf believe what he did?

And yet she'd heard a wolf howl the last time she'd seen Black Wolf—not him making that sound, but a real wolf. She was convinced of it.

Once again the pounding in her head made thinking all but impossible and her father's orders, her future, none of that mattered.

Her legs, sore from the long ride, resisted her effort to stand, but she insisted, because the unanswered questions only became worse when she wasn't doing anything. She'd brought along some *atole* and dried fruit and ate at least half of it. When the rest was gone, she would have to return, but, for now at least, facing her future seemed nothing compared to the need that had brought her here.

Seagulls floated on unseen currents, and she tried to imagine herself up there with them. If she had the keen sight of birds, she might be able to see across the ocean. The thought of what lay on the other side of the ocean briefly distracted her, but because she would never be able to fly, she forced herself to return to the present and reality.

Humqaq.

A place of beliefs beyond her comprehension.

Maybe.

# 17

The wind increased in strength, and when Lucita stood looking down and out at the ocean she was forced to brace herself so she wouldn't be knocked off her feet.

There was something about the wind, energy maybe, that stripped away her weariness and made her feel as if she could run and climb forever. Was this bold creature really her?

No, she admitted, as she began walking again, it wasn't that simple. Her sanity, her need to claim some control over her future, some understanding of the world and her role in it, was at issue, and if she couldn't make her parents understand that, maybe she didn't belong in this world.

Stopping again, she clamped her hand around her wildly blowing hair. Only God knew when one's time to leave this earth had come. Hell waited for those who attempted to alter that timetable, and she loved being alive—yet it would take so little to step to the edge, lean forward, and fling herself into space.

Licking her lips, she discovered that they were salty. Touching her fingers to her cheek, she found it sticky from the moist air. Her hair fought her. Her legs, although tired, felt ready for whatever she required of them.

After releasing her hair, she scrambled to the top of the near-est cliff. Then, once she was sure of her balance, she spread her arms, lifted her head, and let go with something between a cry and laughter.

"Freedom. I feel so free here!"

The wind took her voice and tore it apart before throwing the tiny pieces into the heavens. Still, she felt calmer now and more in control of her emotions. Wondering how her mother would react if she brought her here, Lucita again began her aimless walk. Margarita would be fascinated by the awe-inspiring view, but be-cause she believed God had created everything, she wouldn't question why the cliffs existed or why they'd taken the form they had. If Margarita heard that the Chumash called it Humqaq and considered it sacred, she would pray they would see the light of truth, not listen to another belief.

Certainly not believe.

The wind began a low screaming sound as if trying to break free of some unseen prison, and Lucita tried to remember every-thing Black Wolf had told her about Humqaq, but he hadn't said that much.

"Are you here?" she whispered. Although the wind immedi-ately captured the question, she lost nothing of her words and the deep-felt emotions behind them. "When you come, is it because you feel the same need I did?"

It would be dark before much longer. If she was going to learn anything about this place before then, she would have to hurry her exploration. Putting her mind to this task she'd given herself and refusing to think beyond that, she lifted her skirts enough to keep from tripping on them and headed north.

It didn't take long to discover that she hadn't reached the highest point of land after all, but with the closely bunched peaks and valleys it was nearly impossible to gain a true perspective of what the area looked like. She couldn't imagine any animals liv-ing around the barren cliffs, and yet the occasional faint yapping of coyotes was proof that she wasn't alone.

Not every sound came from the coyotes or the wind as it made its way around the rocks. Another—

Motionless, she studied the great sweep of land, pulled the wild wind into her lungs, absorbed the cry of unseen carnivores, wished she were hearing a wolf instead.

Not a wolf, but something—something so close that it forced a shiver down her spine. Tears dampened her cheeks, and she would have prayed if she'd known whom to pray to.

*Black Wolf? Where are you?*

With every step she took, her memory of what he'd shared with her about Humqaq grew. This was where men came to pray to their spirit, to seek their connection with the great and mysterious worlds of today and of their ancestors.

'Alapay, world of the Gods of the Moon and Sun, home for the First People.

'Itiashup, the earth, which was suspended between the upper and lower worlds and surrounded by a great sea.

C'oyinashup, which was the realm of dark beings.

Both proud and more than a little shocked by her recall, she cocked her head and listened until she was certain she'd found where the disembodied howl was coming from. Possibly the wind was responsible for the sound; she hoped that was it, because she was in no condition to see anyone or absorb any more than she already had.

Reminding herself that any warrior, including one with hatred for what she represented burning inside him, might be here, she took as much care as possible to remain hidden. The boulders were damp from spray, the dampness so pervasive that she half-believed it had penetrated the rocks' core. That plus the wind made movement dangerous, but she couldn't make herself turn around and leave.

Pausing for breath, she studied her surroundings. Because of the way the granite outcroppings ahead were positioned, it was impossible to see more than twenty or thirty feet. She had no doubt that she was close to the ocean, maybe dangerously so, but that didn't matter, because she'd just identified a new sound— clear and fast with rumbling undertones. She realized she was listening to water, not the pounding of waves but similar to it.

Driven by a force she couldn't begin to fathom, she approached the boulders that might house the just-heard sound, only then seeing the thin trail that appeared to lead around the rocks. When she tried to take a calming breath, she found she'd clamped her hand over her mouth. A trail? *It must have been made by animals,* she started to tell herself. And yet, before the thought was fully formed, she accepted that that wasn't it at all.

She'd found where other human beings had walked.

Both afraid and excited beyond any comprehension, she placed her foot on the trail and began following it. The direction she now walked was taking her closer to the rumbling and unseen water.

After a few minutes, she realized the trail was leading her on an almost leisurely journey around the boulders. Now that they were between her and the ocean, she was somewhat protected from the wind, but that didn't improve her ability to draw a mental image of what she was hearing. The water seemed to be laughing, and the howl, or whatever it was, had merged with it, enriching it and chilling her.

When finally she found herself at the highest elevation, she wrapped her arms around her waist and stared out at the distant and hot-burning sun, which would soon begin its nightly descent. Feeling small and alone in a vastness beyond comprehension, she had no idea where she'd spend the night because she couldn't think beyond this moment. What had first looked like a flat area turned out to have a small crater in the middle of it. Walking over to it, she discovered it wasn't a crater after all but a hole large enough for a person to climb into and so deep she couldn't see to its bottom. So little light reached it that at first she wasn't sure what she was looking at, just that the water sounds came from somewhere deep in the shadows.

Dropping to her knees, she leaned forward as far as she dared. Black Wolf had told her that a stream emptied out into the ocean at this point but that it ran underground for a while before spilling out in a sheltered waterfall. In part because the coastline was so rugged, he'd said, its location remained unknown to all except those who understood its sacredness.

She'd found it, been drawn to it by something she couldn't comprehend.

The moisture now spraying onto her wasn't salty and must come from the stream as it burst out of its prison. Because her eyes had adjusted to the shadows, she saw that the waterfall ended in a deep, serene pool. Only when she'd pinpointed where the small stream broke through the rocks did she notice the sturdy rope secured to a nearby boulder at the opposite side of the hole. Its loose end hung over the edge and ended just above the pool. A number of knots, probably handholds, had been tied into the rope.

Looking around, she strained to discover who might be responsible for the rope, but she'd been here long enough to believe no one shared the rocky cliff with her.

But down there —

A shiver of something that wasn't quite fear shot through her because, despite the gloom, she could now make out a dark shadow in the middle of the pool. The shape moved, took on human form, was responsible for the howling.

Backing away, she fought the instinct to leave the stranger with what had to be his prayers, but she'd come so far and had so many questions.

By stretching out on the ground and turning her head to the side, she was better able to hear the stranger's prayer. A man, she determined. The stranger below was a man. Every fiber in her wanted it to be Black Wolf, but he wasn't the only warrior who replenished himself here. Her father and the other soldiers insisted all wild Indians were killers. If they were right and this wasn't Black Wolf, her life might be in danger, but then . . . the mission offered no protection for her.

Her stomach rumbled, but when she took in as much air as her lungs could hold, that seemed to fill her. She would wait here a little longer, wait and watch, and as long as the praying, chanting warrior remained where he was, she would be safe.

Wouldn't she?

Suddenly the wind threw an unexpectedly large amount of moisture at her. Enough reached her eyes that her vision blurred and she was forced to rub them until she could see again. For an instant she couldn't find the figure in the pool, and then—

He'd got out of the water and stood on a small ledge no more than two feet above the pool, staring up at her. She couldn't make out his features and had no way of knowing whether hatred filled his eyes. He was unarmed, naked, his body and long black hair streaming moisture.

Still looking up at her, the man lifted his arms and squeezed water out of his hair. He used his hands to wipe his body dry; nothing about the way he conducted himself gave any indication that he was uncomfortable with his nakedness, and it seemed right to her, primitive but right.

She wasn't sure, but it seemed that he'd cocked his head to one side as if listening to something. Following his lead, she did the same.

The sound began as a deep whisper, grew in strength, spread, faint and yet powerful, part of the earth and yet somehow separate.

Wolf.

Resisting the need to look around, she instead studied the warrior's reaction. He'd again lifted his arms, but this time he didn't stop until they were outspread above his head. He seemed to be swaying; either that or it was she who couldn't remain still. When his howl drifted upward, she felt as if she could reach out and touch it, but before she could make the decision to try, it had slid past her and up into the sky. It should have stopped echoing by now, shouldn't it? There was nothing to hold it, nothing for it to bounce off, and yet it remained.

Became part of the sound coming from the unseen wolf.

Standing, she looked around, but although the predator howl was repeated over and over again and answered each time, she couldn't see anything. Finally, numb and rawly alive at the same time, she turned her attention back to the pool.

The warrior hadn't moved and she wondered if he was capable of remaining with his arms outstretched forever. It shouldn't be any easier to make out his features than it had been before, and maybe her mind was painting something that didn't exist, but she believed she was looking into large black eyes that had locked on her and were asking her to believe.

To believe what?

The warrior's arms slid slowly to his side, and then, without looking down at what he was doing, he picked up something that had been lying on the ledge and tied it around his waist, rendering him no longer naked. Reaching out, he grabbed hold of the hanging rope and pulled it close to him. Then, seemingly effortlessly, he climbed up to her.

Black Wolf.

"You came," he said once he was standing beside her. Despite his attempts to dry himself, his flesh still glistened and his hair stuck to his back. He seemed only half-human, as if he might disappear at any moment.

"I . . . I . . ." Swallowing, she tried again. "If I shouldn't be here, please tell me."

"My prayers are over."

"This is Humqaq, isn't it?" she asked.

"Yes."

"It's incredible. Beautiful. Black Wolf, I heard, not just you but something else."

His features seemed to contract, but she couldn't read his reaction. "Not something, Lucita," he said after a minute. "Wolf Spirit."

"Wolf Spirit." She concentrated on taking a breath and in the act discovered that she wasn't ready for the ramifications.

He adjusted his scrap of clothing un-self-consciously. "Do you want to speak of why you are here?"

"No. Not yet. Maybe . . ."

"Then I will not ask."

*Thank you.* "You scattered my father's horses, didn't you? They said it might have been a grizzly, but—"

"Yes, it was me. And then I watched while they foolishly tried to find our village. Being around them soiled me, and before I return to my people, my family, I must make myself clean again."

"Black Wolf, our beliefs are so different," she said. "For you to worship a wolf—"

"I do not worship Wolf. He is my spirit."

She didn't understand the difference but wanted to. In the few minutes they'd been standing here, the world around them had changed, and now his dark features were painted a subtle red as a result of the setting sun. Everything, she included, carried the same hue, and no matter how much separated them, the sun touched them in the same way; she would never forget that.

"I will tell you this," he went on, "because I feel your heart's hunger."

"Tell me what?"

"About Humqaq."

She started to nod when realization slammed into her. Even before the Chumash could properly comprehend what it meant to be taken into the Church, they were baptized, called neophytes, and expected to work for the glory of that church. In contrast, Black Wolf had waited for her to be ready.

Looking around, she spotted a fairly smooth boulder and sat on it. Black Wolf chose one that placed him in such a position that light from the setting sun spilled over him. According to her mother, the devil constantly placed temptation before God's children, and men, being the stronger, were capable of forcing their will on women. But she could sit alone with Black Wolf and not be afraid.

"This is our belief." His words were accented, reminding her that Spanish wasn't his native language. "Three days after a Chumash dies, his soul comes out of the grave in the evening. That soul first comes to Humqaq, because it has always been where new life enters the world and where that life returns at death. Our ancestors never came here, because they believed the spirits would be disturbed. Instead, they stopped at Shawil and made sacrifices to honor the dead."

"What changed that?"

The corner of his mouth twitched. "The enemy."

"You mean the Spanish."

He nodded. "The ancient ways were becoming mist. Families were being torn apart, and the old people were no longer there to teach the children about where they came from. My grandfather and his father, along with other men, heeded the messages from Kakunupmawa, which said it was time for the Chumash to see the footprints of our ancestors."

"Footprints? In the sand? But the sea washes that away, doesn't it?"

"Not in the sand. In the rocks."

Her head pounded. "How is that possible?"

"It is not for us to question the way of our gods. Do you ask why your God says one thing or another is a sin?"

"Not if it's in the Bible."

"Ha! Your Bible is words from ancient ones written on talking leaves. Our ancient ones spoke in other ways."

"And . . . and some of what they said or did was in the form of footprints in rocks?" she asked in confusion.

"They are marks left behind by the spirits of the first women and children. It is there that the spirits of those who have just died come to bathe and paint themselves. Then they see a light to the west, which guides them to the land of Shimilaqusha. There are no words in your language for that. It is in my heart." He tapped his chest. "And in the hearts of all who believe."

Close to tears, she blinked repeatedly.

"Look around you." Straightening, he swept his gaze over their surroundings. "The spirits of our ancestors are everywhere. We do not need to see them to believe in their existence. When my son is ready, he will open his heart and mind and eyes and ears and take those things into him."

Suddenly weak, she rocked forward and rested her head in her hands. Her head felt as if it were about to explode and she desperately needed to run, but where? Why?

"What is it?" he asked.

But she couldn't answer.

# 18

"Does your father know where you are?"

"No."

Black Wolf waited for her to say more, but Lucita remained silent. At his prompting, they'd returned to lower ground and collected her horse. He'd gone through her pack and given her the last of her dried fruit, but although she chewed dutifully, she seemed to have no awareness of what she was doing. Rarely one of the old people lost the ability to make decisions and others guided the person through his or her declining years, but Lucita was too young for that.

"He will look for you," Black Wolf said, hoping to prompt her to think of the consequences of her actions.

"No, he won't. He left for the presidio."

Alarmed, he grabbed her elbows. "Why? Tell me!"

"Do you have to ask?"

"No. I do not." Releasing her, he stood and walked into the night. He should be asking if her father had spoken of how long he'd be gone and how many men he hoped to bring back with him or whether there'd been talk of another attempt to find his village, but he couldn't put his mind to anything except her. "Why have you told me this?"

"I don't know! I don't know what's happening to me, why I feel the way I do, why I want . . ."

What she'd just said made little sense, but he didn't ask for an explanation. Instead, knowing a great deal remained inside her, he returned to her side and stood with her while gulls called to each other and the sea continued its ageless assault on the shore.

"I have to go back," she said dully. "Be there when he returns."

"Why?"

"What else is there for me?"

Black Wolf slept little during the night and suspected rest came no easier for Lucita, but while she must be thinking about what would happen between her and her father when they were in each other's presence again, it was different for him.

His concern was for her welfare, yes, but it was more than that; he was a man too long without his wife's presence, and Lucita's body spoke of health and loneliness for something he sensed she had no understanding of. She needed him to listen to her and keep her from being alone for these few hours, nothing else; he struggled to remember that.

Finally darkness gave way to morning. He'd just finished sending his thoughts to his ancestors when he caught her staring at him.

"Why did you stay with me?" she asked, her voice carrying no hint of sleepiness.

*Because you are different from anyone else I have ever known. Because you have taken me out of myself and into your heart and mind.*

"Perhaps I want to make you promise to tell me what you learn after your father returns," he said instead.

Her response was to fold her hands tightly together. "What if he doesn't tell me anything?"

"I wish it was different for you, Lucita, but I cannot change what is."

"No, you can't."

"We will travel together until it is time for us to go our separate ways," he told her. "And if you wish, we will not speak."

The way she stared at him puzzled him, but she only nodded. Silent, they went about the task of getting ready to leave. He wanted her to ride so she could conserve her strength, but she seemed to need to walk.

Summer's wilting heat waited on the horizon, warning him to cover as much ground as possible before afternoon sapped them. When he pointed in a slightly different direction from the one she'd started on, she frowned but didn't argue. He'd chosen a trail that followed a higher elevation because the occasional trees and hills would provide them with welcome shade and allow him to see before he was seen. He tried to put his mind on when he would be with his son again, their shared love and laughter, but Lucita was too close and her impact too great for the thought to hold.

Instead, he simply walked beside her until a distant movement caught his attention. A quick glance at Lucita told him she'd seen it, too. Stopping, he shaded his eyes, but even when the truth of it could no longer be questioned, he continued to stare.

"A wolf," Lucita whispered.

"Yes."

"Do we have anything to fear from it?"

"Not this one," was all he could say.

After signaling her to remain where she was, he went on ahead; despite the heat, he shivered. He wanted to look back at Lucita and somehow convince himself that she hadn't seen Wolf, his Wolf, but he didn't try because he knew different.

Unable to concentrate on anything except the meeting to come, he slowly and reverently approached the dark beast. The animal regarded him with eyes as bright as moonlight on fresh snow. His coat was sleek and full and showed no signs of his having survived years in the wilderness. Maybe he breathed; maybe he was beyond such mortal needs.

*I approach you, my spirit. Approach with my heart hammering within me and my mind filled to overflowing. I do not understand. You have always been in my dreams, my thoughts, showed yourself to me during my vision quest, but this . . .*

Step by hesitant step, he covered the ground between him and his spirit.

*Who sent you here, Wolf? Was it Kakunupmawa? And why have you allowed her to be part of this?*

No sound escaped the deep throat. Instead, as if this moment meant everything to him, the creature slipped slowly and gracefully and silently forward. Shaken anew, Black Wolf stopped and held out a trembling hand.

*In joy I accept your gift. In humble awe I take your wisdom into me.*

Close enough now that he could stretch his muzzle and touch Black Wolf's hand, the wolf inhaled deeply. Knowing his spirit was taking in his essence, Black Wolf willed himself to be a warrior. This wasn't the first time they'd come together, but the wonder of it would never leave him, and he would never want it any other way.

The great and deadly mouth opened, revealing teeth capable of tearing him apart. Lost in reverence and awe, Black Wolf kept his hand outstretched. He felt hot breath, proof, maybe, that his spirit lived, and then the powerful teeth closed down around his hand and he felt the tips of Wolf's teeth settle over his flesh, wondered, briefly, if Lucita could see what was happening.

*We are one, my spirit. I take courage from you, give myself up to you.*

His hand remained trapped. Wolf's nostrils expanded and he took another deep breath. The fear that had briefly lapped at him no longer existed. Instead, he felt his chest swell; his eyes filled with joyful tears.

*Your courage is now mine, my spirit. My life is in your care. What do you want of me?*

As if in answer, Wolf opened his mouth and released Black Wolf. Fire burned in the animal's eyes, and Black Wolf returned the gaze, his own hot. Although he waited without breathing, he heard nothing. He had no doubt that his thoughts had reached his spirit and had been understood. Should it not now be time for his spirit to respond?

Instead, Wolf once again extended his muzzle. This time his mouth was closed, upturned slightly as if smiling. When Wolf placed his cold, damp muzzle first on Black Wolf's cheek and then on his forehead, Black Wolf felt as if he was losing touch with himself, flowing outward until he wondered if Wolf had taken everything of him.

*I say you are my spirit, but perhaps I exist for you. Tell me, what do you need of me?*

Wolf's tongue appeared, and he lapped at Black Wolf's face. His heart beating so fast he wondered if it might burst from his throat, Black Wolf buried his fingers in the thick mat of fur covering Wolf's chest. When he did, he felt another heart beating.

*You are real, real to me. And yet you are not one of the wolves who roam this land. Truly your soul belongs in 'Alapay.*

Pressing his fingertips against Wolf's flesh, he closed his eyes. At first there was nothing except the sound of the wind, the sun's heat on his head and exposed flesh, but then he felt himself being lifted, floating, leaving the land of his people.

Wolf was with him, guiding him through night and into the first rays of dawn. He saw spring-green grasses, a sky so blue it left him in awe, deer and rabbits without number, a clean, laughing creek, and he heard children laughing.

Then he stopped moving and together he and Wolf settled onto the lush grass, but the deer and rabbits didn't acknowledge his presence. He'd begun to turn toward Wolf for explanation when movement in the shadow of a great tree caught his attention and he realized a man was walking his way, a man with broad shoulders and dark, run-hardened legs.

*Father.*

The man smiled and continued to come closer until he stood only a few feet away. Although he didn't speak, Black Wolf felt the man's love and joyously returned that love.

*Wolf, thank you.*

\* \* \*

Unsure of how much longer her legs would continue to support her, Lucita didn't move so much as a muscle until Black Wolf rejoined her.

A wolf!

The Chumash warrior had walked out to meet a powerful beast, and they'd stood together, touched each other!

Black Wolf now sat cross-legged on the ground near her, but he wasn't looking at her and hadn't spoken since his return. His eyes had lost focus as if he was locked somewhere she could never go, and yet she understood a great deal. Sitting herself, she reached out and brushed her fingers over Black Wolf's knuckles. Still not meeting her gaze, he turned his hand palm up, and she drew it toward her. Cradling it between her hands now, she stroked his flesh as if the simple contact could free his mind from wherever it had gone.

"I saw him," Black Wolf whispered.

"Who?"

"My father."

"He's dead." She swallowed. "How is that possible?"

"He was at 'Alapay."

"He . . . he is well?" she asked because she had no choice.

Black Wolf lifted his head, but she doubted he saw her. The wolf had remained where he was, watching as Black Wolf slowly walked away from him, and then the creature had evaporated like fog under a relentless sun. She and the warrior were alone, and yet were they?

"Black Wolf." She tried again. "Please, I want to understand." The voice was hers and yet she didn't remember forming the thought that led to the words. "What happened between you and that creature? Why . . . I've never seen an animal do anything like that."

"He is my spirit."

The explanation, although simple, was everything. "Yes. I know," she said.

The haze faded from Black Wolf's eyes, and she saw deep, deep into them, sensed the man's depths. "You believe?" he asked.

*No!* This was insanity, blasphemy! There was only the God of her childhood, the God she'd always worshiped and feared and tried to obey.

"Lucita." Lifting his free hand, he laid it over her cheek, the gesture achingly gentle. "I see pain in your eyes and hear it in your voice."

She couldn't hide anything from this man today. "You must know what I am thinking," she managed. "The padres call your people heathens and your beliefs the work of the devil."

"Then you say Wolf is one with the devil?"

*No! That dark and deadly entity she had always feared would never take a man to his dead father.*

The sky was incredibly blue today, with none of the haze the padres had told her often hung over the valley in the summer. She could easily see where the wolf had stood, remember what had transpired between warrior and animal.

"The only thing I know is that there is a bond between you and that . . . creature."

"That creature is Wolf. My spirit."

"Your spirit. And it allowed me to see it. Why?"

"I do not know."

"Are you sorry? Do you resent—"

"I do not question Wolf's wisdom, Lucita. I never will."

Exhaustion clawed at Sebastian and he'd long ago given up trying to push his horse to go any faster, but as the hastily erected buildings that represented the Santa Barbara Presidio and undeniable proof of the Spanish Crown's presence in Alta California came into view he straightened. Even before he could see the post, he'd heard it—the sounds of men and animals and wagons as familiar to him as his own heart beating.

Still, although he'd gone nearly two days without sleeping in his effort to get here and at the same time scout the land for savages, he reined in his horse and sat looking out at the fortlike structures that had been placed in the narrow shelf of relatively level land between the Santa Ynez Mountains and the Pacific coast. So many of the soldiers here were Mexican-born and -bred, while he'd been raised in Spain. Perhaps that was the difference between them—they'd known a freedom, a wildness, foreign to someone who'd grown up under the Crown's shadow and surrounded by centuries of history and tradition.

It didn't matter, he tried to tell himself, in the end, the only important thing was that they all shared the same goal, that of securing this new land for Spain. Still, as he prodded his heavy-headed mare forward, he forcibly strengthened his resolve. No matter what else concerned Comdr. Bardoniano Herrera, the presidio leader *would* listen. More than listen, Commander Herrera *would* grant him the necessary manpower to bring down Black Wolf and the others.

Nothing less was acceptable.

# 19

_____

"You return."

Black Wolf stepped into the clearing he and the other warriors had transformed into their people's home. After acknowledging the shaman, he took a moment to study his surroundings and again become nothing except Chumash. The valley haze that he usually left behind when he reached the foothills had followed him this afternoon. A large number of men, women, and children were outside, all but a few playing or watching the others play shinny. Recognizing him, many called out a welcome, but out of deference to Talks with Frogs, none came close.

"It is good to hear my people laughing," Black Wolf said. He wanted to see his son and wife, but that would have to wait. "Has there been successful hunting?"

"A young elk. And rabbits."

"Good." Allowing his thoughts to go no further than the present, he told Talks with Frogs that he needed to speak with both him and Walks at Night.

"You have not yet seen your family?" the shaman asked, his features grave.

"I spoke to Dog Girl on the way in. She told me that my son is with other children looking for blackberries."

"Ah. And your wife?"

"I will see her soon."

"Soon, yes." Talks with Frogs' heavy lids briefly slid down to cover his eyes. "But first—"

"First there is much I must tell you and my *wot*."

Talks with Frogs informed him that Walks at Night was in the *temescal*. "He has been there twice already today," the shaman said, sounding more than a little disapproving. "Waiting for me to tell him of the results of my prayers to *miwalaqsh*."

*Miwalaqsh* could mean several things: north, the North Star, or the ceremonial sun staff used during the winter solstice ceremony. As a *'alchuklash*, or astronomer shaman, Talks with Frogs interpreted the movement of the sun, moon, and stars. Surely he had no concern for the ceremony that was months away.

"Why are you not with Walks at Night?" Black Wolf asked as the two headed toward the *temescal*.

"I was waiting for you."

Nodding, Black Wolf waited until Talks with Frogs had stepped inside the ceremonial structure before entering it himself. His grandfather had told him that in the old days all power lay in the hands of the *wots* and shamans. No matter how brave or skillful in hunting a man might be, he would never be considered an equal with the tribe's most powerful men, but the old days were no more. Neither Talks with Frogs nor Walks at Night went near the mission or understood the newcomers' language. He did both, and because of that the other two relied on him for a great deal.

"Much Rain's wife and her unborn are with their ancestors," the shaman said once all three men were seated, their bodies already glistening with sweat. "She is at peace."

"And Much Rain?" Black Wolf asked.

"His heart is heavy. I have shown him the way to healing, but he has not yet begun the journey. Instead, grief and anger fill him. Enough!" Talks with Frogs clapped his hands together.

"Yes, enough," Walks at Night echoed. "Much Rain must walk

at his own pace. Other things concern us. Black Wolf, tell us."

His voice low but steady, Black Wolf told the two men about the corporal's decision to go to the presidio to ask for more help in defending the mission against Indian attack.

"They think we plan to attack?" Walks at Night shook his head in disbelief. "It is not the way of the Chumash to seek battle. Why would they believe that has changed?"

"Perhaps they have made us into what they think we are," Black Wolf said. "Besides, one of their kind is dead, at my hands."

"We know. Much Rain told us."

He tried to remember where he'd been in his telling, but his thoughts snagged on Lucita's role in the leatherjacket's death. She had held the man as life slipped out of him, just as Black Wolf had been part of Willow's dying. For a while hate had flowed between him and Lucita and his heart had closed itself against her and he'd believed he could walk away from her and never want to see her again, but that had changed.

"I do not know when the leatherjacket will return, or whether he will be successful with his request," he explained.

"That is what I felt during my prayers." Talks with Frogs spoke with his eyes closed and sweat dripping off the end of his nose. "His anger is so great that it reaches the stars. A fire burns within the corporal; he can think of nothing except revenge. He is a man with much pride, and that pride has been wounded."

"Yes, it has."

"Ah. Yes. This I say to you: the leatherjacket carries his hatred for us to the place of so many of our enemy, and that hatred will speak for him."

And other leatherjackets will feel and hear that rage and respond to it; Black Wolf had no doubt of that.

"They have come looking for us before," Walks at Night said. "But they were like a single ant trying to eat the leaves of a mulberry tree. However, if there are more of them, perhaps this time they will find us. What do you say, Shaman? Will Mitakuya Iyasin protect us?"

"Ah. You speak as if you believe I can guide the soul of the great unseen, but no shaman can."

"I did not say that." Walks at Night glared at the shaman, then blinked away the sweat threatening to slide into his eyes. "Do not turn my words in your direction. But you have spent much time in prayer and magic making since the Chumash woman's death. Surely if you can hear *miwalaqsh,* you have heard Mitakuya Iyasin as well."

Studying the interplay between the two men, Black Wolf was struck by their complex relationship. No one within the tribe had more power than the shaman, and although Talks with Frog's father had presided over winter ceremonies honoring the sun, Talks with Frogs outstripped his father's reputation because he was also an *'alchuklash,* an astronomer priest. Walks at Night had become *wot* because his father had been *wot* before him, but although he was in charge of all ceremonial objects and costumes and decided who would give the ceremonies and perform the dances, he could not command the tribe. Unless the other braves agreed with his opinion, it would become empty air.

"Talks with Frogs, there is something you must know," Black Wolf said, momentarily ignoring his *wot.* "It is beyond my comprehension to understand its meaning, which is why I came to you."

Walks at Night glowered but said nothing. Looking wise, the shaman waited.

"My soul had much need to pray at Humqaq," Black Wolf began. "I could not return here until I had bathed in the sacred waters and cleansed myself of the leatherjacket's stench."

"That is good. You returned pure," Talks with Frogs said. "What happened?"

*Lucita found me there.* "Wolf spirit," he said instead. "My spirit revealed himself to me although I had not asked him to do so."

"Ah! Yes, yes, this is a matter for much thought." Leaning forward, Talks with Frogs placed his palm on the ground, his whispered chant the only sound. Finally: "Wolf came because he believes you need his protection."

Black Wolf would never doubt that. Just the same, he felt chilled. "I humbled myself before him," he admitted. "Bowed my head and asked what he wanted of me."

"Did he answer?"

He couldn't be sure; despite his awe at being able to touch Wolf, he'd been unable to dismiss Lucita's presence, her role in what had happened. "Wolf's eyes glowed with a red light, and his breath was hot on my flesh."

Talks with Frogs nodded his wise and studied nod, now staring into the fire. When he mumbled under his breath, Black Wolf strained to hear. Walks at Night simply waited, his arms folded over his sweaty chest.

"You say you know where the corporal went," Talks with Frogs said after a long silence. "You stood close enough to him that his words reached you?"

"No." Much as he wanted to protect Lucita—and what existed between them—from these two men, he couldn't. Looking first at his shaman and then at his *wot*, he told them about his meeting with the corporal's daughter. What he kept to himself was where he and Lucita had met, the emotion between them, and that she had seen Wolf.

"This is not the first time the two of you have spoken. Be careful, Black Wolf." Walks at Night's eyes, although small for the rest of his face, dominated. "She may have cast a spell over you."

She had; why else wouldn't he share certain things with the two most powerful men in the village?

"Tell me this," Walks at Night said. He'd angled his body so that his back was partly toward the shaman. "Does the daughter believe her father will attack?"

"She does not know."

"What did she say? Black Wolf, we must know everything."

"That her father is full of anger," he explained. "He wants all of our people dead. He will not rest until the ground runs red with our blood."

Walks at Night recoiled and the shaman pushed his hands outward in a gesture designed to keep evil spirits at bay.

Finally Talks with Frogs cleared his throat. "I have not been to Humqaq for too many moons. When we lived at Tolakwe, it was a simple thing for my father to renew himself there, but now the mission stands in my way." He indicated their surroundings. "Ah. This place will never be the home of my heart."

"Nor mine." Fists clenched, Walks at Night straightened. "Black Wolf, it is a dangerous thing to go to Humqaq, but the Chumash must not forget the home of our ancestors. I say it is better that one makes that journey than none."

Looking deep inside himself, Black Wolf found an image of the way he must have looked as he bathed under the sacred waterfall. His spirit had found him there, and he would forever feel blessed because of it. Humqaq was where his grandfather had taken him when it was time for him to begin the journey to manhood and where he must take his own son.

"If we flee the leatherjackets, we will have to go far from Humqaq," he said, his voice strangely without emotion when what he felt threatened to overwhelm him.

Talks with Frogs rocked back, his voice too quiet. "Your words may be the truth, Black Wolf, but I do not want to hear them because without Humqaq, we can no longer call ourselves Chumash."

The time he'd spent in the *temescal* had left Black Wolf weak and even more in need of sleep, but after cooling himself in the nearby summer-quiet creek, he entered his hut.

As he waited for his eyes to adjust to the gloom, he made a vow. No matter what the danger, he would no longer delay taking Fox Running to Humqaq. Although the boy was young, his father would speak and then speak again of the sacred place and it would become part of Fox Running's soul.

The hut was empty; at least it seemed that way until he heard someone breathing from within his family's room, not just breathing but fighting to bring enough air into the lungs. *Not Fox Running! Please, not my son!*

The prone figure behind the hide covering lay on its side, knees drawn up, one arm outstretched while the other was buried somewhere in a mass of hair — graying hair.

"Rabbit Dancing!"

"Black Wolf? Is that you?"

The last time he'd been here, his wife had been tending a warrior racked by the enemy's illness, but this time it was horribly different.

"Rabbit Dancing," he repeated as he knelt beside her. "They did not tell me you were sick."

"You . . . mean Talks with Frogs?"

He started to nod but stopped as a wracking cough tore through her. "The shaman . . ." She wiped her mouth. "Talks with Frogs has turned his back on me; he resents my healing ways and believes it takes from his power. He would like to hear that I have already died."

"No! I will summon him. He will—"

"Black Wolf, please. There is nothing he can do for me."

She sounded so weak that he wanted to order her to be silent so she could rest, but he'd seen too much death not to know when it threatened.

"I should not have left. My place is by your side."

"Hush, my husband. It is all right. I would not want it otherwise, I will not think only of myself when the lives of all of our people may depend on what your eyes and ears tell you about the enemy."

It wasn't just the enemy. He'd also spent time with Lucita, Lucita who walked and ran and climbed and wasn't hot with fever.

"I told the others to leave me alone," Rabbit Dancing whispered around her labored breathing. "It is the white man's sickness, my husband. My time of dying has come."

"No!"

"Black Wolf, please."

She was asking him not to waste their time together in anger and denial, and although those emotions continued to war within him, he heeded her wisdom.

"That is why our son is with the older children, is it not?" he said as he took her hand and began gently massaging it. He waited for her to warn him not to endanger his own health by touching her, but she didn't. "So he will not see you like this."

"And so, I pray, he will be spared."

Cold dread coursed through him at the thought. A warrior, he would never allow another of the tribe's warriors or the enemy to know of his fear, but this was the woman who had given their son life.

"Listen to me," he said. "I have been to Humqaq; that is why I did not return earlier and why I believe your illness cannot touch me today. While there, I made a vow both to our gods and to Wolf that the day would soon come when Fox Running would join me. They listened and I found peace."

Rabbit Dancing started to sigh, but the sound quickly turned into a sob. "When my time here is gone, my spirit will go to Humqaq so I will always be able to see you and our son, so I will be waiting when your times to leave this earth come."

"I want you with us now."

"I will be." Straightening her legs, she rolled onto her back, hands picking at her neckline as if she found it too tight. "But not in ways we have always known." Her eyes closed and it seemed to take every bit of strength in her simply to breathe. "Keep me in your heart, my husband. Do not . . . do not forget that I loved you."

"As I love you."

Eyes open once again, she smiled. "Your grandfather was a wise man. He saw two people with loneliness inside them and brought them together. When I go to where his spirit dwells, I will thank him for the time I had with you."

"Do not speak as if you were dead. The shaman—"

"Black Wolf, please."

Her eyes seemed on fire, but although he wanted to give her something to drink, he couldn't make himself leave her side long enough to get it. Angry, at what he couldn't say, he asked if the others had deliberately left her alone.

"No. No." Mouth open, she panted. "They only did as I asked. Black Wolf, the enemy's disease rages within me. Whether I eat or drink today makes no difference."

His own eyes burned, but although he wasn't ashamed of crying in front of his wife, the pent-up tears wouldn't come. He couldn't tell whether she was crying or what he saw came from the fever.

"Your son needs you!" he wanted to scream, but reminding her of their child wouldn't hold her back from the coming darkness, would only make what she faced harder to accept and prepare herself for.

"I prayed—" Another coughing spell stopped her, and he waited with her, hurt with her. "I prayed you would return before I died. Black Wolf, our son is too young to understand what is happening to me. I have asked my sister to fill his days with laughter and his nights with warmth to sleep beside. He . . . the day will come when he will call her his mother."

Silent, Black Wolf crouched beside his wife and lifted her in his arms.

"Listen to me, my wife." He spoke with his mouth close to her ear. "Fox Running needs to hear a woman's voice and feel a woman's arms. Your sister is a good mother whose arms will willingly accept yet another child and I am grateful to her for that, but I make a vow to both of us now: our son will not know the pain I did."

"I . . . you—"

"Hush. It is my time to speak." *Maybe it will never be yours again.* "Fox Running holds my heart in his hands. I look at him and know a joy nothing else will ever bring me." A lump clogged his throat, and he waited until he felt enough in control to continue. "I spent too many years without my father's wisdom guiding me. Fox Running needs me, and I need him."

"I know."

Of course she did. "He will be at my side, always."

"A-ways?" She made a feeble attempt to look into his eyes, then collapsed against him.

"Rest your heart, Rabbit Dancing. A wise father does not take his son into battle, and if the time for defending our people comes I vow to keep him safe, but all other times we will be together."

"Battle? War? No."

She should be conserving her strength so she could see and

speak to their son one last time, but, Black Wolf was forced to admit, if she did, she might jeopardize Fox Running's life. That was why he was holding her, not just so she wouldn't be alone, but because, maybe, the pain of never again seeing her child wouldn't cut so deep.

"We are safe here," he told her. "For now. Do not think otherwise."

"No." She shook her head, then panted as if that small effort had exhausted her. "Do not tell me half-truths. I have never been a fool, Black Wolf. Dying does not change that."

Knowing she was right, he told her everything—or almost everything—about his trip to Humqaq, what he'd learned about the plan to have more leatherjackets brought to the mission, the question of whether the Chumash dared remain here.

By the time he'd finished, he'd laid her back on her bed and repeatedly wiped her forehead. She looked so hot and withered that he desperately wanted to bring her some water, but because he respected her wish to have the effort of dying over, he didn't.

She took a deep breath, the sound rattling in her chest. "You are sure the leatherjacket is going to the presidio?" she asked.

"Yes."

"How do you know that?"

He wanted to tell her not to concern herself with that, but it would be the same as a lie, and he would not, could not, do that to her. His hand resting along the side of her neck, he at long last told her both who Lucita was and her role in his knowledge.

"She is not afraid of you?" Rabbit Dancing asked.

"At first, yes, but no longer."

"Because she knows you are not a savage."

He hadn't said much about his private conversations with Lucita, just the ways in which their paths had crossed, but he should have known his wife would look behind his words.

Now, partly to save her the effort of having to ask and partly because he couldn't keep what he felt about Lucita to himself, he told Rabbit Dancing about the young woman who had come to the mission to minister to the needs of neophytes and was learning a great deal about herself.

"She . . . she does not belong there." Rabbit Dancing's eyes had closed long moments ago; she didn't try to change that.

"How can you say that? You do not know her."

"I know—I am *so* tired. . . . Black Wolf, I have never questioned what it is to be Chumash, never thought such a thing could be, but the woman questions her life. Staying at the mission will only make it harder."

"It does not matter," he told his wife. "Her concerns are not mine."

"Yes," she whispered. "They are."

He waited for her to say more, prepared himself to accept her instinct about people, but although her lips were slightly open, trembling a little, she remained silent.

Leaning over his wife's body as if trying to give her some of his strength, he concentrated on her every breath. Finally the harsh effort became less painful and he told himself she was asleep.

"Black Wolf."

Instantly awake, Black Wolf turned toward whoever had just spoken and found himself looking up at his *wot*. "Yes?"

"I have called together our warriors," the older man said. "It is time to talk."

"My wife is sick." He trailed his fingers over Rabbit Dancing's forehead and cheek but received no response. Time was like a dense mist; he couldn't see through it and had no way of knowing how long he'd been in here with her.

"I know, and I mourn for you. But what you told me about the leatherjackets must become known to everyone."

Black Wolf's legs had gone to sleep under the weight of Rabbit Dancing's body. Placing her on her bed, he rubbed his legs back to life. Only then did he lay his hand on her chest.

"She lives?" Walks at Night asked.

"Yes."

After clearing his throat, Walks at Night went on. "Talks with Frogs has completed his magic making," he explained. "The ceremonial ground is ready for us."

"What do you want of me?"

"Do you need to ask? Black Wolf, we must speak of war."

"War?"

"You think I want to say this? But the time of our ancestors is finished, and we can no longer walk in their footsteps. If we are attacked, we must defend ourselves; none will argue with that. But my thoughts are also that perhaps we must strike the first blow."

"My *wot,* this would not be a battle between the Chumash and another tribe. Next to the leatherjackets' weapons our bows and arrows are nothing."

Walks at Night sagged against the nearest wall, and despite the gloom, Black Wolf was convinced that his features had aged. "If we do nothing, will we become what our captured brothers and mothers and children are: slaves? Or perhaps the leatherjackets will hunt us down and kill us."

Black Wolf's throat constricted. Feeling old and tired himself, he placed his lips on his wife's hot forehead and then got to his feet.

"Sit down, Corporal; sit down," Comdr. Bardoniano Herrera encouraged as Sebastian entered the cramped and dark room that served as military headquarters.

Sebastian did so, not because he was allowing himself to be ordered around but because the puffy-faced commander had already returned to his chair and was leaning back in it, his hands folded over his ample belly. Sebastian sucked in what little existed of his own stomach and remained upright.

"First," Commander Herrera began, "please accept my apology for not being able to see you sooner. As undoubtedly you've heard, we are in the process of establishing a convict colony in Santa Cruz; that has taken up a great deal of my time."

It was on the tip of Sebastian's tongue to point out that a colony so far north should be beyond the responsibility of those stationed here, but the truth was he didn't know that much about the deployment of various troops throughout Alta California. It would have been different if he hadn't been isolated at La Purisima. "I'm certain it has," he said mildly.

"Yes, indeed. The viceroy in his wisdom has decided that Santa Cruz is the ideal location for Branciforte, and I would not argue that, since a number of convicts can be shipped there directly. However, others come by land and must be escorted." He shook his head, loose jowls flapping as he did. "And since they do not all come at once—tell me, Corporal, how may I assist you?"

In the two days he'd been here, he'd already sent three messages detailing his reasons for wanting this meeting and had to conclude that they'd either fallen on deaf ears or not been received. Struggling to keep his temper under control, he explained as concisely as possible what had been happening at La Purisima.

"When I first accepted the post, I argued for more manpower," he replied. "However, at the time the viceroy did not believe it was necessary. I believe recent events have proven me right."

"Perhaps."

He wanted to be outside among the soldiers and stock handlers, the various merchants, including Senor Pablo, whom he'd located on board his docked ship, and the camp whores, not in this room that smelled of cigar smoke and sweat. However, until he'd completed his task, he didn't dare allow himself to be distracted.

"Perhaps?" he challenged. "You aren't alarmed by the brazen murder of one of my men?"

"Corporal, you are concerned with a single mission while I must assume responsibility for the security of the entire region."

*A responsibility you could better manage if you ever stepped outside this room.* "That's why I'm here," he said through clenched teeth. "To apprise you of conditions within your region. Commander, I will not be responsible for the consequences should other Indians hear of what has been taking place at La Purisima." He made a move as if to get to his feet, then settled himself again. "I've seen the manpower you have here. There simply aren't enough troops should the Chumash and other tribes go to war against us."

"War?" The word seemed to rumble in Commander Herrera's throat. "You really think—"

"I wouldn't be here if the possibility didn't exist. It has been my experience in over twenty years with the military that gelding the bull while it remains penned takes much less effort than trying to control it once it has broken free."

The beefy man stood, grunting with the effort. "Thank you, Corporal. I appreciate your concern, and your observations." He waved his hand in a dismissive gesture.

"My concern? Is that all you have to say?"

"For now." Herrera's mouth had thinned. "You will receive my decision shortly."

Fists clenched, Sebastian stood but refused to head for the door, yet. "I trust that will be within a few hours," he said. "My time is much better spent at my post than waiting here."

"I understand your concern, Corporal; believe me, I do. However, I intend to consult my advisers first."

"How long will that take?"

Once again Commander Herrera waved his fat hand. "Do not be so impatient. After all, patience as well as the skill to geld a bull is part of what it means to be a military man."

# 20

Lucita had seen it before and been mildly curious about its origin, but this time the violin, although dry and not particularly well made, captured her attention when she entered the sacristy the morning after returning to La Purisima. The instrument hung on a wall to the left and slightly above a particularly dark and somber painting of the crucifixion. In the past, she'd avoided looking at that wall, but her defenses were down this time because she'd come in here for a few minutes of private meditation, as a way of, maybe, coming to grips with what she'd experienced at Humqaq.

Removing the violin from its hook, she looked around for the bow, but if there was one, it wasn't nearby. She plucked the strings, surprised to find the tone much clearer than she'd expected. She *could* make the instrument sing. Hadn't she learned how to play the violin, harp, and flute when her hands were still too small to comfortably hold the instruments?

Stepping outside with her new, if temporary, possession, she looked around for the padres but didn't see either of them. Despite his slight frame, Father Joseph enjoyed experimenting with ways of making the meals more flavorful, and he might be in the kitchen overseeing supper, but she was loath to search for him there because the heat and smoke of the kitchen made her lungs and eyes burn. She considered going to their quarters, only Father Joseph almost never made use of his apartment except at night and Father Patricio kept his door locked and the shutters closed over his small window at all times.

In the end, the smell of baking bread made her decision for her, and she headed toward the blackened adobe oven adjacent to the kitchen. As she suspected, Father Joseph was there, cutting steaming loaves of freshly baked bread into thin slices.

Spotting her, he handed her a piece and explained that he'd experimented with perhaps a little too much garlic. She took it in her free hand, sniffed, smiled, then indicated the violin. "Who plays?" she asked.

"I confess—I am responsible for torturing the poor instrument. It was a gift from Senor Portola. I had mentioned once that I would love to have something to play so I could teach the neophytes a few simple chants, and the next time he came here, he presented it to me."

"What a lovely gesture."

"Yes, it was. I tried to repay him, but he assured me that he'd gained a great deal of pleasure out of his search. He is like that, thinking beyond himself to the needs and wishes of others."

"Yes, he is," she agreed, her heart warming at her memories of the man. She'd barely had a moment to think about him lately and now regretted that.

"I must confess," Father Joseph went on, "I find one excuse after another to delay subjecting my ears and the ears of those around me to what little I'm able to accomplish. It interests you?"

"Oh, yes!" she exclaimed and told him about her years of practice. To her delight, he said he would fetch the bow from his room, where he kept it for safekeeping.

"Nothing would please me more than to teach these children the joys of worshiping God with music, not just with the handful of songs we have been able to pass onto them, but in every way imaginable. In truth, I commissioned Senor Portola to buy three flutes, which are stored with the bow, but my attempts to train the neophytes in their use have met with no little resistance."

She frowned. "I don't understand. I know I've heard flutes at night. Because the sound came from the neophytes' compound, I didn't do more than listen. Otherwise, my curiosity would have been satisfied by now."

"You have not seen what they use?"

When she shook her head, he explained that the Indians, even those who had been born and raised in the mission, insisted on making and using the crude instruments he was forced to call flutes for lack of a better term. A great many had been carved out of bone, with deer shinbones being particularly popular. Others were created from bird bones, often decorated with shell beads placed in precise patterns that, he had been told, represented the night sky in winter.

"I have tried and tried to explain that their so-called music is ungodly and that proof of their willingness to improve their spiritual state would become evident if they'd allow me to show them how to create wooden flutes, but they do not listen. Either that or they are outright defying me."

He sighed. "I daresay these children will test me for as long as the Church and Crown see fit to keep me here. The neophytes would like me to believe that the winter sky means nothing to them—so perverse is their deception—but I know better."

"Why do you say that?"

"Because I would be a fool to ignore the truth, Lucita. In their wild state, their most important celebration comes in the winter. No matter how hard I try or how heartfelt my sermons, they refuse to give up their heathen beliefs; instead, they practice them on the sly. That is why I refuse to allow their primitive instruments to be part of anything which praises the Lord."

Heathen beliefs? When explanations came from Black Wolf's lips, when she watched him purifying himself at Humqaq, not once had she thought that. Still, because what she knew about Kakunupmawa and Hutash had been part of what she and Black Wolf had shared, alone, she said nothing. Instead, she thanked Father Joseph for his offer to loan her the violin. She hoped he would take her to his quarters so she could begin reviving her skill with the instrument, but he only looked over at the building he shared with Father Patricio, a frown marring his usually serene features.

"Perhaps later," he said. Then, to her surprise, he placed his hand on her shoulder and looked into her eyes. "You do not belong here," he muttered.

"What?"

"I'm not sure any of us do."

"Father, what—"

"I should not have said that," he hurried, looking embarrassed. "*He* belonged here. It was ordained that he come to this heathen place, and I live my life in awe of what the sainted man accomplished, but the work left to be done after his death is so daunting."

"He?"

"Fr. Junípero Serra."

She should have known he was talking about the saint who became superior and president of the missions in Baja California and been responsible for establishing the first of the Alta California missions.

"He was indeed a true man of God," she agreed.

"Yes. An inspiration for those of us who must follow in his footsteps."

"Must?"

"A poor choice of words, perhaps," Father Joseph said with the briefest of smiles. "But I must strive to be honest in all things. Lucita, I look at you and see a young woman with great promise ahead of her. You have a mind which constantly questions."

"That's true," she admitted.

"But you should not be here, my child. Mexico, despite its wild beginnings, will soon rival Mother Spain in culture and refinement. That is where you belong, safe from what takes place here."

"I'm not a child."

"No, you are not, although I daresay it would be easier for you if you were. I want to tell you this because I believe we both struggle with the same thing." He ran his hand over the back of his neck, making her wonder if he regretted starting the conversation. "I joined the order when I was ten. It is all I have ever known, all I ever wanted. When I learned I would be coming here, I dropped to my knees and sang praises to God. But . . ."

"But what?" she prompted.

"Many things." His whisper was so faint that she had to strain in order to hear. "Death here is as relentless as the sun. I have prayed over the bodies of so many and overseen their burial. Have their souls truly been saved? We baptize them, call them to prayer, teach them how to go about doing God's work, but . . ."

She'd never seen Father Joseph in such a mood. Always before he'd seemed so determined and content. "I don't know what to say," she admitted.

"There is nothing." This time his attempt at a smile fell short. "Lucita, please heed my warning. Leave La Purisima before it destroys you."

Talks with Frogs had painted his body black to symbolize the seriousness of what was about to transpire, and red slashes indicating pain ran down his cheeks. Seated at the east end of the ceremonial Siliyik, he held up a *Po 'n kakunupmawa* pole made from a debarked holy bush with feathers tied at the top and waited for the other tribe elders to gather.

Black Wolf had hacked a chunk out of his hair to let everyone know he had become a widower but said nothing in response to numerous sympathetic and curious glances. His wife, whom he would never again call by name, was dead, her death coming as he entered their quarters following the earlier meeting with his shaman and *wot*. As soon as this meeting was over, he would carry her into the Siliyik and begin the ceremony that would ensure her soul's journey to Humqaq, but for now, he had to put mourning aside.

He hadn't expected to see Much Rain here since there'd been no sign of his friend earlier and Black Wolf had assumed he'd gone off to pray and seek peace, but the warrior now sat down beside him.

"We are alike," Much Rain whispered. "Two men who have lost

our women. I never dreamed we would come together like this, never wanted such a thing."

Accepting Much Rain's outstretched arm, he clasped it tightly. "Neither did I."

"But we cannot walk back in time."

"No," Black Wolf whispered. "We cannot."

Walks at Night began by telling the others that the corporal had left for the presidio and when he returned he might bring a great many armed and vengeful men with him.

"Black Wolf killed one of them," Walks at Night said. "We all know why." He looked over at Much Rain and Black Wolf. "A warrior cannot call himself a man if he does not cleanse an evil deed; none among us would say he did wrong. But our beliefs do not matter to the leatherjackets. The death of one of us is of no more consequence to them than that of a deer."

"Not a deer," Bear Killer, so named because he had brought down a black bear, said. "If a deer sheds the blood of a hunter, do other hunters then vow to rid a forest of its deer?"

"No," Walks at Night conceded. "They do not, but that is because animals, even cougars and bears, do not know of vengeance. The leatherjackets should understand that and see that we are like them, but they do not."

"Because the Chumash have always run instead of defending what is ours."

Black Wolf had known Bear Killer would say that. The young brave and a number of others like him maintained that the Chumash should have gone to war long before this. However, just as many believed peace would be met with peace because that was how it had always been for the tribe.

Today, wondering how he would tell his son that he no longer had a mother, Black Wolf couldn't put his mind to the direction his people should take.

The argument between those advocating for attack and those who insisted the Chumash would live only if they remained hidden continued. His *wot* wanted him to speak, and in truth Black Wolf wanted to, but the right words remained beyond his reach while he drew strength from Much Rain's presence.

"Wait!" Talks with Frogs' cry cut into Black Wolf's thoughts. "Enough! We are like children fighting among ourselves, blind children who forget that the spirits guide us in all things if we know how to ask."

"What would you have us do?" Bear Killer retorted. "Sit while you make endless magic?"

Silence louder than any shout fell over the assembled men. Even Black Wolf felt himself being brought fully into the present and watched intently as the shaman expanded his chest and lifted his *Po 'n kakunupmawa* high above him.

"Listen to me." Talks with Frogs ordered. "Listen and believe. The arms of the padres and leatherjackets do not reach beyond the valleys, which is why we sought to live here. Now we find that this place, too, may be unsafe. Our women beg us to go where they can raise their children in peace."

The shaman settled his gaze on Black Wolf. "Where children will not grow up without their mothers because those mothers have been taken by the enemy's sickness."

Nodding heads told Black Wolf there wasn't a man among them who didn't want that for the tribe's children. Only it was too late for him and Fox Running.

"What say you, Black Wolf?" Talks with Frogs demanded. "I feel your grief. It surrounds you, eats away at you and makes you weak, but that must not be."

He didn't feel weak, but maybe he didn't know anything about himself today.

"Black Wolf, I say you must cast off your grief, we need you."

"I am but one," he said with the weight of the assembled men's eyes boring into him and Much Rain's hand on his forearm. "Just because I caused the death of one leatherjacket—"

"I am not asking you to do battle for all of us," Talks with Frogs interrupted. "And none would say you should have kept your knife at your side. My wisdom comes from the sun and stars, from the earth and Bear whose eyes see all things, but our spirits cannot reach into the hearts of the enemies because they are without souls. Your eyes, mortal eyes, carry the truth about them."

Maybe the shaman was right. Although he'd said it many

times before, Black Wolf once again described what the mission was like, the complex relationship between padres and leather-jackets, the constant pressure on the neophytes to produce the goods the padres were expected to turn over to merchants in the name of the Crown, the relentless eating away at the neophytes' will to live.

"They are no longer us." Despite the importance of what he was saying, he didn't try to lift his voice above a whisper. "They are like cattle and horses who want nothing more than to be allowed to eat and rest. If we are to live and walk our children into tomorrow, we must think only of us."

"By leaving the land of our ancestors?"

How many times had he struggled with that question? His mind began to form the words he needed to respond, words that had everything to do with safeguarding his son's future, but that wasn't enough.

Looking at each of the village's leaders in turn, he told them about the overpowering need that had sent him to Humqaq. "My soul bursts to life and sings there," he admitted. "And I want my son's soul to sing as well. Each of you, do what you must, but I would rather Fox Running and I die before another sun sets than never again cleanse ourselves there. My wife's spirit waits to make its journey to the place of our ancestors. She vowed to be there for me and our son."

"My wife's and my child's spirits have already gone there," Much Rain said, speaking for the first time. "I will not be whole until I stand at Humqaq and their presence touches me."

All eyes remained on Black Wolf and Much Rain; not a single voice was raised to say they were wrong.

"I hear our warriors' words," Talks with Frogs said at last. "The same words are inside me."

"Then we will fight!" Bear Killer exclaimed. "Fight for the land the gods gave to our ancestors."

Emotionally exhausted, Black Wolf simply listened to the others as one at a time they argued for leaving or staying. When they had all finished, he rose and faced his *wot*. Much Rain, part and parcel of him today, did the same.

"I go now to prepare my son's mother for burial," he said. "But there is one last thing I must say."

It would be dark before much longer. Surrounded by the peace and silence of night, he would be forced to face his wife's death. But first—

"My spirit is strong there," he whispered. "Wolf lives at Humqaq and revealed himself to me there. He waits for my return. I walked to where he waited, touched him, heard his heart beating, and the sound became mine. To never experience that again would be the same as death. I need that and so does my brother." He indicated Much Rain.

The low murmur of voices washed around him and reminded him of how the sacred water felt on his body. As his memory of his union with Wolf grew, a sense of peace filled him, lessening his fear of the coming night's loneliness.

And he allowed himself to face the fact that he hadn't been alone at Humqaq.

Lucita had spent most of the day in the infirmary thinking about what Father Joseph had said earlier. However, she'd managed to strip her mind of everything except offering herself up to her God during evening prayers, and for several minutes she'd actually succeeded in attaining a state of humble acceptance. In her mind, a soft light had played over a green meadow filled with animals. The lion had lain down with the lamb, and she had walked among them, at peace. But then, somehow, she'd lost her grip on the dream.

Now, violin and bow in hand, she stepped outside and sat on a tree trunk not far from the cemetery. The stars were a white-gold tonight, and the moon, although on the wane, cast its own clean and gentle light. She didn't want to think about what would happen when her father returned, what Black Wolf was doing or whether she'd ever see him again, why she couldn't hold onto the state of grace that sustained and enriched her mother's life, whether warfare and death lay ahead.

Pablo Portola could take her away from all this.

Placing the violin under her chin, she began sliding the

bow over the strings and drew a mental image of the pleasure Pablo must have felt when he located it. He was a good and decent man, caring, and she already half-believed she could be content with him.

Shaking herself free, she started a chant, but it seemed so dark in tone when she needed to feel light.

Her mother had once sung lullabies to her and encouraged her to memorize the simple words, and when she'd become old enough to sit quietly in mass, she'd learned hymn after hymn. She'd heard secular songs during her infrequent forays into the city, but she couldn't remember enough about them, or maybe the truth was she couldn't hold onto anything from the past.

When she realized she'd continued to work the instrument while trying to decide what to play, she gave herself up to simply listening to sound, creating, experiencing. True, the instrument had been passed from hand to hand and then left to hang untouched for who knew how long and didn't have the quality of the violins she'd used before, but her thoughts—what there were of them—wrapped themselves around the notes and accompanying mood, and she felt at peace.

She couldn't say how long she'd been playing when she realized she was no longer alone. Children tiptoed toward her but stopped before they'd got close enough that she could make out their features. Just the same, she felt their excitement and wondered how long it had been since they'd truly enjoyed themselves. Black Wolf had told her a little about the games the Chumash children played, but if those diversions continued at the mission, it was while they were in their own quarters and not in the church's shadow.

Switching to a hymn of celebration because of its lively rhythm, she threw herself into the role of entertainer. Some of the children remained standing, but an even larger number sat down just out of reach. A few began clapping lightly in time with the music, and she encouraged them with smiles and nods. She finished the hymn but immediately switched to another, this one slower, simple in words and notes. Her mother had been so proud when she'd learned to play well enough to be chosen for a solo presentation at mass. Remembering Margarita's beaming face, Lucita tried to draw that world from the past around her, but it refused to take form. Maybe it didn't matter, she told herself. Maybe what was important was coming to grips with what her life was now.

Her rebellious mind had just demanded to know what that life would become when her father returned when she realized she now had an accompaniment. Cocking her head to one side, she concentrated. It was a flute, the notes soft and haunting and weightless. Maybe her mood was responsible, but the so-called primitive instrument felt utterly right for the night, for where they were, while hers now sounded just a little out of place.

Still, she couldn't make herself stop playing, and before long another flute joined the first. If she and the Indian musicians came together like this every night, maybe after a while they would teach her the music of their religion.

If she remained here.


Fox Running snuggled against Black Wolf.

"Where is Mama?" the boy asked for at least the fourth time tonight.

"She has gone to be with our ancestors," Black Wolf told his son once again. Then, although he doubted Fox Running could understand everything he was saying, he went on. "She got sick. She tried hard to get well so she could take care of you, but even her knowledge of medicine wasn't enough."

Fox Running yawned, the sound ending in a squeak that made Black Wolf chuckle.

"You have had a full day, little man. Chasing after rabbits is not an easy thing to do."

"Why?"

Despite the heaviness in his heart, Black Wolf again chuckled and gave his son a quick squeeze. "Why? Is that what you say to everything? Your mother said that the time would come when you knew the answers and the questions would cease, but she did not tell me how long that would take."

"Why?"

*Wolf, thank you for this child. He is tomorrow, a reason for me to live.*

"Do you understand—," he began but then stopped himself. He'd been about to ask Fox Running if he understood that Rabbit Dancing would never return to them, but if he did, the boy might cry himself to sleep, and Black Wolf wanted their time together to be filled with peace.

*Their time together.* That was what had eluded him while he and the others debated running versus staying and facing the possibility of war. He wasn't afraid of battle and the thought of death would never fill him with fear, but he wasn't just a man, a warrior. He was also a father, and his son no longer had a mother. Nothing mattered more than making sure his son didn't have to turn to others for the answer to why he was facing the future without either parent.

"Do you remember when you first learned to walk?" He whispered the question. "How angry you got when you kept falling down? How you stuck your arms out and couldn't get your legs to cease moving when you wanted to stop and your mother didn't dare let you get too close to the fire?"

Although Fox Running nuzzled his head against Black Wolf's side, the boy didn't respond.

"You had not yet reached your first birthday when your legs became strong enough to hold you, but you were not content simply to walk. No. You had to run. Everywhere you went, everything you did, you ran."

"Why?"

"Because, little man, because." His wife should be with them tonight. She would have loved to watch and listen, would have laughed with him. "We . . . we did not know what to call you when you were born. We wanted you to have a name which said who you were, and so we called you many things, but none of them were right until we watched you run and saw how joyful running made you."

"Why?"

"Because parents are like that, little man. We laugh when you laugh, cry when you cry. And . . ." He'd almost told his son that parents were willing to lay down their lives so their children might live. "From the beginning you ran like a little fox who chases his tail and tries to nip his brothers and sisters and bumps into his parents. We knew then, Fox Running, that you had named yourself."

He readied himself for yet another question. Instead, the boy sighed deeply and once again snuggled against him. When his grandfather became feeble, Black Wolf had had enough time to travel to the sea and search the shore for a whale carcass. He had chosen a rib bone and used that to mark Lame Deer's grave, but he hadn't known his wife was going to die. Tomorrow he would collect stone slabs or maybe carve a wood grave pole to mark her resting place, but tonight he refused to think about that.

His son was falling asleep, muscle and bone turning soft and warm. Although Fox Running insisted he was no longer a baby and refused to be treated like one, Black Wolf began rocking slowly back and forth as he and his son's mother had done when their infant son had difficulty falling asleep.

Fox Running felt so right in his arms. Whenever he looked at the boy, he saw himself and his wife, but mostly he saw a new human life beginning to walk its own way.

He prayed his arms would be enough and that they would always be there for his son, but maybe not even Wolf could protect him from the leatherjackets.

# 21

The smell. And the heat.

Feeling light-headed, Lucita leaned forward and braced her hands on her knees. When she no longer felt as if she might faint, she straightened and lifted a hand to shield her eyes so she could take in her surroundings. A gray haze clung to the horizon and stripped all vibrancy from the sky, trees, and hills. She tried to bring forth the magic and wonder of the time she'd spent at the coast with Black Wolf, but what she'd see when she reentered the infirmary had left her unable to think of anything except how much she hated that place of death.

Midnight was back and in even more desperate straits than before. His older brother had carried him in early this morning, but in spite of her shock at seeing the infection in his once again gaping wound, she hadn't allowed herself to rail against the filthy conditions and exertion that had been responsible for what had happened.

When dizziness again assaulted her, she forced herself to admit that her thoughts and not the heat were responsible. She'd stepped outside because she needed to fetch more water and would return because Midnight depended on her, but it was so hard! The boy's fevered leg continued to burn no matter how many times she soaked it in the coolest water she could find, and now the boy's entire body felt like an oven. Although he could barely swallow, at least she could bathe him and that way give him a small measure of comfort—and hold onto a nugget of hope that he might survive.

"I hate this place! Hate what happens here!"

Shocked by her outburst, she looked around, but from what she could tell, no one had heard. When she clamped her hand over her mouth, she wasn't surprised to find her lips dry and rough. Her skirt had become caked with dust during her endless treks to the cistern, a bloodstain covered much of her right sleeve, and she was in desperate need of a bath.

Picking up her pails, she squared her shoulders and headed for the cistern, determined to do what she could to clean herself—not that the effort would have any lasting benefits. A number of cattle were being slaughtered today, which meant most of the neophytes were engaged in that disturbing and yet necessary task. Father Joseph had sent out a scout early this morning, but he had seen no sign of her father and whoever might be returning with him.

A long, mournful, and yet achingly intense bellow stopped her in midstride. Shuddering, she tried not to imagine what had caused the cow to utter that sound. Once again her throat, her very being, filled with the words she'd uttered a few minutes ago.

She *hated* La Purisima Mission. *Hated* Alta California.

All except for—no! She wouldn't allow herself to think about Black Wolf! He belonged to a world she would never understand.

Reaching the cistern, she set down her pails and plunged her hands and arms into the clean running water. Using lye soap, she scrubbed every bit of exposed flesh until she was afraid she'd draw blood, and then she dunked her head into the water so she could wash her hair. Finally, she unlaced her shoes, lifted her skirt, and stepped barefoot into the pool. The water felt heavenly.

She'd reluctantly got out and was waiting for her feet to dry when she noticed a boy with Father Patricio. The padre had his arm around the youth's shoulder and was leaning toward him, speaking into his ear as they walked. By contrast, the boy held himself arrow straight and seemed to be straining against the padre.

The two came toward her, Father Patricio continuing to talk, his words so low Lucita couldn't make out more than the barest murmur of sound. Once they were close enough that she could make out the youth's features, she realized it was Midnight's older brother. Most of the male neophytes had high and prominent cheekbones. Their noses were large, at least larger than she was used to seeing, and their chins seemed to have been carved from stone, but this boy had a girl-like quality to him despite his maturing body. His long, shining hair framed delicate and slightly rounded features, his eyes dominating his face.

"Good day, Lucita." Father Patricio acknowledged her with a quick smile. After patting the boy on the head, the padre stepped away from him and indicated her feet. "I see the filthy conditions here have compelled you to attempt cleanliness. I wish you success. Unfortunately, I'm afraid it is a temporary condition."

"I have to agree," she admitted. "You aren't overseeing the slaughtering?" She was surprised she could say the word without her throat tightening.

Shrugging, he glanced back at the motionless boy. "Everyone knows their assigned tasks and the consequences of slackening; they should, given the countless times this chore has been done. However, you are right—I must return before much longer."

The boy, who wore not so much as a loincloth, stared at the ground. Impulsively she walked over to him and touched his shoulder. "You can come see your brother whenever you want." She spoke slowly, emphasizing every syllable and hoping he could pick up at least a little of what she was saying to him. "He's very sick, but I know it would help him to have you there."

Something flitted across the child's features, but he gave no indication he understood a word. She repeated herself, but the result was the same.

"Do not waste your breath, Lucita," Father Patricio warned. Pointing, he ordered the boy to get into the cistern and begin cleaning himself. "No matter how hard Father Joseph and I try, these children are incapable of learning adequate Spanish."

"But . . . I thought you were talking to him a few minutes ago."

"You are mistaken," he said quickly. "Quite mistaken. That one might as well be deaf for all the good my words do."

She wasn't sure. Hadn't the boy reacted—by trying to pull free?

Drawing on what little Chumash she'd picked up in the time she'd been here, she held her arms as if she were rocking a baby while repeating what she hoped was the word for "sick" and then placed her hand over her leg to indicate Midnight's injury. As before, something flashed in the boy's eyes, but he remained silent.

"What is that?" Father Patricio insisted. "What are you doing?"

"Not enough, I fear. My Chumash is so inadequate, but I keep trying. I want him to know that his—"

"No!" Stalking toward her, the priest threw back his shoulders. "I forbid it!"

Shocked, she nearly took an involuntary step backward, but for reasons she couldn't fully explain it was important that she stand her ground. "Why not? He cares for his brother." Her throat closed down, briefly making it impossible for her to speak. "He needs to know—"

"Lucita, these children . . ." He jabbed a finger at the dripping boy. "If we acknowledge their godless ways, they will never understand how misguided they are."

"Learning to communicate with them is hardly condoning godlessness. Besides, if you'd allowed Midnight to take care of his wound for a few more days, this wouldn't have happened."

Red blotches broke out on his cheeks. "I will *not* argue this with you, Lucita."

She had never seen Father Patricio so upset and would have turned her full attention to trying to understand why if she hadn't noticed the boy's reaction. He seemed to be trying to shrink away from the padre, a natural response to the harsh words of course, but it was more than that. His eyes, which had been so guarded a few minutes before, now burned, not just with fear, but with anger as well.

*He understands.*

"I . . . I am sorry," she said because she understood the folly of arguing with him. "This is still new to me. I—"

"Perhaps. I am appalled you even considered learning their language."

She was equally appalled that he wasn't willing to reach out to the neophytes in the most basic of ways. "The sounds they make are so different. I can't help but be fascinated by how they accomplish that."

His frown served as proof that he didn't share her enthusiasm. "Those are inhuman noises, Lucita. Our task is to lift them above their animal-like state. I insist you never forget that."

Father Joseph had never made her feel anything but wanted. Obviously lonely for any kind of communication, he had asked her about life in Mexico City, but although Father Patricio had listened in on a couple of those conversations, he had said little. However, until this moment she'd never had an inkling that he resented her presence.

Her mother was a master at avoiding confrontation, and Lucita had learned a great deal from her, a knowledge she fell back on now. Head lowered in acceptance, she clasped her hands as if in prayer. "I am sorry. I don't pretend to know as much about the neophytes as you do. I simply thought—"

"Yes, yes. Once you have a few more years behind you, you will understand that there are certain levels of intelligence and those who have the ability to reason and lead have the obligation to do so. This one?"—he indicated the boy—"impresses me with his quickness in learning new tasks. I have taken him under my wing with the hope that he might act as a bridge to the others. However . . ." He sighed. "Perhaps my dedication is ill-founded. As you can see, no matter how much I have given of myself to him, he continues to distrust my motives."

"Have you tried this before?" she asked, choosing her words carefully. "Selecting a neophyte with the hopes that he would make it easier to reach the others?"

"Numerous times, Lucita. If nothing else, I am determined." He crooked a finger at the boy.

"Were you ever successful?"

"Successful?" An emotion she couldn't read settled over Father Patricio's features. "He would disagree, but there was one. . . ."

"He?" she prompted, suddenly cold.

"Never mind." Father Patricio waved his hand impatiently. "It was a long time ago and does not concern you. Come, boy."

If it hadn't been for the way the boy's toes curled inward, she wouldn't have guessed Father Patricio's order had any impact on him. The padre's hand snaked out, and he pulled the youngster close to him. He sniffed, then nodded. "It is so hard to get the wild smell out of them," he muttered. "I heard you playing last night. You make that sad old violin sing, and I stand in awe of your talent. Senor Portola will be much impressed. I daresay you have already made a most favorable impact on him."

Although she wondered at the abrupt change of subject, she decided to go along with it. "I love playing. I always have."

"And the neophytes fell right in line. However, by the next time you lead them in God's praises, they will know better than to use their heathen instruments."

Black Wolf had told her he hated Father Patricio. Because he hadn't explained the reason behind his hatred and she'd been loath to question him, she'd understood little. Today, however, no amount of prayer and pleas for tolerance and understanding removed her own displeasure with the padre.

Last night had been so peaceful, a short hour of calm during which she'd felt connected with the Indians. They'd shared something precious, and now Father Patricio had ruined the memory with his threat.

*No, he hadn't,* she insisted as she propped open the infirmary door. Only she had control over her memories and emotions, and last night had been good; she refused to let anything change that.

Black Wolf would have enjoyed it. In fact, with his deep voice, he would have provided the perfect accompaniment.

*Where are you? Are you all right?*

Shaking off the question, she finished bathing the patients and then fed those capable of eating. She was changing the bandage on a woman whose legs had been burned by hot tallow when the bells announcing midday prayers rang. Lucita's first impulse was to use it as an excuse to quit what she was doing because the burned flesh turned her stomach, but so far, the woman hadn't turned feverish. With diligence, maybe Lucita could keep the wounds free from infection. Success in this place of illness was so rare that the woman's being able to walk again might be considered a miracle.

"Father Patricio is wrong," she said aloud, conviction breaking through. "Black Wolf learned Spanish. If he can, so can others."

The woman stopped her moaning and regarded Lucita through narrowed eyes.

"Why I am saying anything?" she continued. "It's just . . . just that I spend so much time alone. Not alone really, because there are so many people here, but . . . alone in my heart."

Using a clean wet rag, she dribbled cool water over the woman's left leg. "The nuns used grease whenever one of the orphans burned themselves, but grease made them cry so, poor things. And I didn't see that it helped the healing. But water—especially if it's cold . . ."

She had to stop chattering. Just the same, when she noticed that some of the strained look had gone out of the woman's eyes, she freshened the cloth and laid it over the wound, muttering that she had hated having to cause the infants and children any pain.

"The orphans had so few needs or wants," she continued. "Some of the older ones were afraid of being touched. I think things must have happened or been done to them to make them like that. But the babies, the babies loved to be rocked."

The woman nodded.

"Do you do that?" she asked around her shock. "Rock your babies?"

"Y-es."

Struck dumb, Lucita could only stare openmouthed at the woman. She started to pick up the cloth, then, remembering she'd just placed it there, let it go.

"How . . . how much of what I've been saying do you understand?"

The faintest of smiles touched the usually taut lips. "Much."

"But . . . but Father Patricio says . . ."

"He does not know. He does not care to know."

What did that mean? "How did you—I mean, are you the
only one?"

"Only one?"

"Who understands Spanish."

"No. No." The woman laughed. "Not all words, true, but . . .
but a number."

"Why didn't you say anything before?"

The woman's eyes closed, cutting Lucita off, but Lucita waited,
and after the better part of a minute, the woman opened them
again. "You speak with a woman's heart," the neophyte said. "My
woman's heart hears."

On the brink of tears, Lucita clasped the woman's hand.
"Thank you for saying that. I—"

"Lucita!"

For one, maybe two seconds she struggled against the march
of time so she could return to when her mother hadn't been here.
"What?" she asked in the end, because she had no choice.

"Prayers have already begun."

Fearing a lecture, she felt her muscles tense, but to her surprise, her mother said nothing more. Instead, Margarita walked
over to where Lucita was standing and looked down at the
woman's burns.

Shuddering, Margarita turned away. "How do you do it?" she
asked. "I know it is my duty to give of myself in here, and I try.
But what I see appalls and sickens me, and I feel so helpless, so
inadequate."

Lucita wanted to ask her mother not to speak like that because
the patient understood her, but if she did, she would be betray-
ing a confidence.

"I have to keep busy," she tried to explain. "And this is something I can do. Mother, go, please. I'll join you as soon as I'm
done."

"Will you? Sometimes I think the last thing you want to do is step inside a church."

Something was different about her mother today. Maybe it was her husband's absence and maybe—what? Whatever it was, Lucita was grateful that, for a few seconds at least, she wasn't being treated like a misbehaving child.

"I don't know how I feel," she said with as much honesty as she was capable of. "These people—" She couldn't call them neophytes, not after what she and the woman had shared. "Their beliefs aren't the same as ours, but they're just as strong. I can't turn my back on that."

Margarita's lips trembled and her eyes became moist. "I know, my daughter," she whispered.

Unable to ignore the pain in her mother's voice, Lucita embraced her. "You can't do my living for me, Mother. Only I can."

"I know." Margarita reached out and pulled her daughter into her embrace. Her heart felt not heavy but full as she absorbed her daughter's strength.

The Indian woman had fallen asleep while Lucita dribbled water over her burns. Well aware of how little sleep she had got since her accident, Lucita decided not to disturb her by re-dressing the injuries. Instead, long after her mother had left for services she remained beside her patient and fanned the air with her hand.

Finally her arm grew so tired that she took a chance on stopping. To her relief, the woman didn't stir. Silence permeated the infirmary, and Lucita felt assaulted by it. Instead of forcing herself to the heart-sickening task of checking to see if Midnight had lapsed into unconsciousness, she walked outside.

A little of the endless haze had lifted, with the result that her world appeared more colorful than it had for days. A rumble of voices served as notice that mass was over and the Indians had gone back to work.

Not knowing what, if anything, she had in mind, she started toward her quarters, but she hadn't covered half the distance before sudden movement to her left stopped her.

*Black Wolf,* she thought before she could stop herself.

No, not him.

The boy she'd seen earlier with Father Patricio had burst out of the padre's quarters and was running as fast as his legs would carry him. She couldn't tell what his destination was, just that Father Patricio was charging after him.

"Stop!" Father Patricio screamed. "Stop or I will beat you within an inch of your life!"

Horrified, Lucita stared. The boy, as unencumbered by clothing as he'd been before, was the swifter runner. However, instead of watching where he was going, he repeatedly looked over his shoulders at his pursuer. Neither of them seemed aware of her presence.

Glancing around, she determined that except for a couple of excited dogs, no one else was close enough to see. Of course Father Patricio's shouts—

"Stop! Damnation, stop!"

The boy kept running, long hair flying out behind him. This wasn't any of her concern. Hadn't Father Patricio made it clear he resented her presence?

But the boy—

Acting on instinct, she sprang in front of the youngster, snagged him around the waist, and clutched his struggling body to her.

# 22

The boy fought her with every ounce of strength in his young body, and Lucita came within a heartbeat of being forced to release him, but he looked so terrified that she refused to give up.

"No, no, no," she chanted. "It is all right. Nothing is going to hurt you. I promise, I promise."

It didn't matter whether he understood or if she could make good on her vow. Right now the important, the only, thing was getting him to relax.

Still, he twisted away from her and kicked, nearly succeeding in freeing himself. Teeth clenched against the sudden pain in her calf, she clamped her arms around him and pulled him tight against her. She concentrated on not letting her legs get in the way of another blow.

"God in heaven!" Father Patricio gasped. "How dare you!"

Pressing forward, he cocked his arm and slapped the boy hard against the side of his head. The child staggered and for a moment sagged in Lucita's arms. She saw the padre raise his arm again and without thinking spun her prisoner away from him. As a result, the blow landed on her shoulder. Although it was a glancing strike, she cried out, desperate to get the padre to come to his senses.

"Stop it!" she gasped. Her heart beat so loudly that she could barely think beyond the sound. "Do not hit him; please."

"He disobeyed me!" Father Patricio insisted. "He knows what is expected of him, and yet he disobeys—"

"Father Patricio! That is enough."

Out of the corner of her eye Lucita glimpsed Father Joseph hurrying toward them. If the two of them opposed her, what would she do?

"What is going on?" Father Joseph demanded, his cheeks unnaturally red.

"This is none of your concern!" Father Patricio shot back. "I do not interfere in your affairs. I expect the same of you."

Lucita had never seen anything approaching animosity between the two men and could barely believe this was happening. In truth, they put her in mind of dogs fighting over the same bone. She wanted to steer the boy to someplace safe but wasn't sure the padres would let her or whether anywhere represented safety.

"Your so-called affairs are my concern because of the way you conduct yourself." Father Joseph spoke through clenched teeth. "To have this take place in public—"

"Nothing has taken place except that this . . . this creature is defying me. And *she* insists on protecting him."

An argument pressed against Lucita's lips, but she wisely kept quiet. The boy had stopped struggling. His hot body trembled, and reacting to his emotion, she continued to hold onto him. If he'd been an infant, she could comfort him, but things had happened to him that she couldn't begin to understand.

"I am sorry you had to be part of this, Lucita," Father Joseph said, belatedly acknowledging her. He started to shift his weight but wound up gripping his knee. "It is—I do not want you to for a moment to think that Father Patricio and I are not of the same accord, but . . ."

His words trailed off and he looked around as if trying to remember where he was and what had brought him here. "It is this place," he muttered. "There are times when the isolation . . . When . . ." He stared long and hard at Father Patricio. "I am not the only one who feels this way."

"No, he is not," Father Patricio admitted, making Lucita wonder how long they were going to continue speaking to her and not each other.

"I understand," she said finally, not because she did but because the silence was making her uncomfortable.

"I pray you do." Releasing his knee, Father Joseph folded his slender fingers together, the knuckles immediately turning white. "There is no intellectual stimulation here, no one of a like mind to converse with, no diversion from the everlasting — the unappreciated work of making the mission succeed."

Instead of saying anything, she warily watched as Father Patricio stepped toward the boy. The child drew away, a nearly inaudible sob oozing from him. She wasn't sure whether his trembling was in reaction to his fear or because he was exhausted. Perhaps it was a little of both.

"Release him to me, Lucita," Father Patricio ordered as she placed her body between him and the child. "Life's lessons are not always what one would wish, but that does not change the necessity."

What lessons? She could understand reluctance to do certain tasks about the mission, but this was deeper and beyond her comprehension. "He doesn't want to be with you. What is so important that—"

"That is not your concern, Lucita! Release him, now!"

"No."

Glowering, the padre reached for her. However, before he could grab hold of her, Father Joseph stepped between them and took Father Patricio's wrist.

"Not now." Father Joseph's voice remained as soft as it always was, but there was no mistaking his determination.

For a moment Father Patricio stared at his trapped wrist; then he tried to tug free, but Father Joseph only increased his grip.

"Not now," Father Joseph repeated. "Lucita, take the boy with you."

"No!"

"Enough!" Father Joseph's voice equaled Father Patricio's in intensity. "You and I must speak, alone."

Holding the boy tight against her side, feeling his emotion and wondering if he could feel hers as well, Lucita spun away. She readied herself in case the child tried to free himself, but he now seemed willing to do whatever she wanted. Apparently a number of neophytes had heard the commotion, because although she couldn't concentrate enough to focus on her surroundings, she knew she was being watched. Her mind felt as if it might explode from the pressure of unanswered questions, but there was no one she could turn to.

Stopping, she tried to look beyond this moment. A dry wind was blowing today, with the result that dust skittered and whirled about and had coated everything with a fine layer of gray. The heavy mission building walls that had once impressed her with their durability pressed around her, trapping her. The everlasting haze clung to the sky, turning the sun a dull orange and stripping the blue from the heavens. The hills that rose on all sides stood like sentries determined to prevent her from escaping.

"I won't let him hurt you again," she vowed. Then, as a rush of love washed through her, she released the boy. For a moment he looked up at her with bright and beautiful eyes and she remembered his compassion and concern for Midnight, and then he ran.

After indecision that went on for too long, she headed toward the infirmary because there was nowhere else for her to go, not now at least. Midnight needed her to help ease what she'd finally come to accept was his dying, but she didn't have the strength for that, yet.

At first glance, the Indian woman she'd spoken to earlier in the day seemed to be asleep, but she opened her eyes as Lucita came closer.

"How do you feel?" Lucita asked.

"All right."

"Good." Weak, she dropped to her knees beside the woman. "What is your name?"

"I call myself Feather."

"Feather. That's beautiful. I am Lucita."

"Lu-cita?"

"Yes. That's right." She took a deep breath, then let it rush out. "I hate in here, the stifling heat, the smells. You must, too."

"Yes."

How simple and yet heartfelt Feather's answer was. "If you want, after dark I will take you outside."

"Outside?"

"Yes. Would you like that?"

The woman's eyes glistened. "Very much," she whispered.

"Of course you do," she whispered. Then, beyond weighing the wisdom of her words, she began telling Feather about what had just happened but had got no further than describing the boy running out of the padre's quarters when the door opened, revealing her mother.

"I heard." Margarita spoke in a low whisper. "Oh, Lucita, you angered Father Patricio. Why?"

Her mother's first and maybe only concern was that her daughter had displeased a man of God. She shouldn't be surprised, but on the heels of what had happened today, she ached for something different. Not leaving out anything, she told her mother everything.

"I wouldn't stand back and watch a child be mistreated," she finished. "I couldn't."

"Lucita, ours is not to question the ways of our priests and padres. Their relationship with God is much closer than ours ever will be."

"That doesn't make what he did right," she protested. "You didn't see that boy. He was terrified."

"Because he is a savage. Lucita—"

"No!" she interrupted. "He's a human being."

Although she'd been intent on what she and her mother were saying to each other, she now realized that Feather was taking in everything. Would, Lucita wanted to ask her mother, a "savage" understand what this argument was about?

To her surprise, Margarita pressed a hand over her eyes, a

ragged breath tearing at the air. "I was once like you," she muttered. "There was a time when I questioned."

"What did you question?" she asked, incredulous.

"It was so long ago, so long. And my parents did to me what I am doing to you." Sighing, she blinked back tears. "Their answer was always for me to immerse myself in prayers, to beg God to show me the way."

"And did he?"

"Yes. Of course."

Her answer had come too quickly, too softly, as if she was trying to deny that it could ever be anything else. "I wish," Lucita whispered, "I wish we could talk to each other. Really talk."

"We do. All the time."

"No, we don't."

"What do you want me to say?"

"I don't know," she whispered. "Maybe nothing."

"You don't belong here." Margarita, too, was whispering. "I pray Senor Portola will return soon."

Lips pinched and pale, Margarita spun on her heels and stumbled out of the room. Through blurred vision Lucita recorded first her mother's figure as a solid, gray shadow and then nothing.

His eyes little more than slits as protection against the sun and windblown particles, Black Wolf studied the small group of men making their way toward the mission. He could have slipped closer and still not risk detection, but he didn't need to see more than he already did. Lucita's father had returned, bringing with him four other men. Four seemed such a small number to protect the mission against what Corporal Rodriguez believed was an Indian uprising, but it was still more than had been before, and all of them were well armed.

No, not all of them, he realized. The man riding beside Rodriguez wasn't wearing the heavy leather padding the others did. He carried himself like a man who had spent much of his life on horseback. After studying him a little longer, Black Wolf realized it was the merchant who'd been at La Purisima a couple of weeks ago and had spent a great deal of time with Lucita.

Nearby movement distracted Black Wolf, and he saw he'd disturbed a beetle that was trying to find a way into the ground. He watched, both amused and filled with admiration, as the small, dark creature dug at soil and pebbles until it managed to cover itself. Was the beetle a sign, a message from Wolf that he should hide from his enemy?

The too-familiar taste of hate filled him and clenched his fist. Two days ago he had held his son in his arms and made a vow to always be there for him. Nothing about that vow had changed, but the shock of his wife's death had begun to lift and was being replaced by reality.

The leatherjackets were here. More of them meant even more repression for his trapped people and more danger for those who had managed to remain free.

The enemy had killed his wife! Their diseases had found her and snuffed out a life, leaving a boy to grow up without his mother!

Despite the effort it took, Black Wolf willed his fingers to straighten. Then he reached for his spear and lifted it over his head, the stone point aimed at Corporal Rodriguez's heart. This man, this enemy, lived to destroy the Chumash. If he could, the corporal would murder old women and children—Fox Running included.

But if this spear found Rodriguez's heart, the killing might end. The padres spoke of serpents. That was what Rodriguez and the other leatherjackets were: serpents. But if he cut off the snake's head—

No, he couldn't do that, because the Spanish were serpents without end and killing one would only bring others. His ancestors had followed the path of revenge when necessary, but that was when the enemy was no stronger than the Chumash. The old order no longer existed.

His throat filled, almost choking off his ability to breathe. Not fighting the sensation, embracing it, he threw back his head and howled.

As the sound reached the soldiers, Rodriguez straightened and scanned his surroundings. Black Wolf! He was sure of it!

His new troops looked at him, obviously expecting an explanation. Even Senor Portola, who'd accepted Rodriguez's offer of protection during the trip back to La Purisima, turned in the saddle, but all he did was nod.

Black Wolf!

"Soon," Rodriguez hissed under his breath as he again took inventory of the fighting men he'd been given. "Soon."

Lucita knew her father had returned long before she spotted him and the others riding into the valley. Ever since Black Wolf had killed Mundo, at least one soldier was always posted on a rise above the mission, and it had been that man who'd brought word.

Now she stood next to her mother as several neophytes rushed out to take charge of the horses. Despite Margarita's prayers of thankfulness that her husband was safe, Lucita sensed the woman's tension. The soldiers were an unsavory lot; none of the three had shaved or otherwise tended to their personal needs in what looked like weeks, and Lucita hoped she wouldn't have to get so close that she could smell them. She couldn't tell much about the other man because he wore a large-brimmed hat that shielded his face.

From the way they stumbled about after dismounting she guessed they'd come all the way from the presidio without stopping to sleep. She should feel sorry for them and make sure they had something to eat and drink, but these men represented increased danger to Black Wolf. And her father—what would he say to her; what would he do?

"Go to him," Margarita insisted. "He is your father."

"He's your husband," she said before giving herself time to weigh the wisdom of her words.

"I mean little to him. You know that."

Surprised by the unexpected honesty, she stared at her mother, but Margarita didn't meet her eyes. Although the last thing she wanted to do was speak to her father, Lucita, still the dutiful daughter, stepped forward and waited for him to acknowledge her.

"There you are!" he said in his booming voice, his expression unreadable. "Come here. Come here."

She did as she was ordered, wincing only a little when he grabbed her arm and pushed her toward the man with the large hat. Recognizing Pablo Portola, she could only gape. His lively eyes caught hers, and in that moment she knew he was glad to see her.

"You're back," she managed.

"At last."

He smiled and she felt as if she'd been enveloped by a warm blanket. "It has been a long time, Lucita. Too long. Unfortunately, nothing goes as smoothly as one would hope. You've been well?"

"Quite, thank you." She didn't remember him being a particularly large man, but there seemed to be more substance to him than before. Either that or her need to have someone to lean on was greater than she wanted to admit.

"Is that all you have to say to him?" her father insisted. "Don't you realize the sacrifices he's made and the effort he has gone to in order to return so soon?"

"Please," Pablo insisted. "There were few sacrifices."

"You must be exhausted," she said in an effort to change the subject. The padres stood off to one side, not looking at each other, tension heavy between them. "I wish we'd known you were coming today. Hopefully there will be food to your liking."

"Yes, yes," her mother agreed. After a glance at her husband, she went on. "We want to do all we can to make you comfortable. Senor Portola, I hope you will tell us what you have been doing since we last saw you."

"I would like nothing better." He hadn't taken his eyes off Lucita. "But first I want to hear how you've been. When your father told me of his determination to bring in more troops, I cursed myself for leaving."

"It couldn't be helped," Lucita said softly. "Please don't burden your mind with that."

"But I do. You're important to me, you must know that." Pablo extended his bent arm toward her in invitation. She slid hers through the crook and allowed him to guide her toward the dining area, where neophytes were rushing about setting up an impromptu meal, but despite the distraction of the man's presence, she sensed something else. Something . . .

It was vital she not look at the horizon or do anything that might make her father suspicious, but in ways she couldn't explain, she *knew* Black Wolf was up there, watching.

Over steaming bowls of hastily prepared stew, Lucita's father gave an exacting account of what he'd accomplished during his time at the presidio. Lucita hated his boasting and anger at the commander's inability to make a timely decision almost as much as she hated the way the soldiers deferred to his every word.

To her mind, he hadn't been as successful as he claimed, since he'd only managed to have three more men assigned to him, but to hear him tell it, the commander had ordered fully half of his available force to help quell the "uprising." Unfortunately, her father explained, a large number of the presidio's soldiers had been sent to Santa Cruz to oversee the establishment of a convict colony.

"I am surprised you were able to return so soon, Senor Portola," Margarita finally broke in. "You are responsible for overseeing your ships, and if there are convicts . . . I understand there are pirates as well."

"Unfortunately, yes. However . . ." Turning toward Lucita, he winked. "There is more to life than work and responsibility. Ah!" He patted his belly. "I do not believe I have ever eaten so much. Lucita, I hope you will join me in a stroll."

"I, ah, the infirmary—"

"That can wait," Margarita insisted while Sebastian glared. "Senor Portola, I fear my daughter will exhaust herself doing the Lord's work. She needs to relax and to hear of the world beyond here."

"I'm sorry," Lucita said to Pablo. "I didn't mean to refuse your offer. It's just that I've done little except work lately."

"Then it's time for that to change."

She rose and again took Pablo's offered arm. As the door closed between them and the others, she felt herself begin to relax, in part because she no longer had to bear her father's stony scrutiny, in part because she'd missed Pablo's concern for her welfare, his understanding.

# 23

---

Although Black Wolf spent two days and nights as close as he dared get to the mission, he was unable to learn anything about Sebastian's plans beyond the fact that the leatherjackets ceaselessly patrolled every inch of the valley.

It seemed a strange and useless thing for them to do, since there were still few men and so much land to cover and, if he wanted, he could slip past them despite the increased risk. However, as long as the leatherjackets remained here, his people had nothing to fear and there was no need for him to risk his safety by entering the enemy's place.

Lucita was often about. Usually he saw her entering or leaving the infirmary, but occasionally she was in the company of the merchant. They seemed comfortable in each other's company, talking and sometimes laughing — something she never did when she was around her parents or him.

Late on the afternoon of the third day, he spotted her walking toward the cemetery, head bowed, her shoulders slumped forward. Behind her walked one of the neophytes, who carried a small, inert bundle in his arms. Someone had died, most likely someone Lucita had been treating in the infirmary. To the padres, the death of a neophyte meant they had to briefly pray over the body before ordering it lowered into a shallow grave. Those who loved the neophyte had to wait until the padres were finished before being allowed to mourn, not by singing and dancing as the Chumash had done since the beginning of time, but with short and silent prayers.

Whoever had died today had been a child; the size of the neophyte's burden made that clear. Lucita loved children and would take such a death hard. Although he hadn't dared risk letting her know he was nearby, he longed to comfort her. Instead, he was forced to remain hidden like a hunted animal until the day had spent itself.

At last evening mass was over and, except for the sentries, the mission had quieted down. Not sure of anything except that he needed to speak to her even though it made no sense and might mean the end to him, he slipped through the shadows until he reached her living quarters. Although he strained to hear, it was several minutes before he'd convinced himself that she wasn't in there. She might have returned to the infirmary without his noticing; there was also the possibility that she had unfinished business at the cemetery. Or she might be with the merchant.

A deep male voice caught his ear, and he pressed himself against the nearest adobe wall, asking Wolf to protect him. The voice became louder and clearer, the sound that of a man confident with both his surroundings and himself. It was only when the man was close enough so he could make out his outline that Black Wolf realized it was the newcomer, and that Lucita was with him.

"No. No. You don't have to do this," she was saying. "You've already been so kind."

"It isn't just kindness, Lucita," the man responded. "You know that. Are you sure you want to do this tonight?"

Lucita didn't immediately respond. Then: "When . . . when he died, I was in shock, but now . . ."

"Shock can be a wonderful thing. While we're wrapped in it,

we're saved from having to face certain painful realities. Wait here, please, while I change boots. Much as I hate to admit it, these was not the wisest purchase I have ever made. No matter what precautions I take, they rub my heels raw."

Black Wolf watched, telling himself he felt nothing, as the man patted Lucita's shoulder before strolling away. She stood alone in the dark looking less substantial than she had a few minutes before, her body still, her head turning first one way and then another.

Wondering if she sensed his presence, he half-expected her to call out to him. Instead, she reached for the door to her quarters, but instead of going inside, she remained where she was and pressed her hand over her mouth. Despite her attempt at silence, a small whimper escaped her.

He started moving as soon as she did, trailing her like a wolf trails its prey, not surprised when she headed toward the cemetery. What did surprise him was when she stopped in front of an olive tree, broke off a branch, and carried it, dangling from her fingers. Reaching the cemetery, she stopped at the entrance.

*Do not be afraid of this place, Lucita. There is only peace here.*

Another sigh made its way to him on the night air, and then, as he'd already known she would, she walked over to the small, freshly dug grave.

"I'm sorry, Midnight," she whispered. "So sorry your life was short and that you never knew freedom. I tried. Please believe I tried to keep you alive. I just . . . I just . . ."

Leaning forward, she dropped the branch on the mound. "Mother saw my tears. So did the padres, but they don't understand. . . . I'm not sure Pablo does either."

"I do," Black Wolf said.

Jerking upright, she spun around. Another whisper of sound—not a cry this time—escaped her lips, and then she was quiet, staring at him, her body alert but not ready for flight.

"Who was it?" he asked, pointing at the ground.

She stared at him so long that he wondered if she'd lost herself in him. "A boy," she finally said. "I don't know how old, still a child. I called him Midnight because his eyes were so dark. He'd . . . he'd hurt himself and the wound got infected and there was nothing . . ."

"You loved him."

"Yes, I did. What are you doing here?" she suddenly demanded. "Haven't you seen the additional troops? My father . . . my father said there wouldn't be any more attacks because of them."

"I did not come to attack, Lucita. At least not tonight."

She sucked in her breath. "I . . . I told myself I'd never see you again."

"Is it what you want?"

"Want?" Although she laughed, the sound was bitter. "No. Oh, no."

They didn't have much time. Hadn't that man said he would return? Still, the threat of danger seemed a little thing now that she'd said what she had. "I have been on your mind?"

"Yes. Yes. Black Wolf . . . My father—don't you care what happens to you? If they find you, they'll capture you or . . . or kill you."

"I know."

"Don't talk like that! You have a wife and a son. They need—"

"My wife is no more."

"Dead?" The way she said the word made him think she never wanted to hear or speak it again.

"Yes," he said, the explanation simple because that was all he was capable of.

"I'm so sorry. How . . . Maybe you don't want to talk about it."

No, he didn't, but at the same time he needed to tell her about his wife's sickness and death, the way he'd held his son, and his promises to him, the sense of loss. However, before he could think how to begin, he heard a door open and close.

"The merchant," he said. "When he comes his arms are empty, but when he leaves his horses and mules are burdened. This time he was not gone long. Perhaps it is because he wanted to see you."

"Please go. It isn't safe."

"Maybe I will silence him."

"No, you won't." To his surprise, she reached out and touched her fingers to his cheek. "Please go, Black Wolf. I couldn't stand it if anything happened to you."

*Nor would I want to face tomorrow if death claimed you,* he thought as he stepped into the night.

Crickets sent a chorus of song into the air, making it nearly impossible for Lucita to think beyond their racket. Although she needed some indication of whether Pablo suspected she'd been with someone, she hadn't spoken since Pablo arrived a couple of minutes ago, and he did nothing to end the silence himself. Seeking both distance from him and time to make sense of the fact that she had seen Black Wolf tonight, she knelt beside the fresh grave. Death came so often here, particularly inside the infirmary, that she'd told herself she was getting used to it, but she hadn't expected Midnight to die. Or maybe the truth was she'd refused to accept the reality behind his ever-increasing fever.

Midnight, dead. Black Wolf's wife, dead.

No matter how much Lucita fought it, the pounding in her head became harder. She tried to tell herself that the noise from the crickets was responsible but knew it wasn't that at all. Her eyes burned, her throat felt as if it might close, and a scream fought for release. Instead, the sound she made belonged to an infant deprived of loving arms.

"Lucita, don't," Pablo said as he pulled her to her feet. Somehow he managed to hold onto the candle he'd brought with him. "You can't keep everything locked up inside this way. It will make you sick."

"I can't help—when is the dying going to be over?" She buried her head against his chest. "When?"

"Never, Lucita. You know that."

Of course she did! Unexpectedly angry, she came within a breath of ordering him not to treat her like a fool, but he'd done nothing to warrant her outburst.

"It's this horrid place," she managed. "Life is held in such disregard here. The padres—I know it grieves them to see so many neophytes die, but they say it's God's will and then go about their work. I can't go on caring for people who are going to die. I can't!"

"You don't have to."

Black Wolf had slipped away, but he might still be able to hear her. Just the same, she was too weak and wounded to temper what she said.

"Midnight trusted me. He . . . he put his life in my hands, and I failed him." Swallowing, she forced down the lump in her throat. "I'm so sick of it. I thought . . . I thought I was doing the right thing when I asked to come here, but . . ."

"You don't have to stay."

Didn't she? Tonight she wasn't sure she was capable of grasping anything except that a child she'd come to love had died under her care. And that Black Wolf's son would have to grow up without a mother.

"You're overwrought," Pablo said. "It is nothing for you to be ashamed of. In fact, I feel honored that you've let down your guard around me. My sweet Lucita, you've worked so hard to prove that you're strong, but you don't have to try around me."

She didn't?

"I need a woman to care for and protect," he continued. "I have wanted that for many years. Lucita, listen to me. I don't want for anything of a material nature. If you and I were to marry, you'd never wonder if you'd have a roof over your head, never again have to be surrounded by the world's unfortunates."

"I'm grateful for your offer," she muttered, all too aware that Black Wolf, who embraced the night as if it was a dear friend, might have heard. "You know I am."

"It isn't your gratitude I want, Lucita."

"I . . ."

"What is it?" He continued to hold her as if he feared she might break. "Perhaps you don't believe you would be happy with me?"

"That . . . that isn't it."

"Then what? You can't make a lasting difference here; surely you know that. No matter how much you might sacrifice yourself, you cannot keep the Indians from succumbing to disease."

"No, I can't," she said as she asked herself if that was what had happened to Black Wolf's wife.

"I hate seeing what this place is doing to you." He indicated Midnight's grave. "Your heart is so big; that's one of the things I love about you."

Wondering if it was possible for a person to fall in love with another so soon, she took a steadying breath and looked up at him. Black Wolf belonged to the shadows; they might be all that kept him alive. In contrast, Pablo had an abundance of confidence about his surroundings.

"You're attracted to a woman who can't stop crying?" she asked in what she hoped was a teasing tone.

"That and more things than I can list tonight. I hated every minute we were apart. You were all I could think about."

"I thought about you, too. A great deal," she added.

"Positive thoughts, I trust?"

When she nodded, his smile lit up his features. "Then I couldn't be happier. There is so much of the world I want you to see. Places where you would be greeted as a princess."

"A princess?"

He chuckled. "I do business with men who would do anything they could to court my favor. They'd take one look at you and know how highly I regard you. There's nothing they wouldn't do for you. Me either.'"

With Pablo, she would no longer have to stand in a crowded cemetery in the middle of the night and remember that the child in the newest grave had been alive a few hours ago. Straightening, she tried to study Pablo's expression, but it was too dark for that, and if it hadn't been for his size and clothing and the way he spoke and a thousand other things, she might have believed he was Black Wolf.

Black Wolf who had killed once and might kill again and would never know material comfort or peace and maybe was destined to die a violent death.

\* \* \*

Lucita was going to leave. Although she hadn't pledged herself to the man, Black Wolf knew it was just a matter of time before she put the mission behind her. He didn't blame her, he told himself as he squatted at the side of the new grave and pressed his palm into the fresh earth, leaving his warrior's mark to help guide the child's journey to the spirit world.

He didn't want her to ever again cry the way she had a few minutes ago.

After picking up a handful of dirt and rocks, he stood. He'd left Fox Running with his wife's sister, not because he hadn't wanted his son with him, but because a three-year-old didn't yet understand the need for silence. He could turn the boy's rearing over to Fox Running's aunt; she had already offered to raise him as one of her own. But Fox Running's smile gave Black Wolf a reason to live, and he would not allow his son to grow up with only vague memories of his father as he'd been forced to do.

When he opened his fingers, what he'd been holding rained down on the grave, and his heart ached.

It was right that Lucita put this behind her with the man she called Pablo. Black Wolf would tell her that so she would have his wisdom to add to Pablo's entreaties. That, he tried to convince himself, was why, instead of returning to the foothills, he'd made a careful circle around the mission until he was within stone-throwing distance of where she lived. Pablo had walked her to the door but hadn't gone inside, and she had been in there long enough to have gone to bed and fallen asleep.

But if she was still awake—

The night guards were behind the church and far enough away that they couldn't have seen him even if the moon had been full, and even if they could, he would lose himself in the distance before their weapons brought him down. Still, he risked drawing attention to himself as he lifted his cupped hands to his mouth and released a long, low howl. No matter how many times he had made the sound over the years, he always gave up a little of himself and became part wolf. It was no different now.

From where he crouched he couldn't see her quarters, but his ears told him what he needed to know. In his mind he saw her step outside, look around, then head toward the sound. Maybe she wasn't the only one to hear, but it was a risk he had to take.

When she stopped, he repeated his earlier cry, so softly this time that the sound barely carried. He imagined how she would respond, maybe wanting to see him again and yet wanting this thing between them to be over. It would be, soon.

"Black Wolf," she whispered. "I can't see—where are you?"

"Here," he whispered back. "You came alone?"

"Yes." She bit off the word, threw it at him really, as she stepped around the corner. "Do you have any idea of the risk you're taking?" she asked in the soft whisper he would never forget.

"Wolf walks with me. I stand in his shadow."

"It isn't enough!" Gasping, she clamped her hand over her mouth. "How can you dismiss armed soldiers?"

"Maybe you will call them to you," he challenged.

"Never. What are you doing here? You almost—if Pablo had seen you . . ."

"He wants to make you his wife."

Although Black Wolf couldn't make out her features, he imagined her quick and startled blink. "You heard."

"Yes."

"I thought . . . I was afraid—don't you care what happens to you?"

"I care very much, Lucita." For a moment he said nothing as he absorbed his surroundings, reassuring himself that no one else was nearby. "I promised my son that he will not grow up without a father."

"Oh, Black Wolf." She reached for him, her nails grazing his upper arm before she pulled back. "I'm so sorry about your wife."

"Thank you."

"Your son, does he understand what happened?"

It seemed a strange thing for her to ask, and yet he should be used to her ability to reach deep inside him and pull out what was most important to him. As briefly and unemotionally as possible, he told her about holding Fox Running while explaining that he would never again know his mother's arms.

"You loved her very much, didn't you?" she whispered.

*Love?* "She was a good woman, gentle and competent."

"A loving mother?"

"Yes." Surprised at how hard it had become to speak, he swallowed. "She was not afraid to die, but she did not want to leave our son."

"You were with her at the end? I'm sorry. If it's too painful to talk about, I understand. But there have been times when you made it easier for me to talk, I would like to do the same for you."

He hadn't called her to him so he could talk about Rabbit Dancing, and yet he wasn't sorry he had. But those words were over, and it was time for other things—as soon as he could gather his thoughts around them.

"You saw me cry tonight, didn't you?" she asked.

"Yes."

"I don't know if that's what a warrior does. Maybe . . . maybe it isn't manly. But if you need to grieve—"

"It is my son's grief that matters," he said even though it was much more complex than that. "Lucita, I heard many things tonight."

"Oh?"

She wanted to touch him—how he knew that he couldn't say, but he had no doubt—just as he wanted to reach for her. However, he didn't dare.

"The words that man said to you."

"Pablo. His name is Pablo Portola."

"This Pablo Portola wants you to become his wife."

"Y-es."

"To go away with him."

"Y-es."

"Is it what you want?"

"What I want?" she repeated.

"Yes. To leave the sickness and death, to forget that there are people called neophytes who do not know what it is to be free, to be free of your father—"

"Stop it!" He sensed movement and guessed she was peering

around her, trying to penetrate the night. He needed to concentrate on his surroundings and learn whether he was still safe, but Lucita stood too close and she had become too important.

"Stop it, please," she said again, a whisper this time.

Wolf was out there. If Lucita asked how he knew that, he would point to his heart. Maybe if he knew how to open her heart to the same knowledge, she would belong here and he would no longer need to tell her to leave, but she hadn't been born Chumash and although she'd reached out in ways the enemy never had before, Wolf sang only for him and his people.

"What do you want?" he asked.

"To be left alone," she said, but he caught a note of desperation in her voice that turned the words into a lie.

"Why?"

"Because I can't think when I'm around you."

Her words made no sense, or maybe the truth was he understood all too well what she'd left unsaid because he felt the same way around her.

Careful to keep his movements so slow and deliberate that she couldn't misunderstand them, he held out his hand, palm uplifted. After a moment, she placed hers in his.

"I am Chumash," he said. "That is all."

"And I'm not."

The truth of what they'd both just said stood between them. "I wish you could see my son, just once," he told her. "My wife said that she saw me in his eyes. His laugh is hers; you would learn something of her from Fox Running's laugh."

"I want . . ." Her voice was husky with unspent tears. "He needs a mother."

"Yes." *Your arms could hold him through the night. Your voice could be the one which tells him about his world.*

Shocked by his thoughts, he reacted by shoving her away. She was briefly off balance but then caught herself, her stare piercing him despite the night.

"Go on. Hate me if that is what you need to do," she insisted. "Hate my father and what he stands for, the other soldiers, our religion. I don't care, Black Wolf! I don't—"

Something that felt like the heat of lightning shot through him. Although she'd already stopped speaking, his hand stabbed the air in warning. Wolf hadn't deserted him; he still felt his spirit's presence, heard his haunting cry, absorbed the warning.

The warning Lucita had heard as well.

# 24

Still as death, Black Wolf stood beside Lucita as the man came closer. He could have run. Every nerve and muscle in him demanded he put self-preservation first and he didn't want to endanger Lucita by being found with her, but he had hidden from this man too many times in the past. After calling his entire being to the ready, he stepped forward.

As he did, the deceptively quiet gray clad figure drew back but didn't run.

"Black Wolf, it is you, isn't it." Whatever the tone of Father Patricio's voice, he wasn't asking a question. He flicked a look at Lucita, then trained his attention on Black Wolf.

"Your eyes are keen, Padre," Black Wolf replied. Taking a moment, he assessed his surroundings. The padre had come alone, which meant Black Wolf could concentrate on him. "Or perhaps I was that careless."

"Careless? Not you, not ever."

"Why are you here?"

Father Patricio gave what might be a chuckle. "Shouldn't I be the one asking you that question?" His gaze again briefly turned to Lucita. "But maybe I already have the answer."

"Will you tell the corporal what you have seen?"

"Would you believe me if I said no?" Snorting, the padre shook his head. "Lucita, what are you doing with him?"

The question served as a stark reminder of the position he'd placed her in, but before he could think of something to say, the padre continued. "Lucita, your mother said you'd gone for a walk—rather abruptly, I might add. It occurred to me that you might have felt the need to return to the cemetery, but now I see—"

"My mother sent you to look for me?"

"No. I took that upon myself. And to find you and Black Wolf together—"

Lucita sucked in her breath, but Black Wolf didn't dare take his eyes off the padre long enough to study her reaction.

"So you and the senorita know each other, do you? I wondered."

"I do not spend all my time cowering from you and the leather-jackets," Black Wolf said in an attempt to turn the conversation around. "You are right. It is not such a hard thing for me to walk about the mission; perhaps I should thank you for that."

"But why? You hate it; don't deny that."

"Sometimes I come to see what my enemies are doing, to learn. And when I do, sometimes I speak to those who live here and they tell me what I need to know."

"Why doesn't that surprise me? No matter how much fear the corporal attempts to beat into the neophytes, they continue to disobey him."

"And you," Black Wolf couldn't resist adding.

"Only a handful. Most are loyal to me."

"Loyal? Hardly."

"You don't know; you'll never know! Lucita, you can't possibly have something in common with this savage."

"He isn't a savage, Father. No matter what you think, he—why did you want to see me?"

"Why? A good question indeed. Senor Portola is a most committed man—a man in love, I daresay."

*Love?* Lucita had asked Black Wolf if he loved his wife. He hadn't fully understood her then, and his comprehension was no greater now. Wondering whether Father Patricio had dismissed his presence or wanted him to believe he had, he remained alert, listening intently.

"He spoke to you about his feelings for me?" Lucita asked the padre.

"Indeed. Indeed. I have seldom had the opportunity to counsel a couple contemplating marriage, but I believe myself equal to the task. After all, one's commitment to marriage is not unlike a parishioner's commitment to the Lord."

Father Patricio's voice had a droning quality like that of sleepy bees, but the tone was deceptive and hid the truth that lay beneath the surface. Black Wolf wouldn't be surprised if the so-called man of peace had a weapon hidden on him. If he did, he was fully capable of using it on anyone he considered a threat.

"Senor Portola asked you to speak for him?" Black Wolf asked. "And you chose now, here, to do so?"

"The Lord's work never ends, Black Wolf—not that I expect you to understand that. Lucita, I must insist you explain what you are doing here with this . . . with this Indian."

"Talking," she answered as Black Wolf silently asked her to forgive him for endangering her.

"About what?"

"Is that your concern?" she shot back. "Tell me, Padre, are you going to inform my father of what you saw?"

"Interesting. Black Wolf asked me the same thing." Father Patricio drew out each word. "Perhaps. Perhaps not. Wisdom lies in taking knowledge deep within oneself and carefully analyzing that knowledge before acting upon it."

The padre had spoken like that so often in the past, his words either meaningless or filled with so much meaning that Black Wolf had been unable to fathom it all. Listening to him now took Black Wolf back to a time and place he didn't want.

"What is it?" Lucita demanded. "You want to threaten me, hold that threat over my head?"

"Lucita, it is not the way of the Lord to be devious. Surely you know that."

"The Lord? Black Wolf, please, go."

She had said the same thing to him a few minutes ago and he had started to obey her, but he couldn't this time, not with the past lapping around him and the future a great unknown. Despite the possibility that Father Patricio was armed, Black Wolf stepped close to the man, expanding his shoulders in a silent message designed to remind the padre who had the greater physical strength.

Father Patricio leaned away but didn't retreat. "Don't," he warned. "If you touch me, Sebastian won't rest until you're dead, even if it means killing hundreds to get to you."

"You throw threats at me, Padre? You do not pray to God to protect you?"

"Stop it!" Lucita hissed. "Both of you, stop it."

Although she barely came up to his shoulders and her arms had never built a house or brought down a deer, Black Wolf believed her capable of risking her own life in an attempt to prevent more bloodshed. That was what made them so different—at least, a part of what made them different. Peace flowed through her veins, beat in her heart, and lived in her eyes, while he had no wish to deny what his hands were capable of.

"Listen to me," he said, not caring what the padre did or thought. "The Chumash have been like frightened rabbits for too long. Strangers come to our land and we hide, and if we cannot hide, we allow ourselves to be taken and made to live another way. But I am no longer a rabbit. I have become a wolf."

"You were always a predator, Black Wolf," Father Patricio said. "That's what fascinates me about you: your potential for violence."

"A man who has seen too many of those he loves die before their time can no longer run and hide, not if he wants to call himself a man."

"If you think your people can attack—"

"That is for you to concern yourself with, Father," he challenged. "I will not tell you the plans of the Chumash."

"No?" Despite the dark, Black Wolf saw the flash of teeth, a warning that Father Patricio was smiling. "You don't understand the power of the Spanish army. You and the rest of your people never will."

"Stop it!" Lucita now stood between him and Father Patricio. Her arm, as she indicated the newest grave, was a shadowed blur. "A boy died today. Tomorrow it might be one of my other patients, the next day yet another one. It *has* to end!"

She'd spoken too loudly. With awareness of the danger he was in gnawing at him, Black Wolf whirled and let the night envelop him. Still, because he was a warrior, he opened his throat, his howled warning splitting the air.

"In here, now!"

Teeth clenched to keep her nervousness to herself, Lucita followed Father Patricio into the sanctuary. With the statue of the crucified Jesus dominating the nearest wall, it seemed the wrong place for them to be. Several candles burned, casting the interior in a soft red glow and adding the illusion of warmth to the gray walls.

Father Patricio dropped to his knees before the crucifix, his prayer an indistinct yet strident mumble, but she didn't join him, not with Black Wolf's howl echoing inside her.

When he was finished, Father Patricio held out his hand indicating he wanted help getting to his feet, and although she hated touching him, she did as he requested. To her relief, he released her as soon as he was standing.

"I have prayed for your soul, Lucita. Prayed every night since you came here."

"Have you?"

In an attempt to gain control over the tension that had wrapped itself around her, she sat on one of the wooden benches. Father Patricio remained standing, his knuckles turning white as he folded his hands over his belly.

"I did so because your mother came to me asking for guidance, because Father Joseph was concerned you would find life here too much of an ordeal, because it is not right for a father and daughter to have so much hostility between them."

Disconcerted because she now knew Father Patricio had all but watched her every step, she forced herself to remain silent.

"Lucita, Father Joseph and I have no greater concern than for the souls of those entrusted to our care."

"What about Black Wolf's soul?"

"He has none."

How wrong the padre was. If Father Patricio had seen Black Wolf at Humqaq or heard him talk about his love for his son, known of his concern for the neophytes, he couldn't possibly think that way.

"You are silent, Lucita? Is it because my words shock you or because you know I speak the truth?"

"The truth?" she echoed. "No, you're wrong. Terribly wrong."

"Am I?" Coming closer, he balanced his weight on widespread legs as if using his body to keep her where she was. "Lucita, I knew Black Wolf when he was a child. I did everything within my power to show him the light, but he refused to see the truth."

"Because he knows another truth," she said, leveling a steady look at him.

Father Patricio's hand snaked out, striking the side of her face before she had time to react. Stifling a gasp, she pressed her hand over her cheek and continued to glare. "You had no—"

"Do not tell me what I can and cannot do! The Lord has seen fit to have me spend these years here. I accept that, but I will never, never allow someone such as you to contradict me. Do you understand?"

Hot eyes settled on her, scorched and warned. Spittle had formed at the side of his mouth, reminding her of her father's affliction, and the priest's flesh seemed to have sagged in the past few seconds, turning him into a vengeful old man.

"Why?" She indicated where he'd struck her. "What did I say that was so wrong?"

"There is only one truth! His truth!" Father Patricio jerked his head skyward.

"Is it?" she asked, wondering at her reckless courage when pain should have made her cautious. "The Chumash had very different beliefs for hundreds, maybe thousands of years. I can't believe they all went to hell because of that."

"Blasphemy!"

"Maybe." The distance between them remained the same, certainly not as much as she needed, and yet she didn't cower. "Maybe not. If I hadn't spent time with Black Wolf, I would believe, like you, that there is only our God. But he opened my eyes."

"He is a savage."

This argument wasn't going to get them anywhere, so why was she trying? And maybe even more important, why did Father Patricio care what she thought?

"Does a savage cry when his wife dies?" she demanded. "Does a savage concern himself with what kind of a life his son will have? Does a savage—I saw him at Humqaq. Heard him praying. Saw Wolf."

Father Patricio recoiled so violently that for a second she thought one of Black Wolf's arrows had found him. The padre's mouth hung open; his hands fluttered to his throat before falling limp by his side. None of the fire had left his small eyes, but the flames now seemed to be directed inward.

"Wolf?" he whispered. "At Humqaq?"

"You know what it means?"

He nodded. "Tell me." It was more of a prayer than an order.

Silently begging Black Wolf to forgive her, she told the padre about seeing the brave and the powerful animal together. She gave no explanation, simply drew a picture of what had happened. Father Patricio started to shake his head, kept shaking it even after she was done, and yet he didn't call her a liar.

"Do your parents know?" he asked through barely moving lips. "Did you tell them where you went?"

"No."

"Have you no concern for your safety? No one goes there alone, no one!"

"I did. And I will never regret that."

He began to pace, his legs taking him from one side of the sanctuary to the other like a trapped animal seeking a way out. Finally he turned to her, his face in shadow. She couldn't say how long they had been in here or how late it was. Nothing mattered except this conversation, this moment, and Black Wolf.

"No one will believe you," he whispered.

*I do.*

Ripples of emotion coursed through Black Wolf, making it impossible for him to think about the rest his body needed. Although he hadn't got any sleep last night, he felt stronger than he'd ever been before, and yet so lonely he couldn't concentrate on the reason for his strength.

He could have killed Father Patricio tonight. Black Wolf had wanted to feel life drain out of the man and for him to know who was responsible as he died.

No, he couldn't have shed the man's blood in Lucita's presence.

From where he stood, in daylight he could see almost the entire length of the mission's water system. The stories the ancient ones had told and retold spoke of a time when lack of rain nearly spelled death for the Chumash. Drought could come again, but because the padres had devised a way to hold the precious water captive, death would not come to the crops and those who tended them. It was a good thing, maybe the only good thing the newcomers had brought with them.

No, not the only thing, he acknowledged. His people now knew how to grow those crops, the worth of horses and muskets, ways of turning clay and straw into walls and ceilings that would protect them from the elements.

His muscles began to cramp, and, thinking to stretch them, he left his hiding place. He was a predator; his spirit had made him one. And yet he was more than the powerful animal whose name he carried. A man, he had been given the ability to reason and plan, to learn from the past and look into the future.

What he saw made him howl.

Father Patricio jerked upright, his hands pressing against the air as if trying to ward off an unseen enemy. From where she sat Lucita couldn't see anything of the world beyond the sanctuary, but she knew.

"Damn him! Damn him to hell!"

The padre's oath rolled off her, and she didn't bother to acknowledge it. Instead, she got to her feet, picked up one of the candles, and hurried over to the door. Opening it, she stepped outside. Although it was now the middle of the night, the air remained hot and dry, the breeze so faint that maybe she only imagined it against her flesh.

The howl had died away. She waited, not breathing, willing its return, but it wasn't repeated. Still, she continued to stare at the darkness as if by force of will she could push it away. Black Wolf was out there somewhere, maybe so far away that he couldn't see her. She hoped so, because his safety meant everything to her. And yet . . .

"He is not human. Sometimes I think he is not human."

Surprised by the note of awe in the padre's voice, she turned toward him, but it wasn't until she brought the candle near him that she was able to make out his expression. Something between hatred and awe lived there, aging him and yet giving him an ageless look.

"Maybe he isn't," she said, not because she believed that but because she wanted to see the padre's reaction.

"You think so? How well do you know him, Lucita? How well?"

She didn't answer.

"You were alone with him, maybe more times than anyone will ever know. He is a man, Lucita. At least, I tell myself he is. And you are a beautiful young woman."

Something had ignited between her and Black Wolf that made her heart beat faster and her body hum with restlessness, but that was all she knew, and she wasn't going to tell Father Patricio that.

"Are you still a virgin?"

"What?" she gasped, shocked.

"Answer me! Senor Portola has asked me to speak in his behalf, but he will not want you if you are no longer pure. If you have given yourself to that savage."

He made it sound so dirty. Even though she had only a vague idea of what he meant by "giving" herself, she wanted to demand he not say such things in her presence.

"Answer me, Lucita! Did you lay down with him?"

"No."

"No?" He blinked. "You are not lying to me, are you? Because if you are—"

"I do not lie."

Relief, along with something else, washed over his features. "Still valuable," he muttered. "Good. Good." She thought he would say more and wondered how she would react this time. Instead, he slipped past her and stood just outside the sanctuary, his back touching the adobe wall, eyes scanning, as hers had done, the night.

Mindful that the corporal hated being disturbed when he was with his men, Father Patricio nevertheless opened the door to the soldiers' quarters and asked Sebastian to step outside with him. Only when the well-armed man was beside him did he relax.

He'd tried to organize what he was going to say but, swayed by Sebastian's quick temper, hadn't been able to come up with anything that wouldn't lead to an explosion. Feeling his way, he brought the corporal up-to-date about his attempts to speak in Senor Portola's behalf.

"Good!" Sebastian exclaimed before he'd finished. "Thank you, Padre. You have done an admirable job of executing your duties." He glanced over his shoulder at the building he'd just left.

"Some of my duties, yes, but I would be remiss if I didn't tell you what I observed tonight."

Even in the dark, he easily imagined Sebastian's impatient glower. For a moment the priest debated letting it go at that, but the corporal had bullied his way around the mission from the day of his arrival, and it was time for him to be brought down to earth.

"Yes?" Sebastian prompted.

"I was just thinking." Feeling in control for the first time in what seemed like hours, he relished the mood. "With the additional military presence here, I would assume La Purisima to be as safe as an infant's nursery."

As he expected, Sebastian didn't say anything.

"It is a shame that that is not the case."

"What are you talking about?"

"Black Wolf," he said, wishing he could see the corporal's expression.

"What about him?"

Before he could think to duck, Sebastian had grabbed his robes and was pulling him off balance.

"He was here tonight," he said.

"Damnation!"

"With your daughter."

Sleep came after a battle Lucita feared she wouldn't win, but although she didn't sit up until she felt morning light against her eyelids, her body told her she'd only got a few hours of rest. Not sure what she was doing or why, she slipped out of bed and dressed. As she was putting on her shoes, the door opened and her mother peered in.

"You're up," Margarita said with a sigh. "And getting ready for mass?"

"Yes," Lucita said, realizing how much she needed ritual this morning.

"I was afraid—where were you last night?"

"I can't tell you, yet. Please be patient with me."

"Patient?"

Lucita nodded by way of answer, and although Margarita continued to give her unfathomable glances, neither of them spoke as they made their way to the church. Inside, the heat was even greater than outside, the result of several hundred bodies packed close together. Both padres were already there, as was Pablo, who nodded but said nothing as Lucita sat beside him.

This place, she thought, had served as her introduction to life at the mission. She'd changed a great deal since that first day, and yet the rhythm here remained the same. Maybe it would help if she could take comfort from prayer and song, but she would have to stop thinking, stop feeling, for that to happen.

"Your father wants to see you after mass," her mother whispered in a choked tone.

"And so do I," Pablo whispered from where he sat.

* * *

After mass, a hand on her forearm prevented her from falling in line behind her mother and Pablo. Looking up, she found herself staring into Father Patricio's eyes. Red-rimmed, they told her that he, too, had got little sleep.

"Now," the padre said. "Your father does not want to wait."

If only her legs felt steadier, she thought as she entered the soldiers' quarters, her mother and Pablo behind her. Father Joseph was already there, along with her father, who stood in the middle of the room, his arms folded over his chest. No one sat.

Incapable of breathing, Lucita struggled to steel herself against the padre's next words. She stared fixedly at him as if her desperate glare could keep him silent.

"Perhaps," Father Patricio said, "it is because I have not known Lucita long and do not know her the way you do, but I cannot convince myself that she is capable of deception."

Was this the way Black Wolf had felt when he had to live here? Was this why he'd risked everything by seeking freedom? Trapped, she could only wait.

# 25

Hunger gnawed at Black Wolf, but the call wasn't strong enough to pull him from his thoughts. He'd remained on the slope above the mission throughout the night, dozing yet always alert. The breeze had carried the sound of bells announcing morning mass. Now that was over and the neophytes were eating before starting on their assigned tasks.

When he began digging in the dirt, at first he paid no attention to what he was doing, but bit by bit what seemed to be random designs turned into a human figure draped in a heavy gown.

"Do you feel my presence, Padre?" he asked. "Did you hear my final howl last night?"

Once again silent, he filled in the details of eyes, nose, and mouth. When what to him represented the padre was finished, he placed his hand over it because this way Father Patricio might sense him.

"You saw," he said. "Do not deny it! You called me a liar when I sought to speak about Wolf, but you followed me and saw."

It had been a spring morning several years ago when he'd spotted the padre on his way to the upper canal. Instead of fading into the wilderness, he'd approached Father Patricio, even calling out so the man would have no doubt of who he was. The padre had pulled back in alarm, but Black Wolf had said he meant him no harm and then handed over his spear as proof. The padre's eyes had said what he wanted to do with that spear, but Black Wolf had challenged him to see him as a man, an equal.

Aware that their time alone together might be short, he'd first caressed the marking on the back of his wrist and then clutched his charm stone. The padre's reaction had been to insist that those things served as proof of Black Wolf's godless state. That was when he had scrambled onto a nearby boulder and, ignoring the now inconsequential figure below him, sent out a prayer. Wolf had answered, first by announcing his presence on the wind and then by revealing himself at the edge of the trees.

Wolf had stood tall and proud, tail erect, head lifted, eyes intense. He had walked out to meet his spirit, not stopping until Wolf was close enough to touch and be touched. Then, his thoughts on the constant wonder of what existed between them, he'd placed his hand in the beast's mouth. Wolf had closed his teeth around his fingers as he'd done in Lucita's presence, the pressure increasing until Black Wolf couldn't have freed himself without causing damage to his flesh; there'd been no pain.

They'd remained like that through countless heartbeats, united and sharing what needed no words, before Wolf raised his muzzle to the sky and howled his mastery of the world.

And Father Patricio had seen.

"Do you make a lie of that day?" Black Wolf asked the dirt figure. "Do you tell yourself that your eyes deceived you, that you can deny what happened, or does your soul know the truth?"

Her father seldom sat, and Lucita suspected he wouldn't today as long as he had things to say and orders to give. In contrast to his piercing glare, her mother stared at the ground, somehow less substantial than she'd been a few minutes ago.

*No matter what he says, I will not let you be blamed. What I do must not reflect on you. You are not responsible, only I, only . . .*

Wrenching herself free of the silent chant, she noted that Father Patricio stood near Father Joseph, but if the two had communicated in any way, she was unaware of it. Only Pablo acknowledged her presence.

"This feels like an inquisition." Pablo directed his observation at her father. "I did not intend anything like that."

"You do not know my daughter."

There was an angry-looking scratch on her father's wrist and, despite everything, she wished she could take care of it for him, but that necessitated touching him and she couldn't do that.

"We are here to discuss two things." Sebastian squared around so he faced her full on. "If the decision was mine alone, there would only be one issue. However, life is never simple."

Her father wasn't a philosopher. He saw or heard; he reacted.

"I must say I am pleased to learn that Senor Portola is kindly disposed toward you. Given the little time the two of you have had to get to know each other, I was not sure he would approach me so soon."

Pablo had asked for her hand in marriage; she had no doubt of that. Why, then, were the others here? Except for her mother, it shouldn't be anyone else's concern.

"Senior Portola is an . . . an intelligent man," she came up with.

"He would not have become so successful in his business if he wasn't." Her father sounded impatient. "He has much to offer a woman—wealth and position."

"Yes, he does."

Sebastian's quick frown was the only warning she needed that she'd spoken out of turn. "What two men discuss between themselves is not the concern of women," he continued after a glance at his wife. "Women's interests are those of home and hearth, children and religion, although with your mother, the Church has always come first. No." He held up his hand. "Don't try to deny the truth."

When Lucita said nothing, he briefly rubbed the scar at the corner of his mouth. "Because of women's natural limits, it is up to men to provide for them."

Knowing the futility of argument, she waited.

"Senor Portola, I offer you my daughter. She has a remarkable degree of intellect for one of her sex and has learned a number of skills which you may find useful. I cannot pretend she does not have shortcomings, not the least of which is her refusal to accept her role in life."

"They aren't shortcomings to me," Pablo assured Sebastian. "I find everything about her utterly charming."

Scarcely believing this conversation was about her, Lucita risked looking at Pablo. His dark eyes seemed so soft and gentle, nothing like Black Wolf's glittering strength.

Her father was far from finished. He told Pablo about her violent opposition to marrying Ermano and how she'd begged her parents to allow her to accompany them here.

"I would have been surprised if there had not been other men in your daughter's life, Corporal," Pablo said. "Tell me, Lucita, do you have any opposition to what is being proposed here?"

"Opposition?"

"I am concerned you have not yet had time to determine whether you are capable of falling in love with me or, if not love, at least sufficient affection. In truth, I have just begun to learn what makes you unique and fascinating. I must ask—the reasons you turned your back on Senor De Leon, do they hold true for me?"

"Oh, no! You . . . you have always shown yourself to be most kind."

"And he was not?"

"No," she whispered.

"Then"—he smiled his ready smile—"perhaps I have passed the first hurdle."

"Indeed you have," she admitted, which garnered a faint nod from her mother, even a grunt she took to be approval from her father. "I appreciate your honesty."

"I have been told that one of my greatest faults is my insistence on being blunt." Despite his words, he sounded not the slightest bit embarrassed. "Lucita, I would rather we were having this conversation in private, but your father has just informed me that he is embarking on a major strategy designed to ensure the mission's safety. I would be remiss if I remained silent today."

"A major strategy?" She couldn't keep alarm out of her voice. "Father, what is he talking about?"

Sebastian's eyes narrowed. "What I plan is none of your concern."

But it was and nothing either of them said or did would change that. Just the same, she fought to keep her emotions under control.

"I . . . I would never pretend to possess the necessary knowledge for leading troops," she amended. "But if you believe our safety is at risk, Mother and I need to know that."

Whether her father believed her interest went no further than that or not didn't matter. What did was learning, somehow, what he had in mind.

The good side of her father's mouth twitched, and he pressed against the offending muscle. "Haven't I always protected you? I would trust you have no doubt of my ability to continue to do so. You have received a marriage proposal, Lucita. We await your response."

*A marriage proposal.* "I . . ."

"Sebastian." Her mother spoke for the first time. "How can she respond while surrounded by an audience? Such matters should be conducted in private."

Ignoring his wife, Sebastian leveled his gaze first on Pablo and then on Lucita again. Feeling as if she was unraveling, she struggled to imagine herself traveling to the presidio with this gentle and yet worldly man. The trip would be a long one, but with each mile they traveled she'd put more of the mission behind her. Never again would she have to stand in a crude cemetery while a small boy was buried. Never again would she force herself to enter an infirmary and spend her days in futile attempts to save the lives of those who had no defense against the illnesses her people had brought with them.

With Pablo she could explore the world. She would think for

herself, make her own choices and decisions. Free from her father's harsh criticism, she might gain a sense of self-respect she could barely imagine. No longer would she be forced to sleep within thick adobe walls.

"Senor Portola," she began, not at all sure of what she was going to say, "I don't believe myself worthy of you."

"But you are; you are."

She'd known he was going to say that and silently thanked him, then prayed she was doing the right thing. Thinking to place her hand in his and by the silent gesture put her future, her life, in his keeping, she started toward him. As she did, her attention was drawn to the faint light coming in the small window to her left. She could see little, just a portion of the livestock corral and beyond that the gently rolling hills that Black Wolf called home.

Humqaq.

"Lucita!"

Startled, she pulled her attention, if not her emotions, from the wilderness and faced her father. Until this moment she'd held the small belief that beneath his soldier's exterior some part of him loved her. She no longer did.

"I don't have an answer for you, Pablo." Her voice refused to reach beyond a whisper. "Not yet."

The call of a wild turkey settled over Black Wolf, but although he knew who was responsible for the sound, he didn't respond until he'd finished a handful of the blackberries he'd picked a short while ago. His answering wolf cry swirled around him; then the breeze caught it and threw it into the sky.

A few minutes later, Much Rain came into view. His friend acknowledged him with a welcoming nod, but no hint of a smile touched his lips.

"I wondered if I would find you here," Much Rain said. "What keeps you at this place? If I had any choice, I would never again look at the enemy's walls."

"What brings you here, my friend?" Scooping up some of the berries, he handed them to Much Rain. "Nothing forces you."

"Maybe," he said on the tail of a frown. "Maybe not. Black Wolf, I have done much thinking. Without my wife beside me, life has become like a dry creek bed."

"I am sorry."

Much Rain lowered himself to the ground and began sorting through the berries, eating only a few. "I spoke to the shaman, took his herbs, and prayed for a night filled with telling dreams, but they have not come."

Much Rain hadn't looked at him since their initial greeting. Remembering times when his own musings lay tangled inside him, he waited.

"My house has become too small," Much Rain continued after a long silence. "I look around and see my wife's relatives, my relatives. They take up so much space that there is none left for me."

"That can happen."

"Did it for you? When your wife died, did you feel as if you had grown to the size of a grizzly? You wanted to roar in pain and rage but were afraid that if you began, you could never stop?"

"Much Rain, listen to me," Black Wolf insisted. "What you and your wife had was far from what I shared with mine. She was my wife, yes, but she never held the same place in my heart that yours did with you."

Leaning forward, Much Rain idly picked up and then discarded several berries. "What I had was rare; I know that. She and I chose each other. When we came together in bed, it was with joy and laughter."

What was that like? Black Wolf considered reminding Much Rain that he was a young brave and would surely find another wife, but although Much Rain knew he was expected to marry again, perhaps no one would ever fill the holes in his heart caused by Willow's death.

"What do you want of me?" Black Wolf asked.

"What?" Much Rain pressed his hand over his eyes, breathing deep and slow. "I do not know. I—when I awoke this morning, all that mattered was that she was not beside me and I would shatter into a thousand pieces, like ice, if I did not do something. I started to walk. And while I walked, I tried to look into the future. When you do, what do you see?"

A few minutes ago Black Wolf had nearly convinced himself that he had nothing to think about except filling his belly and watching to make sure the leatherjackets didn't begin a new search for his people, but that was before Much Rain found him. Now, forced to face the question, he admitted he'd only been putting off the inevitable.

"I am not a shaman," he said. "I cannot stare at tomorrow."

"But surely you have thought beyond today."

Not just tomorrow, but the rest of his life. "I see my son becoming a man. Nothing is more important to me."

"What kind of a man? Free or slave?"

"Free!"

"Can you promise him that? Can you?"

Wolf, his spirit, protected him and made it possible for him to walk within the shadow of the mission walls; he would always believe that. But Fox Running was too young to have made his spirit search and thus walked exposed and naked.

"You could not promise your wife that she would live to be an old woman," he said. "Do not ask me to do more."

"I did not mean to." Much Rain briefly met his gaze. "Black Wolf, there is none among us whose relationship with his spirit is closer. You say that your woman did not live in your heart, but your son does, just as my wife lived in mine."

"Yes."

"That is why I am here. To ask you, Black Wolf, what lives inside you."

"Freedom," he said without having to think about his response.

"Is that all?"

"You think it is not enough?"

"I have no answers," Much Rain whispered. "I want to hate the enemy. When I think of what the leatherjackets did to her, an earthquake builds inside me, but then the earthquake is gone and nothing is left except grief."

"I do not want that for you!" he said as he gripped Much Rain's hand. The leatherjackets never touched each other; maybe they thought it unmanly. But how could he call himself a man if he didn't offer comfort to a friend in pain? "If I could find a way to make you believe in tomorrow, I would do it."

Sighing, Much Rain nodded. "I think . . . maybe it is not answers I need from you. Maybe it is enough to know you will listen."

"No, that is not enough."

When Much Rain stared at him, he gathered his thoughts around him and then began. "I became a warrior because Wolf was strong within me. I am still a warrior, but becoming a father has changed me and made me look beyond myself.

"That is what I thought about the last time I went to Humqaq," he continued. "I opened myself to the First People, Evening Star, the Gods of the Moon and Sun, the Great Unknown, and those beings filled me. I am Fox Running's father. Wolf has become my father, but he is guided by the spirits of our ancestors. No matter what the padres say, this is what I will always believe."

"Humqaq," Much Rain whispered, his eyes misting.

"It is where our hearts and souls belong. Without that place with its memories and spirits, the Chumash are nothing. You and I are nothing."

Groaning, Much Rain picked up a blackberry and placed it in his mouth. "If the leatherjackets have their way, soon we will no longer be able to go there. Maybe soon there will be none of us left to make the journey."

"We have only today," Black Wolf said. "And the belief that because we have Humqaq we will face tomorrow."

Much Rain sighed but didn't drop his gaze. "Once I laughed and sang because I believed a woman and I would face that time together, but now I am alone."

"No, you are not! Her spirit, our gods, the memories of our ancestors wait for you at Humqaq, but only you can seek them out."

"Come there with me."

"I cannot."

"Why?"

"Because . . ." Scanning the sky, Black Wolf spotted a distant hawk floating on an unseen breeze. "You need to begin your journey to tomorrow, but I am caught in today."

# 26

His anger would have been better. Instead, silence pounded at the walls, the impact so great that Lucita thought she might scream.

Perhaps ten feet away, her father stood staring out the same window that had held her attention a few minutes ago. Father Joseph had slipped close to her mother as if trying to give comfort and put distance between himself and the military man, but Father Patricio only watched from beneath lowered lids, what might be the threat of a smile on his lips. Pablo hadn't spoken, and she couldn't force herself to look at him, or maybe the truth was she didn't dare take her eyes off her father.

"You refuse?" Sebastian asked.

"Not refuse. I need more time." *Time to comprehend the hold Black Wolf and his world has on me.*

"What do you want—for Pablo to shower you with gifts?"

"No, of course not. Father, so much has happened since I came here; I'm confused. I—"

"Are you?"

There was something deadly in the simple question. Warned and terrified of what he'd say next, she remained silent.

"You think me a fool, but I am not."

"Sebastian, please," her mother moaned. "Your daughter would never—"

"Quiet, woman! This daughter of yours who professes to be so enthralled with the way of life here? I wonder what you would say if you knew the truth?"

*No!*

"Shall I say the words, Lucita, or will you, finally?"

"I don't know what you want."

"Don't you!" Gray-red splotches appeared on Sebastian's cheeks, and the injured side of his face spasmed uncontrollably. "I know what happened last night."

Suddenly colder than she'd ever been, she could only stare at Father Patricio. In an insane way, she waited for him to at least apologize for what he'd done, but a man who feels regret doesn't allow his smile to grow.

"It was my duty to tell your father about the savage, Lucita," the padre insisted. "Surely you know that."

A thousand useless excuses slammed through her, but she dismissed them. "He isn't a savage."

"Lucita!"

"He isn't, Mother. He's a Chumash warrior named Black Wolf. He—"

"I know his name," her father interrupted. "He's a killer."

*Killer.*

"Go on, Daughter; deny that he was responsible for Mundo's death."

"Mundo killed Willow," she said, her voice strong and level.

"Willow?" Sebastian demanded. "What are you talking about?"

If self-preservation were all that mattered to her, she would have remained silent, but she couldn't let the others believe Black Wolf was a cold-blooded killer; she couldn't! Dividing her attention among everyone in the room, she told them how Mundo had come across Willow and beaten her to the point of death when she tried to fight him off. Margarita looked in shock. Father Joseph kept shaking his head like a weary dog while her father's eyes hardened even more and Father Patricio stared without blinking. Pablo didn't look at her.

"How do you know this?" Sebastian demanded.

"Black Wolf told me." She kept her gaze steady, bold even. "And I believe him. He speaks Spanish nearly as well as we do. He isn't a savage; neither are the others he lives with. That's . . . that's what—there's so much hostility and hatred, the Church and military treating the Indians like animals. I—"

"Enough!" Sebastian stalked toward her, stopping when he was so close that she could smell his hot breath. Grabbing her, he yanked her with him as he stalked from the room. Despite her need to concentrate on what was happening, she stole a glance over her shoulder, catching a glimpse of the tears forming in her mother's eyes and the disbelief on Pablo's face.

Because resisting her father would only infuriate him more, she concentrated on keeping up with him. A number of neophytes stopped what they were doing to stare at them, but no one made a move to interfere. At first she thought he was taking her back to where he'd imprisoned her before. Instead, he made his way to the church, every boot step vibrating through her, and, after opening the heavy door, shoved her in ahead of him.

"Go on!" he bellowed. "Repeat what you just said, only this time do it in God's house!"

Knocked off balance, she fell to her knees but quickly scrambled to her feet. Her heart felt as if it might burst from her chest, and yet although she had never been more afraid of her father, her emotions went far deeper than that.

"My daughter." He planted himself between her and the door. "My daughter fornicating with a savage!"

"I haven't! Father, I—"

His fingers formed a fist. "I'm not interested in your lies, Lucita. If you were a man, I would have already killed you."

"Don't let that stop you."

"What?"

"You hate me. Why should it matter to you whether I'm alive or not?"

"It doesn't."

Pain slashed through her, but she struggled to keep her reaction to herself. "Then why—"

"Why are we here? How little you know of a soldier's life, Lucita. When Father Patricio came to me with his story of seeing you and Black Wolf together, I no longer wanted to call you my daughter. My first thought was to marry you off as quickly as possible. No matter what happens between you and me, I must still face my superiors. I *will* hold my head high. If everyone believed I had arranged a successful marriage for you, the truth would never have to come out. But—"

He cupped his hand over his chin, looking like a man contemplating a mathematical equation. "But heart and soul I am a soldier. I know my duty."

She understood his rage and even his anger, but this coolly deliberate way of speaking made her half-sick with fear. Struggling against the emotion, she looked around as if fascinated by her surroundings.

"That's why I wanted to come to La Purisima," she insisted. "Because I believed I had a duty to serve God's children. But I was wrong."

He waved his hand as if dismissing her, but as long as he didn't shout her into silence, she'd fight to make herself understood.

"The Indians aren't God's children; I now believe that. For thousands of years they embraced their own deities and were at peace with that belief, but we're trying to take that from them. It isn't right."

"If you believe that, you are the only one. Enough! I have no intention of arguing this point with you."

"Then why—"

"Why did I want us to be alone?" His laugh reminded her of a crow's shrill cry. "Because there's something I want from you. Once I have it, I don't care what you do—because you are no longer my daughter."

*"No longer my daughter."* "What is it?"

"How bold you are. How brave." This time his laugh sounded

forced. "Oh, yes, you would have made a good soldier. One thing." He held up his forefinger. "And then I will never have to speak to you again."

"Why? Because you are going to kill me?"

"Do not tempt me."

Their voices echoed in the empty high-ceilinged room— strange that she hadn't noticed that before. In the silence that followed his last words, she found herself being drawn to him, not because she held out a desperate hope that they could salvage anything in the way of a relationship, but because the man would always be her father. He held himself as he always had, straight and tall, refusing to let the years and miles and battles have their way with him. There were flecks of gray in his hair and tiny grooves around his eyes. His mouth had once been gentle, hadn't it? The child who still lived inside her remembered that he'd laughed as she toddled after him, held her, kissed her.

Now nothing remained except the memory.

"Where is he?"

*He.* "I don't know."

"Do not lie to me, Lucita."

He leaned closer and invaded her space, but she refused to shrink away. He'd said she would have made a good soldier, and in some perverse way she wanted to prove him right. "I'm not lying."

"No? How many times have you met with him?"

"I don't remember."

Something that might have been pain flickered in his eyes. "Why? What does he—never mind! The thought of you with that murdering savage disgusts me."

Black Wolf had killed because a soldier had ended the life of one of his people, but reminding her father of that would serve no purpose. "He's an intelligent human being," she said, conviction coating every word.

"Don't waste your breath, Lucita. The only thing that matters to me is defeating my enemy. Now, where is he?"

"Why won't you believe me? I told you I—"

"You think you can defy me? How little you know of a soldier's ways. If you believe nothing else of me, believe this. I have ways of forcing you to bring him to me."

Something was making him restless, and Black Wolf knew better than to ignore that. Although he'd sent Much Rain off with the rest of his berries, he didn't seek distraction by looking for something to eat. Instead, he crouched on a mound of earth and felt the day's heat seep into his feet and the top of his head.

The wind had all but gone to sleep, which was often its way when summer beat down around everything. Like the animals and birds, maybe the wind, too, ran out of energy under the relentless sun, but he didn't dare.

Awareness touched him with the strength of a hummingbird's feathers, first reminding him of the need to constantly survey his surroundings, then forcing him to his feet. There was little about the land to hold his attention, just softly rolling hills and dry grass shimmering with heat waves. The sky was hazed and in the distance it was impossible to tell where the land let off and the heavens began, but because he could see for miles in all directions, he became convinced that what he felt had nothing to do with his immediate world.

He pulled air deep into his lungs, but although his senses were keen, they told him nothing. Perhaps he was reacting to the things he and Much Rain had said and shared. Perhaps . . .

*Lucita.*

When her name touched him, he wrapped himself around it, held it close, tested and tasted, found no danger.

Not danger to him, but . . .

*What is it, Wolf? I trust what my body tells me about my world, but this is not about me.*

Not all of the grayness came from the hazy sky. Some of it, a hard and powerful shape coming toward him, stood apart. On legs that felt strong enough to carry him to the ends of the earth, he walked toward his spirit until they stood only a few feet apart. Wolf's eyes were both red and black, his teeth white and sharp, his nostrils flared. The powerful chest could survive the strongest arrow—not that any warrior would ever raise a weapon to Wolf.

*My heart embraces you, my spirit. I take your presence into me and know I am blessed.*

Wolf never spoke. What he thought and believed had always come to Black Wolf in the form of emotion. Today he felt an icy ripple down his spine.

*You warn of danger. To me?*

A brief nod of the great head.

*To my people?*

A shake.

*Then who?*

Wolf leaned forward and lowered his head, his snout pressing against Black Wolf's chest.

*Danger to my heart?*

A nod.

*To someone I hold close to my heart?*

Another nod.

*To my son?*

A shake.

Lucita would never know what had transpired between her father and Father Patricio, and even if she did, it wouldn't have mattered. All that did was that the padre had opened the church door and was stepping inside.

He wasn't alone.

"What are you doing?" she demanded when she realized that the boy she'd rescued from Father Patricio stood behind the padre, his hands tied behind him and a rope around his neck. "My God, what are you doing?"

"Stacking the deck," Father Patricio replied. After closing the door, he pulled the boy with him to where Sebastian stood.

"Father, what is this about?"

"I am *not* your father, Lucita! Not any longer. So you believe you know more about how this child should be treated than Father Patricio does, do you?"

"He's afraid of him." This wasn't happening! How could her father possibly care about this child? He had no use for him, no reason—

"You have the weakness all women do." Sebastian's voice held no more emotion than if he'd been discussing the weather. "That's why, no matter what I said, you would never succeed as a soldier. The value you put on life will always stand between you and what must be done."

"What must be done?" she forced herself to ask.

"I swallowed my pride when I requested more troops. All around me mission commanders with no more soldiers under their command provide the padres with safety. I know what they were thinking, the way they judge. But they don't have to deal with someone like Black Wolf."

"He's just one man. He—"

"Ha! If Indians throughout California hear he killed a soldier and received no punishment, they'll lose their fear of us. There are so many of them. If they go to war—I will not be responsible for any bloodshed. I will not."

"No one would blame you."

"Wouldn't they! Listen to me, Lucita. I am a soldier; that is the only thing I am. It is my duty to vanquish my enemy, by whatever means necessary."

"I . . . know."

"I hope you do. And today the means . . ." He pointed at the cowering child. "Perhaps you know where Black Wolf is; perhaps you don't. But I have no doubt that you can, once again, contact him—if the need is great enough."

The boy stared at her, his eyes speaking of fear and defeat, but no matter how much she wanted to protect him, she didn't dare, not now.

"You're a woman, Lucita," Sebastian continued. "Weak in the ways that make a man strong. Tell me, what value do you put on this child's life?"

*I would die to protect him.* But if she told her father that, he'd use it to his advantage. "He is only one," she said against the lump in her throat. "He means no more and no less than the others."

An appraising look settled over Sebastian's features, and although she knew he must resent having to do so, he gave her a begrudging smile.

"A thinking answer," he said. "I would be wise never to underestimate you. However . . ."

His arms had been hanging at his side, but now he folded them over his chest and walked over to where Father Patricio and the boy stood. The child shrank back as far as his tether would allow.

"What are you doing?" The question escaped before she could stop it.

"You say this boy's life means no more or less than the others'. You've seen neophytes die. Didn't you bury one yesterday?"

She didn't answer.

"I understood you shed tears at that child's death. You don't want to cry again, do you?"

*I hate you.*

"No answer, Lucita? No matter." Taking the rope from Father Patricio, he yanked. Off balance, the child had no choice but to lean against Sebastian's side.

"Stop it! You're hurting him."

"Hurt? You don't know the meaning of the word."

She'd felt both on fire and as if she might freeze since this insane conversation with her father began. Now both sensations attacked at the same time, and it was all she could do to remain in control of her senses.

"He is an innocent! He has nothing to do with this."

"But he does, Lucita. He does."

As if to lend weight to his words, Sebastian grabbed a handful of the boy's hair and pulled his head back, exposing his throat. Although her father's knife remained at his side, she had no doubt of what he was capable of.

"What do you want of me?" she asked, the words the most difficult she had ever spoken.

# 27

A wolf could never be taken prisoner. He'd seen it attempted once, leatherjackets wounding a juvenile and running it until the creature could no longer move. One of the men had thrown a rope over the wolf's head and then approached on foot, other ropes held ready to tie its legs. Any other wild animal would have given up, but not this one. With the last of its strength it had charged the leatherjacket, desperate teeth reaching for the man's throat, when no Chumash had ever had reason to fear a wolf attack.

The animal had died under a rain of blows as the other leatherjackets came to their fellow's defense, and Black Wolf would always believe it had sought its own death.

Today Black Wolf felt more animal than human. Trapped, not by a rope but by his inability to get any closer to the mission, he had no way of answering the questions pounding through him.

Something was wrong. Danger danced in the wind.

And his heart knew the danger was aimed at Lucita.

Three times he had attempted to approach the mission from different directions, but every one of the leatherjackets patrolled on horseback, more alert than he'd ever seen them. The neophytes continued to go about their chores although they often stopped to talk among themselves. Father Joseph was spending the day with those preparing hides for shipment, but although Black Wolf spotted Father Patricio several times, it seemed that the padre wasn't concerning himself with the mission's work.

Corporal Rodriguez didn't show himself until late afternoon. Then, striding with the weight and purpose of a man with much on his mind, he called one after another of his followers to him before going into his quarters.

Black Wolf saw no sign of Lucita. Once, her mother appeared at the sanctuary door and looked around, then went back inside, and although her actions puzzled him, he had no way of learning what she was doing.

As the sun began to set, he made up his mind. With the God of Night on his shoulder and Wolf in his heart, he would learn more even if uneasy teeth caused by Wolf's warnings nipped at him.

Even though her father had closed the shutters to the one window in the storeroom, enough light filtered in through the small crack that Lucita was able to take some small comfort from it. If she'd been able to see more, maybe she could distract herself by finding safe places for her mind to go.

"What do you want of me?" she had asked her father when fear for the boy Father Patricio called Yucca all but overwhelmed her. By way of answer, he'd tightened the rope around Yucca's neck, and she'd reacted like any mother animal protecting her young, but before she could attack her father, Father Patricio had grabbed her and then Pablo had burst in, ordering her released and demanding to be told what was happening.

Her father's explanation had been brief; he was determined to put an end to the danger from the Chumash, and his daughter was the key to getting his hands on Black Wolf. He was the mission's military commander and within his rights, and nothing Pablo said or did would change his course, eventually.

Maybe there was a spark of humanity in her father after all, she'd thought when he said the last; maybe he didn't hate her as much as she believed. And maybe he was willing to hold off on his plans while he worked at appeasing Pablo, whose wealth and ability to move among a great many people, some of them influential, carried weight.

Whichever it was, her father had locked her in here after informing her that he was giving her until nightfall to rethink her position. If she wasn't ready to reveal Black Wolf's location by then, he'd carry out his threat to kill Yucca.

Where was Yucca? Even with his hands tied, the boy had tried to slip away while the men were arguing, but her father had turned him back over to Father Patricio, and because she hadn't seen or spoken to anyone in the hours since then, she'd fought wave after wave of fear for the child.

And for Black Wolf.

When the bells announcing evening mass rang, she tried to distract herself by mentally placing herself inside the church, but the last time she'd been there it had been at her father's insistence. If God condoned her father's cruel treatment of Yucca, she didn't want to know, but how could it be otherwise? And how could she ever again pray to a God who allowed something like that to happen to a child?

God's will?

No!

By pressing her face against the slit between the two shutters, she was able to follow the lengthening shadows, but finally she could see nothing, not even her hand in front of her face. Her father hadn't said when he would come for her—not that that surprised her, because he wanted the waiting to tear at her. He was winning that battle, might have already won if it hadn't been for Black Wolf.

Was Black Wolf no more than a man, a brave, a warrior? Yes, he had grown larger in her mind because of his spiritual belief, but even when she told herself that his belief was no different from hers and couldn't possibly make him more than he was, some small but insistent part of her refused to believe that.

Because she had seen Wolf.

That was why she hadn't yet caved into her father even though he held Yucca's life in his hands. Every emotion and nerve in her screamed to put an end to Yucca's fear and suffering, but if she did that, she would be responsible for Black Wolf's death.

*Not dead! He couldn't die!*

She'd just pressed her hand to her throbbing forehead when she caught the whisper of a sound beyond the shutters. After a moment, the sound came again, perhaps closer this time. *Black Wolf!*

*No, please — please don't take the chance!*

"Lucita? Lucita, can you hear me?"

Unnerved by her mother's voice, Lucita had to swallow twice before she could make herself respond. "What are you doing here?" she asked as an image of Margarita, fluttering hand at her throat, eyes wide, with too much white showing, formed in her mind.

"You are all right," Margarita whispered. "Thank God."

"God had nothing to do with this," she hissed. "Where is he?"

"He? Your father?"

"Yes, my father." She nearly choked on the word. "Is he with you?"

"No."

"Where is he?"

"Drinking. Drinking and cursing. Lucita, there is so little time. You have to hurry."

She could hear her mother's ragged breathing, knew the older woman was fighting tears and fear, wondered not if but when Margarita's courage would desert her.

"You have to leave. Otherwise . . ."

*Otherwise my father will kill me, or force me to forfeit Black Wolf's life.*

"How did you know where to look for me?"

"Pablo."

Frowning, she realized she'd given the man who'd wanted to marry her only fleeting thought during her hours of imprisonment. He wasn't part of her life, not really. Free to come and go as he pleased, she had told herself, he'd waste no time putting distance between himself and what was happening at La Purisima.

True, he had intervened today, but in his place, she would want nothing more than to turn her back on the entire experience.

"Did you hear me?" her mother asked. "I have been with Pablo."

"He told you what happened?"

"I did not want to hear. My prayers—I told him I had to pray for your soul, and for your father's soul, but he would not be silent."

Only half-understanding what her mother was saying, Lucita mentally stretched her hand through the darkness until she found the older cheek.

"Lucita?" Margarita's voice caught. "It is better I never see you again than for your father to treat you this way."

"What are you saying?"

"Pablo will take you with him. He promised that the two of you will leave tonight. You will be safe."

*Leave? Free?* "What about you?"

Silence, hot and alive, stretched between them. Then her mother sighed. "Your father will not harm me with his men and the padres around. He knows they will talk and his commanders might consider him incompetent; he—he would do anything to prevent that from happening. It . . . Pablo told me he will take all blame, that everyone will believe it was him who stole you away."

"And Sebastian can save face. Yes, that would mean a great deal to him."

"Not just a great deal," Margarita whispered. "Maybe your father will leave me here and go somewhere else. I . . . I think I would like that."

"You really want . . ."

"I . . . there isn't time. He knows when to stop drinking. Soon he'll—can you run?"

"Yes." *In a heartbeat.*

Her mother's explanation was brief. Lucita was to count to thirty. By that time Margarita would have reached the door and lifted the lumber that held it in place. All Lucita had to do was slip through the opening. If God was on their side, the noise would be minimal and they could make their way to the corral where Pablo waited with two saddled horses. But if what they were doing alerted Sebastian or any of the other soldiers—Margarita didn't finish the sentence.

After waiting through the count, which seemed to take forever, as she reached the final numbers Lucita heard wood scraping against wood and then the leather hinges protesting. Placing her shoulder against the door, she pushed and stepped forward, joining her mother. Too close to hysteria, Lucita reached for her but managed only a half-embrace before Margarita began hurrying her through the dark.

Margarita stumbled twice, nearly pulling Lucita off balance as well, but somehow they reached the corral without falling or, Lucita prayed, drawing attention to themselves. Even as she half-walked, half-ran, she struggled to comprehend what she was doing, and the reality that she had no choice.

Not if she was going to live.

Or Yucca.

Or Black Wolf.

As her mother had told her, Pablo was at the corral, rocking back and forth in what she took to be agitation. Remembering what he'd witnessed earlier today, she struggled to face him; it didn't matter that they could barely see each other.

"Do you know what you are doing?" she forced herself to ask. "If my father learns you helped free me—"

"He will, because I have no intention of keeping the truth from him," Pablo said, his voice expressionless. She sensed movement and then felt his hand brushing against the side of her neck. "In fact, if I had not been concerned that he might take his wrath out on you or others who are dear to you, I would not have offered him a quantity of liquor. Instead, I would be confronting him as we speak."

"No! You don't know his wrath."

"His wrath." Pablo laughed but kept his voice low. "He has no jurisdiction over me, and he knows about my military and business connections. Lucita, the world is far more complex than what you have experienced here. There are forces, pressures on the military—never mind. We will have ample opportunity to discuss that once we are away from here."

*Away from here.* "I—"

"Lucita, please. Go now."

Margarita's voice, weighted with fear, gave her something to concentrate on. "I don't want to leave you, Mother. Pablo, can't she come with us?"

"No!" Margarita gasped. "It is all right. This is where the Lord wants me to be. He will look over me."

"But if Father divorces you—"

"Divorce?" Margarita spoke the word not as if it was something vile and incomprehensible, but almost as if it had become a friend. "As long as I can serve the Lord and you are safe, nothing else matters."

"But—"

"Lucita, go."

There was no changing her mother's mind. Still, the thought of never seeing her again stripped Lucita's muscles of strength. Ignoring the restless horses and Pablo's obvious impatience, she clasped her mother to her.

Tears seeking escape pounded at her temples, but she refused to let her mother's last memory of her be that of her sobbing. Perhaps Margarita felt the same way, because although her voice was husky, she sounded in control.

"I love you," she whispered. "I will always love you. From the moment of your birth, I prayed you would share my depth of faith, but you do not."

"No, I don't," she answered truthfully.

"Open your heart and soul. That is all I ask."

She had, she nearly said, but didn't because her mother would never understand what she'd found during her search. Still embracing the woman who had given her life, she focused on Pablo. "You don't have to do this," she said.

"I want to show you the world, dear lady."

*The world? She couldn't think beyond this moment, this place.* "Yucca, where is he?"

"With Father Patricio, I'm sorry to say."

"No!" Afraid her outburst had carried, she clapped her hand over her mouth. "I can't leave him. I can't!"

Rocks scraped Black Wolf's knees and dug into the palms of his hands, but he ignored the discomfort and continued forward, careful to keep his body low to the ground. He had always wished he'd never been to this place and knew nothing about it, but tonight he was glad the mission was nearly as familiar to him as Humqaq.

His first stop had been at the infirmary, but although he'd risked detection by slipping inside, he'd seen no sign of Lucita and the woman he'd spoken to had said she hadn't seen her today. That wasn't right.

The sound of loud male voices had come from the barracks, and although he didn't take a chance on getting close to it, the shouts and laughter told him that the men, Sebastian included, were drinking.

Neither Lucita nor her mother were in their quarters; the silence told him that. He'd been about to make his way to the church when his straining ears picked up the sound of her voice but not what she was saying. Despite the night, the stars told him she wasn't alone; with her were her mother and the merchant. Slipping closer, Black Wolf saw that Pablo Portola held two saddled horses.

Two?

As he watched, Pablo grabbed Lucita's shoulders, but she silently fought him.

Without giving himself time to think, Black Wolf launched himself at the man, and they landed on the ground together. Taking advantage of the fact that the back of the man's head had struck the earth, Black Wolf yanked his knife free and pressed it against the exposed throat.

"Black Wolf, no!" Lucita stood over him.

"I will kill—"

"No!" Taut as a bowstring, she hovered over him. "Please, no."

"He would have hurt—"

"No, he wouldn't. Please, Black Wolf, Pablo is my . . . my friend."

"A friend does not inflict harm on another," he wanted to tell her, but her fear spoke to him.

"Let him up, please."

Two heartbeats became three and then four, but finally he did as she'd asked, not because rage didn't still hum through him, but because Lucita had asked and he couldn't refuse her. The man she'd called Pablo sat up and rubbed the back of his head. Although he was no longer touching Pablo, Black Wolf knew Lucita's "friend" had begun to tremble. Good. Fear made a man unwise in battle.

Standing so close that she could have grabbed the knife in a quick lunge, Lucita didn't acknowledge her mother, whose ragged breathing overrode every other sound.

"What are you doing here?" she demanded. "It's dangerous. So dangerous."

"I know."

"Then why—"

"Wolf."

Her hand now flattened against her chest, she stepped back. "Wolf," she repeated.

"His spirit came to me, whispered of great risk."

"But you came anyway. Why?"

"You."

Sucking in her breath, she reached out as if to touch him; then her arm dropped by her side and, in a voice choked with emotion, she told him everything that had happened that day.

"You are leaving with him?" he asked.

"I can't stay here."

"Lucita," her mother said anxiously. "You know him, don't you? Your father was right about that. How long—what—I do not believe this."

If Lucita wanted to explain, she would have to do it another time, because he'd already been here longer than was safe. "Go then," Black Wolf said. "Leave with that man, now."

Emotion rolled out of her, a wave of heat and feeling he didn't understand but couldn't ignore. "I can't," she managed.

*Because of me?*

"Not without Yucca," she said before he could ask the question that should only be between the two of them.

"Forget Yucca," Pablo said. "Lucita, you cannot help anyone except yourself."

"No. I—"

"Who is Yucca?" Black Wolf interrupted.

She told him with a minimum of words, but that didn't blunt his reaction. "He is with Father Patricio?" he forced himself to ask.

"Yes."

Yucca might be safe tonight, but as long as the boy remained with Father Patricio he was at risk, something Black Wolf knew all too well. "Stay here," he commanded. "I will free him."

"No!" Lucita grabbed his wrist, the touch sending lightning through him. "Black Wolf, if something happened to you . . ."

Covering her hand with his, he looked down at her. "Wolf walks at my side. The child belongs with me."

Black Wolf hadn't been inside the padres' private quarters since Lame Deer rescued him and had believed he would never again feel those hated walls close around him, but just as his grandfather had risked everything for him, he would do the same for Yucca.

After leaving the others, he'd made his way to the small, solid building. Now, although a part of him remained with Lucita, he concentrated on what had to be done. Lucita would leave with Pablo and be safe with him; the man had been urging her to get on one of the horses. Her mother, crying now, had been saying the same thing. As for Lucita, she'd held onto his arm until he pulled free but said nothing.

He had no words for her either, just the prayer that she would find happiness in the world of her birth.

The arched door to where the padres lived was closed and might be locked from the inside, but its greatest weakness was in the leather hinges. Using the knife that had so recently been at

Pablo's neck, Black Wolf sliced through what he could reach of the leather and then stepped back.

He would have only a few seconds in which to act, sudden attack followed by grabbing the child and running. Maybe, if Wolf's strength was in his hand, his knife would find Father Patricio's throat, and although killing the padre might spell his doom and maybe the end to everything his people still had, he wanted to watch the man die.

There wasn't time to think of death, only time for action.

When he shoved, his shoulder encountered more resistance than he'd expected, but he continued to push, his feet digging into the earth. Finally the barrier gave way and the door crashed to the ground, nearly taking him with it.

Father Patricio had been sitting at his table, a candle spilling light onto an open Bible, but he'd already sprung to his feet by the time Black Wolf entered. The priest's mouth, opened in disbelief, revealed yellowed teeth. Yucca, kneeling in front of the padre, looked just as shocked.

"Yucca!" Black Wolf ordered. "Come. Now."

The boy's head jerked back as if he'd been slapped, but before Black Wolf had to repeat himself, he stood. Lucita had said that Father Patricio had tied the boy's hands, but he was free now. Yucca took a hesitant step toward Black Wolf, then looked back at Father Patricio.

"Black Wolf!" The padre's eyes glittered with candle-red highlights. "What are you—"

"No more!"

Although the collapsing door had made enough noise that surely everyone at the mission had heard, these few seconds with Father Patricio had to be. His knife in his upraised hand, Black Wolf started toward the other man, who reacted by grabbing the Bible and clutching it to his chest.

"You call yourself a man of god?" Black Wolf asked. "There is evil in you. No savage would do what you do. You call yourself civilized. I call you Devil."

"Go away. My God, go away."

It would take so little to free Father Patricio's blood from his veins; just a quick, hard slice of the knife and Black Wolf could forget what he'd endured at the man's hands.

"Devil," he repeated.

"Help!" Father Patricio screeched. "Help!"

The hot smell of urine reached Black Wolf, and from Yucca's reaction he knew the boy had noticed it as well. A quick lunge, knife blade against flesh, and the smell of blood would fill the room.

"Help! Help!"

"Black Wolf!" Lucita screamed from behind him. "Run!"

# 28

Reaching out with his free hand, Black Wolf grabbed Yucca's arm and pulled him close, then turned and ran. Yucca stumbled over the collapsed door, but Black Wolf held on, and in a couple of seconds the boy had regained his balance.

Despite the dark, Black Wolf was able to make out several figures running toward them from the leatherjackets' barracks. Instinct said that safety lay in putting the mission behind him, but it was no longer that simple.

Changing direction, he sprinted toward Lucita, dragging Yucca behind him, because she had yelled out a warning and he couldn't leave without acknowledging what she'd done.

"Black Wolf, please!" she grasped. "Leave! Take him and go!"

"Come with me."

A heartbeat passed and then she took a half-step toward him; he sensed the emotion behind her movement and felt his heart swell.

"What is it?" Sebastian bellowed from somewhere behind him. "What is happening?"

"Black Wolf!" Father Patricio screamed. "He tried to kill me!"

"Did you?" Lucita insisted. "Did you?"

"Yes!"

The pounding footsteps increased in strength, and despite the disorganized cries, he knew it would only be a matter of seconds before the leatherjackets found him.

"Come with me," he repeated.

"Lucita, no!" Voice trembling, the mother locked her arms around her daughter. "He tried to kill—"

"Get out of here, Black Wolf!" It was Pablo. "Go, now!"

Black Wolf couldn't touch Lucita without letting go of Yucca or his knife, and he didn't dare do either. Just the same, he felt her along the length of his body and in his heart and prayed it was the same for her. "Lucita?"

"I can't. Oh, God, I can't!"

It was over between them. This time he might never understand had ended with her words, and because the name of her God had escaped her lips.

Whirling, he ran toward the space between the corral and the grain storage shed, no longer needing to hold onto Yucca, whose speed suddenly matched his. Just beyond them darkness and freedom waited. He would be safe there, he and this child who was so much what he'd once been and what his own son would be in a few years. And nothing else mattered.

Once again Father Patricio cried out, but Black Wolf didn't try to make sense of what the man was saying. Sebastian, sounding too close, cursed, but Black Wolf didn't waste time trying to determine where he was; instead he continued to run. Once again Yucca stumbled and fell, instantly stopping Black Wolf. The child cried out, his high voice telling the leatherjackets where they were.

"Get up!" Black Wolf insisted. "Run!"

"My ankle—"

Leaning down, he grabbed Yucca around the waist and hauled him to his feet. "You must!" he ordered. Before he could say another word, he heard a sound like thunder and something hard and hot slammed into his side.

Yucca screamed.

Despite the sudden awful burning, Black Wolf felt light-headed, and his knees threatened to buckle, but if he lost his footing, he would become a deer whose legs had been shredded by a wolf's teeth.

*Wolf, hear me! Give me strength.*

"Run, Yucca," he ordered. "Run for your life!"

Had Black Wolf been shot? Lucita thought she'd seen him stagger immediately after the musket's explosion, but she couldn't make herself face that awful possibility. All that mattered was that by the time her father and the others reached where she'd last seen or thought she'd seen Black Wolf, he and Yucca had fled.

She couldn't say for sure how much time had passed since then. After milling about for several minutes, two of the soldiers had run back to their quarters and returned with several burning branches, which they used to light the area where Black Wolf and Yucca had last been seen.

It *had* been Black Wolf, an excited Father Patricio insisted. The savage had broken into his bedroom, stolen Yucca from him, and certainly would have killed him if Lucita hadn't cried out.

"You warned him, didn't you?" Her father loomed over her. Even in his stocking feet and his breath smelling of whiskey, he remained a formidable presence. Her mother, who had risked so much by freeing her, stood beside her, as did a remarkably composed Pablo.

"What do you want me to say?" she asked her father, feeling strangely detached. "You heard me."

"Oh, yes, I did."

He'd laid down his musket, but although she believed he wanted nothing more than to strike her, his hands remained fisted at his sides.

"Do you want me to apologize?" she asked, challenged maybe. "I won't. Nothing you do or say will change what I did. I . . . I am not sorry."

"My daughter," he said, his voice cold, "if I had one, would not have made a mockery of her heritage." He seemed about to say more, but perhaps he had remembered how many ears would hear what passed between them. Turning toward his wife, he demanded an explanation.

"I freed her." Although soft, Margarita's voice carried more conviction than Lucita had ever heard from her. "I will not have her treated like a criminal."

"You disobeyed me? How dare you!"

Instinct warned Lucita to do nothing more to incur her father's wrath, but it was too late for that. "Don't blame her," she insisted. "It is me you hate, not her."

"Hate?" He leaned closer. "Hate! I wish you were dead."

Pablo, who had said little, stood only a few feet away. She thought he might intercede in her behalf or attempt to calm her father, but he remained a silent and strangely impassive figure.

Before she could think of what, if anything, to say, one of the soldiers called out that there was something Sebastian needed to see. As he stalked away, Margarita clamped cold fingers around Lucita's shoulder.

"Go, now. Before—Pablo, please make her . . ."

"Yes!" Sebastian cried triumphantly. "I knew I had hit him."

*Black Wolf wounded?* Casting caution aside, Lucita rushed over to where her father was staring at the ground. At first she saw nothing, but then someone moved one of the burning brands and she spotted the dark, glistening stain.

Dropping to her knees, she touched the damp pool with a trembling finger. Her nerve endings recorded a telltale stickiness, and when she brought her finger to her nose she smelled blood.

*She'd known it; buried where she'd hoped she wouldn't have to acknowledge it was the memory of how, for a few seconds, strength had left Black Wolf and he'd come close, too close, to falling.*

"No!"

Back on her feet now, she struck out, connecting with her father's side. Cursing, he shoved her away, then came after her. Grabbing her, he began to shake her so violently that her head snapped from side to side.

"Stop it!" Whoever had yelled—she couldn't concentrate on

anything except her father's fury—was trying to pull them apart. "Corporal, stop it!"

"No daughter . . . no daughter of mine—"

"My husband, for God's sake, you are killing her!" This from several feet away.

"God?" Sebastian bellowed. "No! She is the devil's child!"

Her father's right hand was being ripped off her, his nails tearing through fabric and gouging her flesh. From somewhere deep inside she summoned the strength to fight him herself, kicking and sinking her teeth into his left wrist like the wild animals the padres said the Chumash were. Bellowing, he swung at her. His fist connected with the side of her jaw; her knees buckled, and she fell.

On hands and knees, she shook her head in a desperate attempt to clear her senses while above her the sounds of a violent struggle, blows and curses, filled the air. Once again her mother screamed, sounding no more civilized than she felt. First one and then both of the horses squealed. Although the world around her refused to come into focus, Lucita forced herself to stand.

Suddenly the fighting stopped; nothing was left of it except deep and ragged breathing, and by slow degrees she made sense of what had happened. Her father and Pablo had come to blows and blood flowed from each of their noses, but neither looked beaten. Rather, like enraged dogs, they stood glaring at each other while the soldiers, the padres, and her mother looked on.

Pablo spoke first. "Nothing has changed, Lucita," he said, his tone an island of calm in an insane world. "I still intend to leave tonight. I trust your father has the decency to allow you to collect your belongings so you can accompany me."

Not speaking or acknowledging her, Sebastian scooped up his musket and started toward the horse corral.

"What are you doing?" Lucita demanded, although she already knew.

If Sebastian heard her—and he must have—he gave no indication. "I have no daughter," he had said.

"Lucita." Pablo spoke softly, his breathing already under control. "It is time to leave."

"You will take her?" Margarita, crying, asked. "Keep her safe?"

"I promise."

Margarita sobbed and made the sign of the cross. "Thank you," she murmured. "Thank you. Lucita?"

Her father had become one of several shadows touched by torchlight. In a moment he would slip into the corral, select one of the horses, saddle and bridle it, and ride out after Black Wolf and Yucca—Black Wolf who might be dying.

"Lucita?"

An animal with sharp teeth had clamped its jaws around Black Wolf's side and refused to let go. The pain receded just a little when he didn't breathe or move, but if he gave into the need to do those things, his life would end before morning.

Yucca had asked him twice about his injury, crying a little when he didn't answer, but after that the boy had fallen silent. As long as they were on level ground, Black Wolf was able to walk unaided, but whenever he tried to climb, his legs turned into those of an old man and he was forced to loop his arm around the boy's shoulder for support.

His wound had bled profusely at first, but now when he touched it, he found no fresh blood, thanks to the dried grass he'd pressed against his side. As long as he continued to move, strength would remain in him, but if he stopped for any length of time, he might not be able to stand again.

Wolf had warned him of danger. If he'd been a wise man, he would have heeded the warning and would have never returned to the enemy place, but his heart had beaten with fear for Lucita, and wisdom had turned into frost before a bright sun.

"Do not leave me, Wolf," he whispered. "Listen to the words of a foolish man and tell me what I must do."

"Black Wolf," Yucca said anxiously. "Who are you talking to?"

"My spirit."

"Your . . . spirit?"

Had Yucca been taken so far from his heritage that he didn't know what the word meant? Before Black Wolf could make himself ask the question, the answer came to him in memories of what he'd been like when Lame Deer brought him back to the people of his birth.

"I speak of ancient things, Chumash wisdom," he said around the gnawing in his side. "When we are where we belong, I will tell you. Show you."

"How? The soldiers are following us; you know they are."

Soldiers, not leatherjackets, but perhaps it was better that today's children spoke a new way. "I know," he said, then stopped and listened. His heart put him in mind of a drum in the hands of an angry child, making it difficult for him to hear anything else, and he asked Yucca to listen with him.

"Nothing," Yucca said after a while. "Maybe . . ."

"Maybe what?"

"I am not sure. Black Wolf, are we safe out here? Father Patricio said wolves and bears would attack me if I tried to leave."

"Wolf is my brother. He will not harm you."

"Your brother—" Yucca started, then stopped.

In the distance, the morning sun was beginning to make its presence known as a thin band of light and promise from the east. Humqaq lay to the west. Humqaq. Home.

Too late.

Too late.

Straightening in the saddle, Lucita pressed her hand against the back of her neck in an attempt to work the tension out of her, but even a lungful of air wasn't enough to push the horrible thought from her mind.

Hours ago, she'd grabbed the horse Pablo had saddled for her and galloped away from the mission, leaving behind her crying mother and a silent, staring Pablo. Lucita had tried to tell herself that her father couldn't possibly care what she did, but the attempt at self-deception didn't last because Sebastian was at his core a soldier and the same drive that had sent her in search of Black Wolf and Yucca ruled him.

Her father, whom she had to admire despite everything, had hunted down many an enemy over the course of his career. He didn't know which way Black Wolf had gone and that would slow and frustrate him, but he would search until he had the answer. She had no doubt of that.

If she were Black Wolf and wounded, what would she do and where would she go? Those were the twin questions that had sent her toward the hills, because if nothing except the instinct for survival was left, surely Black Wolf would want to return to his people. The shamans—that was what the Chumash called their healers, wasn't it?—were there, and he needed their care. But even more important, his son was in the village.

Would Black Wolf want his son to see him the way she imagined him? After hours of riding and occasionally hiding from the scattered but searching soldiers, she believed she had the answer, not because of what she knew about the man, but because of what she'd learned about blood ties from her mother. When she thought her daughter's life was at risk, Margarita had put that daughter's life before everything else.

Black Wolf wanted and needed his son.

When her horse attempted to stop to graze, Lucita dug her heels into the animal's side, grateful that dawn had begun to touch her world even if that increased the risk of the soldiers spotting her. As she caught her first glimpse of the distant hills where Black Wolf said his people lived, she tried to imagine him making his way there, his need for his son lending strength to his legs.

*No!*

How could she have been so stupid! Yanking on the reins, she pulled the horse to a quick stop. She'd thought she'd found the answer to where to search for Black Wolf in her mother's behavior but hadn't looked at the whole of it. True, Margarita had risked everything by coming to Lucita's defense, but her action hadn't been either rash or unthinking. Before freeing her, Margarita had made sure Pablo was willing to take her to safety. And Margarita had believed the padres would protect her from her husband's wrath.

Black Wolf knew what Sebastian was capable of, his need for revenge. He wouldn't risk his son's life by going to him now.

*Where, then?*

The wilderness that had felt right and comfortable such a

short while ago now loomed in all directions. How could she possibly find the warrior in this vastness?

"Rest, please. You will kill yourself if you keep going."

"I will rest when I have reached the home of my ancestors."

Yucca groaned but didn't say anything. Nothing remained of night, which made their traveling easier. Black Wolf's side, although it still throbbed, no longer commanded so much of his attention, and he felt less like a dying animal trying to return to its den. A few minutes ago, at his prompting, Yucca had dug up some roots and bulbs so they had something to eat, and although he was still thirsty, the food had revived him a little. At the rate they were moving and needing to sleep before much longer, it would be late tomorrow before they reached Humqaq. He still believed that bathing in the sacred water would do more for his body than anything the shaman gave him, but during the hours of walking and thinking the need to see the hidden falls had become less overpowering.

He'd told Yucca about Humqaq, where it lay, and the centuries-old trail leading to it and had been relieved to learn that the boy had heard about the place. Perhaps, Black Wolf thought, the time would come when the leatherjackets and padres left this land and the Chumash would be free to return to the way of their ancestors.

Perhaps.

All about them were songbirds, some of them blending into their world, others marked by bright blues, reds, and yellows, trying to fill their small but always hungry stomachs. Pointing to a tree with a woodpecker on it, Black Wolf was explaining that their feathers were used in *Po 'n kakunupmawa,* the sun pole, during winter solstice ceremonies when a new, deep sound caught his attention.

Yucca heard it, too. "Horse," the boy said.

# 29

The land lay barren in all directions, the dry rolling hills lulling Lucita's senses until she could barely remember what had brought her out here or whom she'd left behind. She carried with her the memory of Pablo's last words to her, and for some reason they held more weight than what her mother had said.

"You have to make a decision, Lucita," he'd said. "You. No one else can."

She didn't know whether he'd still be there when she returned, if she returned, or whether there was anything between them.

Not that it mattered today.

Only Black Wolf did. Black Wolf who lived in a world far different from her own.

Straightening and stretching her back as she'd already done more times than she cared to admit, she forced herself to concentrate on her surroundings. She'd wondered if she'd spot any of the soldiers now, but the land's vastness had consumed them.

The trail she was on had been laid down by generations of Chumash feet, and although it was seldom used these days, she prayed—not sure whom she was praying to—that the time would come when the Indians were once again free to openly make the journey to Humqaq.

Maybe she would bring her mother here, maybe even her father.

A flash of red against a tree's dark background distracted her from the insane thought. Black Wolf had told her that woodpeckers were highly prized because of their bright feathers, which were used in a number of ceremonies, and that whoever killed one of the birds always prayed to the tiny creature's soul.

*Do you have a soul, little bird? Black Wolf believes you do, you and the tree you are on, the ground from which the tree grows, the sky above, the smallest insect.*

The woodpecker paid her no mind, its beak drumming with surprising strength against the trunk. It must be seeking out insects to eat, but if Black Wolf was right and even ants and grubs had souls, did the woodpecker ask forgiveness every time it filled its stomach?

The question was the product of a mind too long without sleep, she told herself as she let her horse pick its way over a jumble of rocks. If she did manage to make it all the way to Humqaq, perhaps she would bathe where Black Wolf had, hoping the cold water would revive her.

If Black Wolf gave her his blessing to do so.

Something moved, the movement not quick and random like that of a bird and too large for the country's small animals yet not big enough to be that of a soldier. Standing her ground, she waited for whoever it was to reveal himself.

"Yucca?"

The boy came toward her, his hand upraised to shield his eyes from the sun. From his jerky gait she guessed he'd been on his feet for hours, but her sense of relief at having found him was greater than any concern for his physical condition.

"I knew—I hoped . . . ," she began. Then the only question that truly mattered burst from her. "Where is he?"

Yucca pointed behind him. "He waits for you."

There was something profound about Yucca's words, she soon discovered, although she found Black Wolf sitting on an exposed tree root, his legs outstretched as if he had nothing better to do than watch the day's dawning. Unable to bring her gaze to his side, she concentrated on his bright and clear eyes, the way his hair clung to his neck, his deep, even breathing.

Barely aware of what she was doing, she dismounted and hurried over to him but stopped when she was still too far away to touch him, suddenly scared.

"You knew where I was going," he said.

"Yes, finally."

"How?"

"I . . . I don't know."

"I think different."

A gust of wind skipped over her cheek and calmed her a little. "At first," she said, "I had no idea how to go about finding you, but I tried to put myself in your place. If I was a wounded Chumash warrior, I would need to go to Humqaq."

He nodded and made a move as if to get to his feet, but instead of completing the gesture, he remained sitting, and she settled herself on the ground a few feet away.

"I prayed . . ." She swallowed and began again. "I was afraid you had been so badly injured that—"

"I am not." He lifted the wad of grass away from his side and showed her a raw furrow surrounded by healthy flesh. "At first my mind closed down and I was like an animal seeking a place to die, but Wolf walked with me last night."

If Black Wolf believed that, it was the truth.

"You did not stay with your people," he said.

*My people?* "No."

"Why not?"

"I don't know!" she cried out, shocked that she'd revealed so much. "Everything happened so fast. I was afraid for Yucca and for you and the soldiers were yelling and trying to decide where to look for you and my mother was crying and I—maybe what I did made no more sense than your decision to go to Humqaq."

He said nothing to indicate his reaction to her explanation, but she thought she saw empathy, maybe even understanding, in the way he continued to look at her.

Yucca stood behind her and to her left, but although she wanted to ask the boy how he was and try to explain why her father and Father Patricio had done what they had—as if she had words for that—her eyes had bonded with Black Wolf's and everything else would have to wait.

"What are you going to do?" she asked. "Continue on to Humqaq?"

"Yes."

*Good.* "And after that?"

Lifting his left hand, he first ran it through his hair and then used it to scrub his cheek. "I do not know."

*Not know? No!* "But you have to." She couldn't keep the desperation out of her voice. "Your son—you want to see him, don't you?"

"Yes. But this morning that is all I am sure of."

Maybe that wasn't so bad after all, she told herself. He had been wounded, after all. Naturally he had suffered some degree of shock, and with that, along with the loss of blood and the hours he'd spent walking, she couldn't expect him to be as clearheaded as he'd always been.

"I know it seems as if there's incredible distance between Humqaq and your village, but after you've rested a bit, you'll be able to return."

"And after that?"

She was sitting in such a way that a rock dug into her thigh, but she couldn't put her mind to how she might end the discomfort, not now that Black Wolf had thrown his question at her. Now that it was light, her father or some of the soldiers might have come across the trail with her horse's hoofprints on it and be on their way here, but that, too, had to wait.

"I can't answer that for you," she told him. "I am not Chumash."

"But you knew where I would go."

"Y-es, finally."

"Tell me, when you prayed, were your prayers to your God?"

*No.* "Don't ask me that! I'm so confused right now. I can't believe I did what I did, leaving like that."

The desperation in her voice shocked her into silence. Staring at her hands, she gave up trying to avoid his question. Yes, she had prayed—she would never try to tell either of them otherwise—but that wasn't what had thrown her into so much turmoil.

"Do not retreat from me, Lucita," he prodded. "It must not be like that between us."

"I know." Saying that made things a little easier. "I—you are Chumash. You've shown me what it is to be Chumash. And when I was afraid for you, I prayed to your gods."

"Are you still afraid?"

What was he trying to do to her? "Yes." With an effort, she kept from looking back the way she'd come. "My father will never give up. He'll hunt for you until—"

"And for you."

"Yes! Yes, for me, too. Is that what you want me to say?"

"I do not want for us to be together like this or for last night to have happened, but I cannot change the truth. Lucita?" He leaned forward and locked his gaze on her until she had no choice but to return it.

"You are afraid for yourself, are you not?" he asked.

"Yes."

"Ah. And a man or woman stalked by fear turns to help beyond him- or herself. When you think of yourself, who are your prayers to?"

Her father had called him a savage. Her mother and the padres believed the Indians were simpleminded, but that was because they didn't know them the way she knew Black Wolf; the others hadn't been allowed close to a Chumash heart.

A rustling sound behind her distracted her, or maybe the truth was she allowed herself to be distracted. Yucca had brought her horse close and was removing its saddle. She thanked him for tending to it and then asked Black Wolf when he would start for Humqaq again.

"Not until night," he told her, his eyes no less intent than they'd been when he asked his question. "Today I hide, and rest."

"Of course." After repositioning her legs, she ran her hands over the ground until she found a dry oak leaf, which she crumbled between her fingers.

"What about you, Lucita? What will you do?"

Opening her hand, she let the crushed leaf fall to the ground. She reached down to pick up another but left it where it was. There was nothing here to slow the wind, and it made a singing sound as it slipped along the ground pushing the grasses first one direction and then another. She spotted a trio of butterflies either caught in the breeze or relishing the random movement.

"I think I would like to be a butterfly," she said. "To let the wind guide everything I do."

"You are not a butterfly, Lucita."

"No." She sighed. "I'm not."

Although he said nothing, she felt and understood his unspoken question.

"I don't know what I'm going to do."

Both Yucca and Lucita had fallen asleep. From where he sat, Black Wolf was able to keep an eye on them, the grazing horse, and perhaps a quarter-mile of the ancient trail they'd already covered.

Lucita slept like a child with her knees drawn up against her body and her head resting on her bent arm. She'd admitted she was hungry, but although he offered to tell her what roots were safe to eat, she'd muttered that that could come later and then stretched out on the ground.

The effort of standing forced him to grind his teeth together, but if he didn't move, his body would stiffen. Leaning against a tree, he took in his surroundings until they were as familiar to him as his son's face.

Lucita had been right. Nothing mattered more to him than Fox Running. His son's memory had given him the strength to keep going through the night and even now forced him to look into the future when he wanted his mind to remain still and silent.

Never again would he go to the mission. As long as the corporal and Father Patricio remained there, the risk was too great—

not that he wanted it otherwise today. He belonged here, at Humqaq, or in his village surrounded by his people with his son by his side.

Perhaps, then, he had not lost so much. Some blood, yes, but nothing else that mattered. More than that, he had repaid his debt to his grandfather by giving Yucca his freedom. Like Black Wolf, the boy would feel like an outsider at first, but with each passing day he would become more Chumash and less neophyte.

Lucita had lost everything.

Maybe.

The man called Pablo had offered her a new way to live. If she returned to him, she could leave the mission and put her father's hatred behind her and even if she never saw her mother again, at least she would be safe.

And happy?

Pushing away from the tree, he waited until he was sure his legs would hold him, then walked over to Lucita and knelt beside her.

"I wish I could walk this journey for you," he whispered. "If you had been born Chumash, you would turn to your spirit for the truth within your heart, but that is not so. The search must be your own."

She stirred and muttered something he couldn't understand but didn't waken. When she was once again still, he leaned forward and touched his lips to her closed eyes.

"Lucita! Yucca! Awake!"

Galvanized by Black Wolf's shout, Lucita surged to her feet. Still half-asleep, she rubbed her eyes, then looked wildly around.

Black Wolf stood beside her horse, the reins caught in his strong fingers. With his other hand, he pointed.

"Soldiers!" Yucca gasped. "They see us?"

"Not yet," Black Wolf answered.

But soon. There were three of them, the lead figure all too familiar. "Run!" she screamed at Black Wolf. "You have to run."

"I cannot."

The awful finality in his voice tore through her, and, stumbling a little, she hurried to his side. "On horseback!" she insisted. "Please. You can do it."

"I will not leave you."

"*I will not leave you.*" As the sound of approaching hoofbeats reached her, she took Black Wolf's free hand and held it against her breasts.

"My father won't kill me. No matter what he said, he won't."

"He may make you wish you were dead."

How did this man know so much about her and the people who made up her life? "No, no," she tried to deny. "Pablo. My mother, the padres—"

"Not Father Patricio."

"But the others." No matter how hard she tried, she couldn't keep desperation out of her voice. "They wouldn't—"

"Is it what you want?"

Not knowing what he was talking about, or maybe the truth was she wasn't ready to face the question, she increased her grip on his wrist. He was part of this land, *was* this land. If he died, something precious and timeless would die with him.

"Yucca," she gasped as the approaching horses broke into a canter. "You have to think of him."

Not trying to break free, Black Wolf held the reins out to Yucca. "Go," he ordered the boy. "To Humqaq. What I told you about it will guide you there, and my friend will find you."

Although Yucca's eyes were wide with fright, he managed to hoist himself onto the horse's bare back. "Black Wolf, please," he begged. "Come with me."

A shake of the head served as Black Wolf's answer. A heartbeat later, he lunged forward and slapped the horse's rump. As the animal sprang forward, he turned back toward her.

"What do you want, Lucita?" he asked.

# 30

────────

Her father and the two soldiers with him reached them before Lucita's mind could do more than slam up against Black Wolf's question. Every nerve in her screamed at the warrior to run, but she was thinking with a woman's mind when forces she'd just begun to understand ruled him.

He was magnificent, wild and yet controlled, boldly facing the man who'd tried to kill him.

Sebastian yanked his horse to such a violent stop that the animal screamed. The others remained behind him, obviously deferring to their commander. Pulling his sword free from where it hung on the saddle, Sebastian aimed it at Black Wolf's chest.

"No!" Without a thought to her own safety, she placed herself between the two men.

"Get away from him!" Sebastian ordered.

"No. I won't let you hurt him. Don't you understand, I can't!"

Black Wolf grabbed her and tried to move her aside, but when she resisted he ceased his efforts, and she gave silent thanks. His hands remained on her, drawing her father's attention to that.

"You are his whore!" Sebastian's cheeks flamed red. "My daughter, a savage's whore."

"No! I'm pure. A virgin."

"You think I would believe anything you say?"

"That is your decision, Corporal." What she'd just said made her throat burn, but she wasn't sorry. Only then did she realize Pablo was on her father's left. Something crackled in the air between the two men, but she didn't dare allow herself to be distracted by it.

"I will not run from you," Black Wolf said, his tone calm, cold. "It is time for us to stand face-to-face."

She expected her father to shout Black Wolf down or, worse, finish what he'd begun last night, but for one of the few times in his life, the man said and did nothing. He looked old this morning, not beaten, but something had been lost. It was as if he'd left something of the soldier behind.

"I am Chumash," Black Wolf continued. "Once I cowered from the leatherjackets, but if I allow that to happen again, I can no longer call myself a man."

"A man!" The soldier snorted. "You are a savage."

"To you, perhaps. But that is because you have chosen not to understand the ways of my people. What say you, Corporal? Do you believe the same as him?"

The good side of her father's mouth worked; then, still silent, he clamped his lips together and turned his attention from Black Wolf back to her.

"You have made your bed, Lucita." He bit out the words but spoke softly. "Now you must spend the rest of your life in it."

Had she? Intent on the drama taking place around her, she felt a lifetime away from knowing the answer to that. Before she could begin to comprehend what faced her, Pablo urged his horse close to her father's. Nothing about the way he carried himself or the look in his eyes gave away what he was thinking. Had it just been a few days ago that she'd sat talking to him about the life they could share, the world beyond Alta California that they would explore together? She'd thought she'd wanted it—had wanted it—but now . . .

"What is in your heart, Corporal?" Black Wolf broke the silence. "Is it in you to see me as your equal? To settle this thing between us man to man?"

"Let me have at him, Corporal," the soldier hissed. Lifting his musket, he aimed it at Black Wolf's chest. "One shot, that's all it'll take."

"No!" Once again she squared herself in front of Black Wolf, but this time he easily pushed her aside. Looking up, she found something in his eyes that kept her where he'd placed her. A warrior, those beautiful and expressive eyes said, did not hide behind a woman's skirts, even if those skirts might save his life.

"Lucita?" Pablo pressed. "This is between your father and him. What is it going to be? Either you return with me, or I leave alone."

Pablo represented her one and only way out of this existence. In her heart she believed this confrontation between her father and Black Wolf would have come whether she was part of it or not. Black Wolf didn't need her, not in any way she could see or touch, and what did he have to offer her? Certainly nothing like Pablo did.

"What is it going to be, Lucita?" Sebastian asked.

How had her body become so heavy? It took every ounce of strength she possessed just to stand upright. "You don't understand!" she cried.

"I understand enough."

Maybe her father did. She would never again be the child waiting for one of his rare hugs, never again know what it was like to be protected by his position in life. Pablo was offering her protection and security while maybe all she'd ever know with Black Wolf was running and hiding.

No. Black Wolf had made a vow to never run again, and his decision might kill him today.

"Leave," Black Wolf said.

"You can't—"

"Lucita, your way is not mine. You will never understand what it is to be Chumash."

Nothing had ever hurt as much as his rejection; she bled in places that would never show but would leave her scarred for the rest of her life. Only dimly aware of what she was doing, she stepped away from Black Wolf, but instead of walking toward Pablo, she remained apart from everyone.

The air smelled of heat and summer, of dirt and rocks and dry grass, but there was more to it than that . . . a hint of something—

The sea.

Humqaq.

Wolf had been at Humqaq.

Closing her eyes, she searched within herself for the memory. There'd been a closeness between Black Wolf and his spirit that transcended anything she'd ever experienced, as if warrior and beast shared a single mind, a single thought, the same heart even.

"Lucita?"

Pablo. But she couldn't think of anything except that extraordinary memory. Eyes again open, she fixed her gaze on Black Wolf, who seemed to have forgotten where he was and stared, not at the men who had come to kill him, but at the horizon.

Throwing back his head, he stretched his arms toward the sky. The howl began deep in his chest, rose slowly, first touched the air, and then became part of it. Pablo, who had begun to back his horse, stopped. Her father increased his grip on his musket, as did the soldier with him, but no one spoke.

Black Wolf's howl went on and on like a restless and endless wind, both beautiful and hard, ancient and utterly right. His eyes were nearly shut and she couldn't see anything of that most expressive part of him. Crying a little because of the loss, she discovered that her own throat was trying to make the same sound, trying and maybe succeeding, but she couldn't be sure because only what Black Wolf was doing mattered.

"Silence!" her father bellowed. "If you are trying to call your warriors—Lucita, what in the name of the devil are you doing?"

*Trying to understand, maybe trying to find myself.*

A dark mist began to form at the base of a great spreading oak at the top of the nearest rise. She might not have yet noticed it if Black Wolf hadn't opened his eyes and she hadn't followed the line of his relentless gaze. After taking a deep breath, Black Wolf again called out and the mist grew and took on shape and definition. Shaking, she stepped toward the form but stopped when she could no longer sense the warrior's presence.

"What . . ."

"The devil!"

"No, not a devil," she told her father. "Wolf."

If anything, she felt weaker than she had a few minutes ago, and yet she would somehow find the strength she needed for whatever was happening. All eyes were now on the massive creature slowly walking toward them. From behind her, someone moved, but she couldn't make herself look at anything except Wolf.

Black Wolf began chanting in the harsh and yet lyrical Chumash language. Wolf was his spirit, whom he trusted to show him the way to walk in both this world and the one that came afterward. Black Wolf had opened his soul and heart to accept Wolf and, because of that, feared nothing. He didn't want to leave his son, but if that was what Wolf had decided for him, he would accept.

"You can't die!" she cried. "I won't let—Black Wolf, please."

"Damnation, what is happening?"

Her father would have to find his own answers, because Black Wolf cared about nothing except greeting Wolf and she couldn't take her eyes, her emotions, her soul, off what was taking place between a man and his spirit.

Looking as if he existed in a world all his own, Black Wolf stretched his arms even farther and waited. Wolf, glossy fur shining in the morning sun, superbly muscled body striding effortlessly, headed unerringly toward the warrior.

*You cannot die. If you do, I will die with you.*

In just a few more heartbeats, the two would meet and she could cease her desperate prayer because Wolf, surely, would not let anything happen to Black Wolf.

A new sound spun her around, shattering her although she already knew what caused it. The soldier had placed his musket against his shoulder, his arms ridged to support its weight, the barrel aimed at Wolf. Before she could so much as cry out, an explosion split the air.

Wolf had to have been hit! No more than fifty feet separated soldier and animal, and the man's grip on the weapon had been so steady, his features so determined.

Wolf—

"You missed!" her father bellowed.

"No! I didn't—here, I'll show you!"

Urging his horse close to her father, he dropped his weapon and snatched his commander's musket. By contrast, Black Wolf still hadn't moved a muscle and seemed unaware of what was taking place around him, as did Wolf, who continued walking toward the warrior.

Shocked into immobility, Lucita watched the soldier load and prime her father's musket, barely breathed as he again aimed at Wolf. She could have tried to stop him, but—

The second blast was even more terrible and forced a shriek from her. This time Wolf glanced at the soldier, but that was all. No red stain ruined his magnificent coat.

"You can't kill him!" she cried out as strength flowed through her veins. "You can't because he isn't of this world."

"No! I swear, Corporal. I swear . . ."

What did she care what her father and the soldier said to each other? Ignoring them, she focused on Black Wolf and his spirit as they came together, absorbed the energy and love between them, and believed that a little of that love touched her as well. With his arm now resting on Wolf's shoulder, Black Wolf acknowledged her.

"I heard you call to him," he said to her. "The sound came from your heart?"

By way of answer, she extended her hand toward the massive carnivore. After a moment, Wolf touched her fingers with a cool, moist nose and she didn't ask how he could have substance and be impossible to kill because she knew that he existed as flesh and blood only for those who understood, who believed.

"Lucita?" For the first time in her life, she heard uncertainty in her father's voice. "What—"

"Listen to me, Corporal," Black Wolf interrupted. "You tried to kill me. Because we are enemies, I understand why, but I will say this to you."

A glance at her father assured Lucita that he was hanging onto every word.

"I could have ended you," Black Wolf continued. "It would not have been a difficult task; my arrows are straight, my arms strong."

"Why didn't you?" her father asked after a long and charged silence.

His attention sliding back to Wolf, Black Wolf spoke over his shoulder.

"Because I am a human being, one who could not kill the father of the woman who understands."

"They will return. Your father may think about what I said, but the time will come when they remember only what today was to have been about."

Although she nodded agreement to what Black Wolf had just said, Lucita didn't take her eyes off where she'd last seen her father and the others. They had left a few minutes ago, the soldier who'd tried to kill Wolf lashing his horse into a gallop, Pablo and her father going much more slowly.

"He believed," she said as realization of what she'd seen sunk in. "My father has always said that the only things he trusts are his own senses."

"It will not change him," Black Wolf said. "Maybe today he is different, but tomorrow he will look inside himself and see only a leatherjacket."

"I know," she whispered.

She'd sat down because standing had taken more energy than she possessed and because she needed to be closer to the earth. Black Wolf remained standing with his fingers buried in Wolf's fur, oblivious to his wound. She smelled the animal smell of the wolf, heard air going in and out of his deep lungs, and yet there was something not of this world about him.

"You could have gone back with them," Black Wolf told her. "They would not have turned you away."

"It doesn't matter." It seemed to take a long time to say the words. "That isn't where I want to be."

"Where then?"

*Where?*

"Just—just before you called to Wolf, I smelled the sea," she said by way of answer. "It made me think of Humqaq."

"Humqaq was in my heart as well."

*I know.* "Black Wolf, your spirit accepts me."

She looked up and into the animal's deep, dark eyes and knew she would never see anything more beautiful. "Humqaq sent me a reminder of that acceptance," she continued.

"You believe that?"

*Yes.* Needing to be held, she said, "A little while ago you told me I wasn't Chumash, but I can touch Wolf. Would Humqaq reach out to me if I had no understanding of what it is to be Chumash?"

Instead of answering, he stepped away from Wolf and held out his hand to her. Accepting his challenge, his promise maybe, she placed her hand in his, feeling the heat Wolf had left there.

"I said you were not Chumash because I wanted you to remember where you came from," he told her once she was standing in front of him. "I would not take you from that."

"I . . . thank you."

"Lucita, only you could decide whether to leave your past."

She had, she thought as Black Wolf wrapped his arms around her and the emptiness inside died. No matter what she'd been when she came to this land, she was no longer that child, and the journey that lay ahead was a new beginning, one she wouldn't have to make alone.

Still wrapped within Black Wolf's warmth, she stretched a hand toward Wolf, palm down so the creature, the spirit, could make the decision whether to accept her. Wolf's nostrils on the back of her hand burned her flesh, and the heat slid throughout her.

"I love you," she whispered. She wasn't sure whether she was speaking to man or beast, maybe both. "You are so fierce, so powerful, and yet . . . yet you can be gentle."

"You understand that?" Black Wolf asked.

"Yes, now."

"Why?" he asked as Yucca and her horse came into view.

"I . . . I think you know."

When Black Wolf ran his hand down her shoulder, she understood his need to make her part of him because the same need filled her.

"I want to meet him," she said from her heart.

"My son?"

"Yes."

"And then?"

"And then I want to learn how to be a Chumash."

# Available by mail from

## TOR ▲ FORGE

**1812 • David Nevin**
The War of 1812 would either make America a global power sweeping to the pacific or break it into small pieces bound to mighty England. Only the courage of James Madison, Andrew Jackson, and their wives could determine the nation's fate.

**PRIDE OF LIONS • Morgan Llywelyn**
*Pride of Lions*, the sequel to the immensely popular *Lion of Ireland*, is a stunningly realistic novel of the dreams and bloodshed, passion and treachery, of eleventh-century Ireland and its lusty people.

**WALTZING IN RAGTIME • Eileen Charbonneau**
The daughter of a lumber baron is struggling to make it as a journalist in turn-of-the-century San Francisco when she meets ranger Matthew Hart, whose passion for nature challenges her deepest held beliefs.

**BUFFALO SOLDIERS • Tom Willard**
Former slaves had proven they could fight valiantly for their freedom, but in the West they were to fight for the freedom and security of the white settlers who often despised them.

**THIN MOON AND COLD MIST • Kathleen O'Neal Gear**
Robin Heatherton, a spy for the Confederacy, flees with her son to the Colorado Territory, hoping to escape from Union Army Major Corley, obsessed with her ever since her espionage work led to the death of his brother.

**SEMINOLE SONG • Vella Munn**
"As the U.S. Army surrounds their reservation in the Florida Everglades, a Seminole warrior chief clings to the slave girl who once saved his life after fleeing from her master, a wife-murderer who is out for blood." —*Hot Picks*

**THE OVERLAND TRAIL • Wendi Lee**
Based on the authentic diaries of the women who crossed the country in the late 1840s. America, a widowed pioneer, and Dancing Feather, a young Paiute, set out to recover America's kidnapped infant daughter—and to forge a bridge between their two worlds.